NOWHERE TO HIDE

R. PATRICK
GATES

PINNACLE BOOKS
Kensington Publishing Corp.
www.kensingtonbooks.com

PINNACLE BOOKS are published by

Kensington Publishing Corp.
850 Third Avenue
New York, NY 10022

All Kensington titles, imprints, and distributed lines are available at special quantity discounts for bulk purchases for sales promotions, premiums, fund-raising, educational, or institutional use. Special book excerpts or customized printings can also be created to fit specific needs. For details, write or phone the office of the Kensington special sales manager: Kensington Publishing Corp., 850 Third Avenue, New York, NY 10022, attn: Special Sales Department; phone: 1-800-221-2647.

ISBN-13: 978-0-7860-1826-0
ISBN-10: 0-7860-1826-7

First printing: October 2008

10 9 8 7 6 5 4 3 2 1

Printed in the United States of America

Unmasked

The doorbell rings, rousing Billy from his memories.

(Someone's here! Now's your chance! Quick, get moving! Run to the door, tell them you're trapped in here with The Monster!)

Awkwardly, Billy tries to turn his head in the cramped space and peek out from behind the cabinet to try and see who is there, but The Monster enters the kitchen from the dining room, passing within inches of his hiding palce.

(That was too close!)

Billy waits a moment, then manages to stick his head out from behind the cabinet just enough to be able to see with his left eye. The Monster is standing a few feet away in the breakfast nook, its back to him, a towel in its hand, wiping the blood from the living room floor off its palms and fingers. The bell rings again. The Monster goes to the door and looks through the edge of the curtain to see who's on the back porch.

"The paperboy," The Monster mutters. It takes off the rubber Spider-Man mask and puts it on the counter. Billy tries, but can't see its face. With its back still to him, The Monster wipes at the front of its shirt, then takes the shirt off and tosses it and the towel to the floor by the kitchen sink. From the rack of coat hooks to the left of the kitchen door, it takes one of Billy's father's gray hooded sweatshirts and puts it on.

Billy stares at the back of The Monster's head, at its hair, black like his own . . .

(It looks like—)

. . . and lowers his eyes to take in the rest of the thing: the shape of its body, its pants, and even the shoes on its feet.

(It *really* looks like—)

Billy gasps. As if it heard, The Monster looks his way, and he sees its face for the first time . . .

Books by R. Patrick Gates

GRIMM REAPINGS*

GRIMM MEMORIALS*

THE PRISON*

'VADERS*

FEAR

JUMPERS

TUNNELVISION

DEATHWALKER

*Published by Kensington Publishing Corp.

Special thanks to Peter Senftleben at Kensington for his honest, and persistent, editorial work on this book. It is a much better book because of him. Thanks also to my brother, Tim Gates, for his always valued assistance with proofreading and law enforcement information. Any errors dealing with the latter are mine.

This book is dedicated to my family.

O, what man may within him hide,
Though angel on the outward side.

—William Shakespeare

Out of the mouth of babes....

—Psalms

Friday
afternoon

(*Hide!*)

He stands in the kitchen . . .

(*The Monster*—)

. . . frozen to the spot.

(—*is* here *in YOUR house!*)

He can't move.

(Ladies and Gentlemen! The Monster is *in the house*!)

He is mesmerized by The Monster's eyes, which are the only part of its face that he can see through the rubber pullover Spider-Man mask it wears over its head— *his* Spider-Man mask from last Halloween, the one he thought Kevin had stolen or thrown away on him just to be mean!

The Monster's eyes are gleeful with rabid hate and insanity. They captivate him.

(Don't look at it!)

Right *now* he is hearing *its* breathing through the mask, ragged and growling.

(Don't listen to it!)

Right *now* he smells it: a mixture of foul breath, body odor, and something else. Something *worse*.

(Don't smell it!)

He knows that smell; he's smelled it before, the time he found the dead cat behind the garage—it is the smell of *death*.

It is *horrible*!

It is partly that smell that prevents him from moving.

The noxious odor makes him dizzy to the very edge of fainting.

(Don't look now, but that's not Spider-Man, it's the M-O-N-S-T-E-R standing there and that isn't a candy bar it has for you, it's a crowbar!)

"You know," The Monster growls, its voice and words muffled under the mask. It is a poor imitation of a human voice, but at the same time, it is *familiar*.

(No it isn't. Don't think that.)

"There's an old saying . . ."

Billy hates its voice.

"Children should be *invisible*!" The Monster laughs.

The sound grates on Billy's ears. It is the sound of a selfish beast filled with madness and loathing for everything and everyone, but especially for itself.

"Actually," The Monster goes on, "that isn't a saying at all." The thing takes a step toward Billy. "I just made it up!" It laughs again, loudly exaggerating it into the sound of howling and barking as it throws its head back like a dog howling at the moon. Like a big evil dog that will just as soon bite you as look at you.

"It's time to get invisible, Billy-boy."

It knows my name!

(Stop it! Don't think about it, or you'll never get away!)

The sound of his name on The Monster's lips, coming from The Monster's mouth, is like an electric shock, jolting him from his paralysis.

(In the nick of time! A second more and your head is going to be dented 'cause—)

The Monster is swinging the crowbar.

Billy backpedals and trips over a leg of one of the kitchen chairs. He crashes to the floor on his back. The curved, clawed end of the crowbar passes close enough to his head that he can feel a breeze from it.

The Monster's second swing is from above its head, straight down at Billy's upturned, frightened face. He rolls to the right. It just misses. The clawed end of it pierces the red and brown linoleum floor and sticks there. The Monster struggles to pry it loose.

Billy crabwalks backward, scrambling out from under the table until his head and shoulders hit the dividing half wall between the kitchen and the breakfast nook.

The Monster gives up on the stuck crowbar and crouches. It looks under the table at him and winks.

Billy pulls his legs under him and stands.

(Run, idiot!)

The Monster copies him and also stands. The table is between them.

(Run *now* or The Monster's going to get you for sure!)

Billy can't move.

(Don't do it!)

He looks at the Spider-Man mask and into The Monster's inhuman murderous eyes gleaming through the eyeholes.

(DON'T DO IT!)

. . . and sobs in terror.

"Daddy! Help me!" Billy screams as loud as he can.

"Sorry, kid," The Monster growls. "Daddy's not home."

The Monster shoves the table hard, pushing its edge into Billy's upper chest and shoulders. He is thrown back. His head slams into the wall and the table edge pins him there before his now slack body can slump to the floor.

The void of unconsciousness envelops him as The Monster's claws close round his neck. In the depths of a darkness that out-shadows the darkest night he has ever seen, images come to him on a feeble current of alien thought that becomes his own:

A room steeped in shadows. A single bed. A single student desk with a chair. A single, small table by the bed with a single lamp on it. On the bed sat a boy; his face familiar.

"Hello?" the boy whispered. There was no one else in the room. "Hello? Are you still there?"

No answer came from the shadows, which suddenly deepened and stretched away from him, forming into a rising tunnel with a patch of vertical rectangular light at the top, as from an open doorway. A voice came from the light:

"You're a fucking animal!"

A shadow moved in the light, blotting it out for a moment—a monstrous head. Something was coming; he could feel it with every fiber of his being.

Something bad was coming.

He turned and fled into the front hallway to the living room door. His mother was lying on the floor behind the couch. He asked her what she was doing but used her first name, "Molly," instead of "Mom," something he never did. The television suddenly came on by itself and he was drawn to the shining screen. There was a game show on. He looked at the host, Drew Carey, and gasped, "He looks like Sir!"

Billy had no idea who Sir was or why he felt such fear at the sound of his name. A news bulletin came on the television—police warning women in the Poughkeepsie, New York, area of a serial rapist on the loose.

But we live in Blackstone, Connecticut, he thought as the television, and the room around it, faded away and he rose back to consciousness.

Billy opens his eyes and closes them again. He breathes slowly. The air is cool and smells funny, yet familiar—a smell he doesn't like. He tries opening his eyes again. Everything is dark and blurry. His head hurts worse than the time his older brother, Kevin, threw the baseball at him and knocked him out.

His head isn't the only thing that hurts.

The more he wakes the more every part of his body hurts—his head, throat, arms, legs, back, stomach—but that doesn't hurt from injury; his stomach hurts from *fear*, from *terror*. A feeling so intense it twists his gut into a knot.

What happened? he wonders.

(I don't think you want to know.)

In a rush it comes back to him. He just got home from school. He walked in the kitchen door and announced, "Mom! I'm home," the way he did every day. The house was quiet. Too quiet. No sound of the TV on in the living room even though it was time for what his mother called, "my story," the soap opera, *General Hospital.* That didn't really bother him at first or catch his attention, but he didn't hear the baby crying; his four-week-old baby brother, Jimmy, always seems to cry whenever Billy's mom tries to take a break to relax or watch something on television, as if he *knows* and doesn't want her to. But the house wasn't filled with the grating sound of his crying.

(That kid's crying could wake the dead.)

That's something his dad said the first night Jimmy and Mom came home from the hospital, and Jimmy cried all night long. Billy thought it funny when he heard it, but after thinking about it, he was afraid. Being afraid, however, is something seven-year-old Billy Teags is used to. He is afraid of so many things—spiders, snakes, high places, the dark, the bogeyman in his closet . . .

(And sometimes under the bed—don't forget under the bed!)

. . . his older brother, Kevin, kids at school and on the bus, teachers, the cellar—the list is quite long. But the thing that Billy is most afraid of is . . . *The Monster.* The Monster he's known about for a long time and whose presence he sensed in the house when he got home today and realized it was too quiet.

(Where was it hiding?)

He isn't sure . . . can't remember. . . .

(You called out to Mom and went to the front hall-way.)

That's right; he was going to go upstairs, figuring Mom was in the nursery with the baby, and that's probably why he wasn't crying.

Now it all comes back to him. He didn't get scared until he saw the kitchen wall phone had been ripped out. It lay smashed on the floor.

(That's when the Monster jumped out!)

The Monster had been hiding in the breakfast nook, ducked down behind the half wall that separates it from the rest of the kitchen.

(Before you even made it to the hallway, The Monster nearly grabbed you.)

He can't believe The Monster was in his house! His home. Waiting for him.

(The Monster *is* in your home, right now, and it ain't the first time!)

But where?

(Good question. Do you really want to know the answer?)

Billy ignores the familiar voice; the side of him that's always cracking jokes and getting him in trouble. He rubs his eyes despite the pain it rouses in his head. He is in a dark, quiet place, lying on something hard and cold, like stone. It smells musty. He blinks several times and raises his head, causing a throbbing painful pulse in his temples. He realizes he isn't in complete darkness; there is just enough dim light to see by. Slowly his surroundings become clearer.

(You're in the cellar.)

Billy *hates* the cellar. The cellar is dark and creepy. The cellar is full of spiders.

(And now it's the home of your friendly neighborhood *Monster*!)

The image of the thing wearing his Halloween Spider-

Man mask—even though it is an adult mask and too big for him, Billy loved it—comes back to him, and he shudders. He looks around but can't see The Monster.

(You've *never* been able to actually *see* it—except in your dreams—until today, but it's always been there, hasn't it?)

Billy sits up quickly only to be rewarded with an increase of the throbbing pain in his head. He swallows with difficulty; his throat hurts more than his head.

(The Monster tried to strangle you!)

The image of Drew Carey hosting a game show flashes through his mind, bringing fear with it.

"Sir," he mumbles uncomprehendingly and rubs his neck. He looks around. He's lying at the bottom of the cellar stairs, looking up at the kitchen door at the top. Another image comes—the upward tunnel with the light at the top like a door.

(Same position, different cellar.)

From the pain in his arms, shoulders, legs, back, and sides that rivals the pain in his head and throat, he guesses The Monster threw him most of the way down the stairs after it choked him.

(But where is *it* now?)

Gingerly, he gets to his feet and scans what he can see of the large, cluttered basement. There is no sign of The Monster.

(What about the workshop?)

Trying not to make a sound, Billy steps out past the stairs far enough so that he can see the door to the workshop under the stairs, at the back of the cellar. The light isn't on inside. All is quiet there.

The sound of footsteps upstairs.

(*That's* where it is!)

The footsteps cross the kitchen floor. They near the door at the top of the stairs.

(It's coming! Hide!)

He runs a few steps and stops, unsure of where to go. The cellar is so crammed with boxes and furniture and just plain junk that it is a veritable obstacle course to maneuver. With so much stuff, it should be easy to find a place to hide, but everywhere he looks seems obvious and flimsy.

The footsteps stop right outside the door at the top of the stairs.

He makes up his mind, choosing what he thinks is an obvious place out of sheer desperation and because it is closest—right under the stairs. Shivering with fear and disgust, he ducks through cobwebs and climbs over an old lawn mower until he is lying on the floor right up under the bottom of the stairs, with dust in his eyes, the smell of oil from the lawn mower in his nose, and the sensation of *things* crawling on his bare arms and legs from the cobwebs clinging to his skin. It is all he can do to remain there, keep quiet, and not start bawling.

(Do that and you're dead meat.)

A moment later the cellar door opens, and the heavy tread of The Monster's feet start down, then stop after just a couple of steps.

"Shit," The Monster swears softly. "I thought I strangled that little bastard!" The Monster continues down, stopping on the last step, the one right over where Billy lies curled up.

"You're pretty tough, kid. Why don't you come out now? I just want to talk to you. Maybe we can work something out." The last few words degenerate into a sinister giggle. "No . . . really. I mean it. I just want to talk."

The Monster steps to the bottom and walks away from the stairs.

"Come out, come out, wherever you are! Olly-olly-oxen-free!"

Billy puts his hands over his ears to keep out the awful sound of The Monster's voice and to keep himself from crying.

(If you crybaby now forget it, kiss-your-butt-bye-bye, see-you-later-alligator!)

The Monster grunts. From the sound, Billy guesses it is looking under the oil tank in the rear left corner of the cellar. If he is correct in his judgment of where The Monster is, it means it is the farthest from him and the stairs as it can possibly be. If he is going to make a break for it . . .

(Now is as good a time as any.)

He doesn't move. He *can't* move. Terror keeps him paralyzed, but he rationalizes his cowardice by telling himself that the Monster will catch him before he can ever make it up the stairs.

(Don't be chicken—*brawk-buc-buc-bra-awk*! You can't wait here until it catches you and eats you! I bet you'll be finger-lickin' good!)

"I know you didn't get upstairs, kid, so you've got to be down here somewhere," The Monster growls in a low voice, more to itself than to Billy.

Billy knows it's only a matter of time before The Monster finds him. No matter how cluttered the cellar might be, it is, after all, only so big. All The Monster has to do is keep searching. Sooner or later it will look under the stairs, or look in the workshop and from the workshop doorway, it will easily see Billy's hiding place.

There are only two ways out of the cellar, not counting the windows, which are too high for Billy to reach without climbing on something. The easiest way out, under normal circumstances, is the stairs up to the kitchen. All he has to do is crawl out from under them, dash around the railing and the post at the bottom, and scoot up. If he's right about The Monster being over by the oil tank, then there are a jumbled pile of boxes, trash bags filled with old clothes, an old, defunct humidifier the size of a small desk, a stack of drawers belonging to a long ago thrown out dresser, several bald snow tires, a rusted tackle box, many stacks of tied newspaper bundles atop and around a portable, fold-up card table, and a pair of narrow, louvered, wooden closet doors leaning precariously against the support post nearest the stairs and in danger of toppling given the slightest nudge, between it and him. There is a narrow, barely discernible pathway through all the junk, but it is not a path that can be maneuvered quickly without bumping into stuff and knocking it over.

The other exit from the cellar is through the workshop to the bulkhead door to the outside. The cellar is really two rooms—the main cellar, where The Monster is and which contains the furnace, washer-dryer, a double sink, a large, upright storage freezer, the water heater, oil tank, chimney, plus all the junk—and a second room under the stairs at the rear right corner, under the kitchen, which was converted into a workshop complete with a large workbench topped with shelves filled with Ball jars containing screws, nuts, nails, washers, and a wall rack upon which hang a wide variety of tools. The workshop was part of the main cellar at one time, but was sectioned off with a wood-framed wall of sheetrock. There had been an old wooden door on the workshop entrance, but it now leans against the wall next to the entrance where it used to hang.

The workshop is the only part of the cellar that is free of stored clutter. The workshop belongs to Billy's father, who is a clean, neat person—he often calls himself "Felix" for reasons unbeknown to Billy—and his mother is the opposite—his dad calls her "Oscar" for equally mysterious reasons. His father refuses to clean up the main cellar since his mother is responsible for cluttering it up—she hates to throw anything away—

and will not allow her into his neat little workshop sanctuary.

In the workshop are the stairs leading outside through a rusted metal bulkhead door that is never used. Billy's father padlocked the door on the outside, to keep anyone from breaking into his workshop and stealing his tools.

(So there's only *one* way out of here, Dumbo, and if you don't use it you're going to be one sorry soldier!)

It has to be the stairs to the kitchen then, and it has to be soon.

(No shit, Sherlock! Why don't you waste some more time figuring out what you already know!)

The sound of boxes crashing to the floor startles him. He can't see anything without crawling forward and peeking out from under the stairs, but he doesn't want to risk it; he has no idea where The Monster is now. There are so many stacks of various size boxes in the cellar he can't tell which one made the noise. He hears The Monster bump into something else that makes a scraping sound on the floor. The Monster curses loudly. Billy guesses The Monster is on the other side of the furnace. If he makes a break for it now and is really quiet, he might be able to reach the stairs without The Monster seeing him. The Monster has to go around the chimney, the large tackle box, the pile of old tires, the water heater, and the unstable piles of newspapers before it gets to a clear path to the stairs. Once Billy starts up the stairs, though, he knows they will creak and that will surely give him away.

But he might just have enough of a head start.

(So get moving!)

Maybe . . .

(What are you waiting for?)

. . . maybe not.

(Don't chicken out now! You ain't got forever!)

His will says *go*, but his feet and legs say *no!* They are more attuned to his fear and can't hear the command to *run* through the terror.

"I can hear you bree-athing!"

(Told you! Run! Now! Do it! Do it! The Monster knows where you are!)

Billy's breath sticks in his throat, but he forces his legs and feet to work by pushing himself out of the narrow space with his hands. His lower limbs respond as though he's mired in mud. His legs are sluggish with fear. He can't get them to move any faster.

(This isn't the way it's supposed to be.)

Billy agrees. He envisioned quickly and nimbly extricating himself from his hiding place and maneuvering around to the stairs like an Olympic athlete.

(More like some juicy bug struggling to move in a spider's web!)

It seems to take forever to get out of the cramped space under the stairs. Slowly, cautiously, Billy crawls out on his hands and knees before raising his head to risk a look around. Directly in front of him is a stack of old newspapers, tied into large, roughly square bundles that provide cover but require him to get off his knees and stand almost upright for him to be able to see over. He does so, rising just enough to peer over the top of the stack and scan what he can see of the rest of the cellar. His eyes flit over the washer and dryer in the far left front corner, next to the deep, white, double utility sink, and move right, over a load of gray, fake wood paneling stacked against the wall next to the laundry area. The freezer, chimney, furnace, and water heater block his view of the middle part of the cellar, but what he can see of the space to the right, beyond them, appears empty.

That means The Monster is behind the stuff around the chimney that is too tall and bulky for Billy to see over or around. The shortest route for The Monster to get to him—to its left, around the chimney—is blocked by a loose pile of trash bags filled with old clothing heaped on top of the large humidifier, in front of which are stacked more bundles of newspapers. It isn't an impenetrable barrier, but it will slow down The Monster enough that Billy hopes he can get upstairs to the kitchen and outside where he can run to a neighbor's house for help.

It all depends on him getting to the stairs as quickly and quietly as possible before being discovered.

Psyching himself up, he turns left and creeps toward the support post at the bottom of the stairs, to which the railing is attached. All he has to do is get around that, and he can run up the stairs and not worry about how much noise he is making.

Thinking of that, Billy realizes something isn't right. Just as his foot nudges an old, rusted wire hanger on the floor that makes a loud scraping sound, he realizes what it is—not only can't he *see* The Monster, but he can't *hear* it either!

(It's *listening* for *you!*)

The silence increases the sound of the hanger scraping on the floor tenfold, making it seem, in Billy's ears, to reverberate around the cellar with the volume of a crash of thunder.

There is a sudden flurry of movement as the pile of trash bags explodes off the humidifier, crashing everywhere. One bag hits the stack of newspapers. They topple over into the sink. The rest hit the louvered doors leaning against the other nearby support post a few feet to the right of where Billy stands. The doors fall over and crash directly into the stairs, leaning at a severe angle in front of Billy. They block his path but leave a space of about three feet beneath them through which he can still escape.

(It's coming!)

Knowing he has to move, but unable to take his eyes from the junk toppling like dominoes, certain that The Monster is going to come leaping over the falling debris any second and cut off his escape, Billy wants to scream, but doesn't have enough breath in his panting lungs to produce a sound equal to the terror he feels.

But The Monster isn't there in the gloom behind the falling trash bags and newspapers. The Monster isn't leaping over the junk and lunging for him, knocking the folding doors aside and pushing over everything in its path in its frenzy to get at him.

Billy's mind races. *If The Monster isn't in front of me, where is it?*

(Don't stand there! It's probably sneaking up on you!)

A voice from directly behind him: "Peek-a-boo I see you!"

(Told you!)

It tricked him, pushing over the bags and setting off the domino sequence of falling junk as a diversion while it ducked around the other side of the furnace and water heater and got behind him. Its familiar yet horrible eyes through the mask are gleeful with its successful subterfuge.

(Run! Run now or forever be in pieces!)

The Monster looks left and grabs something leaning against the wall next to the doorway to the workshop— Billy's father's ax. It holds the woodchopper firmly in both of its hands. Billy turns and faces The Monster but stumbles backward right into the louvered doors, which keep him from falling.

The Monster chuckles.

(Run, stupid!)

The Monster's chuckle turns into laughter, then stops abruptly. "You're trapped, Billy-boy! Come here, I want to *ax* you something!" Its laughter explodes again.

Without turning his back on The Monster, Billy swiftly

drops to his hands and knees and scampers backward under the louvered doors as fast as he can.

The Monster leaps forward, swinging the ax into the folding doors just as Billy gets out from under them on the other side. The top door splits in two, but the ax blade gets stuck in the one beneath it.

At the crash of metal into wood, Billy jumps up, grabs the post at the bottom of the stairs, and ducks around it as splinters fly by.

Furious, The Monster tries to pull the ax free of the door but only succeeds in pulling the door up with it, sending the two pieces of the broken top crashing straight back into the Monster's face. The Monster ducks and lets go of the ax handle.

Seeing his chance, Billy clambers up the stairs as fast as he can, using his hands on the steps, as well as his feet—

(Running like a monkey!)

—in his panic to escape.

"Get back here, you little rat bastard!" The Monster roars.

Billy doesn't stop and doesn't look back. He can hear The Monster grunting and the wooden doors banging as it works the ax loose.

"You're only making it worse for yourself!" The Monster warns.

Billy reaches the top of the stairs and grabs the knob with both hands. Slippery with fear-sweat, his fingers slip off. Below, he can hear the wrenching squeal of the ax blade coming free of the wooden door followed by The Monster grunting as it heaves the door out of the way. *Crash!*

"You'd better come back down here, right now. Chop-chop!" The Monster says, panting from its exertions.

Billy grabs the doorknob again with both hands and

turns it. The greasy metal handle finally turns, the latch clicks, and he throws his weight against the wood. It swings open. He falls onto the kitchen floor.

Got to get out of the house, he thinks frantically.

(Now *that* sounds like a plan.)

The kitchen door leading out to the side porch and the left side of the house is a few feet to his right. He gets to his feet and runs to it.

(Hurry! It's coming!)

Billy wipes the palms of his hands on his shirt, grabs the doorknob, and turns it.

Nothing happens. The door is locked.

(It wasn't locked when you got home from school! The Monster did it!)

A frightened, high-pitched keening grows in Billy's throat and escapes from his mouth as he fumbles with the lock button on the doorknob.

(You're trapped!)

He can hear The Monster coming up the stairs, still breathing heavily, but not hurrying, as if it knows he'll never get the door unlocked in time.

"You are making me work *way* too hard for this, Billy-boy-o," The Monster grunts.

(Now would be a good time to open the door and GET THE HECK OUT OF HERE!)

The lock button pops. He tries the knob again. The door still won't open. He looks above the knob. Three-quarters of the way up the door the sliding bolt-lock is shut. He reaches for it, but Billy is small for his age and the lock is too high.

(It's too late anyway.)

The Monster staggers from the cellar, huffing and puffing.

Billy backs away from the door.

"Nice try, kid," The Monster whispers and feints a lunge at him.

Billy stumbles backward until he is up against the refrigerator door. The Monster comes at him slowly, a crazy gleam in its eyes through the mask.

Billy is frozen with fear.

"Don't you want to *ax* me something?" The Monster says quietly. It rears back with the ax, like a left-handed baseball player with a bat, and swings it with all its might. At the last second, Billy's fear thaws enough to let him dive to the floor. He feels the wind of the blade as it whistles a fraction of an inch over his head. It plunges into the refrigerator door with a loud, metallic *thunk* and a sound like air escaping a vacuum-packed can hisses into the room.

"Goddamn it! Not again! Fuck!"

(Sounds like the fridge is taking a leak!)

A nervous giggle escapes Billy's lips even as he scrambles across the floor past The Monster and into the adjacent smaller breakfast nook. He gets to his feet next to the kitchen table and looks around frantically, wondering what to do.

(Find some place to hide! Jump out a window! *Anything*, but you can't just stand here!)

With a sound like nails being pried from wood, only much louder, the ax head comes free of the refrigerator door.

Billy dashes into the front hallway.

(Hide! Hide! Hide!)

He can't think straight.

"I'm coming for you, Billy-boy!" The Monster says from the kitchen. "Wait up, would ya?" it adds and giggles, sending shivers through Billy.

Straight ahead is the front door, which they never use and keep locked all the time. To his left are the stairs . . .

(Is that blood?)

. . . to the second floor, but there is no way out of the

house from up there. Under the stairs is the downstairs bathroom.

(More blood on the floor!)

It's only a half bath, with a toilet and a sink, and has nowhere to hide, unless he can squeeze into the cabinet under the sink, but he doesn't have time for that. The Monster is too close.

(It's coming around the corner!)

"There you are, my little pork chop. And I do mean *chop*!" It raises the ax over its head and charges into the hallway.

Billy screams and cringes, stumbling off balance and falling on his side. He hears the ax blade strike something with a thick, wooden sound and looks up. The ax head is caught in the top of the door frame between the hallway and the kitchen.

"Son-of-a-fucking-*bitch*!" The Monster roars, looking up. With a heaving grunt, it tears the ax head free of the wood, sending splinters showering down upon its shoulders.

(Better run! Better hide!)

Billy scrambles to his feet and runs into the living room. Before he knows what is happening, his feet go out from under him, and he hits the floor hard, landing right on his tailbone. Pain shoots up his spine, and he stifles a cry and looks at his hands. They are wet, coated with a dark purple, slippery substance. It looks like grease, or paint, as though someone spilled one of his plastic bottles of poster paint all over the living room floor.

(It wasn't me!)

He looks around and gasps. The floor, the couch, the wall to his right, are all spattered with the same dark liquid that is on his hands.

Sticking out from behind the couch something catches his eye.

A foot.

(It's wearing one of Mom's sandals!)

He freezes and stares at it, feeling a sense of déjà vu.

(Move! Move! Move! You can't stand here and gawk! You got to hide! The Monster will be here any minute! Yeah, it's Mom, and yeah, she might be dead, but if you don't hurry up and hide you will definitely be dead!)

Billy looks at the blood on his hands; his mother's blood.

(Go!)

"You know, I think that's your color!" The Monster is directly behind him, standing in the archway between the living room and the front hallway.

Instinctively, Billy rolls to his right. The ax comes down dead center of the spot where he just sat. The floor shudders with the force of the blow. He tries to regain his feet, but the slick puddle of blood won't let him. It's just as well. The Monster yanks the ax head out of the floor and swings sideways at Billy. He ducks and rolls farther into the large room, on top of the oval braided rug that covers the floor in the center and around which all the furniture is situated.

The ax hits the wall, sending out an explosion of horsehair plaster and bits of gold and silver flowered wallpaper. The Monster leaves it there and takes a step toward Billy, bent over, its arms reaching for him.

The bloody floor comes to his rescue. Just as Billy did, The Monster slips in the gore; its feet fly out from under it. It sprawls facedown, its head and shoulders on the rug just a foot and a half from Billy, the rest of its body on the floor with its feet in the doorway.

With the rug under him providing traction, Billy gets to his feet and starts for the open French doors that separate the living room from the dining room, but stops. The Monster remains on the floor, its face in the rug, the lower half of its body in the blood. And the thing is *laughing* hysterically.

Another sound catches Billy's ear. It's the glass doors on the tall, narrow bookcase against the wall to his left rattling. The piece of furniture sits on an uneven part of the old pine floor and has always rattled whenever anyone moves in the room. Billy has been yelled at many times by his father for running through the room and causing the cabinet to rock and shake so badly it was in danger of falling over.

(That's it! Do it!)

Billy lunges for the bookcase, stepping dangerously close to the laughing monster still lying on the floor. He pulls the left side glass door open hard by its brass handle and keeps pulling. The piece of furniture doesn't need much to get it going. It leans forward so quickly that it almost topples over onto Billy. Luckily he realizes in time that he is too close and takes a step away from it as it falls over.

It crashes onto The Monster's head and shoulders. The glass doors shatter and books, knickknacks, DVDs, and CDs cascade onto The Monster's neck and shoulders. The weight of the cabinet and its contents drives The Monster's face into the rug again. The evil creature lets out a loud groan, a soft grunt, then is quiet.

Billy stands immobile, looking at what he's done. The Monster's shoulders, back, and left arm are under the bookcase; the rest of its body isn't moving, but that isn't what keeps Billy staring. For the first time since laying eyes on The Monster, he's not too frightened to notice that The Monster's clothes—its jeans and plain maroon shirt—look familiar.

(Never mind its clothes.)

But . . .

(Don't think about that now! Did you kill it?)

Billy takes a deep breath and a cautious step forward. He leans over The Monster. He can't hear it breathing.

(Yeah! You killed it! Oh yeah! Way to go! Ding-dong! The Monster's dead!)

Being careful not to step in the blood again, Billy moves even closer. He wants to pull the Spider-Man mask off. He wants to see The Monster's face.

(Are you crazy? What if it *ain't* dead?)

Its hand twitches.

(What did I tell you!)

Billy jumps back and almost stumbles.

"You are in *real* fucking trouble now, kiddo," The Monster groans, its voice muffled by both the mask and the rug.

Billy staggers back and away. The bookcase starts to rise as The Monster uses its arms against the floor to push it up. Billy looks around.

(Get out of here!)

He doesn't know where to go.

(*Anywhere*! Just go *now*!)

He turns and goes through the open French doors into the dining room. A scream nearly escapes his lips, but he clamps his hands over his mouth. Lying to the left, just under the edge of the dining room table, is his eleven-year-old brother, Kevin. His face is turned away. His head lies in a pool of blood, but Billy can tell it's him. Despite the blood, he recognizes Kevin's Boston Red Sox pajamas.

Billy begins to cry.

(No! No! No! It's bad, it's bad, but you can't lose it now! Not now! The Monster's getting up! Come on! Come on! Don't lose it now!)

Billy can't help it. The tears come hot and fast. Though he and Kevin fight a lot, and Kevin picks on Billy relentlessly, he's still his brother, no matter what.

(And now he's dead. The Monster killed him and it's going to kill you, too, if you don't *do* something!)

The Monster moans and grunts behind him as it struggles out from under the bookcase.

(Run now! Stop looking at Kevin and run! Try the back door again! Try the front door! Try anything!)

Somehow, Billy manages to pull his eyes from the sight of his slaughtered brother and move through the dining room to the other door that leads back to the kitchen. Behind him he hears the bookcase crash as The Monster finally manages to push it off and free itself.

"Think of it this way, Billy-boy," The Monster says, out of breath as it gets slowly to its feet. "I did you a favor. You hated that fucker Kevin anyway, didn't you? Truthfully—how many times have you wished he would just *drop dead?* Huh? Am I right? Well, now he has. He'll never tease you again." The Monster chuckles. "You don't have to thank me. It was my pleasure."

Billy tries to block out The Monster's words, but what it says is true. More times than he cares to remember, he's said that he hated Kevin. He said it just the other day when Kevin, who was sick with the flu, held him down and coughed in his face in an attempt to get Billy sick as well.

(He couldn't stand it that him and Jimmy got sick, but you didn't.)

"I hate you! I hate you!" Billy screamed, and Kevin let a drop of his saliva fall into Billy's mouth.

(You just said it 'cause you were mad!)

And just as many times he's wished his older brother dead. Like last summer when Kevin went through a phase where he carried a safety pin around with him everywhere he went and took every opportunity to jab it into Billy whenever he was foolish enough to turn his back on his brother, or when their parents weren't around. After the third or fourth stab, always in the butt, Billy started seriously wishing his brother would croak.

(You didn't *mean* it! Who wouldn't wish that after all he's done to you?)

Then there was the time shortly before that. Mom made Kevin take him along when he went out to play army with a bunch of the older neighborhood kids. In front of all his laughing friends—

(Not all of them laughed. Donny didn't.)

—except Donny Desmond, Kevin gave Billy a canteen that he had peed in, telling his little brother it was lemonade Mom had packed special just for him. And Billy fell for it, taking a big swig before he realized what it was and started puking. He ran home with cruel laughter ringing in his ears. Kevin got in a lot of trouble for that stunt.

(Yeah . . . and he got his revenge, too—Indian sunburns first thing in the morning and last thing before bed, every day and night for two weeks!)

Billy remembers something his mother said when, in the heat of humiliated anger, he had told her, "I wish Kevin was dead!"

"Don't say that, Billy. He's your brother, and no matter how much he teases you, he loves you. You know, you should always be careful what you wish for. It just might come true."

Be careful what you wish for. It just might come true!

Well . . . now it has. Kevin is dead, and *he* wished it. He stops next to the kitchen table. "It's my fault," he blubbers softly.

(No! It isn't! It's The Monster's fault. It killed Kevin and it's going to kill you, too, if you stand around crying and blaming yourself!)

He has to get out of there. He has to get help. Even if Kevin does look to be beyond help, maybe he is still alive. Billy has to get someone to help; someone to get rid of The Monster and help Kevin.

"And Mom," he whispers aloud.

(But there was a lot of blood in the living room.)

He doesn't want to face that, even if he knows it's true.

(Okay! Don't even think about that now! Maybe that's not even her. Maybe she's okay and out shopping, or she took the baby to the doctor, but you can't waste time with that now or you'll be dead, too!)

The Monster will be on him in a moment. He doesn't have enough time to pull a chair over to the kitchen door so he can climb up and undo the bolt and the front door is too far and locked anyway. There is only one place close enough and good enough for him to hide. Just this side of the dining room entranceway, set kitty-corner next to the breakfast nook window, is a tall cabinet his mother likes to decorate with knickknacks that reflect the season or the closest holiday. Though it is May, each shelf still holds items from St. Patrick's Day. There is just enough room for Billy to squeeze behind the cabinet and get completely out of sight.

He puts his back to the wall and squeezes through the narrow space. He scrapes his chest and left cheek against the edge of the cabinet, but he manages to get behind it a moment before he hears The Monster step into the dining room.

The space behind the cabinet is tight but allows just enough room for him to stand in the corner with his face against the back of the piece of furniture. He remains as still as he can and concentrates on breathing as soundlessly as possible. He closes his eyes.

(Don't do that! This isn't baby-hide-and-seek, you know, where if you can't see The Monster it can't see you!)

Billy doesn't care. He's hurt and scared. He just wants to stay behind the cabinet and never open his eyes again. He wants to sleep. Kevin is dead, and he wished him that way. His mom is probably dead, too, and that, too, is probably his fault somehow. He just wants to go to sleep and never wake up, but he can't stop thinking about Kevin, can't stop remembering the last time he wished his older brother dead.

(Why drag that up now? Let it go!)

It was just last week, before Kevin and Jimmy got sick. He was walking through the school yard, on his way to his bus, when Kevin came up behind him. Kevin could be so silent sometimes.

(He calls it, "walking like an Indian.")

Billy never heard him until Kevin was right on top of him, shouting, "Aaaaah!" right in Billy's ear. Billy jumped in fright, and Kevin swiped his World Champion Red Sox baseball cap and took off with it.

"Hey! Baby Einstein!" Kevin taunted, using the nickname Billy hated most of all the names Kevin called him.

(Twenty-three at last count.)

"Let's see if you can figure out how to get your hat back!"

The other kids in the yard all laughed at that. They thought it was really funny. Billy blushed hotly and chased his brother, but Kevin was way too fast. He danced around Billy, dangling the hat within his reach, only to snap it away when Billy tried to grab it.

Billy started to cry. He didn't want to . . .

(Could you be any more embarrassed?)

. . . but he couldn't help it. He started to cry, and once he did, the floodgates opened, and he bawled. Screaming, "I hate you, Kevin!" he turned and ran to his bus, falling and tearing a hole in the knee of his new jeans, scraping the skin beneath in the process. He was stumbling up the stairs to the bus, the laughter of the other kids still ringing in his ears, when he heard, "Hey! Crybaby Einstein !" He turned and saw Kevin standing on the sidewalk behind him. He threw the baseball cap in Billy's face.

"Here's your widdle hatty-watty, Baby Cryin'stein," Kevin said in an exaggerated baby voice.

The kids standing around really thought the variation on his nickname was hilarious and laughed and jeered. With hot tears of anger warming his already flushed cheeks, Billy ran down the bus aisle until he found an empty seat at the very back of the bus.

"I hate him!" he thought furiously on the ride home. "I wish he would die! I wish he would get some horrible disease . . .

(Like the cancer that killed Grammy?)

. . . and he would die slowly." With his active imagination, Billy dreamt up an image of his older brother lying in a hospital bed, tubes running out of his nose and an oxygen mask over his mouth just like Grammy before she died. His body covered with open tumors that leaked blood and pus onto the sheets. He would moan and cry out in pain, pleading with Billy to call the nurse or doctor to give him something to take the pain away. And Billy would just stand there saying, "You want your shotty-wotty, crybaby? Cry for me!"

Billy smiled to himself at the image. It made him feel a little better until he heard his brother's laughter from the front of the bus. Billy peeked over the seat in front of him and saw Kevin teasing Sally Simons, a pretty blond girl in Billy's class.

Kevin is such a jerk, he thought.

(How did you end up with such a jerk for a brother?)

Billy spent the rest of the bus ride home using his vivid imagination to cook up various gruesome tortures and deaths for his mean older brother. He imagined him chained to a dungeon wall while rats ate his eyeballs. He imagined him swimming in an ocean and a great white shark biting him in two. Each successive image, more gory and gruesome than the last, made him feel better. By the time he reached his stop he was almost feeling good.

Being in the back of the bus, Billy lost sight of Kevin, who got off the bus before him. On the sidewalk, Billy looked around, wanting to keep Kevin in front of him and in sight on the walk home from the bus stop, but Kevin was gone. Disappeared.

He's up to something, Billy thought. I just know it.

(He's hiding somewhere, and he's going to do something else mean to you.)

Billy started for home, looking warily over his shoulder every few seconds and keeping his eyes alert for any sign of his brother. Rounding the corner of Ledgemore Street, not far from the bus stop and less than a block from Warren Street and home, two older kids from Kevin's class stepped out from behind a hedge and stopped him.

"Hey! Here's the little crybaby Einstein now!" one of them said. Billy didn't know their names, but he knew they weren't friends of Kevin. That made him hate his brother even more—it was bad enough that he had to put up with being picked on by Kevin and his friends, but now kids Kevin didn't even like were following in his brother's footsteps.

The one who spoke leaned into Billy's face. "If I take your hat, Baby Einstein, will you cry for us like you did back at the playground?"

Too late, Billy tried to run. The bigger of the two kids snatched his hat off his head, while the other stuck out his foot and tripped Billy, sending him sprawling to the sidewalk.

"You gonna cry now, Baby Einstein?" the bigger one taunted.

Billy did want to cry. He could feel the tears building, threatening to escape, but he fought them. He started to get up. There was a sudden blur of movement behind the two bullies. The larger one fell to the ground next to Billy, almost on top of him.

It was Kevin. He reached over and snatched Billy's hat from the bully's hand, then shoved the other kid into the bushes along the sidewalk.

"Leave my brother alone, assholes!" Kevin threatened. "The next time you touch him I'll rip your heads off and take a shit down your throats!" Kevin helped Billy to his feet and placed his cap back on his brother's head. The stunned bullies watched them walk off together, Kevin's arm protectively around Billy's shoulders.

"You know, Dorko, you got to stop letting people push you around," Kevin said as they walked away.

Feeling like crying even more than before, but for a different reason, Billy mumbled, "Thanks, Kevin."

Kevin turned toward him, a nasty smile on his face. "Thanks nothing. Nobody but me picks on you, Slimeball Swillbucket!"

(I hate that name!)

With that he punched Billy hard in the arm, grabbed his hat, and took off running for home.

Hunched behind the cabinet, his mother's words: *No matter how much he teases you, he loves you—*

(I guess that's what she meant.)

—come back to him, bringing silent tears. Kevin was mean, that's for sure, but he always stuck up for Billy whenever Billy was in trouble, whether from other kids or Mom and Dad. He remembers a time when he accidentally broke a vase while running through the dining room. It was a wedding gift from his mom's favorite aunt and an expensive antique or something. His mom was royally pissed off. Mom and Dad immediately blamed Kevin, who usually was the culprit when something got broken. Though Kevin knew that Billy had

done it, he never said a word and took the punishment
without ever turning his little brother in. Of course after-
ward, he cornered Billy and gave him an Indian sunburn
that left his forearm red and sore for hours.

The doorbell rings, rousing Billy from his memories.

(Someone's here! Now's your chance! Quick, get
moving! Run to the door, tell them you're trapped in
here with The Monster!)

Awkwardly, Billy turns his head in the cramped space
to try to peek out from behind the cabinet and see who
is there, but The Monster enters the kitchen from the
dining room, passing within inches of his hiding place.

(That was too close!)

Billy waits a moment, then sticks his head out from
behind the cabinet just enough to be able to see with
his right eye. The Monster is standing a few feet away in
the breakfast nook, its back to him, a towel in its hand,
wiping the blood from the living room floor off its
palms and fingers. The bell rings again. The Monster
goes to the door and looks through the edge of the curtain to see who's on the back porch.

"The fucking paperboy," The Monster mutters. It
takes off the rubber Spider-Man mask and puts it on the
counter. Billy tries but can't see its face. With its back
still to him The Monster wipes at the front of its shirt,
then takes the shirt off and tosses it and the towel to the
floor by the kitchen sink. From the rack of coat hooks
to the left of the kitchen door, it takes one of Billy's father's gray hooded sweatshirts and puts it on.

Billy stares at the back of The Monster's head, at its
hair, black like his own . . .

(It looks like—)

. . . and lowers his eyes to take in the rest of the
thing; the shape of its body, its pants, and even the shoes
on its feet.

(It *really* looks like—)

Billy gasps. As if it heard, The Monster looks his way, and he sees its face for the first time: the high forehead, the long thin nose, the deep-set dark eyes and small mouth—an adult version of Billy.

(Dad!)

The Monster *looks like his father.*

"If you're nearby, Billy-boy, and thinking of trying anything—*don't!*" The Monster whispers loudly.

(Now it even *sounds* a little like Dad, too!)

Billy can't believe it; he doesn't *want* to believe what is now obvious. . . .

(The Monster ate Dad!)

Billy is staggered by the knowledge. Like the monster in the movie *The Thing,* which he watched not too long ago with his dad and Kevin, The Monster ate his father and now is able to look like him!

(But not *exactly* like him—Dad's not left-handed!)

He sees the truth of that; the more he looks at his father he can tell it's *not* really his dad. It's a close replica, but there's something not quite right . . .

(It's weird how it can look like Dad but *not* look like him at the same time!)

The realization that *everyone* in his family is gone suddenly overwhelms Billy. His mother, and his brother, Kevin, killed by The Monster, and now his dad *eaten* by the thing. He fights back the urge to scream and cry.

(I know it's bad, but don't lose it now.)

For a moment he thinks about shouting to the paperboy and asking him to run for help, but The Monster's warning makes him think better of it. Instead he slips out from behind the cabinet while The Monster is peeking through the curtain again. Avoiding looking at Kevin's body, Billy crosses through the dining room, back into the living room, heading for the front hallway.

(Get in the bathroom! Hide in the cabinet under the sink. The Monster won't think to look there.)

Driven by the voice in his head Billy avoids the blood on the floor, but can't help noticing his mother's black marble rolling pin, covered in blood and gore, lying on the coffee table next to the couch. He stumbles past it to the hallway. The doorbell rings again, keeping The Monster in the kitchen. Billy stops in the living room doorway and looks back over the way he just came.

(You're leaving bloody footprints!)

He takes off his sneakers, shoves them under the end of the couch, and tiptoes across the hallway to the bathroom. The door is open, and he slips inside. He squats and opens the cabinet door under the sink. He is faced with a couple rolls of toilet paper, a large refill bottle of liquid hand soap, a spray bottle of cleaner, and the drainpipe for the sink. Billy looks past the bathroom products. The cabinet isn't very wide, but it's deep. He can fit in there, though it will be cramped, and then put the cleaner and stuff in front again to hide him further.

He pushes the toilet paper and plastic containers aside and squeezes in, pushing his legs past the pipe. He manages to turn himself in the cramped space until he is sideways with his hips jammed under the curve of the drainpipe. He reaches back and puts the soap, spray cleaner, and Charmin back in place. He grabs the bottom edge of the door and softly closes it.

"Mom," he whimpers softly in the darkness of his new hiding place.

(This can't be happening!)

"Dad . . . Kevin . . ."

(It's got to be a dream; a nightmare!)

Tears stream down his face, and he starts to tremble. Silently, he weeps. The grief grows in him until his shocked, exhausted psyche can handle it no longer. He falls into a shallow, nervous state of escapist sleep.

* * *

He was flying.

He loved dreams of flying, only this dream was different than his other flying dreams. Those were happy, carefree, exhilarating dreams, but this one had the feel of the dreams where he saw through the eyes of The Monster . . . saw it kill. . . .

Suddenly he was no longer flying, he was falling, and falling fast. He could feel the air rushing up at him, blowing his hair back, making his eyes water, pushing against the flesh of his face, making his cheeks ripple, and blowing down his throat, choking him when he opened his mouth. He passed through a cloud and into clear, bright sunlight.

Below, stood a house.

His house.

He fell toward it, faster and faster. Just when he thought he was going to smash right into the roof speeding up at him, his descent slowed. Instead of crashing into the slate tiles covering the top of the house, he sank into them and through them into the attic and then the nursery. He passed right through that room and floated down into the kitchen and kept going, into the cellar where he landed on the floor of his father's workshop, which was right below the kitchen.

He was on his knees, facing the workbench. He could see a large, deep, dark hole in the wall under the workbench that he had never noticed before whenever his father had let him help with one of his projects. A chill air came from the hole, making him tremble—not from its coolness, but from the slimy feel of it on his skin. The air coming from the hole felt alive. He had the sudden fear that the air was evil, and that just by letting it touch his skin, he was letting that evil infect him, letting it into his body and mind.

The darkness in the hole did the impossible: it got darker.

And began to move.

Something was in there, coming closer, slinking and slithering along. Two shining orbs appeared, growing larger and larger. He realized they were not human eyes; they were yellow, alien, hungry *eyes. A shape began to form in the darkness and came closer. A moment more and it would be upon him. Below the eyes he could now see the outline of a body, huge and furry; its arms massive; its claws long and daggerlike. Drooling fangs filled its mouth. The Monster that came from the hole in the wall could have just as easily come straight from one of his nightmares. He screamed. The thing lunged and passed right through him.*

Suddenly he was rising through the air, up through the cellar ceiling into the kitchen. He could hear Baby Jimmy crying up in the nursery and another sound, someone on the porch. A moment later, the back door opened and his father walked in. But his excitement and joy at the sight of his father was quickly and brutally squashed as the horror from the workshop burst through the cellar door. Its massive arms wrapped around his father, and its sharp claws dug into his flesh. Dad never had a chance. The thing opened its cavernous mouth. A roar came from it, matched by a scream from Dad, and both blended together into the sound of a baby crying.

The man-beast-monster did not eat *his father, so much as* absorb *him. As soon as it did, the monstrosity started shrinking. The living, breathing, horror, tooth, fur, and claw began to change, taking on a familiar form.*

Dad—but not Dad.

The Monster.

Billy whimpers softly in his sleep and the dream retreats, changes.

His eyelids twitch.

A flash of light.

He opened his eyes and there she was—Mom. All warmth and softness, smelling like goodness. She wrapped his baby body in her tender arms and cooed her love to him. He slept secure in her protective embrace. . . .

He moaned.

He was sick.

Measles. She was there, caring for him, loving him. She sang a song of soothing. He breathed in the soft scent of her skin.

"I love my little man. Yes I do!"

He smiled. He laughed

The dream changed . . .

His fifth birthday party. The house full of people—aunts, uncles, Grampy, cousins, and neighbors. They all came bearing gifts, just for him. It was his special day. He was king.

The excitement of the day kept his adrenal gland pumping a steady flow of energy into his small body. His cousins and he raced through the house, weaving in and out and under and around the people milling about eating his mother's lasagna. He tried to be patient. Before the party, his mother told him that he would have to wait until everyone was done eating before he could blow out the candles on his cake and open his gifts. As he played, he kept a constant check on the people eating and how much was left on their plates. When some of the overweight guests headed back to the buffet table for seconds, he groaned and looked pleadingly to his mother but got no help there. She was more than happy to dish out second helpings to anyone who wanted more.

Finally, everyone had their fill. His mother was pouring the coffee. The food was put away.

"Now Mom? Can I open my gifts now?"

"Not yet, honey. Soon. Your dad's not here yet. He'll be home in a minute, okay?"

Reluctantly he agreed, then had a strange thought: Dad's not coming home. *For a moment he was very frightened, almost to the point of tears. But it was silly to think that for no sooner did the thought pop into his head then Dad came through the door, a gift-wrapped package under his arm.*

The candles were put on the cake and lit.

"Happy Birthday to Billy," was sung. Then he was tearing

into gifts wrapped with Pokemon, Spider-Man, and Trans-formers paper.

A box of two hundred crayons and a Spider-man coloring book—"Wow!"

Megatron and Optimus Prime action figures—"Cool!"

An art set—"Pretty cool."

Pajamas—"Not cool!"

He tore through his gifts, stopping just long enough to ooh and aah appropriately over each one and say thank you to the giver, even if he wasn't crazy about the gift. He opened presents of books, clothes, toy trucks and cars, and birthday cards with money inside.

He saved the one from his dad for last. From the shape of it he thought he knew what it was, but his father had told him he was too young for them, and that they were dangerous. He looked at the package hopefully, then at his father who smiled and nodded.

Encouraging.

His mother came in from the living room where she had just served the last of the coffee to the adults who were watching a basketball game on TV. She was smiling until she saw the shape of the gift from his dad. Her smile faltered.

Another encouraging sign.

He ripped the Spider-Man birthday paper furiously, freeing the gift inside. And there they were in all their glory, the things he had most wanted and was sure he would never get. After all, both his mother and his father had said he was too young for Wheelies, the sneakers with wheels in the heels that would let him glide as though he were on roller skates. They were too dangerous, they had told him. He could get killed or seriously injured on them.

But here they were! His mother looked angry and pulled his father aside. He couldn't hear what she was saying, but his father was laughing and patting her shoulder. Her angry expression softened.

It was going to be okay.
He could keep the sneakers.

The joy and excitement he feels brings him up from the depths of sleep to the surface of consciousness. In his ears, his father's and mother's voices echo:

"Promise us that you'll be careful, Billy," his father said, followed by his mother, "We just don't want to see you get hurt. We love you, little man, and we just want to protect you. . . ."

He wakes in the cramped darkness, his bruised body hurting more than before. His neck feels swollen as much from emotion as from The Monster's strangling him; he can barely swallow. He opens his eyes and can't remember where he is. A surge of panic courses through him. Then it all comes back . . .

(Coming home to find The Monster in the house—)
. . . the chase . . . finding Kevin . . . and Mom . . . The Monster in Dad's clothes and more. . . . He remembers the dream of his father being absorbed by The Monster when he got home from his trip and wonders if it was just a dream, or another incident of being able to observe The Monster while it killed.

(But The Monster in the dream was nothing like the one after you now. Speaking of which, you got to figure out a way to get out of here.)

But he can't think, doesn't want to think. He wishes it was a bad dream, but his gut tells him different. He wishes he could just wake up to find his mother and Kevin and father alive and leaning over him, reassuring him that it *was* just a nightmare and everything is all right now.

(But it isn't.)

The wish reminds him of the other dream he just had, a good dream of a happier time. He thinks of his parents' words just before he woke up. "We want to protect you." Tears bubble up inside him. They hadn't even been able to protect themselves. Never mind him. And *he* certainly wasn't able to protect *them*.

But then, they never believed him about The Monster. . . .

(Especially after you called the police!)

In the hazy aftermath of sleep, he dozes and remembers:

"I saw it, Mom."

It was at dinner two days after his second dream of The Monster. His parents were talking about the police finding two more bodies of a mother and baby murdered in the basement of their apartment building.

"I saw it," *he repeated, putting his fork down on his half-eaten plate of macaroni and cheese. He suddenly wasn't hungry anymore.*

"You saw it? Where? On the news today? You shouldn't watch that stuff, honey," *his mother scolded gently.*

"No, I saw it. I saw it happen."

Suddenly his mother and father looked terrified. His father stopped eating and stared at Billy while his mother leaned close to him, her face a picture of fear and worry.

"What do you mean, you saw it? Where did you see it?"

"In a dream. I saw the lady and her baby dead. They were killed by a monster wearing a mask just like in the dream I had the night you and Jimmy came home from the hospital." *Billy tried to keep his voice steady even though he felt like crying.*

The look of worry on his mother's face disappeared and his father grinned and shook his head. He went back to eating. His mother let out a sigh of relief.

"Oh Billy! You had me worried there for a minute," *she said with a laugh.*

"But it was real, Mom!"

"I know, honey. Sometimes dreams can seem very real, but they're not. When did you have this dream?"

"Sunday night."

"The night after you watched horror movies with your father, who should know better?"

Billy nodded. His mother snuck a wink at his father.

"You know why you had that dream, don't you?" *she asked.*

"Because I got a overactive 'magination?" *Billy asked, repeating something his parents often said about him.*

His mom laughed. "Yeah, I guess that's one reason. That combined with watching those scary movies with your dad and Kevin gave you that bad dream, hon. What were the last two you watched, John?" *she turned and asked Billy's dad.*

"*The Thing*, from the fifties, was the 'then' classic," his dad replied, "And John Carpenter's version of it was the 'now' classic, which is kind of stupid since it was made twenty or thirty years ago, but I guess—"

"It's okay, John. You answered my question. I don't need a commentary," *Mom said, cutting him off. To Billy she continued,* "Yeah. It's no wonder. Now Billy, I've told you before, movies like that, and TV shows, and stories about monsters are just make-believe. You know that, right?"

He nodded hesitantly.

"All that stuff comes out of someone's imagination. Someone with a fantastic imagination just like yours," *his dad explained and added,* "Billy, if those movies are going to scare you like this and give you nightmares, maybe we shouldn't watch them anymore."

Billy was torn then—the horror movies did scare him, but he loved when he and Kevin and Dad piled onto the couch with a big bowl of popcorn every Saturday night at seven, and he got to stay up to eleven to watch, Horror Film Classics—Then and Now, *a weekly program on the Turner Classic Movie Channel.*

"But I like watching them," *Billy replied, his lower lip trembling, tears filling his eyes.*

"We know, sweetie," *his mother told him, shooting his dad a stern look.* "That's why you need to remember there's nothing to be afraid of from those movies. Monsters aren't real."

"This one was! I saw the monster in the mask follow them down into the basement of their apartment building. It hit the lady in the head with a shovel and then used a broken golf club to stab the mother and her baby. It stuck them together!" *he explained.*

His mom looked at his dad, who shrugged and helped himself to more macaroni and cheese. "Honey, that nightmare was caused by hearing about the recent murders and the movies you watched. And you do have a very vivid imagination—a wonderful imagination—but you let it get carried away sometimes, that's all. Now go upstairs and get ready for your bath."

As Billy went up the stairs he heard his father say, "Sometimes that kid's imagination scares me." *A moment later he added,* "I guess he shouldn't watch horror movies with me and Kevin anymore."

To which his mother replied, "That was weird. How did he know the mother and her baby were killed in the basement of their apartment house? And he was so specific about the shovel and a broken golf club. Where'd he get that? I heard the first report on the news just a little while ago. They didn't say anything about them being found in a basement or stuck together with a broken golf club. Where's this coming from?"

"He heard us talking about it. It reminded him of his dream, which obviously had a basement, a shovel, and a broken golf club in it, so he's just fused it all together until he thinks that's what he dreamt," *his father explained dismissively.*

In spite of his parents' explanations and assurances, Billy wasn't able to let it go. Even in the face of what his alter ego told him, warning him not to do something stupid like call the police, Billy went into his parents' room at the top of the stairs and dialed 911.

"Blackstone Emergency. Your call is being recorded. Please state your name, address and the nature of your emergency."

"My name is Billy Teags and I live at sixty-two Warren Street," *Billy answered automatically and went on.* "I saw a monster kill someone," *he said, as low as possible, not wanting his parents or Kevin to hear him.*

"It's a crime to make prank calls to nine-one-one, son."

"I'm not!" *Billy said indignantly.* "I really saw it. The Monster killed the mommy and her baby!"

Just then he heard Kevin coming up the stairs. Afraid of getting caught, Billy hung up the phone.

"What are you doing in Mom and Dad's room?" *Kevin asked as he reached the top of the stairs and saw Billy in their parents' room.* "You know you're not supposed to be in here. Were you on the phone? Who were you talking to?"

"No one."

Kevin looked at his younger brother suspiciously. Slowly, a mean smile spread across Kevin's lips. "You know, Bill," *he said quietly, casting a quick glance over his shoulder and toward the stairs,* "I know your dream about the monster was real, and I know which monster it is."

Billy didn't know how to react; he wasn't sure if Kevin was teasing him or telling the truth.

"What do you mean?" *he asked cautiously.*

"I mean," *Kevin said,* "that I know what the monster is—it's a shape-shifter like in the movie, *The Thing*. It can make itself look like anyone it wants. It could be your teacher, or that girl, Sally, in your class that you like. Heck, it could even be . . . Mom or Dad!" *Kevin stepped closer, his hands hooked into claws held out in front of him, reaching for Billy.*

"It could even look like . . . me!" *He grabbed Billy, twisted him in a headlock and cried,* "Monster-noogies!" *He raked his clawed hand back and forth across Billy's head.*

The next day, after school, a police car showed up at the house. Billy was in his room reading when Kevin came running in.

"The cops are here. I just heard them tell Mom that you called them last night from our phone, and you were stupid enough to leave your name and address. Mom told them about your stupid monster dream." *Kevin laughed.* "I can't believe what a dumb shit you are. Now they're probably going to arrest you."

They hadn't. Both of his parents, however, did have a long sit-down talk with him, after the police left, on the seriousness of what he had done. But Billy only wanted to know if the cops believed his story.

"No, Billy," *his father said harshly, irritation in his tone,* "they didn't. They don't solve crimes and find killers with dreams. You caused them to waste time coming here 'cause they have to check out every clue, every call about these things. They could have been working on real clues."

"But did you tell them I saw the monster stab the mother and baby with the broken golf club like I told you?" *Billy asked with a pleading look directed at his mother.*

"As soon as they heard you called about a dream, Bill," *his father answered instead, his voice on the edge of angry now,* "they didn't want to hear any more. You're lucky they were nice guys 'cause they warned us that making phony calls to the cops is serious business. Do it again and you'll be arrested and sent to jail."

He opens his eyes. They drip tears . . .
(No one except Bradley ever believed you.)
. . . and now his mother and Kevin are dead and . . .
(The Monster ate Dad.)
. . . the evil thing looks enough like him to fool almost anyone—
(But not you!)
—his face, his hair, his arms and legs. Even though Kevin was teasing that time, he was right and hadn't known it—The Monster *is* a shape-shifter like the alien monster in the movie, *The Thing*. Now it looks like his dad and acts like his dad, but not completely. The features are a little too hard and The Monster *is* left-handed, his dad, right. Two more things give it away—its *eyes* and its voice. When Billy looks into its eyes he *knows* that it isn't his father; not his *real* father. And its voice is the growl of the beast, of The Monster, not Dad.

Tears come.
(Stop it! Stop it! You don't have time for this. You can't hide in here forever! The Monster will find you!)

Low moaning sounds come from his throat. He tries to stop them, but the moaning becomes louder. He can't help it. The sound is in danger of bursting forth as a full-pitched wailing when he hears footsteps in the hallway and the sound of The Monster humming.

Billy slaps his hands over his mouth and holds his breath. It sounds like The Monster is right outside the bathroom.

"Where are you, you little bastard?" he hears it say softly. "You can't hide from me forever. This house is big, but it ain't that big."

The Monster lets out a long slow breath. Billy cringes as he hears it step into the bathroom, then the sound of toilet paper being pulled from the roll. Next comes the sound of The Monster blowing its nose.

"Let's see," The Monster muses aloud in a low voice, "I checked the entire downstairs. I know you didn't climb out a window 'cause I would have heard you, plus they're all still locked from the inside. You didn't get out the front door either because, likewise, *it's* still locked from the inside."

Billy hears the toilet flush.

The Monster leaves the bathroom, and a moment later Billy hears its heavy, though muffled, footsteps going up the stairs which run right over the downstairs bathroom.

(Now! Get out now!)

He's tempted to burst from the cabinet and make a run for the kitchen door, but he has to wait until The Monster is all the way upstairs. Then he can get to the kitchen, pull a chair over to the door, get on it, undo the chain bolt-lock, and get out of the house. He figures he can run across the street and get the neighbor, Mr. Velardo, to call the police. But he has to wait, otherwise The Monster will hear and catch him.

The Monster's footsteps reach the top of the stairs. Billy hears it walking down the upstairs hall. The house is old, and whenever anyone walks around upstairs it can be heard downstairs as the ceilings and beams in the house creak. Billy pushes aside the toilet paper and cleaners and opens the cabinet door a crack to hear better. It sounds like The Monster is in the upstairs bathroom looking in the linen closet for him.

(Hell-o-o! Earth to Billy! Etter-bay am-scray ow-nay!)

Billy pushes the cabinet door all the way open. He starts to get out, but suddenly both legs cramp, causing deep severe pain in his calves. He doesn't know how

long he was asleep, but he's been in the cabinet space
too long. His legs already hurt from being thrown down
the cellar stairs; now the pain is so intense he almost
cries out and starts bawling.

(Might as well just yell, "Come and get it, Mr. Monster!
Dinner's ready!")

He crawls on his stomach out of the cabinet. He
straightens his legs, stretching them as quietly as possible without making any noise.

(If you think your legs hurt now, wait until The Monster *chops them off*!)

Billy lies on the bathroom floor, crying silently. He is
tired, hungry, and in more pain than he's ever felt in
his young life. He's in a state of shock that would make
a weaker child comatose. He doesn't want this to be
happening anymore. He wants the bad dream to end.
He wants to wake up and have his mom and his dad and
Kevin and the baby all there safe and sound and . . .

(Stop crying and think!)

He opens his eyes.

If The Monster ate Dad, and Kevin is in the dining
room, and Mom is . . .

(You know!)

Where is the *baby*? He ponders that question and the
cramps in his legs suddenly subside. The muscles relax.
He stretches the left one more but gets a spasm. The leg
jerks involuntarily. His left foot nudges the front of the
cabinet, knocking a bottle of mouthwash off the edge
of the sink. Almost letting out a shriek, Billy squirms
and twists and slides his body over the tiled floor in an
attempt to catch the bottle. It slips through his hands
and lands with a soft but painful *thump* on his chest.

(Yes! He makes the game-winning grab!)

He quickly wraps both arms around the large bottle
and hugs it as he tries to hear where The Monster is and
if it heard and is coming.

The house is very quiet. Billy holds his breath, contorting his face in an effort to open his ears wider to hear any sound of The Monster's movement.

There is silence in the house.

Gathering his courage, he places the mouthwash on the floor next to the cabinet and gets to his hands and knees. He crawls to the bathroom door. He sticks his head out but can see nothing but the empty hallway. He listens and can hear nothing.

(Now would be a good time to get out of here, don't you think? Run and push a chair to the door and undo the lock?)

Slowly Billy gets to his feet and stands on his sore legs. Moving as quickly as he can and still be quiet, he starts for the kitchen. Halfway through the hallway, he hears The Monster walking along the upstairs hallway directly over him.

(Go now! Move!)

From just above him, Billy hears The Monster say in a singsong voice, "I can hear you!"

It freezes him.

The Monster is coming downstairs.

Billy can't move. He hears The Monster on the top step. Two more and it will be at the top landing, and he'll be able to see its feet. Still he can't move a muscle to save his life.

(Scream! Run to the door! Hide! Do *something*, but don't just stand here and waste these precious moments!)

Billy can see the tip of one of The Monster's shoes as it steps onto the first landing. That's enough to break his frozen panic and get him moving. He ducks into the living room, avoids the blood on the floor, jumps over the downed bookcase, and runs into the dining room keeping his eyes averted from the horror that lies there. Soundlessly, he slips under the dining room table at the end opposite Kevin. He hides amid the chair legs, his back to the bloody body that used to be his brother. If The Monster goes into the living room, he can slip into the kitchen, maybe stay ahead of the beast. Maybe find a way to escape.

(That's a lot of maybes!)

It feels so strange to be under the table like this. Just last night he had sat here, having dinner with his mother . . .

(Don't think about it.)

. . . and the baby; Kevin was still sick with the flu and up in his room . . .

(At least baby Jimmy might be alive—you *can* think about that.)

. . . and Dad was away on a business trip. He was due home tomorrow, Saturday, but Billy now figures he came home early and surprised The Monster like in his dream.

But last night it was just him, Mom, and the baby. They had meatloaf for supper with mashed potatoes, gravy, and broccoli. Billy hates broccoli. So does Kevin. His dad hates it, too, but his mother cooks it at least once a week anyway, insisting it's good for them. Billy always hides the gross stuff under his mashed potatoes and hopes his mother won't notice, but she always does. Then he has to gag them down anyway. Last night, however, his mom didn't even mention the broccoli hidden under the remnants of mashed potatoes on his plate. She just took his plate away without a word. She was upset. She had just learned of the latest murders; the bodies were found in Coggshall Park. Though Billy had seen it in another dream, he didn't tell her about it. He learned his lesson after the incident with trying to tell the police.

He dropped his fork just before she took his plate, and he didn't pick it up because the baby, who was sick with the flu, also, and lying in his portable bassinette in the living room, started crying and throwing up. Billy hurried over to wipe Jimmy's chin with his napkin and forgot about his fork.

The sound of The Monster reaching the bottom of the stairs interrupts his thoughts. He listens as The Monster goes into the kitchen.

"It's okay now, Billy-boy."

Its voice sends a chill through him.

(It sounds more and more like *Dad*! The Monster can impersonate him almost *perfectly* now!)

"I was just kidding around before. I'm not going to hurt you. I was just playing a little joke."

Oh, how Billy wants to believe it really is his dad; he wants everything to be normal again.

(Are you kidding? Look behind you, that's Kevin, *dead*, and guess who killed him? That thing out there in the kitchen, that's who. So you can forget about normal; normal has gone bye-bye. Normal hit the road and said, "See you later, alligator!")

In the silence, Billy can just make out the sound of The Monster chuckling softly to itself.

(It almost had you fooled, didn't it? When are you going to learn? Don't listen to it!)

Billy can hear it breathing. The sound seems to come from everywhere at once. Suddenly Billy realizes that The Monster has been moving as it talks to him. Now he has no idea where it is, whether it's still in the kitchen, in the front hallway, or . . .

(Right behind you!)

He quickly turns and looks.

Not there.

A drop of sweat crawls down the side of his nose, making it itch uncomfortably. Somewhere, not too far away, a floorboard creaks slightly, not loud enough for him to pinpoint its location exactly. It might have come from the hallway or the kitchen or even the living room, which is blocked from his view by the low-hanging table-cloth. Billy doesn't dare move. The drop of sweat slides down to the tip of his nose and hangs there maddeningly. Instead of dropping off, the sweat drop remains, becoming an itch, then a tickle. He dares to move and rub the sweat away, but it is too late. He's going to sneeze. He holds his breath, blinks his eyes, scrunches up his face, and puts his index finger under his nose—anything to ward off the sneeze. It's no good. The sneeze is building, tingling and burning in his nasal passages all the way up to a point right between his eyes. The sneeze is going to come no matter what.

(And The Monster will hear it and change back to its *real* form as it charges in, fangs dripping, claws bloody and ready to shred you to pieces, and suck you in just like it did to Dad!)

Billy shudders at the memory. Sometimes . . .

(Like now?)

. . . he wishes he could turn off the voice in his head; the voice of his wise-guy alter ego. Sometimes, it really isn't a good thing.

(Thanks. I love you, too.)

Billy grabs at his nose with his left hand and squeezes it, attempting to stifle the nasal explosion that is trying to erupt. There is a soft sound in the room—a footstep? Or is it just his imagination?

(Sounded like a footstep to me.)

He was so involved with his nose that he can't be sure of what he heard—if it is The Monster or not. The table-cloth hangs so low—almost to the floor—that he can't see more than a few inches of hardwood floor around the table. The sneeze will wait no longer. Helpless to stop it, he can at least hold it in enough that only a tiny squeak escapes.

He strains to hear The Monster, wondering if it heard him. All seems quiet.

"Gesundheit!"

(It's in the room!)

The Monster's feet appear suddenly at the edge of the table, just under the long tablecloth. The cloth lifts. The Monster bends over. Billy is too paralyzed with fear to run.

(Last night—)

The Monster wears the Spider-Man mask again. Billy remembers from his dreams of the thing that it likes to wear a mask when it kills. It looks at him through the eyeholes, making him shiver.

(Last night you—)

The Monster reaches for him, its eyes gleaming.

(Last night you dropped a fork—)

The Monster laughs. It has him, and it knows it. Now its eyes are laughing at Billy, too.

(Last night you dropped a fork *and didn't pick it up*!)

In the cramped space under the table Billy lurches away from The Monster's grabbing claws. He rolls onto his back and slides around between two chairs, using his feet to push himself over the slippery hardwood floor.

(There!)

He sees it . . .

(The fork!)

. . . right where he dropped it next to the leg of his chair. It's just a few feet from where Kevin now lies all bloody and dead.

Billy grabs for the fork but is prevented from reaching it when The Monster's clawed hand catches on his pants leg, snagging him.

"No!" he screams in panic and terror. He lunges forward, straining for the fork. His finger touches it but only manages to push it away. The Monster pulls him back. Billy kicks and feels the heel of his right foot connect with The Monster's left arm, loosening the pressure of its grip for just a second. That's all Billy needs. He lunges for the fork again, and this time his fingers close around it before The Monster can pull him back.

The Monster drags Billy toward the edge of the table. Its rhythmic grunting and breathing sound like the workings of some strange machine. Billy doesn't resist but rolls toward The Monster, trapping its hand under his butt. With all his might he stabs the fork into the tender skin on the inside of The Monster's left forearm.

The tines of the fork aren't very sharp, and his seven-year-old muscles aren't strong enough to push it in far enough to do any real damage, but it does break the skin; it does stick in The Monster's flesh and draw blood. Best of all, it surprises The Monster and startles it into letting him go. Billy scrambles away, crawling quickly under the table and out the other side.

"Aaaarrrrrrrggghhhh!" The Monster screams like a character in a comic book. It is such a corny and fake-sounding scream that it almost makes Billy chuckle despite his fear. He gets to his feet on the other side of the table and runs into the kitchen. There is a loud bang from behind him. The Monster swears loudly and furiously. Billy realizes The Monster must have hit its head on the underside of the table as it tried to stand and come after him.

(Good!)

The Monster lets out a stream of curses. Billy is certain it will come charging after him any second. He only has three choices as far as he can see—he can run to the cellar, or duck into the living room via the front hallway . . .

(And get trapped like a rat, you rodent.)

. . . or run upstairs.

(Bingo! That's your only real choice.)

He grabs one of the kitchen table chairs as he runs by it, and pulls it to the floor. It falls with a loud clatter.

He hopes it will hinder The Monster's pursuit. He heads into the front hall and up the stairs, grabbing the newel post and looking toward the living room in the same motion. The pool of blood is still there, spread over the highly polished hardwood floor. A scream builds in his chest at the sight of the blood, and no matter how much he tells himself not to think about it, he can't help but remember to whom the blood belongs.

(It'll belong to you if you don't move it!)

A shadow falls over the dark red puddle and a second later The Monster steps over the gore and into the hallway, its eyes red and wide and hateful with murderous intent behind the mask. Its hands are up and ready to tear into him.

"Mommy!" Billy squeals in fright, not even realizing that he does.

"I don't think she'll be helping you," The Monster says in a mock-sorrowful voice. The sleeves of its sweatshirt are pushed up. A trickle of blood from the superficial fork wound runs down the inside of The Monster's left forearm.

Billy flings himself up the stairs, scrambling on hands and feet to climb away from The Monster as quickly as possible. The thing starts after him, but the ringing doorbell again stops it. The Monster turns toward the kitchen.

(Go! Go! Go!)

Billy goes.

His foot slips on blood on the edge of the next step. He falls and bangs his knees and scrapes his chest on the edge of the steps above it. There is blood on every step.

(Ignore it!)

He keeps scrambling and finally manages to make it to the top.

He stands and rubs his bloody hands on his pants. His chest aches.

(Is there *anyplace* left that doesn't hurt?)

The doorbell rings again.

Billy listens to The Monster go into the kitchen and hears it swear, "Fuck! What now?" It is no longer imitating his dad; its voice is growling and harsh again. A moment later, it comes back to the doorway between the kitchen and the hallway and its voice gets louder.

"It's your little buddy, Bradley, at the door. If you make a sound, or try to call for help, I won't hesitate to pull him inside and gut him like a fish."

(That's right! Bradley was coming over to play video games after school.)

Bradley Goldberg is Billy's best—

(Only!)

—friend. With Kevin sick, Billy had been looking forward to an uninterrupted afternoon of video game play with Brad.

(Not!)

The Monster chuckles. "I know you'll do the right thing," it says, adding "Sucker!" under its breath.

Billy waits for The Monster to answer the door, but it doesn't.

(Uh-oh! What's it doing?)

He imagines The Monster standing in the shadows of the kitchen like it did before, spying through the curtain and waiting for Brad to leave.

Billy knows The Monster is right. Bradley won't stand a chance if he tries to warn him. He knows The Monster will be true to its word and Brad will die.

Something tugs at him as he wishes he could get a cry for help to Brad without endangering his best friend; something about Brad and being *upstairs* that can help . . .

(That would be nice.)

. . . He and Brad were up here not that long ago—

(The day after the cops came 'cause of your call!)

—when he told his best friend about how he had

called the cops to tell them about his dreams. Brad is the only person who believes him. He's the only person Billy has been able to talk to about his dreams and The Monster who hasn't laughed at him and made fun of him, like Kevin, or treated him like a child who can't tell the difference between a dream and something real, like his parents. Brad is the only one Billy dared tell about the dreams where he is thrust into The Monster's head while it's stalking and killing its victims.

(He didn't laugh or think you were nuts.)

Billy turns and looks into his parents' bedroom, directly across from the top of the stairs.

(I wouldn't hide in there.)

Hiding isn't what he has in mind. Something else. He was telling Brad about how he dialed 911 and it comes to him. He realizes he's been staring at the thing from the moment he looked into the bedroom.

(Oh yeah!)

It's right there . . .

(How stupid can you be? It was right in front of you all along!)

. . . on the night table by his parents' bed. The upstairs phone!

(Rescue!)

Billy runs to the bedside and snatches up the receiver. Before it's even to his ear he dials 911, the way his mother taught him. But there is no sound on the line, no dial tone. He depresses the hang up button and releases it. Still nothing. No sound. No buzzing on the line.

(No rescue!)

His mother and father taught him how to use the phone in an emergency . . .

(And boy! is this ever an emergency.)

. . . but they never told him what to do if the phone didn't *work* in an emergency.

(Guess they never planned on us being stuck in the house with a monster smart enough to screw up the phones!)

Billy puts the receiver down and looks around, checking the two bureaus, the dresser, and night tables on both sides of the bed. His mother has a cell phone—his dad's is broken—but she usually keeps it in her purse or her pocket. He doesn't see it. He takes a cautious step back toward the hallway. The Monster is still nowhere in sight. The doorbell has stopped ringing. Brad left. Brad's *safe*!

(So where's The Monster now? Waiting for you to go back downstairs?)

Billy expects to see it coming up the stairs for him any second, but the hallway and stairs remain empty. He doesn't know what to do.

(Maybe it's already up here—hiding in the hallway.)

Billy doesn't think so; he would have heard it. . . .

(But you were distracted by the phone.)

Could The Monster have snuck upstairs then?

(Yes!)

Tiptoeing, Billy crosses the room to the door. He peers around the edge of the door frame, exposing just his right eye as he scans the hallway. It's empty.

(But that doesn't mean The Monster ain't lurking in the bathroom or in one of the other rooms, or just around the corner that turns into yours and Kevin's room at the end.)

He knows that.

(If it *is* hiding down there, you can run downstairs and try to unlock the door again or find an open window, but do it quick.)

But Billy can't bring himself to attempt it, not knowing for sure where The Monster is hiding. He steps cautiously into the hallway and nearly drops dead with fright when a floorboard creaks loudly beneath his feet.

"Is that you, honey?"

The Monster is still downstairs in the kitchen.

(What's it doing down there? It's got you trapped up here. Why isn't it coming after you? I don't like this one bit.)

Billy agrees. He knows he has to hide and fast. Whatever The Monster is up to it's sure to be something bad. For a moment, Billy harbors the thought of just doing nothing, not hiding, not running, not anything. Just give up and stand there and wait for The Monster to come.

(Are you crazy? While you're at it, just lie down in the middle of the highway, drink poison, or take a long walk off a short pier. Do you want to die? Do you?)

Billy knows what the answer to that question *should* be, knows what a *normal* person would answer, but after everything that's happened he feels decidedly *un-*normal.

(As opposed to when?)

His brother is dead. As far as he knows . . .

(Unless Mom lent her favorite sandals to the person lying in a pool of blood behind the couch in the living room—)

. . . so is his mother, and his father has been devoured by The Monster. Why should he feel normal? *How* can he *possibly* feel normal?

(Actually, think about it—for someone in your position, feeling like you do, wanting to just lay down and give up *is* probably normal, but you can't. You don't have time! Don't you hear The Monster coming?)

Actually, he doesn't. The stairs, which creak loudly under the slightest weight, are silent. Billy steps into the hall and cranes his neck to see—no monster on the stairs.

(Got to make a decision here: fly or fry?)

Shut up! He tells the voice in his head. *Just shut up for once and listen. What do you hear?*

(Taps?)

No . . . it's nothing.

He can't hear The Monster at all.

Where is it?

(Good question.)

Billy goes to the railing that runs half the length of the upstairs hall. He leans as far out as he dares to be able to see downstairs.

(Hello-o! Why are you doing this when you could be yelling out a window or even climbing out one?)

Billy goes to the window at the top of the stairs and looks through the open slats of the Venetian blind.

(Never mind.)

It's at least a twenty-foot drop from the window to the flagstone front walk below.

(You'll kill yourself.)

He slips back into his parents' bedroom and goes to the window that overlooks the porch at the front of the house. He can see no one on the street beyond the porch roof. He tries to lift the window, but the windows are the original ones the house was built with, and even his father, who is strong, has trouble getting them open and closed they stick so badly.

(Now what?)

Good question. He glances around the room one more time; fleetingly considers hiding under the bed . . .

(The Monster will be able to see you under there as it comes upstairs!)

. . . but immediately dismisses the idea. He goes back to the hallway and listens. Now he hears The Monster in the kitchen.

(What's it doing?)

The mangled refrigerator door groans as it opens and closes. A pop, a hiss, and a slurping, gulping wet sloppy noise follow, and then a metallic crunching sound. The noises evoke images in Billy's head of The Monster opening the refrigerator door, taking out one of Billy's father's beers, slamming the door, popping the top on the beer can, and guzzling it down before crushing the empty aluminum can. Just like Billy's father used to do.

Anger surges in Billy. *The Monster is drinking my dad's beer!* He never cared about his dad's beer before, but now the thought of The Monster slurping it down makes Billy so angry he wants to bawl his eyes out.

(Snap out of it!)

The Monster burps loudly, and its voice breaks the silence. "You can stay up there if you want, Billy-boy, or you can come down now. As soon as I'm done down here, I'll be coming for you, and it won't be pretty if you make me work for it." The Monster punctuates the statement with another loud wet burp.

(Don't listen!)

He tries not to, but the truth of The Monster's words fill Billy with a crippling despair. The Monster is right; he can't get away. His only option is to find another place to hide—and there are very few of those left—where he can wait in trembling terror for The Monster to find him and murder him the way it murdered the rest of his family.

Why *not* just give up and get it over with? Why torture himself with fear, with hiding and listening to The Monster search for him, getting closer and closer until . . .

Wouldn't it be easier to just give up now?

(No! You can't be a quitter!)

His dad always said that the worst thing anyone can ever be is a quitter. And though Billy is certain his father is gone, consumed by The Monster, he knows that if Dad *were* still around he would tell him, "Don't be a quitter, Billy."

Billy quickly assesses his situation. He can't get any of the second floor windows open.

(Not that it matters with no one outside to yell to.

Even if there were, I guess Mr. Monster would be up here in two seconds flat if it heard you hollering out the window.)

Billy supposes it would. The Monster is downstairs, so going down there is out of the question. There really is only one option left open to him.

(As long as you don't count suicide.)

While The Monster is busy doing whatever it's doing downstairs, he has to find a place to hide. But there is something else he's forgotten. . . .

(The baby!)

That's it! Before he can hide he has to check on Jimmy.

(I wouldn't be too hopeful of finding your baby brother alive; that kid has *never* gone this long without crying.)

In the house below, Billy hears The Monster walking around. It sounds as though it's still in the kitchen. Billy moves stealthily along the upstairs hallway. From many a game of hide-and-seek he's played in the house, he knows which parts of the hallway floor creak. He avoids these and the spots of blood leading from the nursery to the stairs.

(Not a good sign!)

At the same time he listens for any sign that The Monster is coming upstairs after him. Billy goes as quickly and directly as he can to the nursery at the end of the hallway, just before it takes a left turn into his and Kevin's room. The door is open. The floor is covered with blood. More blood drips from the closet doorknob and runs down the wooden door panels. A pool of the red stuff beneath the knob is large and has a sheen to its surface.

(Whose blood is it? The baby's?)

He steps across the threshold and over the blood to the end of the crib. He stands on tiptoes to see over the crib's baseboard.

(Jimmy is there!)

He slips around to the side, whose bars remind him of his trip to Benson's Wild Animal Farm in New Hampshire last year, and looks through; Baby Jimmy is definitely in the crib.

(Be quiet! He's sleeping!)

But there is something wrong. Billy moves closer.

(Don't wake him up! Don't make him cry!)

Billy's baby brother lies unmoving, his eyes not completely closed.

(The Monster got him, too?)

A gut-wrenching sob escapes Billy.

(Shhh! The Monster!)

He stifles his crying, forces it back into his chest where it becomes a hot knife of pain. Scalding tears squeeze from the corners of his clenched eyes.

(Don't lose it now!)

He turns away from the crib, but is faced again with the bloody doorknob on the closet door and the pool of blood congealing on the floor. It sickens him.

(Don't hurl now!)

He staggers back into the hallway.

(Listen!)

From downstairs he hears The Monster moving stuff around; sounds like furniture.

(Stop wondering what it's doing and find someplace to hide, or try another window! There's got to be *some* way out of here!)

Billy shakes his head; he knows if he can't open the window in his parents' room, he won't be able to open any of the other second floor windows. Even if he could, he remembers now that all the outside, winter storm windows, except for the one at the top of the stairs, are still down; his father was supposed to put them up when he got home from his trip, and Billy and Kevin were going to help him. They had helped their father put

them down with great difficulty last fall when he winter-
ized the house, and Billy definitely knows he can't open
those. Besides, all of the windows are just as high as the
one at the top of the stairs. He'd break his neck jump-
ing from any of them.

Hiding is his only option.

(But where?)

Something tantalizes the edges of his memory. He
wracks his brain to remember what it is.

(You'd better hurry up! How about you try and fool
The Monster for now and buy some time?)

He goes to the bathroom door and listens. He hears
more furniture being moved around, then silence. He
steps into the bathroom and pulls the shower curtain
closed, letting it make a lot of noise in the quiet house.
He wants The Monster to hear.

(Good idea!)

Without a sound, Billy creeps back into the hallway.
The Monster's heavy tread sounds in the downstairs
hallway.

(It's coming!)

The sick knot in Billy's gut tightens.

The Monster's footsteps stop.

(Don't crap your pants! That shower curtain thing is
good, but if you think it'll fool The Monster, then your
smarts have been overrated.)

Billy ignores the remark and keeps on. He tiptoes
past the nursery to his and Kevin's bedroom and slips
through the half-open door. He knows his attempt to
fool The Monster won't, but maybe it will slow it down;
it'll have to check it out just to be sure. And that will
give Billy just enough time to reach what he's finally remembered—the *perfect* hiding spot.

He discovered it two years ago, at Easter, shortly after
his fifth birthday. The family had recently discovered
that Grammy—Billy's mother's mother—was dying of

cancer. His mother had decided to have a big family re-
union and cook a massive ham dinner for her parents
and their surviving brothers and sisters, plus all her siblings—three brothers and two sisters, and their spouses
and children. The house was crowded with relatives—
Billy's aunts and uncles, great aunts and uncles, close
cousins and a few distant ones, plus Grampy and Grammy.

Despite the pall that hung over the adults, Billy and
his cousins, not understanding how ill their grandmother
was, or how little time she had left to live, had fun. Billy
loved having all his relatives there any time other than
his birthday. He loved the feeling in the air when the
house was full of voices and laughter and sometimes
even singing. He loved running around the house, in and
out of adult legs and under tables and around furniture,
chasing cousins, being chased, laughing, screaming, giggling.

It was after dinner when he found the perfect hiding
place. The adults were in the living room, trying to sit
comfortably with their ham-swollen bellies to watch a
movie called *The Passion of the Christ*. The kids, Billy and
Kevin and their cousins, were at the kitchen table,
which was always designated as the "kids' table" at holi-
days while the adults ate in the dining room. They were
all eating chocolate cream pie when Kevin suggested
they play hide-and-seek.

After several rounds of "one-potato-two-potato-three-
potato-four," Uncle Bob-the-state-policeman's daughter,
Sherry, who was Kevin's age, was picked to be IT. She
stood with her face to the closed cellar door and started
counting by ones to fifty. Cousins scrambled everywhere.
Ronnie, Aunt Phyllis and Uncle Jim's seven-year-old,
scooted into the dining room and hid under the vacant
table with its long cloth hanging nearly to the floor providing good cover. Bowie, Aunt Sally and Uncle Bill's six-
year-old Dakota Fanning look-alike daughter, ran into the

living room and hid behind the couch. Brendan, Uncle
Mike and Aunt Marie's ten-year-old, sucked his stomach
in enough to squeeze in behind the knickknack cabinet
in the corner of the breakfast nook. And Dominic, who
was Aunt Gina and Uncle Ted's five-year-old, started following Billy as he headed upstairs right behind Kevin.

Kevin took the stairs two at a time and outdistanced
Billy and Dominic quickly. Billy was six months younger
than Dominic, and a lot smaller than his cousin, but
Dominic was a whiner and acted like the younger child.
Billy couldn't stand him. As fast as he could Billy fol-
lowed his older brother up the stairs.

"Wait up!" Dominic cried, his voice high-pitched and
needling. Sometimes it made Billy shiver with disgust to
hear it. "Wait up" was the last thing Billy intended to do.

"Find your own hiding place!" Billy said over his
shoulder. Behind him, wimpy Dominic started to blubber.

"I-I-I don't know where to hide!"

Billy cringed but felt bad all the same. He let Dominic catch up to him at the top of the stairs. Below, he
could hear Sherry counting: ". . . twenty-seven, twenty-
eight, twenty-nine . . ."

In his parents' room, Kevin was slipping into the
closet.

"Hide under the bed in my mom's room," Billy directed Dominic, who was only too happy to do as told.
As soon as his cousin was wedged under the bed, Billy
headed for his room and the large closet. He pushed
his way into the deep end and discovered pieces of
wood nailed onto the wall there like a ladder, which al-
lowed him to climb to the single shelf at the top of the
closet. The shelf was large and more than long and
wide enough for him to lie on and keep most of the
piles of off-season clothing stored there in front of him,
giving him something to hide behind and lie on.

He had won the game of hide-and-seek with that hiding place and it had become his secret place ever since. He'd told no one about it, not even Brad.

(Yes! That's the place!)

Billy goes to the closet, moving soundlessly through his and Kevin's room, and pauses outside the door. He listens for The Monster. Faintly, from the kitchen, he hears The Monster open the refrigerator door again and a repeat of the beer-drinking sounds. Maybe The Monster will get drunk, he hopes, and fall asleep.

(Yeah, and maybe you shouldn't depend on maybes.)

He hears The Monster crunch the beer can and toss it into the plastic trash barrel with the swivel lid on it near the kitchen closet door.

"Okay," The Monster says, out of breath.

Billy hears it walk into the downstairs hallway. He hears its feet upon the stairs as it says: "But we *should* if we want them to buy it."

(We?)

For a moment Billy wonders if The Monster has someone . . .

(Another monster?)

. . . with it, but the stairs creak again, and he must hide. He slips inside the closet, leaving the door open in the hope it might fool The Monster into thinking he isn't in there.

(Fat chance with your luck!)

The closet is the largest in the house—bigger than the bathroom—and used by his mother to store anything and everything that she can fit in there. He retreats to the deep end, sliding between stacks of cardboard boxes and pushing through two rows of hanging clothes as he goes. In the darkness he feels for the rear corner of the closet where his winter coat hangs on a hook and covers the ladder. As quietly as possible, he takes the coat down, puts it over his shoulder, and climbs to the shelf. He replaces his coat on the hook to hide the boards, and then slides behind the piles of his and Kevin's summer clothes still in winter storage even though it's May.

There is a muffled creak of wood from somewhere in the house.

(The Monster's upstairs.)

It's followed by a low, mean chuckle.

(It's in the hallway.)

"Time for fun and games! Nothing better than a good old game of hide-and-seek," The Monster says, laughing after as if it cracked a joke. "I hope you're not hiding in one of the clo-sets!" The Monster singsongs. "That would be too ea-sy!"

(Maybe it can read your mind!)

Billy listens to The Monster, and a fresh cold wave of fear washes over him. From the sound of The Monster's voice, it's definitely upstairs, maybe in the hallway . . .

(Or in your room right outside the closet door!)

No matter. Either way it's too late to find another hiding place. He's just going to have to trust that The Monster won't think he can get up on the shelf.

"Surprise!" The Monster yells and there is a loud bang. From the sound, Billy guesses it's the closet door in his parents' bedroom next door.

There is silence for several minutes before it is split by a loud crash and the sound of splintering wood, but no longer from next door. The only thing Billy can imagine is that The Monster kicked in the bathroom door.

"I'm com-ing Billy-boy," The Monster croons, singing its words still. Billy hates it when The Monster calls him "Billy-boy."

(Don't think about that now.)

He can't help it. It makes him shiver and feel sick.

He hears a new sound—the shower curtain being pulled back. The Monster is definitely in the bathroom.

A few moments later there is the squeak of another door opening, and he guesses The Monster is in the nursery. He hears it moving around, searching for him.

Then silence.

Billy waits.

The Monster should be coming into his room next.

(Better hold it together.)

He takes a deep breath and tries to control his trembling.

The door to his room opens slowly. The hinges creak loudly as they always do. Billy can hear The Monster humming to itself as it moves around the room like a housewife straightening up. The humming fades along with any sound of the thing.

Billy holds his breath.

(Get ready, here it comes.)

He strains to hear if The Monster is right outside the closet door, but his heart is pounding in his ears so loudly he can hear nothing else.

(Bet The Monster can hear it, too.)

Billy hides his face behind the clothes and waits, trying to prepare himself for The Monster inevitably attacking the closet and tearing out everything inside as it searches for him. He hopes he doesn't scream . . .

(You scream, you die.)

. . . and he hopes The Monster doesn't look under his coat, see the ladder, and realize he's hiding on the shelf.

He waits.

Nothing.

Maybe The Monster isn't even going to check the closet.

(Yeah, right! The Monster's not as dumb as you look.)

Shhh! Billy commands the voice in his head. He strains to hear any sound of The Monster in the room beyond the closet door. He's only been listening for a few seconds, but it feels like hours.

(Where the heck is it?)

Billy is just about to sit up and take a peek when he hears a softly spoken swearword come from *within* the closet below him.

He freezes.

(The Monster is *in the closet!*)

"Where the fuck is that little shit?" The Monster mutters to itself in a harsh whisper.

Light suddenly blinds Billy as The Monster pulls the string that lights the bare bulb almost directly over where he lays hiding. He shuts his eyes tightly and listens to The Monster search the closet again. He feels the shelf shake as The Monster moves the clothes on the rack below, looking behind them and finding nothing. Suddenly, the walls and the shelf Billy lays on shake violently as The Monster knocks boxes over and pulls clothes from the racks, throwing them into the room behind it. It is breathing heavily now.

"Where the hell is he?" it whispers in frustration. "He can't have got by me!"

The closet light goes out, and Billy watches colored doughnut-shaped images of its reflection sail across his darkened vision. He listens to The Monster leave the closet and wants to whoop for joy.

(Don't get carried away, or you'll get *carried* away . . . in a coffin!)

He feels a momentary surge of pride at having outwitted The Monster.

(For now, at least.)

The horrid creature never thought to look behind the coat hanging on the hook; never saw the ladder.

"I know you're up here somewhere, Billy-boy," The Monster says. It sounds like it is near the bedroom door. "You know you can't get away. You know you can't get out of the house. I've got all afternoon to find you."

Billy senses it is unsure of the latter statement.

"You can't get away. It'll go easier for you if you just come out now."

It actually sounds *uncertain*.

(Well, sooner or later *someone* is bound to find out it's in here, and what it's done.)

"The longer it takes for me to find you, puke, the worse it will be for you!" The Monster sounds nothing like his father now, and there is no exaggeration or cruel playfulness in its voice any more—only rage.

Abruptly The Monster leaves the room, and Billy hears it go back downstairs. He can't believe it.

(It has to know you're upstairs somewhere. What's it doing? What's it up to? Is there someone at the door again?)

He didn't hear the doorbell, but maybe someone knocked.

(That must be it; being in the closet you couldn't hear it.)

Billy thinks about climbing down and going into the nursery, which is over the kitchen with a window that overlooks the porch. From there he might be able to see who is out there as they leave and maybe get their attention, but the sound of The Monster's muffled voice again stops him. He's pretty sure it says, "All right, honey. Time to go."

(What?)

He hears furniture being pushed around again, and then a new sound, a faint, *scratchy* sound, a sliding sound that he's heard before but can't quite place.

(Now what's The Monster up to? Never mind—you don't want to know—it can't be good.)

Billy lies back and closes his eyes again. He feels suddenly exhausted and limp. The high-voltage terror that has kept him in shock and honed to a razor-sharp edge suddenly drains away. He can't believe it's only been a couple of hours since he got home from school. It feels like The Monster has been chasing him *forever.*

The heat of the closet begins to work on him, making him drowsy. He'd like nothing better than to be able to just go to sleep . . .

(And roll off the shelf! You can't sleep here, you idiot!)

He has to stay awake. He shakes his head.

(Stay awake or you are dead meat.)

The odd sound fades, but he can still faintly hear The Monster moving around. Billy raises his head and listens. The familiar yet baffling sound resumes a few moments later, softly at first, then louder.

(Maybe The Monster is barricading the doors with furniture so you can't escape.)

But then it can't escape, either.

(Maybe it doesn't want to.)

The sound sparks a memory—helping Mom do wash at the local Suds Yer Duds coin-operated laundry last year when their washing machine broke down. Billy tried to carry a large clothes bag filled with dirty laundry, but he couldn't do it. He had to drag it. That's what the sound from downstairs reminds him of; it doesn't sound like furniture, it sounds like that big bag of clothes did when he dragged it across the floor.

The sound sparks a new image in his imagination— The Monster dragging his mom by the ankles through the living room and into the front hallway.

Tears come hard at the thought.

(Oh Khee-rist! Here you go again, crybaby!)

He can't help it; what else could that sound be?

(Lots of things! Maybe The Monster is taking out the trash—you know, getting rid of evidence.)

Emotion makes Billy's eyes heavy and his eyelids

droop. If only he could make it all go away just by closing them; if only he could sleep.

(That's just what The Monster wants. Stay awake!)

He opens his eyes.

(Wide! Wider! The Monster *wants* you to doze off so
it can creep up on you and get you and that'll be the
end, and The Monster will win and get away scot-free.)

Billy rubs his face with his hands. If only it wasn't so
damned hot in the closet.

(If you can't stand the heat, get out of the closet.)

He doesn't dare leave the safe haven he's found.

(Then deal with it.)

It had been an unusually hot May this year and everyone was predicting a scorching summer. Those fore-
casts had been so numerous that Kevin claimed to have
overheard their parents discussing putting in an above-
ground pool in the backyard for the summer.

(That ain't happening anymore.)

No, it isn't, and the realization pierces Billy as painfully
as a physical wound. There are going to be a lot of things
that will never happen. . . .

(Shhh! The Monster!)

From downstairs, the sound of dragging stops for a
few moments, then resumes. Billy estimates The Monster is in the downstairs hallway.

Dragging Mom!

(Don't listen!)

Billy can't ignore it; he is certain now that The Monster is dragging his dead mother through the downstairs . . .

(But where?)

. . . to the *cellar*! In each of his dreams of The Monster murdering, except the last one, The Monster left its
victims in cellars.

(That's right!)

He wants to cry. He wants his mother. Wanting her and knowing she's dead bring tears that he can't hold back. Lying on the shelf in the darkness, listening to The Monster drag his mother to the cellar, Billy cries until the tears run into his ears, making them tickle and itch.

He sits up.

The scraping fades a little, and he imagines The Monster in the kitchen now, dragging Mom across the floor to the cellar door. Then it will drag Kevin down there . . .

(Don't do this!)

. . . then it'll come for Jimmy and . . .

(Don't go there!)

. . . what it will do with the baby and Mom is too horrible to think about. But Billy can't help it. He's seen the other mothers The Monster has killed; their babies stabbed through and pinned to them. He knows that's what The Monster wants to do now. That's why it's dragging Mom into the cellar.

(You can't do anything about that!)

Maybe he can.

(What?)

If The Monster can't *find* Jimmy, then it can't stab something long and sharp through him and Mom and stick them together like a human shish kebab.

(Too risky! Don't even think about it!)

But it's something he knows he *has* to do.

"I can't let The Monster do that to Mom and Jimmy," he vows, his lips moving soundlessly. Billy sits up and slides to the end of the shelf. Carefully, he removes the coat from the hook and puts it over his shoulder. He turns onto his stomach and reaches out with his right foot, groping for the nearest wood brace–ladder rung so he can climb down. There is a scary moment when he can't find the foothold and thinks he is going to fall. He slips lower. Just as he can't hold on any longer and is too far off the shelf to pull himself back up, his heel catches the wood.

(Close one!)

He plants his foot carefully, climbs down, and lays the coat on the floor.

(This ain't a good idea.)

The closet door is open, but very little light from the room penetrates into the deep end where he is. With only one window, Billy's bedroom is never well lit naturally, especially on gloomy, rainy days like today.

Billy drops to his hands and knees and crawls under the few clothes The Monster didn't pull from the rack. He doesn't want to risk making a sound with a hanger sliding or clothes falling and alerting The Monster to his whereabouts. He stops and listens. Faintly, the sound of swearing comes to him, followed by the cellar door opening.

Billy waits until he hears The Monster move again with a grunt and a loud *thump* on the cellar stairs. He stands and walks lightly to the open bedroom door.

His heart is racing.

(Go now while The Monster is making so much noise!)

There are a succession of grunts and *thumps* from downstairs. Billy pictures The Monster dragging Mom down the cellar stairs—a horrible image of her head bouncing off each step, her hair flopping and the blood flying. . . .

(STOP!)

He stays close to the wall, where the floor is less likely to creak, and crosses to the nursery in four steps. He avoids the blood and quickly moves around the crib. He looks at Jimmy.

(This is crazy!)

He looks around. The closet's no good . . .

(This won't end well.)

. . . and not under the crib.

(First place The Monster will look.)

He spies the baby's laundry hamper, a round wicker basket with a matching lid almost as tall as Billy.

(It'll find him there, too.)

The only place left is the bureau, or one of the other rooms.

(You don't have time for that!)

Then it has to be the bureau. The bottom drawer looks big enough.

"Son of a bitch!" The Monster cries loudly enough to be heard from the cellar, startling Billy as he kneels in front of the baby's dresser to slide the bottom drawer open.

(The Monster will hear!)

He does it anyway, with barely a sound.

(That's enough! The Monster heard! It's coming!)

But The Monster isn't; he can hear it climbing the cellar stairs, ranting almost incoherently about a cut it apparently got on its hand while it was in the cellar. Its speech is punctuated with swears—the F-word and the S-word, mostly—every few seconds.

(It's trying to fool you! It's sneaking up on you!)

The large bottom drawer is filled with baby blankets on the right side, but the left side is nearly empty but for one pair of Jimmy's thick woolen winter pajamas.

(Give it up!)

He goes back to the crib.

(Don't you think The Monster can hear you every time you move around?)

It doesn't matter; he has to finish this. He unhooks the side cage and lowers it the way he's seen his mother do plenty of times. Carefully, gently . . .

(You can't wake him!)

. . . he lifts Jimmy from the crib, cradling his head just like his mother showed him.

(Doesn't matter.)

Quietly, he places Jimmy on top of the pajamas and pulls two blankets from the other side over him, being careful to keep it from covering his face.

(Why? It's not like he's going to suffocate! *You* should be worrying about The Monster. Can't you hear it coming?)

He closes the drawer as gently as he handled the baby.

(The Monster's in the kitchen *right below you!*)

He freezes and listens. There is the customary *clang* and lurch throughout the house's old pipes as the kitchen faucet is turned on and off too quickly. Footsteps cross the kitchen . . .

(Here it comes!)

. . . and go into the dining room.

(Kevin!)

Billy stands.

(The Monster's in the dining room to drag Kevin down into the cellar.)

He turns to leave . . .

(No! The dining room is *under* your room! If you go back to the closet now The Monster will hear you for sure.)

He realizes that's true. He's been lucky; if The Monster wasn't so loud most of the time it probably would have heard him by now.

(So don't push your luck.)

He remains immobile in front of the bureau and waits.

(Wait until it's going down the cellar stairs again.)

He listens; hears nothing.

(What if The Monster isn't going for Kevin? What if it went through the dining room into the living room and the front hallway and is sneaking up here right now?)

He's about to move when he hears the loud groan of furniture legs scraping against a wooden floor.

(Sounds like the dining room table.)

He is tormented once again by the dreaded sound of The Monster dragging a body—Kevin this time; he's sure of it—to the cellar. It seems to last an eternity, but eventually he hears the cellar door bang open.

(Now!)

A loud tumbling crash startles him into movement. Swiftly and silently he leaves the nursery and goes back to the closet as The Monster's roaring laughter covers any noise his movement might make. Once inside he drops to his hands and knees and crawls to the deep end. He picks up the coat and uses the wooden cross supports to climb back onto the shelf. After rehanging the coat and hiding the ladder again, Billy lies still and breathless.

The Monster is still laughing.

(The Monster threw Kevin down the cellar stairs!)

Billy bites his lip not to cry.

(Don't!)

The Monster's laughter fades. It's moving through the house again. Loud footsteps on the stairs.

(It *wants* you to know it's coming so you'll be even *more* a-scared—is it working?)

Billy holds his breath and closes his eyes.

(I'll take that as a yes.)

Listen!

(The Monster is in the hallway!)

He follows The Monster's heavy tread to the nursery. There is a momentary silence broken by, "What the fuck?" The Monster bellows. "Where the fuck is the baby?"

Billy is seized with trembling.

(Don't shake! You *shake*—you *rattle*!)

"Billy-boy! This ain't funny!" The Monster roars.

Billy struggles not to wet his pants . . .

(Hold it!)

. . . but with every word The Monster roars the urge to pee grows stronger.

(Get a grip. Don't think about it.)

A loud series of wood-snapping *cracks* erupts from the nursery.

"Where's the baby, Billy-boy?" The Monster asks in a suddenly soft voice that frightens Billy even more than its roaring. It makes him want to do number two in his pants as well as number one.

(Try to think of something else.)

He can't.

(Something happy.)

He can't remember what *happy* is . . .

(Your birthday! That's it! You were happy then!)

It was just two months ago.

(Seems like years!)

It was the best birthday ever; March 8, the day he turned seven years old. He remembers his mom saying: "He might be only seven, but he's wise beyond his years. He's got the mind of a thirty-year-old," to the other moms that came. It was Mom's idea to have a party where he could invite kids from school—no relatives. He tried to tell her that other than Bradley, he didn't have any friends at school, but she thought he was just being silly and went ahead and got the names and addresses of all of his classmates and sent them invitations, care of their parents. Billy was upset at first—

(And afraid!)

—but when he realized he was going to get *two* birth-day parties with the obligatory family party held a week later, he was all for it. His mom had complained earlier in the year about the seemingly endless parade of birth-days for extended family members, going on about how ridiculous it was; the family was getting too big for so many parties. She claimed that Billy's aunts and uncles—

her brothers and sisters since his dad was an only child whose parents were both dead—only wanted to cash in on as many gifts for their kids as they could get. But when it came time for Billy's birthday she insisted on him having a family party in addition to one with his friends. She ignored his father's suggestion that she be the one to set a precedent and start a new tradition. She argued that none of her siblings would take the hint, and Billy would end up losing out.

His father laughed at her then, which made her mad. With only a month to go before Jimmy's birth, his mother's belly was swollen and hanging low, almost between her legs. She had to waddle like a duck when she walked. She looked funny. One day Billy laughed at her trying to walk up the stairs, and she burst into tears. His father explained to him later that women get very emotional when they are going to have a baby, and that it wasn't his fault. His father said having a baby growing inside a woman did funny things to her body and her mind, and it was sometimes hard for her to control the way she felt or acted. His father told him it was like having a different person inside you. Billy kind of knew what he meant by that—his alter ego was like a different person sometimes even though he knew it wasn't.

I wish I didn't laugh at Mom that day.

(You said you were sorry! Go back to the happy memories.)

He was indeed happy to turn seven. It was a milestone for him. Seven meant second grade in the fall. Seven meant he was a big boy. Though Billy loved first grade with Mrs. Petrie, he was very excited about going into second grade. He was even more excited about the coming summer vacation. The day of his birthday was like a preview of the present weather: summer weather, hot and sunny; short-sleeves weather.

The party was outside, in the backyard where his father had set up the large canvas canopy that he usually only put up for the Fourth of July and Labor Day family cookouts. It was a strange day, as his birthdays always seemed to be. It was supposed to be a happy day—the second happiest day of the year, after Christmas, according to his dad, though Billy placed it third after Christmas, then Halloween. That was due to Billy never feeling really happy on his birthday; at least not as happy as he thought he should. Part of it had to do with playing host. His mother insisted that he do his part and wait on his guests and let his cousins or friends play with any of his toys that they wanted to. It was supposed to be *his* day, and he resented having to share his new presents and spend so much time making sure everyone else felt at home. None of his cousins had to do that. At their birthday parties they were the centers of attention and given their own way no matter how bratty they acted. But Billy's mom always said, "I don't care what other people do."

And that was only part of it. The other part was hard to put into words, or even think about in a way that could be examined. It was just a feeling, a mood. It started as soon as he woke on his birthday, and continued to grow throughout the day. It was a sense of fear and sadness combined. If the words had been part of his vocabulary, Billy would have said it was a feeling of sorrowful apprehension, of sad anxiety, that really had nothing to do with the party and the presents he anticipated. Actually, it wasn't even that; it was more like a memory of apprehension and anxiety that he didn't understand at all. It only happened on his birthday—his true birthday. If the party was held on a day other than his actual birthday, he was fine. But come his true birthday, it would start.

This past birthday, as had every other birthday, started with an odd, yet familiar dream—never the same one but all of them similar—just before waking.

He was at Disney World with his mother and father and Kevin. Though he had never actually been there, he had watched enough programs about it on the Disney Channel that his sleeping mind was able to re-create the park in detail. It was one of those dreams where he was completely immersed in the reality of the dream; all his senses experienced it.

It was Easter and they were there for the Annual Easter Egg Hunt. Roger Rabbit was leading the Easter Parade down Main Street USA, and as soon as it passed the hunt was on. Kevin found three eggs right away: beautiful gold, silver, and bejeweled ones that dazzled the eyes, but when Billy looked, he found none, or, if he did see one, it was taken by another child before he could get to it.

An announcement came over the public address system: "The lucky boy or girl who finds the special, magical, black Easter egg will win a week's free stay in the park for his or her entire family!"

And there it was! The black egg the public address announcer had just spoken of. It was sitting under a dwarfed palm tree, right at the curbside, not five feet away. Before Billy could move, Kevin came down the street toward it. Billy lost all hope; Kevin would surely see it. Which was okay; he'd still get to go to Disney for the free week as part of the family, but he had really wanted to find the egg, had wanted so badly, for once, to be the hero.

The unbelievable happened. Kevin walked right by the egg, and hope surged again in Billy. He dashed forward as fast as the dream would allow and grabbed the ebony egg before any of the other children could beat him to it.

It was hot in his hand. And slimy. He held it to his ear and heard a baby crying, then realized the crying wasn't coming from within the egg; it came from nearby, from his mother's swollen belly. And Billy knew, at that moment, that it was him

*in his mom's stomach, crying, making the egg in his hand
grow hot.*

*A different sound came from the egg. He listened. The sound
of growling.*

He woke from the birthday dream that day with a
feeling of déjà vu, on the brink of remembering he'd
had similar dreams every year on his birthday since his
first birthday, but the stuff of sleep was too elusive. Besides, he'd had too much to look forward to.

The sounds of The Monster searching for the baby
stop. The abrupt silence pulls Billy away from his memories.

A few seconds later The Monster says, "Little cock-
sucker!"

(It's in the *room* again!)

Billy holds his breath and closes his eyes. He focuses
once more on the memory of his birthday to keep the
terror away.

His first birthday party this year—the one with kids
from school—was much better than he had thought it
was going to be.

(You were afraid no one except Brad would show
up.)

But his fears were unfounded. Most of the class came
and treated him as though they really were his friends!
Billy was dumbfounded by it and couldn't understand
why—

(Either they just wanted cake and ice cream or their
parents made them to be polite.)

—but he was glad for it, whatever the reason.

Further to his surprise, he got a lot of cool stuff from
his classmates, with the emphasis being on action figures and toys rather than stupid clothes like he usually
got from some of his aunts and uncles and always from
Grampy and Grammy before she died. That in itself
made it better.

After opening his gifts and duly thanking everyone—in addition, his mother would make him write a personal thank-you note to each kid and their parents—they had cake and ice cream and orange soda. Then the games began. Billy's mom went to a lot of effort to devise games and activities for the partygoers to play, to keep them occupied. Though Billy thought they were dumb—games like, "Pin the Tail on the Donkey" and, "Charades," and activities like a three-legged race in the yard and a treasure hunt where kids searched outside for hidden candy and small toys—he joined in and had fun.

To tell the truth, though, as soon as the presents were opened and the cake and ice cream consumed, Billy would have been glad to see everyone but Brad just go home, and he didn't care that much whether even Brad stayed. If everyone left he could play with his new stuff and not have to share it. Then he could plug his new PS3 games in and have some real fun. His mother, though, was adamant about him showing his guests a good time and participating in all the games and activities.

He finally got a break during the treasure hunt. He didn't care if he got any candy—he was still full from the cake and ice cream—and he didn't care about the toys, which were cheap things like balsa wood gliders and plastic water pistols. He snuck into the house, but just as he was about to go into the living room to play his video games, his mother and Mrs. Goldberg, Brad's mother, came inside. Billy had to duck down behind the kitchen counter. If his mom saw him in the house, she'd make him go right back outside and join in the stupid treasure hunt.

Billy was upset and silently repeated a swear word he often heard his father say. If his mother and Mrs. Goldberg stayed in the kitchen, he'd never be able to get into the living room to play his games. He was so upset that he didn't pay much attention at first to the grown-ups talking while his mother made a pot of coffee, until he heard his name. Then he was all ears.

". . . Billy almost never kicked inside me, not like this one. I hope that's a good sign that he'll be different once he's born, too. John didn't want me to have another one, you know, after Billy, but I so want a little girl. The first three months with Billy were really tough. He was sick all the time. There were times when I was actually afraid he might die. It really was hard on us. He cried so much. It got to John more than it did to me. Sometimes, when Billy was really in pain, John couldn't stand his crying. He had to leave the house on many an occasion to get away from it, it bothered him so bad. I think if John had to be with Billy twenty-four hours a day, seven days a week, like I was, it would have driven him insane. I mean, it really can make you understand, and even have sympathy for, those parents that injure their kids or even kill them just trying to get them to stop crying. There were plenty of times I just wanted to shake Billy to get him to shut up. It must be especially hard for single parents. They don't have anyone else to help them out. You know it's not the baby's fault that he's crying, but you get to a point where you're almost ready to do anything to shut him up."

"Oh, I know what you mean," Mrs. Goldberg said. "Bradley was bad, too. He used to sleep all day and stay up crying all night. I was a basket case until my husband's Jewish grandmother visited one day. When I told her what the baby was doing, she picked him up and turned him upside down three times, then put him back in his crib upside down. And you know, it's crazy, but it worked. From that day on he slept at night and was awake during the day, just like normal."

The closet door slams shut suddenly, disturbing the

air around Billy and startling him back to the present. He almost screams . . .

(No! Disaster!)

. . . but doesn't.

"Okay, Billy-boy," The Monster says out in the room.

Billy swallows the whimper that wants to push the stifled scream out.

"I'm through fooling around. It's time to come out and tell me where you put your baby brother."

(The Monster can't find Jimmy!)

Billy feels a surge of triumph.

(Take it easy; you know what happens sometimes when you get too worked up.)

Billy tries to relax and breathe evenly, calmly. It's true. When he gets excited sometimes he starts breathing too fast and gets dizzy. He even passed out once on the first day of kindergarten.

He hears The Monster moving around in the hallway, then its voice: "He can't be in the attic. There's no way he could get this door open."

Billy can picture the thing standing below the pull-down attic door set into the hallway ceiling.

"Okay, so you're not in the attic," The Monster says, speaking softly to itself.

Billy has to strain to catch its words.

"Where might you be?"

Billy is surprised The Monster doesn't sound more upset. The hateful glee that had underscored its voice is back and even more pronounced now.

(It sounds like it's having *fun*, like it's enjoying the hunt.)

"You know, you little puke, *you* hiding on me is one thing, but hiding your baby brother . . . well. That's just not fair," The Monster pouts. "Not fair at all. No fair! No fair!"

(It sounds like a little kid!)

"I have to say that I still think you're in one of the closets, Billy-boy. I guess I just missed you the last time. So-o-o-o-o-o-o, it looks like I'll just have to rip each one apart until I find you, and your brother, my little bunnies. Then I'm going to make you watch what I do to him and your mother!"

Billy cringes at the thought.

The Monster's footsteps retreat down the hallway to Billy's parents' bedroom. It whistles, "Pop Goes the Weasel" loudly as it tears open the closet door, making it bang against the wall. The whistling goes on, but is sometimes covered by the sound of The Monster tearing clothes and hangers out of the closet and throwing them on the floor. There is the sound of boxes falling and being tossed aside. He can hear shoes being kicked around on the wooden closet floor. Immediately following is the sound of wood being wrenched from its nails.

The way the wall behind him shakes Billy guesses The Monster is ripping the very shelves out of the closet in its fervor to find him and Jimmy.

(Maybe we should have hidden in a drawer, too.)

The Monster is going to tear every closet apart until it gets him. It's being very thorough this time.

(Get out of here! Hide under the bed or behind the curtains. Anywhere! It'll be busy ripping the closet apart, and you can sneak out behind it.)

Billy doubts it, but also knows the voice in his head is partly right. He must find another place to hide. He has no choice. If he stays in the closet The Monster is sure to find him . . .

(Wait a minute!)

. . . and when it does it will hurt him to make him tell it where Jimmy is.

(Ever wonder why those boards are here like a ladder in this closet?)

Billy looks up. Slowly, he raises his head and gets up

on one elbow for a closer look at the ceiling above him. A joint in his shoulder pops painfully; the noise is deafening to him. If The Monster wasn't whistling and tearing up the two closets in his parents' room, it would surely have heard. It sounds like a gunshot to Billy. He can see a faint line running through the wide boards that make up the closet ceiling over him. The line makes a square about three feet by three feet. He reaches up and touches the board that is against the rear wall.

(It moved!)

The wide board in the ceiling directly over his head lifted. It is loose.

(That's it!)

So are the others. All of them.

(It's a door! This must have been the original door to the attic; that's why the boards are on the wall like a ladder. It was probably too hard for an adult to use, so someone in the past put in the pull-down attic door in the hallway!)

Billy lays back and looks at the ceiling. In the dark of the closet it looks normal above him; he can't see the outline of the door. He reaches up again and tentatively pushes the board again. It moves. He pushes some more, lifts the wood, and pushes it aside into the attic.

(Do another one.)

He does the same with the board next to it, pushing it up into the attic then off to the side also.

(Yes! That's it!)

Billy sits up and cautiously sticks his head through the opening. Hot stale air washes over him. Using both hands he lifts another board and pushes it aside, widening the hole. There are two more boards that make up the trapdoor and look like they can be removed, but the space is big enough for him to get through.

(All right then! Get up there! It's the perfect hiding place.)

That's true, but it could also be a trap. The only other way out of the attic is through the hallway door, and Billy doubts he can open that door. There is certainly no way out of the house through the attic.

(But The Monster won't look up there for you. It's safe for now.)

Yes, as long as The Monster doesn't see the ladder or find the secret door in the ceiling of the closet in his room when it tears it apart . . .

(Don't even think that!)

. . . he'll be safe.

Grabbing the edges of the opening with his hands, Billy pulls himself up and climbs into the attic. Carefully, he replaces the ceiling boards. The Monster's rampage covers any sounds he makes.

(You'll be safe up here! I'm telling you, The Monster won't check up here, and it *won't* find the trapdoor in the closet.)

Billy hopes so. He doesn't want to think about the alternative. If he does, he'll get so scared that he'll start crying and won't be able to stop. The Monster might even hear him, especially if he gets the hiccups like he often does when he cries. He crouches over the secret door in the top of the closet, his feet on the two rafter beams that run parallel to either side, and replaces the boards. He knows from his dad that he has to be careful to step on the wooden beams in the attic or on the planks of wood his father laid over the beams to create a walkway, or he will go crashing right through the flimsy plaster ceilings of the second-floor rooms below.

He doesn't dare move around in the attic with The Monster on the second floor. He listens to it, trying to pinpoint its location. He thinks it's in the nursery.

(Tearing apart the closet by the sound of it.)

He hopes it doesn't think of searching the bureau drawers. Despite the sounds of destruction, The Mon-

ster still whistles like a happy worker. Under cover of
the noise The Monster is making, Billy stands carefully
on two wooden beams adjacent to the secret door in the
closet ceiling.

The sounds of destruction suddenly stop. The Monster's whistling ceases.

(It heard you!)

He freezes where he is.

(It'll be up here in a flash!)

Billy waits, listening for the sound of squeaking springs
on the attic door as it opens. Instead, he hears a muffled
grunt, then The Monster swears.

"Fuck!"

(It's in your room.)

Billy crosses his fingers and tries to imagine what the
closet looks like from The Monster's point of view. He
wonders if it will see the outline of the trapdoor in the
ceiling, or the crack between the boards, or if it will pull
his coat from its hook and notice the boards like a ladder nailed to the deep inside wall.

He hears the closet door open and squeak on its old
hinges. The Monster is in the closet now, pulling the
rest of the clothes out and throwing them on the bedroom floor. The Monster isn't whistling so happily any
longer. As his brother Kevin would say, "It's pissed!" It
growls with rage as it tears the closet apart. The Monster tears the shelf off the closet wall, its nails shrieking
in protest at being so rudely awakened from their tightly
embedded sleep. The attic rafters shake. He hears the
shelf crash to the floor and imagines The Monster flinging it aside.

Several seconds of silence follow before Billy is
nearly jolted from his perch on the plank by a tremendous pounding on the closet wall that shakes the entire
attic and the house itself like an earthquake tremor. Lit-

tle dust falls flow from the slanted roof beams over Billy's head.

Billy feels like cheering . . .

(Don't get carried away!)

. . . but allows himself only a small victory smile instead. The Monster is in a *rage* because *he* . . .

(Little seven-year-old *Billy Teags*!)

. . . outsmarted it.

(The rotten *bastard*!)

Not wanting to make any sound while The Monster is in the rooms below him, Billy decides he's better off remaining still. Oh so slowly, he lowers himself onto the nearest wide plank and lies on it, stomach down, resting his head on his arms folded under it on the plank. He breathes quietly through his mouth for fear of inhaling dust into his nose and sneezing again, and listens to The Monster go from bedroom to bedroom again, overturning furniture and searching everywhere it can think of in its efforts to find him and Jimmy.

Billy prays the bottom drawer of the bureau in the nursery doesn't open when The Monster surely will knock it over.

(Cross your fingers!)

He does and closes his tired eyes . . .

(Don't go to—)

. . . and yawns.

(—sleep!)

Friday
evening

A nightmare of being stalked by The Monster through a labyrinth of tunnels chases Billy up a long stairway to startled wakefulness and an overwhelming urge to pee. Fear tingles in his spine as the fragments of the dream fade and the realization he dozed off and was helpless and defenseless while he slept sets in.

(What if you had rolled off in your sleep?)

He still lies stretched out on top of the wide, thick wooden plank nearest the closet trapdoor that his father laid across the attic rafter beams so that he could walk around easily and get to all the stuff that is stored up there. There are five planks in all, forming a crude circle around the attic, starting at the depression that is the door down to the upstairs hallway and leading around the chimney.

The sounds of destruction coming from below when he fell asleep have stopped. The house is quiet. He wonders with a growing sense of dread if The Monster is quiet because it found Jimmy.

(Nothing you can do about it.)

It seems there is nothing he can do about anything.

(Not true! You can stay alive.)

What if The Monster doesn't give up and leave? Billy wonders. Sooner or later it's going to look in the attic just to rule it out. He has to face it: if The Monster stays in the house, he may have to leave the attic and try to escape or get help somehow. While he was asleep . . .

(How long?)

. . . he figures The Monster must have finished its search upstairs for him and Jimmy. If it's on the first floor again, he can't hear it. That might mean it found Jimmy and is in the cellar . . .

(And it might not.)

. . . skewering the baby and Mom together.

(Maybe The Monster is resting, and you just can't hear it because you're too far away.)

Billy stands unsteadily on the plank and looks around the attic. He wonders how long he slept, and what time it is.

(How about what day?)

Could it be Saturday? Could he have slept all night? Dim light that could be either the light of dawn or sunset shows in weak rays through the louvered chrome ventilation window set into the front face of the gabled peak of the old Dutch Colonial. Billy walks slowly and laboriously to the window and makes it without causing a sound. He peeks through the slats. The rain has stopped, and the sun is low at the front of the house which faces west, he remembers, again from his father. Sun's going down. It's still Friday. He wasn't asleep that long.

(Man! You're lucky The Monster didn't come up while you were out.)

Though feeble, the light provides enough illumination for Billy to see the attic now that he isn't preoccupied with worrying about The Monster. Under the makeshift boardwalk and between all the rafter beams on the floor of the attic, pink insulation billows like a kid's forgotten stash of cotton candy. To the right, under the slant of the roof across from the large, square brick chimney that rises through the center of the attic, a big, rectangular black chest sits across several rafter beams. It is surrounded by three stacks of boxes that also straddle the rafter beams. On top of the chest stands a tall pile of old magazines. On the face of the chest two broad brass buckles secure the lid with thick leather straps.

To the left of the air vent at the front of the attic are more boxes on a makeshift wooden platform his father put there. He can see a tinsel Christmas wreath sticking out of the top of one of the boxes and remembers that all the Christmas decorations and lights are over there. Billy turns around. On the attic floor by the door to the hallway, tucked under the slanted roof, are a line of paint cans placed on a narrow short board. Their tops and sides are caked with dried colors. In the middle of the rear wall, under the peak of the house, is another air vent.

Billy turns back to the vent behind him. It's low enough that he can see through it if he stands on his toes and pushes up the bottom slat. He sees the branches of the maple tree in front of the house. He looks down onto the porch roof and street below.

(So close and yet so far!)

Billy shivers despite the stuffy hot air of the attic. He is deathly afraid of heights, and the view through the vent makes him dizzy with vertigo. He has to pee badly.

"Come out now, you little shit, and tell me where Jimmy is!"

Startled, Billy's bladder nearly lets go, and he comes close to losing his balance and falling into the insulation between the floor beams. The Monster sounds far away; it must be on the first floor. Its bellowed command is followed by renewed sounds of destruction.

(It's going to tear the house apart!)

He doesn't care, as long as The Monster hasn't found Jimmy yet. Frightened by The Monster's voice, he turns away from the vent. He can't stand listening to it. It makes him want to pee so badly it hurts. It makes him want to seek out the deepest, darkest corner of the attic, curl up, close his eyes, and pretend that he's somewhere else, somewhere safe.

(Oh yeah, that'll make it all go away—and maybe you can get The Monster to change your diaper, baby, while you're at it! Just before it *kills* you!)

Billy forces himself to walk carefully and quietly to the cans by the drop-down door. One of the cans is an empty coffee can with a rag in it. Carefully, he unzips and pees silently on the rag.

(You can't just curl up and block out what is going on. The Monster isn't going to give up.)

He has to face it. There are only two ways he's going to survive this: he's going to have to figure out a way to get out of the house, or send a message for help. He puts the can down and thinks about it. If he's lucky . . .

(Which you're not!)

. . . The Monster could give up searching for him . . .

(Doubtful!)

. . . thinking he has escaped. It could leave the house and try to get away before it gets caught.

(Keep dreaming!)

Okay . . . so that probably isn't going to happen. It's a harsh fact, but, for whatever reason, The Monster seems determined to find him and make him tell it where Jimmy is so it can make him watch while it impales Mom and Jimmy like marshmallows on a stick before it finally kills him, too.

(It can't kill you if it can't find you.)

That's true, and he can't think of a better place than the attic to hide in; it's the last place The Monster would think to look for him knowing he can't reach the hallway ceiling door to get up here.

(At least hiding buys some time for you to try and think of a way to escape.)

Billy tries to block out the sounds of The Monster's

rampage in the house below. He goes to the chest and looks at the pile of magazines on top of it. He takes one off the stack. It's a *National Geographic.* That's his mother's favorite. She proudly displays each new issue on the living room coffee table.

(Yeah, unless it has pictures of some primitive tribe that live naked in the jungle, then you never get to see it!)

Billy puts the magazine back carefully, but the stack teeters, threatening to topple over. He grabs at it in a panic, righting the sliding magazines just in time.

(Phew! That was close!)

He feels slightly sick imagining the crash the magazines would have made if the pile had fallen over.

(Why don't you just jump around and yell, "Here I am, Monster! Come and eat me!")

To make sure they won't fall again, he painstakingly straightens the pile, carefully easing each magazine into line with the one on top of it. In the process, he notices a large, vinyl-covered book wrapped in plastic behind the magazines on the chest lid. After fixing the last magazine, he carefully extricates the book. He sits cross-legged on the wide plank in front of the chest. Cradling the album between his knees, he unwraps it.

It's the old family photo album, so full of pictures jammed in every space from cover to cover that it bulges. He opens it and is greeted with a plethora of memories: his parents dancing; Mom icing a birthday cake; Dad dressed as Santa Claus; Mom looking very pregnant, eating a banana split topped with hot dog relish; his older brother Kevin as a newborn, in Mom's arms, sucking on a bottle. There are many more.

A picture comes to Billy's mind of his mom pasting photographs in the album with him. Just after his birthday this year they finished filling the album with pictures of the family. For Christmas, Billy and Kevin had given her a new photo album that Dad helped them buy. When this one was full she wrapped it in Saran Wrap, and his dad brought it up to the attic for storage. His mom was so excited about filling the new album with pictures of Jimmy. She was looking forward to it so much.

Billy fights back a tear.

She'll never get to finish it now.

(Oh boy! Let's keep moving here. Moving right along. Before you know it you'll be bawling.)

The crash of furniture in the house below makes Billy tremble, but as he stares at the pictures in the album, turning the pages slowly, a sense of calm spreads over him. The next few pages contain photographs of his parents when they were still dating: sunny summer beach days, sparkling white ski scenes, party scenes of men and women sitting around a tiny table crammed with beer and wine bottles.

Billy turns another page and comes to photos of his mother's bridal shower. These are followed by many pages of pictures of their honeymoon. The handwriting—his mom's—below the picture identifies the place as one he's never heard of: The Virgin Islands. Billy knows there is another entire album of wedding pictures, taken by a professional photographer, somewhere in the house, probably in the chest.

His sense of calm grows into a feeling of warmth seeing so many pictures of his parents happy together. Each picture holds a different memory: him, Kevin, and Mom running though the lawn sprinkler in the yard on a hot summer's day; Dad helping Kevin open a Christmas gift two years ago—a new bike—followed by a series of pictures showing Kevin riding it. There is a picture of him and Kevin helping Mom ice a Father's Day cake, and another of Dad carrying a sleeping three-year-old Billy in his arms. Though each picture is different, each one brings a feeling of warmth to Billy as he looks at them. The feeling is so good, so strong, even the knowledge that his family will never be happy . . .

(Or alive.)

. . . like that again can ruin it.

Not until he turns the next page, that is, and sees the photo of his mom in the hospital, holding him, a newborn, in her arms. Underneath the photograph, in Mom's flowing handwriting: *Me and my beautiful best boy William Randolph Teags*.

The sadness creeps in once again. The impact of what's happened, of who is dead, suddenly overwhelms him. It makes him want to scream with the pain of the grief he feels. It's so strong it rips into his mind, bringing the threat of a blackout with it.

Billy doubles over. His sobs come hard and fast, but he manages to keep them soft. He tries to push the sad thoughts from his mind . . .

(Too late!)

. . . but the damage is done. The full weight of all that's happened since he got home from school that afternoon becomes a crushing load as it hits home that never again will his mother hold him and cradle him in her arms or kiss him all over, giggling, the way she used to. Never again will his father take him to the playground or let him sit on his lap and steer the car up the street they live on. No more will his mom tuck him in and tell him a story at night. No more will his dad play catch with him and Kevin in the backyard. No more will he and Kevin play hide-and-seek in the house on rainy days or flashlight tag in the neighborhood with friends on hot summer nights.

Everyone is dead.

(You're not!)

There's no getting away from it, no denying it.

The dead legs behind the couch are indeed his

mother's. The body under the dining room table is Kevin. He hid the body of Baby Jimmy himself in the bottom drawer of the nursery dresser. And no matter how much The Monster imitates his father and makes itself look like him, Billy knows his father, too, is dead, devoured by The Monster just like in the movie, *The Thing*. Even though Kevin was only teasing him when he told Billy The Monster was the same as the one in the movie, he was right. The Monster *is* capable of eating people and then making itself look like them. Tears well in him and run in large silent drops down the crease of his nose and into his mouth. Their salty taste reminds him of days spent in the sun at the beach building sand castles and bodysurfing in the cold water of the Atlantic with Mom, Dad, and Kevin. The tears come harder and the sorrow builds in his chest until it is a solid hurtful lump that surges into his throat.

He wants to just let it all out.

(No!)

To cry.

(Uh-uh!)

To wail.

(Not a good idea!)

To scream his grief, but he dare not make a sound. The Monster is still loudly trashing the house below and probably wouldn't hear him, but he can't take the chance. Besides, he's afraid if he really does let it all out, it might become uncontrollable, unstoppable.

(You might just cry yourself crazy!)

Billy wipes the tears from his face and tries to take slow deep breaths to melt the hurtful lump of sorrow stuck in his throat.

(Think of something else. Think of something . . . *happy again!*)

He doesn't want to. He's tired and hurt.

(Come on!)

He tries, but it's a halfhearted one. It isn't going to

work this time. He doesn't want to remember how happy his life was before The Monster came and will never be again. He sits cross-legged on the plank in front of the trunk, the photo album cradled in his arms. It would be so nice just to lie down and go to sleep again and forget everything—forget about The Monster, forget about his mother and father, forget about Kevin, forget about little Jimmy. He just wants to forget about *everything*, going all the way back to when he first became aware of The Monster's presence in his life.

He looks down at the album in his lap and lets a few more pages slip from his fingers and fall from the force of gravity. He catches glimpses of snapshots of him taking his first steps; Kevin tearing open more Christmas presents; last Halloween when he'd worn the Spider-Man mask The Monster stole and is wearing.

(Forget that!)

He comes to a page with photographs from his seventh birthday this year. He's blowing out the candles on his cake, his mother by his side, her belly heavy with unborn Jimmy.

(*That's* when all this started! This nightmare really began when *he* was born! It's little Jimmy's fault!)

Billy feels a twinge of hate for his baby brother. It's quickly countered by shame and guilt. It isn't the baby's fault; after all he is only a baby.

(Well . . . it's *somebody's* fault!)

Yes, it is, and Billy knows whose. It isn't Jimmy's fault, or Kevin's, or his mother's, or his father's. And it certainly isn't *his* fault.

(*It's The Monster's fault.*)

It *is* The Monster's fault. If it hadn't come none of this would have happened. His mother and Kevin would still be alive and Dad . . .

(Wouldn't have become Monster Chow!)

"It *is* The Monster's fault!" Billy whispers. As if on

cue The Monster roars louder than ever. Billy can tell it's at the top of the stairs. It sounds as if The Monster is ripping apart the stair railing. There is a booming *thud* that makes the whole house shake, followed by the *crack* of splintering wood and the sound of pieces of wood crashing to the first floor. Before Billy can wonder why The Monster is doing that, its voice comes thundering up to him.

"Come out you little puke!" The Monster bellows. "I haven't got time for this shit, Billy-boy! You're screwing everything up!"

Billy leans over, head turned, listening. He detects a note of desperation, maybe even fear, in The Monster's voice.

(Oh yeah! Like it's really going to be a-scared-a-you!)

Maybe not him, but something else . . . a feeling . . . he's not sure where it comes from, or how he knows it, but he's suddenly sure that The Monster is afraid. It *needs* to find him and Jimmy, but it needs him more because if it doesn't find him and kill him it's going to get *caught.*

From just below the front left quarter of the attic floor, the sounds of destruction go on. Billy pictures The Monster kicking apart the railing and the ornate balusters—a word his dad taught him for the spokes that connect the handrail to the steps—that his father worked so hard on restoring. Billy had heard the story many times of how half of the balusters had been missing when they bought the house and moved there from Poughkeepsie just before he was born. The remaining balusters had been so beautifully carved that his dad had vowed to match them. It took him four years of weekends spent searching antique shops, flea markets, and yard sales throughout Connecticut and eastern New York for matching ones. With a smile, Billy remembers the day his father came running into the house to announce that he'd found a house in Hartford that was being torn down and had the exact same balusters in it. And best of all, he told them nearly dancing with excitement, was that the guy tearing the house down let him have them for *nothing*!

"I lucked out!" he cried and dragged four-year-old Billy, eight-year-old Kevin, and Mom outside to show them the backseat of his car piled with dusty looking pieces of wood. They weren't initially impressed, but after his father lovingly restored each baluster, sanding and staining and polishing, the stairway was perfect. It was the part of the house that his father was most proud of.

(And now The Monster is destroying it.)

Anger builds in Billy, displacing the subsiding grief, pushing it aside, but not too far. It remains like an open wound.

Why won't the thing just stop? he wonders, trying not to hear the sounds of destruction.

Why does it have to wreck everything? Why can't it just go away and leave me alone? Hasn't it done enough? Hasn't it destroyed everyone I love?

(Yeah . . . and now it wants to destroy you, too!)

The tumult of The Monster's destructive rage suddenly stops. The house grows quiet and still. Billy waits, expecting any moment to hear The Monster wrecking something else, but the silence grows longer. Billy holds his breath, straining to detect some sound of the evil creature. There is nothing. Then, very faintly, Billy catches something—the trickling of water. It's followed by a grunt and a rolling, rattling sound repeated several times. Billy realizes it's the toilet paper coming off the roll dispenser in the upstairs bathroom. The toilet flushes.

(The Monster went to the bathroom. I guess even monsters have to go sometimes!)

Strangely, that knowledge makes Billy feel better. It takes The Monster down a notch, making it a little less

threatening and a little more vulnerable somehow. If even
The Monster has to take a dump just like everybody
else, then it follows that it also has to get tired and sleep
sometimes just like a normal human. If he can remain
hidden from The Monster a while longer, maybe it will
go to sleep, and he can try and sneak out.

(Maybe you should sing it a lullaby. *Not!*)

Billy wishes he hadn't fallen asleep in the attic before. He can see night settling through the ventilation
windows. He definitely slept long enough for The Monster to have been able to nap at the same time as him.
As far as he knows The Monster is well rested.

(I told you not to fall asleep!)

Billy shakes his head. *What is past is past and you can't
do anything about it,* his mother always says.

(And didn't she also say that there are no such things
as monsters?)

That brings the sting of tears.

(Sorry.)

The bathroom door slams, startling him. Anxiety tingles through his nerves. A wave of itchiness rolls over
his back. Billy strains to hear what The Monster is doing.
He hears floorboards creaking. He starts to move closer
to the door that opens on the hallway so that he can
hear better . . .

(Stop! The Monster will hear you! It's right below
you for crying out loud!)

. . . and freezes. He almost forgot. If he moves around
too much in the attic, the ceilings of the second-floor
rooms might creak. Just like all the floors in the house
creak. There are plenty of times that he can remember
being in the living room or the dining room and hearing his brother or mother or father walking around upstairs and being able to tell exactly what room they
were in.

He has to stay still.

(Perfectly still!)

As long as The Monster is on the second floor he can't move.

(What about when it's on the first floor?)

Billy ponders that. If it's really quiet in the house The Monster might even hear him from the first floor. Sounds have always carried everywhere in the house. The hallway floorboards creak below him. It sounds like The Monster is walking back and forth at the top of the stairs. Pacing. Like a caged animal. But it has to sleep sometime.

(Sure about that?)

All he can do is wait and hope. After all, if The Monster has to go to the bathroom, it *has* to sleep, too.

(Maybe. Maybe not.)

Billy frowns. His right foot is growing numb. Slowly, he closes the photo album on his lap. He lifts the book off his legs and uncrosses them, stretching out his right one, careful not to make a sound. He shakes the foot carefully to get the circulation going again. It doesn't help. The numbness is spreading to his left foot and leg. Below, The Monster continues pacing. Billy is afraid to move, afraid of making a noise. With both legs numb, any movement he makes will be awkward and probably knock the stack of magazines crashing off the trunk.

(Just stay still!)

That's easier said than done. Billy's never been the type to be able to sit still for very long, even when he's reading a book. To do it now . . .

(Means the difference between life and death!)

. . . with nothing to keep his mind occupied is going to be difficult. Add to that the growing discomfort in his legs . . .

(Be a man! Suck it up!)

. . . and he knows he's in trouble. He tries to get his mind off his limbs, but it's becoming more and more difficult to remain still. He thinks of the book he just finished reading: *The Hobbit*. He wishes he had a ring like Bilbo Baggins in the book that could make him invisible.

(But that's just a made-up story, and this is real!)

He knows that.

(This is *really* real!)

The Monster is real.

(It sure ain't make-believe.)

It's a real-life, surefire monster—the kind his mother and father assured him, more times than he cares to remember, do not exist, especially in his bedroom closet . . .

(Or under the bed!)

He guesses Mom was partly right. There are no monsters in his closet or under his bed. Monsters are too smart to hide there.

(Monsters hide in plain view, behind the faces of ordinary people you love and trust.)

The doorbell rings faintly. It sounds like the kitchen door again. Hope flares inside him. Maybe it's someone come to save him; one of the neighbors heard The Monster on its rampage, or happened to look in the window and see it . . .

(All the shades are closed.)

. . . chasing him and called the cops. He entertains a wild hope. Maybe it's Mom's brother, Uncle Bob, the state policeman. He'll have other policemen with him, and they'll bust in and kill The Monster.

(Yes!)

Kill it!

(Kill it *dead*!)

Billy wants more than anything to see The Monster dead. He wants to make it pay for Mom and Dad and Kevin and Jimmy. . . .

The Monster curses loudly. The sound startles Billy. It sounds like The Monster is right there in the attic with him. A moment later he hears it descending the stairs to the first floor. Now is his chance to move. He carefully places the photo album on top of the chest and tries to stand. He nearly crashes to the floor. His legs are now so numb they barely hold his weight. He sits on the plank with both legs extended in front of him and massages them. The needles and pins sensation starts, and it's all he can do not to cry out. He *hates* that feeling. The sensation is so uncomfortable he doesn't know what to do. He wants to stand and jiggle and slap his legs to drive the needles and pins out, but doesn't dare risk a noise. Even though The Monster is on the first floor, it might hear him in the old house and discover his hiding place.

There are suddenly no sounds from the house below.

(The Monster's not answering the door.)

It must be keeping quiet waiting for whoever rang the bell to give up and go away. He looks longingly at the attic ventilation window. Though he can see it is getting dark outside, he still would like to look in the hope that someone is out there. Maybe he can whistle to them or something.

(You don't know how to whistle.)

Then maybe he can push something through the vents that will fall to the street and get their attention. He takes the *National Geographic* off the pile again. It's just thin enough to fit through one of the vents and maybe draw the attention of anyone out there. Carefully, he stands and tries to take a step. The awakening nerve endings in his feet explode with pain. There is no way he's going to be able to cross to the window, which entails walking tightrope-style on the planks his dad put down without making a sound. He knows he'll fall for sure and go crashing right through one of the second-floor ceilings. Then The Monster will definitely have him. . . .

(For breakfast, lunch, *and* dinner!)

Despondent, he carefully puts the magazine back.

(Don't give up! You'll think of something!)

The doorbell does not ring again. The hope that had been kindled by it is now dashed. He feels so bad, it's several minutes before he realizes The Monster hasn't made a sound and still hasn't come back upstairs. Billy tries another cautious step. The needles and pins sensation is nearly gone, but it's too late to catch whoever was at the door. They're certainly gone by now. He tries a deep knee bend, flexing his legs, and cringes at the crackling sounds his knees make when he straightens. Moving quietly and carefully along the planks, Billy crosses to the attic door and lies next to it, listening for sounds of The Monster from below.

He hears nothing. A few moments later he detects an odd electric humming sound that baffles him until he figures out that it must be the refrigerator. It sounds broken after The Monster chopped it with the ax. Billy strains to hear more, listening beyond the sound of the refrigerator. Farther away he can suddenly hear the cacophony of renewed destruction. The Monster is apparently back to its plan to tear the house apart until it finds him and Jimmy. The sounds are too far away though for The Monster to be on the second or even the ground floor. When the chimney, which runs from the basement up through the center of the entire house and through the middle of the attic just a few feet from Billy, shakes, sending dust raining down, Billy knows where The Monster is—the cellar!

(Now's your chance to get out of the house!)

Billy isn't so sure.

(Whaddya mean? It's down in the cellar again—you can sneak downstairs and get out the back door before it even knows you're gone. Or if you're afraid it might hear you, hide in one of the rooms on the first floor that The Monster has already searched, then sneak out when it goes upstairs!)

Billy thinks about it for a while and decides to go for it.

The plan is quickly killed when he hears the cellar door bang open and The Monster return to the kitchen. But it doesn't come directly upstairs. It remains on the first floor, and no matter how much Billy strains, he can't hear what the thing is doing. Billy carefully stands and goes back to the chest and the photo album. There is a picture sticking out of its pages that he didn't notice before. He pulls it out and looks at it. It's a shot of him as a newborn with his mother on the day she brought him home from the hospital. It makes Billy think of when his mom brought Jimmy home. He didn't know it then, but that was also when The Monster must have got in the house, hiding in the cellar and in the shadows of night, waiting for its chance.

(It's hard to believe that was only a month ago.)

The night Baby Jimmy came home, Billy had his first dream of The Monster and being inside it. At the time, waking screaming from the nightmare, he was so frightened he wasn't able to remember right away what the dream had been about. His mother, of course, came running when he screamed and woke crying, but that only made him feel worse. He knew his mother was still getting better after having Jimmy and needed to rest, but there she was, as always, ready to comfort him. She wasn't angry or short with him. She hugged him and reassured him with loving words and insisted that he tell her about the dream. She always made him tell her his nightmares; she said by telling them he could get them out of his brain, and then they wouldn't return when he went back to sleep.

"I saw someone standing in a dark place," he told his mother. "I . . . I was like, floating over them and, far away, I heard the baby crying." Billy paused a moment, unsure of how to say what had happened next. "Then I saw it standing in the shadows! I saw . . ." He faltered, afraid to name the thing that terrified him; afraid that doing so would make it appear.

His mother smiled and nodded uncertainly. "What honey? What did you see?"

"The Monster," Billy answered, softly, warily.

"Billy, you know there are no such things as monsters!" his mother said in a tone of voice that said, *Come on, I thought you were a big boy!*

And that was just it—he was a big boy; before that night he had thought monsters were just make-believe.

(Or only lived in dreams.)

He didn't tell her the rest of the nightmare then; of how suddenly he was inside The Monster, in its body, in its head.

How he *became* The Monster.

He saw through its eyes as it stalked the night, looking for a house—the right house. He thought its thoughts as it prepared to do awful things. He knew when The Monster knew it had found the house it was seeking. He felt its moment of feeling smothered as it put on a heavy rubber mask. He smelled the noxious rubber and looked through the eyeholes at The Monster's world. He went along in helpless terror, hoping . . .

(Praying!)

. . . he would wake up.

He didn't.

He saw, smelled, heard, felt, and tasted everything the same as The Monster. And he became enraged along with The Monster when it heard the baby crying. The Monster was in a cellar. Billy thought it was his cellar. From the house above came the sound of a baby crying. He thought it was Baby Jimmy. The crying grew louder and more piercing. Then he was moving, propelled along inside The Monster as it climbed the cellar stairs. As it stepped into a hallway and not a kitchen, Billy realized the Monster wasn't in his house.

(Not yet!)

He saw a door getting closer. The baby's crying came from behind it. The wailing went up a notch at The Monster's approach, reaching a new level of irritation, as if the baby was afraid, as if the infant knew The Monster was coming to hurt him. He was subjected to the awful experience of smothering the baby with a pillow. He wanted to weep as The Monster beat the poor mother to death in her own bed with her bedside lamp. But worst of all was when The Monster carried both bodies back to the cellar, laid the baby on the mother's stomach, and impaled them both together with a long knitting needle it had found in the house.

He'd thought nothing could be worse than that . . .

(But you were wrong!)

Soon after leaving the house where the mother and baby lay in the cellar, Billy and The Monster stood outside another house.

His *house*.

And it was going inside.

That was the most terrifying thing of all—frightening enough to bring him awake screaming.

The baby was crying.

He looked to the hallway and in the darkness saw a shadowy figure right outside his door, about to go into the baby's room—The Monster!

But then the hallway light came on, and he saw it was his mother. She'd been in the nursery attending to the crying Jimmy.

His sense of The Monster's presence disappeared.

As he had finished telling his mom about his dream, he heard his father's footsteps on the stairs. A moment later he appeared in the bedroom doorway with his jacket on, one hand over his ear to block out Jimmy's crying from the nursery next door.

"Sorry I'm so late, Molly. I had a last-minute emergency claim that I had to process—poor family lost its house in a fire over in Stinson. What's wrong here?"

Billy felt shame for not being a big boy, the way his father looked at him when his mother related he'd had a nightmare. But he'd known from that moment on that The Monster—no make-believe monster or boogeyman—

(A real live grinning evil monster!)

—was hiding somewhere in the house, or very close by.

With his father there, he tried to explain about The Monster. It wouldn't be the last time he did so, but it would have the same end result as the rest—they didn't understand or believe that his dreams were real.

"This wasn't like the stuff on TV and in movies. I know that isn't real," he told them. "But this was real. I was inside a monster, an actual living monster, and it was in the house! It was right there in the hallway." He pointed a trembling finger toward the door.

At that moment Kevin rolled over on the bottom bunk and fell out of bed, something he does—

(Did!)

—often, and Billy and his parents burst out laughing. But the laughter didn't last; the sound of it made the baby cry louder, and it changed to that high-pitched, nails-on-chalkboard kind of cry that he had. It took Billy's poor mom hours to settle him and get him to stop. It bothered Dad so much he tried to sleep on the couch downstairs with headphones on, listening to CDs of old Beatles tunes, but ended up returning to work several hours earlier than normal.

Eventually everyone else also got back to bed that night. As Billy lay there, listening to the night sounds of the house settling around him, his thoughts went back to the dream. It upset him that he wasn't able to make his parents understand that he knew the difference between real and make-believe and that The Monster of his dreams was real and had somehow got into *their* house!

Billy looks up from the photo album. He can hear The Monster coming up the stairs to the second floor again. It stops at the top of the stairs before going into Billy's parents' bedroom.

Silence follows.

(Be quiet.)

He knows The Monster won't look in the attic; it has no reason to think he can be up there.

(Yeah, but . . . *it* doesn't really *need* a reason, does it? Remember the old *vice versa?*)

The *vice versa* was a term his dad liked to use a lot. He was always inserting it into his speech, especially when he talked about his job. One day Billy asked him what *vice versa* meant and his dad tried to explain:

"It's like . . . what's true for one thing is true for another." That didn't cut it with Billy, and his dad tried again. "It means that two things could be switched and you wouldn't notice. Like this plaid on my shirt—you could say it's red and black, or *vice versa*, it's black and red. It doesn't make any difference; it's the same thing."

Billy kind of got it then, or at least he said he did. But it wasn't until The Monster showed up that he truly came to understand what *vice versa* meant . . . in more ways than one. He wondered if *he* dreamed of The Monster and was able to be inside its head, did The Monster dream about him and get inside *his* head, too? He'd known from his first dream of The Monster that he and it were connected in some way, and he worried that whenever he sensed The Monster's presence, as he often

had before he came home from school today and found
it in his house in the guise of his father, could The Monster sense *him* equally as well?

(And if you think about The Monster and picture
where it is and what's it doing, can it, *vice versa,* do the
same?)

He doesn't know.

(And you don't want to find out, *so don't think about
it*!)

Billy tries to distract his thoughts by mentally humming the theme to *Star Wars,* his and Dad's favorite
movie, and by looking at the photo album again.

He opens the back of the book. The last eleven pages
are a series of eight-by-twelve-inch family portrait pictures—one per page—taken every year at Sears since
Kevin was born. The last one in the book is from last
year. Kevin and he look cramped and uncomfortable in
their suits and ties. It reminds Billy of last week when
they all went to Sears again to get a new family photo
with the newest member of the family, Jimmy. The new
photo replaced the one in his hand and now hangs on
the living room wall.

Trying to get the latest picture taken with Jimmy was
a disaster. The baby wailed incessantly and nothing
Billy's mother tried could quiet the infant's terrible cry.
It wasn't until Billy held Jimmy, while his mom searched
for something in her tote bag to quiet him, that he
stopped crying.

Billy smiles at the memory; it was like a miracle.

As soon as he held Jimmy, the baby clammed up and
started cooing peacefully. And when Billy went to hand
Jimmy back to his mom, he started bawling again until
Billy took him back. Finally the only way they were able
to get the picture without Jimmy screaming was for Billy
to hold him.

"You saved the day, kiddo," his father told him after, and his mother agreed. Billy felt very special that day.

(That kid cried almost nonstop right from the start.)

Billy remembers Jimmy had something called "acute colic" because he was allergic to milk and dairy products. He heard his mom tell his dad that's what the doctor had said. His mother cried and said she felt like a terrible mother because she couldn't breast-feed her own baby, but Billy's dad told her it wasn't her fault, even cow's milk made Jimmy cry.

(Cry ain't exactly the right word—he went beyond crying. That kid *wailed*. He *shrieked*. He *screamed* nonstop.)

The doctor prescribed a soy milk formula, but even then things didn't get much better. The soy formula was gross—it smelled bad when Billy's mother mixed it and even worse after it had gone through the baby. Jimmy didn't like the taste of it, and when he did drink it, more often than not, he puked it right up again.

(And through it all he *cried, wailed, shrieked,* and *screamed*!)

While his dad tried to block the noise by listening to loud music through his headphones, or just left the house to get away from the horrible crying, Billy's mother walked Jimmy up and down the stairs since the jostling motion of doing so seemed to be the only thing besides a ride in the car that would quiet him. Even standing still and bouncing him didn't work—he had to be carried up and down the stairs, or he'd scream. When that didn't work his mom did the only other thing that could quiet Jimmy; she took him for a ride in the car.

(That kid could scream for *minutes* without ever taking a breath!)

And if he wasn't crying he was spitting up or having diarrhea. If the crying didn't keep them all awake, the smell did.

His parents quickly became frantic over Jimmy's crying. He overheard them talking of how he, Billy, had cried a lot as a baby, but it wasn't the kind of shrill, cutting cry that seemed to set nerve endings on fire like Jimmy's. Billy's mom was so exhausted within just two days of Jimmy coming home and crying almost nonstop that she called the doctor but got his answering service. It took the doctor three hours to call back.

(Three *horrible* earsplitting hours!)

Billy's father was furious and said that they should take the baby to the Oak Ridge Country Club since it was Wednesday, and that's where they'd find the doctor, along with all the other doctors, playing golf.

"I'd like to see him tee off with this screaming in his ear!" his father said with grim humor.

After the doctor returned the call the baby's formula was changed again. Things got better for a little while.

(But not by much!)

It took several days on the new formula before Jimmy stopped crying constantly.

(But he still cried a *lot*!)

That he did.

(Way too much!)

It was enough to get on everyone's nerves and make them cranky. The first week Billy's mother kept telling them that things would get better; the baby would get better; they'd get into a routine then everything would go back to normal.

(Hah!)

A week later and Jimmy was still crying more often than not. During that time Billy had his second dream of being inside The Monster while it murdered a mother and her helpless baby in the basement of an apartment building in the housing project by the river.

Another trip to the doctor was made. Special stomach medicine was prescribed for Jimmy. Like a miracle it finally worked. Jimmy got better, and Billy stopped dreaming of The Monster. The murders, too, seemed to stop . . .

(But only for two weeks!)

. . . then Jimmy and Kevin came down with the flu and the constant, horrible, shrill crying resumed, only ten times worse than before. It was then that Billy knew The Monster was back. He was in school the day after Jimmy and Kevin both woke up during the night with the flu, and Jimmy cried nonstop until Billy left for the bus. He was exhausted and fell asleep at his desk just after lunch. A dream came upon him that wasn't like the other dreams he'd had of The Monster—in this dream he was inside *someone else.*

He was running along a path through woods.

A thought popped into his head that wasn't his: "It's so nice to have some peace and quiet for a change."

The voice frightened him—it wasn't his voice or the voice of his alter ego, but that was okay, as long as it wasn't the voice of The Monster. He concentrated on it and a sudden fleeting image burned brightly across his mind's eye—a child lying in a spider-ridden, cramped place of shadows, locked in a dark cellar, hugging his knees and crying—and then it was gone.

He was running fast, not from something, but just for the sake of running. He was scared, but the feeling passed when he realized that he wasn't inside The Monster again. He ran faster. It felt good to run and leave the frightening image of the boy in the cellar behind. He took joy in the sound of his sneakers hitting the dirt path, and in the sound of the wind blowing past his ears, his breath rushing in and out of his lungs. It was so quiet in the woods, so peaceful and calm. It was too peaceful and calm for The Monster, he thought.

The running path took a downhill turn. There were treacherous tree roots and loose stones underfoot that could send him for a nasty spill. He looked up and caught a glimpse of sparkling silver water through the thin spring foliage—a lake.

He recognized it as Mirror Lake, in the heart of Coggshall Park, not far from his house. He was in the section of the park called the Arboretum where all the plants and trees were identified by small plastic signs on long rusted metal stakes stuck in the ground near them. Sounds of people—children laughing, a mother warning her child not to climb on the large rocks along the shore, a car radio playing loudly and a young voice singing along just as loudly—carried to him on the wind. They were pleasant sounds. With every passing second he became surer that he wasn't inside The Monster. The question of who he was inside, however, began to concern him. He'd never made a connection like that with anyone other than The Monster. He'd never been inside a normal person.

(Sure about that?)

But normal didn't last.

A new sound suddenly split the air like feedback from a microphone turned up too loud.

A baby crying.

Close by.

He felt something deep inside him build and swell, rising like dirty water in a backed-up toilet.

The Monster.

It flooded his mind so suddenly he could do nothing. The Monster flowed into him, and he became it—a great, drooling horrible beast, all fangs and claws charging through the woods, heading in the direction of the baby crying. With every step it took, running faster and faster, Billy could feel The Monster's rage and desire for blood and silence grow to an overwhelming need that could not be denied. He couldn't escape, no matter how much he tried; the evil thoughts and blood lust of The Monster filled him like a cancer.

He was moving fast through the trees, heading toward that awful sound. The Monster started to shed its clothing as it ran until it was naked. Suddenly he knew what The Monster's intentions were as he watched its right hand grab one of the metal stakes with a sign on it that identified a tree or plant.

The end of the stake was dirty and sharp.

He wanted to shout out a warning to the woman in the woods ahead, but he could do nothing. He could only watch, listen, and feel. The feeling part was the worst of it, especially when The Monster gleefully hit the woman repeatedly over the head with the metal rod and used it to impale her and her live baby, pinning the kicking infant to her, and both of them to the ground the way it had in the other dreams; like the way Mrs. Petrie pinned notes to the class message board with thumbtacks.

Billy had screamed then. He screamed so loud, he propelled himself awake. He screamed so loud he startled Mrs. Petrie into knocking her Styrofoam cup of coffee over. When she angrily asked what was wrong, Billy couldn't tell her. The other kids laughed at him, except for Brad, but that was better than the way they would have reacted if he'd told about his dream—a dream he was sure had really happened. Thanks in part to Kevin, and partly to his being the smartest kid in the class, Billy was already a target of derision from most of his classmates; he could just imagine what they would do and say if he suddenly said he'd screamed because he dreamed he was inside a monster. Mrs. Petrie punished him by making him sit in the "Time-Out" corner and stay in at afternoon recess.

(It's hard to believe that was Wednesday, just two days ago.)

And then Thursday, the TV news reported the discovery of the bodies in Coggshall Park.

(And today The Monster was waiting for you when you got home from school. It must know you saw it kill that mother and baby.)

Billy comes out of his reverie and looks up from the

photograph. He thinks The Monster is still in his parents' bedroom. Still quiet.

(Why? What's it up to?)

Billy wonders what time it is.

(Are you sure it's in Mom and Dad's bedroom?)

He shrugs.

(What's it doing?)

He can't say.

(Maybe it's . . . *sleeping*!)

Billy holds his breath. If The Monster *is* sleeping he might be able to . . .

(But then again maybe it knows where you are, and it's sneaking up on you right now!)

Billy lets his breath out slowly. He listens as hard as he can, not moving a muscle, but hears nothing from The Monster. Billy looks to the attic vent window and sees that the streetlight in front of the house is on. It gives just enough illumination for Billy to see by. Suddenly there is a noise from below, from his parents' bedroom. A soft grunt and the sound of The Monster moving through the room.

(It's going back downstairs!)

Another sound, outside, catches his attention. A car pulls up. With The Monster downstairs, he figures it's safe to move. Doing so gingerly on his stiff legs, and still holding last year's family portrait photo, Billy crosses the plank walkway to the ventilation window. Looking through the bottom metal slat of the vent he can see, just to the right of the porch roof, at the edge of his vision, the next-door neighbor, Mrs. Luts, getting out of her car at the end of her short driveway. She goes around to the trunk and opens it, revealing a half dozen or more plastic grocery bags piled inside.

Billy almost shouts to her . . .

(The Monster will hear!)

. . . but thinks better of it.

(There's got to be some way to get a message to her to get help!)

Billy looks at the family photograph in his hand and remembers something. He reaches in his left pocket.

(Yes!)

During art today in school, he broke a black crayon and stuffed the bottom piece of it into his pocket. He takes it out and quickly kneels and places the family picture facedown on the plank in front of him. Hurriedly, he scribbles a message on the back in bold block letters:

Help! I'm trapped in the house with a monster.
It killed my family.
Everyone's dead. Call the police.

He signs it: Sincerely, *Billy Teags*, the way Mrs. Petrie taught him to sign a letter. Though the photographic paper is thicker than Billy is used to, he manages to fold it into something he only recently learned how to make— thanks to his dad teaching him—*a paper airplane*.

Billy stands and looks out the window again. Mrs. Luts is still taking grocery bags from her trunk and carrying them inside, but there are only two left. Billy tries to push the paper airplane through the vent slat, but the paper is too big and stiff. He compresses it and forces it through.

He has a moment of exhilaration that immediately fades as the plane takes a disappointing nosedive straight to the porch roof about ten or twelve feet below the attic window and stays there.

(Figures.)

Moving as fast as he can without making any noise, Billy goes back to the chest. He gets on one knee and opens the photo album again. He tears a smaller picture—one of him in diapers in his playpen—from its pages. On the back he scribbles:

Help! Call the police!

Moving swiftly, he returns to the window just as Mrs. Luts closes the car trunk and carries the last two bags inside.

(Too late! Should'a known!)

Billy feels like crying. All the adrenaline-charged energy the possibility of rescue via Mrs. Luts roused in him quickly dissipates. He is suddenly weary. His eyelids grow heavy and, as if infected by the sleepiness of his eyes, the rest of his body becomes weighed down. It longs for sleep. Depression and exhaustion seep through him.

(You can't sleep now!)

He knows he shouldn't, but staying awake and alert is getting harder by the minute. Being in a constant state of terror is exhausting. He has to find someplace to lie down for a little while . . .

(Before you fall down!)

. . . and stay quiet and rest without sleeping until he knows the location of The Monster in the house and what it's doing.

(Let's not find out—remember the *vice versa*!)

Then maybe he can think of some way to escape. The plank he stands on in front of the vent window is the widest in the attic. Billy drops to his hands and knees on it and lies on his stomach. A few minutes later he thinks he hears The Monster in the kitchen and imagines the beast in the refrigerator getting something to eat.

(Stop it!)

Billy lets out a sigh and tries not to think about how hungry he is, but he's more tired than hungry. Now, as long as he has an idea of where The Monster is and what it's doing he can . . .

(I wouldn't do that!)

. . . close his eyes for just a little while. . . .

"It's okay, honey. Everything is fine. It was just a dream."

Billy opens his eyes and looks at his mother.

(Just a dream!)

Could it be?

He sits up in bed and looks around. It's early morning and the sun, just peeking over the horizon, shines on his mother's red hair. Billy thinks she looks so beautiful.

(Yeah! It was all just a dream!)

"You're okay?" Billy says to his mother. She gives him a funny look.

(More importantly, *you're* okay!)

"Yeah, I'm fine, Sweetie, but I'm not the one who woke up screaming bloody murder a minute ago."

"Where's Kevin?" Billy asks urgently.

"He just went down to breakfast. You woke him, but it was time to get up for school anyway," she answers, pulling the covers back at an angle so he can get out of bed. She goes to the tall dresser he shares with his older brother. She opens the bottom drawer and takes out a pair of dungarees and his favorite Spider-Man T-shirt. An image of The Monster in his Spider-Man mask flashes before his eyes.

(But that was a dream!)

She places the clothes on the bed next to him as he swings his legs out from under the covers and sits at the edge of the mattress.

"Get dressed. I'll make you chocolate chip pancakes. If you don't hurry your father and your brother will eat them all."

"Dad's okay, too? And baby Jimmy?"

His mother's look becomes one of smiling concern. "Of course they are, Billy. Why wouldn't they be?"

Billy shrugs.

(Just a dream.)

That's it. If everyone *is* okay then it must have been just a dream—a scary dream.

(*The* scariest dream *ever*!)

. . . but a dream nonetheless. In fact, the details of the dream are already fleeing, becoming vague in the manner of dreams.

Billy gets out of bed . . .

(*Was* it a dream? If this is real why isn't the baby crying?)

. . . *and sat on the living room floor. The television was on*—American Idol—*and the windows were dark. Nighttime. His mother sat with her legs folded beneath her on the couch, reading* Discover *magazine. His father was in his recliner right behind Billy, who sat cross-legged on the braided rug as close to the television screen as he could get without his parents telling him to move back.*

(Is *this* the dream? *This* already happened, remember?)

He does. It was a scary moment.

"Hon, listen to this," *his mother said, sitting up a little and motioning with her magazine at his father.* " 'According to the results of an experiment conducted in Oslo, Norway, by scientists at the University of Oslo, male children, especially between infancy and age seven, appear to have some sort of telepathic relationship with their fathers.'

"They don't say just a few kids do, they say all boys have this thing. This connection with their fathers. It's stronger in some than in others and seems to reach its peak in boys around age seven. It says here that in most kids it's more of an empathetic connection, but there have been a few cases that showed a true mental connection between a son and his father, especially in times of trauma or stress. Isn't that amazing?"

Billy's father nodded his head vaguely, eyebrows raised, but his eyes never left the TV screen.

"Are you listening to me, John? Did you hear what I just said?"

Billy looked at the screen, then back at Dad. His father was staring at him with a funny look on his face, then he blinked, glanced over at Mom, and said, "Sounds like a bunch of baloney to me. I can't believe they get money to study crap like that. I heard of one study that got five million from the government to study the effect of methane gas from cow shit on global warming!"

"Watch your language, please," *Billy's mother scolded, but laughed just the same.*

Billy turned back to the television. Suddenly he felt The Monster in the room, watching him. He whirled around, searching frantically, but it wasn't there. His father looked at him curiously again as he crawled over to look behind the recliner.

"Lose something, Bill?"

"No," *Billy replied.*

"What are you doing?"

Billy looked behind the couch . . .

(The Monster's not there—when are you going to learn that it hides in plain sight?)

. . . and leaned against the door in the backseat of the car. Opposite him at the other door, Kevin sat playing with his GameBoy. His father was driving, and his mother was in the front passenger seat. The baby was strapped into a car seat between Billy's mother and father. And, of course, he was crying.

(Big surprise!)

"What are you doing?" *his father asked again, only he wasn't speaking to Billy this time.* "You couldn't leave him be, could you? He was quiet."

Jimmy screamed louder, as if in an effort to drown out his father's complaining.

(Remember this? This already happened, too; you were on your way to Sears for the new family picture. In a minute the car is going to—)

Billy was suddenly thrown into Kevin as his father cut the wheel, swearing and blasting the horn at the same time. Billy's mother shrieked, Kevin yelled, and Jimmy bawled even louder. Suddenly Billy heard a snatch of The Monster's voice inside his head, clear as a bell, just for a second:

Shut up, you fucking brat!

Billy's mother yelled at his father to slow down and watch where he was going, and the voice went as quickly as it had come, leaving Billy wondering if he really heard it or just imagined it. The car swerved again, and Billy was certain he was going to be thrown from the seat. He looked down. It was too dark in the backseat. For some reason his eyes wouldn't focus. . . .

Billy opens his eyes more.

He is no longer in the back of the car; he's lying on a board barely wide enough for his body. He lifts his head to look around and nearly rolls off it.

(Don't do that!)

Slowly the confusion of sleep fades from Billy. His situation, all that has happened, comes crashing back upon him. He lowers his head to the plank again. The knot in his stomach returns bigger and tighter than before. The aches and pains in his bruised body reawaken, joined by the fierce pain in his throat where The Monster tried to strangle him. The steel clamp of terror that has had hold of the back of his neck, forcing his jaws to remain clenched, renews its efforts to snap his head from his neck.

For several sorrowful minutes, Billy lies there, eyes closed, weeping silently and wishing *this* was the dream he could wake from. He wishes everything could be fine again. He wishes his family could be back together again and happy. He wishes The Monster didn't exist.

He lifts his head in the darkness again. He is afraid to think about The Monster, but he can't help wonder where the creature is lurking. He can't hear it now.

(Maybe it's asleep for real now.)

The house is quiet.

(It's got to be asleep!)

A surge of adrenaline sweeps through Billy.

(Now's your chance!)

He rises to his knees, and his hope plummets. The attic is so completely dark now he can't see anything more than a foot away. The vent window casts no light in from outside—the streetlight out in front of the house is no longer on. A while ago Billy had noticed that sometimes it went out and came back on later. He asked his father about it and was told the streetlights did that regularly so that they didn't get overheated and burn out.

(You can do it; just be *careful*!)

Billy looks over his shoulder but can't even see his feet. Without some kind of light he's never going to be able to walk, or even crawl, without making a sound to the section of the attic where the secret door is. He silently curses himself for not staying next to the door.

(Yeah, that was pretty dumb. What if The Monster had come up through the regular door when you were sleeping?)

At least if he had stayed next to the secret door he would be sure of having an escape. Now he's stuck where he is until the streetlight comes on again, or, if it's near dawn, for it to get light enough for him to see.

(And by then The Monster will be awake and nice and refreshed from its nap and raring to go.)

"I wish I knew what time it is," Billy says softly. He lies down again and puts his head on his arm. Silent tears of despair return. He cries himself back to sleep. As he dozes, he doesn't notice the gray light of dawn seeping through the rear vent window across from him. If he had, he might have got up and looked out the front attic window where he would have seen a breeze stir the paper airplane he made. It skitters over the porch roof and off the edge. It spirals down and comes to rest in front of Mrs. Luts's car at the inside edge of her driveway, right next to the walk leading to her kitchen door on the side of her home that faces Billy's house. By the time the plane comes to rest, Billy is asleep, but it is a fitful, terrifying sleep.

He was back in the dark room, the hospital room, with the boy on the bed that he visited before when The Monster was strangling him. The sound of a child crying reverberated in the night air. The boy got off the bed—Billy noticed the windows of the room were covered with wire mesh on the outside—and went out into the hallway, following the sounds of sadness.

There was a desk at the far end of the hallway, with a lamp on it that cast a small circle of light around a nurse sitting there. Behind her, writing on a handheld chart, was a muscle-bound attendant—Billy automatically knew his name was Roy, and that he was mean. The boy snuck along the right-hand wall, nearly out of sight of the two at the desk, until he came abreast of the room the crying came from.

"You'd better quit that sniveling, Ritchie. You don't want me to come in there," *the burly attendant called, his back still turned. The nurse said something to him, and he laughed.*

The boy silently pushed the door open—the sound of crying grew louder for a second—and he slipped inside, immediately pulling the door shut behind him. The room was an exact duplicate of the boy's. Sitting in the corner of the bed, huddled against the wall, was another, smaller boy, with long blond hair in a bowl-cut style.

"Shhh!" *the boy said to the blond child. The smaller boy*

raised his head. Looking at his angelic face, Billy knew—but didn't know how he knew—that the blond's name was Ritchie Tomlinson, and he had set his nine-month-old baby sister on fire and burned her to death. For reasons Billy could not fathom, he felt a sense of admiration for what Ritchie had done, that was countered by an intense desire to shut him up.

"If you're not quiet, Roy is going to come in here and balance your books," *the boy said.* "Why are you crying?"

The blond boy didn't answer. He sniffed and averted his eyes again.

"You feeling guilty about your sister again?" *the boy asked. Billy could hear disgust in the boy's voice.*

The blond nodded feebly. The boy sat on the edge of the bed. "You know, Ritchie, it's like we talked about. There's only one way that you can make it right. One way to make up for what you did, you know that, don't you?" *he said, his voice full of understanding and concern. The blond boy nodded again.* "You know what we have to do, Ritchie."

Another nod from the smaller boy.

"Good. Believe me, it's the right thing, Ritchie, and I'm going to help you, just like I said I would."

Out of his pajama top pocket, the boy took a cracked disposable lighter and a book of matches. "See? I told you." *The boy picked up the lighter and held it up for the blond boy to see.* "It's got a leak. I just twist it like this and the lighter fluid comes out." *He twisted the transparent, blue plastic casing and drops of clear fluid fell onto the blond's feet and the bedspread. The boy leaned over the blond, twisting the lighter so that its flammable contents got on Ritchie's legs, arms, chest, and even on his hair.*

The boy stood and opened the book of matches.

"Ready, Ritchie?"

The small boy looked doubtful, afraid. "Wait!" *he said, reaching for the boy.*

"Too late," *the boy said and lit a match. With the same motion of striking it, he let the flaming match go. It soared through the air like a medieval burning arrow and landed on Ritchie's left arm. Flames sprouted and spread quickly. As Ritchie started to scream, the boy slipped into the closet and sat there, the door open a crack, watching the flickering lights of the fire on the wall and humming soundlessly as he listened to Ritchie scream and then the attendant and the nurse rushing into the room. After it was all over, after the attendant put Ritchie out with a fire extinguisher, and they rushed the blond boy off to the emergency room, the boy went quietly back to his room.*

When Billy wakes, a little over an hour later, he is cold and hungry and actually feels more tired than before. He thinks about the dream he just had . . .

(It was like the other one.)

. . . and shudders at the thought of the little blond boy being set on fire and burning to death.

(Why did he do that? What does it mean?)

He doesn't know.

(Maybe it's better you don't know.)

He stretches his arms carefully. The attic is chilly and gloomy, but at least he can see. Daylight shining through the rear air vent, which faces east, casts bands of yellow across the inside of the attic roof, allowing him to move around without taking a misstep off a plank and crashing through the second floor's ceiling. Looking at the light he figures it's early, six or six-thirty. If he can find out where The Monster is and if it's still sleeping he might be able to escape.

(Then get moving!)

Billy sits up on the plank. He pinches his nostrils and forces air into his nose to unblock his ears.

(The better to hear you with, my dear Monster!)

He listens carefully, holding his breath to catch the slightest sound in the house. Far away he hears the off-key hum of the damaged refrigerator, but it is almost immediately drowned out by a rumbling sound coming up through the chimney—either the furnace turning on, or the water heater. From outside comes the sound of a car going by.

(But do you hear The Monster?)

Billy slowly gets to his feet, wavers off balance for a moment, nearly topples, then straightens. Very faintly, another sound reaches him. He cocks his head to the right, then the left, trying to pinpoint the direction of the sound. It seems to be coming from the other end of the attic. Moving in slow silence, Billy crawls over the planks to the chimney where he stops and listens again. The rumbling from the cellar stops, and he can hear the sound better. Before, it was like papers being rustled together, but being closer he can now tell it's the sound of a person—someone crying softly.

(Who could be crying?)

The Monster?

(Hah! Monsters don't cry, they *eat* and *kill*!)

Another thought occurs to him; maybe it's *Kevin*! Maybe he isn't dead after all! Maybe he was just *hurt* by The Monster!

Or maybe it's Mom!

(You really think so?)

Maybe . . . it's *Dad*! he thinks, hopefully. *Maybe The Monster didn't eat him! Maybe it just made itself look like him. Maybe it copied him from one of the pictures downstairs. . . .*

(But the monster in the movie, *The Thing*, had to eat people before it could *look* like them!)

Maybe *this* shape-shifter doesn't have to do that, he reasons. Maybe it can just see a picture of someone and make itself look like that person. And maybe it can only look like that person for a short time unless it *does* eat them—maybe that's why The Monster wears a mask like the Spider-Man one it stole from him.

(Did you ever think that *maybe* The Monster is trying to trick you?)

Billy ignores that. It *can't* be The Monster. He *refuses* to believe it is The Monster playing a trick. He *needs* to believe it's his dad, or Kevin, or Mom; he *needs* to believe that *one* of them at least is still alive.

He almost calls out to the crier.

(No! Don't be crazy! No matter how much you *don't* want to believe something that ain't gonna make it so! Remember how much you didn't want to believe in The Monster in the first place?)

It's true. He first became aware of The Monster when he was just a baby. It's a knowledge he has lived with for as long as he can remember; a knowledge that has grown stronger the older he gets. He tried to ignore it at first, chalking it up to what his mom called his "overactive imagination—"

(You do live in a fantasy world most of the time.)

—until the dreams started.

(Even then you didn't want to believe. Are you going to keep your head in the sand?)

Billy blocks out the accusing voice. He is too scared, too sad, too hungry, too much in pain, and too exhausted to argue. It *can't* be The Monster playing a trick, that's all. It *has* to be someone he can *trust*. With a renewal of hope Billy continues slowly to the plank that runs by the chest and over to the far rear left corner of the attic where the secret door leads down into the closet. The sound of sobbing grows louder the closer he gets to the door. Someone is in his and Kevin's room. Billy stops midway on the plank and holds his breath, listening as hard as he can. Is it Kevin?

(Doubt it.)

Is it Mom?

(Double-doubt it.)

He can't tell. He crawls a few more cautious inches forward to the very edge of the secret door in the top of his closet.

He can hear the crier very clearly now . . .

(It's not Kevin!)

. . . and it isn't his mother. But he knows the voice. It's . . . *his father*!

(Dad? It can't be him! It's just The Monster looking like him; just because it looks and sounds like Dad doesn't mean it is Dad! Remember how it tried to trick you before in the dining room?)

Billy doesn't agree. He *knows* when The Monster is near; he can *sense* it, and he senses now that this is not The Monster. Somehow his father is back and alive. Somehow he managed not to get eaten by The Monster. Maybe he even killed it after coming home and finding the fiend masquerading as him.

(Something—)

"Dad!" Billy mouths soundlessly.

(—is not right!)

Billy shuts out the voice. He doesn't want to listen. He's certain *that* is his father down there, crying. He can *feel* it.

Poor dad probably came home from his trip and found Kevin and Mom, and that's why he's crying. He'll be glad to see me and know I'm still alive!

(This is a mistake!)

Billy removes the first two boards from the trapdoor . . .

(This is your last chance! Listen! Don't do it!)

. . . and pulls up the third.

"Dad!" he cries, sticking his head through the opening. With the closet door wide open and all the clothes and stuff that had been in it thrown on the floor, Billy can clearly see his father's legs as he sits on Kevin's bottom bunk bed. "Dad! Up here!"

"Billy!" his father sobs, bending over and looking at him. He smiles and gets off the bed. He comes to the closet door.

Suddenly the sense Billy has about his father disappears. He realizes . . .

(You were *wrong*!)

. . . he was *horribly* wrong. The realization hits Billy so hard and so suddenly he nearly falls out of the attic and into the closet.

"It's about fucking time," his father says in a low, emotionless voice—the voice of *The Monster*.

Billy looks into his father's eyes, but what had just been his father's eyes a moment ago are no longer there. The Monster's eyes look back at him now and they are dry.

It tricked him.

(Told you so!)

The Monster charges at Billy. He nearly loses his grip and topples headfirst into the closet, but rights himself and pulls his head back barely just in time. He scrambles backward on all fours and comes close to slipping off the plank.

"Game's over!" The Monster crows. Its hands appear at the edges of the secret door and a second later its head pops up as it tries to pull itself through. But the opening is too narrow for it. It doesn't realize it can widen the door by removing more boards. The Monster hangs there for a moment, looking at Billy and grinning.

"We can do this the easy way or the hard way, Billy-boy. You can give me the baby and climb down, or I can come up through the regular door and get you. I know . . . you're thinking you can just jump down through this door when I come up through the other one, and you *could* do that. Actually, that will make it easier 'cause you can't get out of this room and downstairs without going by the attic door, and when it's down, the hallway is blocked and you won't be able to get by it. So . . . I'm going to get you, puke, no matter what. It's inevitable. I'm sorry, kid, really, but it had to be this way."

Billy feels sick. The Monster fooled him, was able to fool him because of one simple reason. . . .

(Mistake!)

Even though it could look like Dad, Billy never thought The Monster really *was* his father.

(One and the same!)

"If I have to chase you any more, well . . ." The Monster raises its eyebrows and Billy gets the message—he will pay horribly if he doesn't come quietly now.

(Don't do it.)

"Okay," The Monster says with a sigh. "If that's the way you want it." The Monster lets go. Its head disappears through the opening.

(Get up! Get up! He's coming for you!)

But Billy doesn't care anymore. He feels too sick, too weak, too heartbroken. "I was wrong," he mutters. Tears well in his eyes, flooding his vision until the attic around him becomes a watery blur. "The Monster didn't fool me, I fooled myself. The Monster didn't disguise itself as Dad—it *is* Dad. I knew it all along. I just didn't want to believe it."

(So what? So you made a mistake. Don't make another one! Get over it and do something. Come on! You've got to get out of here. The Monster is coming and you're trapped.)

"What's the use?"

The attic door leading to the hallway opens with a rusty squeak of its hinges and springs. The wooden ladder clatters as it slides down and unfolds. Light shoots up into the attic in wide beams, creating a mystical, almost supernatural effect.

"Last chance!" The Monster calls up through the opening. "Come down and bring the baby with you!"

On the plank near the secret door into the closet, Billy curls into a fetal position and begins to cry. Fear drains him of every ounce of strength. The realization that his own father is The Monster saps him of the will to live.

(You can't give up!)

A shadow fractures the upward shafts of light pouring into the attic and grows larger as The Monster climbs the ladder. It stops at the top, surveys the room, and sees Billy lying on the plank near the other door. It stands still for a moment listening to him crying. Several emotions cross The Monster's face—sympathy, sadness, fear, and finally grim determination. It crosses to where Billy lies and crouches next to him.

"Where's the baby?" his father asks, his voice normal.

Billy turns and looks up into his father's face. The hatred isn't there anymore but the eyes are still wrong; the eyes are still crazy and mean.

(*Monster* crazy and *Monster* mean.)

Billy thinks of his mother, dead behind the couch, now in the cellar; of Kevin with his head in a pool of blood, under the dining room table, now also probably in the cellar; and of Baby Jimmy lying *lifeless* in the bottom drawer where Billy hid him. Now The Monster-that-is-his-father is going to make *him* lifeless.

(But it needs to find the baby!)

He hates to face it, but it's true. His father . . .

(Is *nuts!*)

. . . is the real monster.

"You're crazy, Dad," Billy says in a small, terrified, pleading voice.

"As a bedbug, Billy-boy, as a bedbug," his father replies, only now he has the voice of The Monster again, and the fatherly gleam in his eyes is gone. The eyes go beyond crazy and mean and become hard as stone and full of pure hatred for every living thing.

From its back pocket The Monster pulls out a steak knife.

"Where's the baby, Billy-boy? Tell me."

Billy shakes his head in refusal.

(Wrong answer! It's going to hurt you now. Do something!)

The Monster raises the knife. It catches the light in a flash of silver.

It is a spark for Billy. Before the knife can descend, he suddenly uncoils from the fetal position and kicks out with his right foot, planting it squarely in the crouching Monster's chest. The Monster is caught completely off guard and loses its balance on the not too wide plank. It lets out a breathy grunt and sprawls backward, arms and legs splayed. The knife flies from its hand. It lands on the pink insulation between the rafters and keeps going, smashing right through the attic floor. There is a great cracking, crunching sound. The Monster lets out a roar of anger and fear. The entire house shakes as it crashes through the ceiling of Billy's parents' bedroom.

(Yes! I knew you had it in you!)

Billy scrabbles to his feet. He looks down through the huge gaping hole The Monster's fall created. Below, he can see his unconscious father on the floor, next to the battered dresser. From the blood on top of the piece of furniture, and on his father's face, Billy guesses he landed on it first and bounced off. His body lies twisted and unmoving amid the shards of the dresser's smashed mirror littering the carpet.

(I think you killed him!)

"Good." Billy doesn't care; is glad even.

(He deserved to die after all he's done, right?)

Billy stands looking down at his father's prone figure for a long time. He doesn't cry; there are no more tears to shed. Emotionless, he watches plaster dust sift down from the broken ceiling, falling like snow onto the prone figure below.

Nearly ten minutes pass—ten unusually quiet minutes inside his head as his alter ego remains oddly silent—before Billy moves. Slowly, carefully, he crosses to the attic door that leads down to the hallway. He glances back once at the light shining up through the hole in the attic floor, then goes down the creaking, squeaking ladder.

The house seems strangely quiet after all The Monster's ranting and raving. Billy stands for a moment in the upstairs hallway and looks at the destruction The Monster wrought. More than half of the second-floor railing is gone. The newel post at the top of the stairs is leaning precariously over empty space.

But now the house is quiet, silent.

(Silence is good.)

Silence means his father-the-monster might really be dead, or at least hurt too bad to be any more danger.

(You'd better hope so!)

At the bottom of the attic steps Billy goes to the nursery door and looks in. The room is a disaster. The wicker laundry basket is crushed, the crib smashed into several pieces with its mattress up against the closet, thankfully covering the blood there. The bureau he hid Jimmy in lies facedown on the carpet. The Monster never thought to look in its drawers. He turns to go downstairs and sees what his father mentioned before—with the attic stairs down, the hallway is blocked. He's going to have to fold the bottom part of the stairs up, and then the whole thing will rise into the attic automatically on its springs. But the bottom section has to be lifted and folded up first.

Billy bends over and grabs the edge of the second step. He tries to lift the bottom section of four stairs. It won't budge. He gets down on one knee and reaches around, trying to pull the section up from behind. The stairs screech as they come a half inch off the floor and no further; they are too heavy, and the hinge that folds the bottom section onto the top is rusty. Billy plants his feet, grabs the edge of the bottom step and lifts with all his might. Struggling, he manages to get the bottom section high enough that he can bend his knees and get his left one under to support the steps and give him a moment's rest. He gets a better grip and lifts again. The section folds up onto the one above it with a rusty screech of its hinges. With a loud *sproing*, momentum and the recoiling springs take over, and the door rises back into the ceiling.

The sound echoes throughout the house and fades. Billy walks down the hallway, kicking aside bits and pieces of plaster, the railing, and the balusters, and goes to the doorway of his parents' bedroom. He hears nothing from within. He peers around the door frame. The bedroom is a mess. The damage is more than what his dad crashing through the ceiling caused; all the furniture is overturned. The mattress and box spring lean against the wall and the bed frame is ripped apart. All the clothes from the closet are strewn about the room, as are the contents of the dresser and bureau. Two huge sheets of cracked, plastered gypsum board, which made up the ceiling, hang all the way to the floor. Fine white plaster powder blankets everything as if there had been a quick and furious blizzard in the room. Large pieces of the broken gypsum board lie on the bedsprings and the floor. By the leg of the bed's cracked footboard lies the ceiling light fixture, smashed and tangled up in its wiring.

Billy takes it all in but notices none of it. He wants to see only one thing—that his father is still in there, and still out cold or dead. But he can't see him; the hanging ceiling and the bed block his view of the area where his father is.

(I think it's time you got out of here!)

Billy steps into the room, turning his head to and fro in an attempt to see his father's body.

(What are you doing? Get the hell out of here while the getting is good!)

Billy doesn't listen. He *has* to go in. He *has* to know if his father is alive or dead.

(Or faking it and waiting for you to go right over so he can grab you easy as pie!)

He knows the risk; still, he has to see with his own eyes. It's funny, in a way, but he isn't terrified any more. When he believed that a shape-shifting monster had taken on his father's form he was scared to death. Now that he knows there is no monster, just his dad . . .

(Sick, crazy Dad!)

. . . he's no longer afraid.

(You *should* be afraid.)

He knows that, too, but he isn't; he feels only sadness. He doesn't know why his fear is gone; maybe it has something to do with the fact that he realizes his mother was right after all when she told him there were no monsters—not the kind he imagined to have disguised itself as his father anyway. The only real monsters are *people*: sick, crazy, violent people.

(Like Dad.)

A piece of plaster crunches underfoot as he steps closer to the hanging portion of the ceiling. He stops and listens for any sound from his downed father. There is none. Billy can't even hear him breathing. He steps sideways, closer to the bed, and attempts to peer around the jagged edge of the fallen ceiling section. It's too high for him; he can only see the top of the dresser and its shattered mirror. He tries to push the piece of ceiling aside, but the cracked gypsum board gives way and breaks off in pieces in his hand. He tosses the pieces aside and breaks off more, whittling the plaster board down to a level he can see past.

The first thing he glimpses is a foot.

(That's not a foot. It's just an empty sneaker!)

But it's his *father's* empty sneaker.

(Where's his foot? For that matter, where's his leg? His body?)

There is movement in his peripheral vision. Billy looks up. Reflected in a large jagged shard of the dresser mirror that didn't break free of the frame, is his father, standing behind him, forehead bruised, blood trickling into his right eye, arm raised, and fist poised to strike.

Billy turns but doesn't have time to utter a sound, much less scream, before the blow falls and connects with his nose. . . .

The world disappears in an explosion of bright light.

Saturday morning

In the darkness. . . .

He tries to remember, but random thoughts run rampant, shoving cohesion aside.

In the darkness, when they're sleeping. . . .

What?

He doesn't know, cannot remember; cannot stop the supersonic flight of thoughts, images, memories that keep him from a chain of reasoning. He tries to concentrate. Tries to force himself to remember what he had been thinking about. He was looking at the boy bound on the workbench in the cellar, and listening to the flies buzzing in the room, and he'd thought . . . *what?*

(Time for a tune-up!)

A sharp needle of pain drills through his eyeballs and into the back of his head. The knife of pain is so bad he smacks his forehead with the heel of his hand in a futile and childish attempt to hurt the pain back.

He runs both hands vigorously over his face.

Think, damn it! Think!

He looks at the boy again and starts to cry. The tears bring back that which he wants so badly to forget.

"I can't stand it anymore!" *A woman's voice, tearful and fearful.* "This was a mistake. I can't handle it."

"What's the big deal? Just make him stop." *A man's voice, harsh and gravelly.*

"But I don't know how. He just keeps crying and crying, and it's driving me crazy. I'm afraid I'll hurt him."

"So?"

Silence.

He was aware of being in a tightly enclosed, padded place. A bassinette. A hand suddenly appeared and clamped over his face, blocking his nose and mouth.

"See? It's easy to make him stop crying. Do it enough times and he'll learn. Kids are like animals. You got to train them. *Severely* or they turn out all fucked up."

The hand was rough and callused and smelled like tobacco.

"Stop it! You'll hurt him."

The hand lifted. There was the sound of a loud slap, and the woman's voice cried out in shock and pain.

"What *I* say goes, darling. Don't ever forget it. And if I say the little puke stops crying, he'll stop crying."

"No!" *the woman cried, but it was all she said. Her protest was cut off by the sound of repeated blows falling in rhythm with grunts from the male voice. The woman sobbed and shrieked, but those did not last. Very quickly, there was only the sound of fist striking flesh.*

"And don't get any ideas about running off, darling. You're not going anywhere, *ever*, and neither is *the boy*."

I don't care—I don't care—I don't care—I don't care, he repeats in his head like a mantra, silencing the voice from the past and dispelling the memory. The chant brings another memory—a song his father used to sing to the tune of "Old Brown Jug."

(*"I don't care! I don't care! Hitler's lost his underwear!"* That was a good one.)

He sings the ditty to himself, mumbling the words and melody as he looks at the prone figure on the workbench. Like a ray of sunlight piercing a cloud, it comes back to him—*in the darkness, when they're sleeping, children are protected by angels.*

Who used to say that? Was it Molly? His mother? Funny . . . he can't remember, but it doesn't matter—the saying isn't cause for panic. It isn't true. It was never true in his life, so there is no need to remember who said it.

(Whoever said it is a liar.)

As if he heard, the boy opens his eyes and looks at him.

(You're blind!)

Billy blinks, but his vision doesn't clear. He has a buzzing in his ears, as though there are big fat house-flies droning about nearby. The residue of a swirl of foreign images and sensations still clouds his mind's eye so thoroughly it takes away his normal vision as well. For a moment, he is thrilled at the sight of his mother walking through the kitchen door and tossing her keys on the table, but the moment doesn't last, and he knows, without verbalizing it, that what he is seeing happened yesterday. He looks at his mother's face, and she melts into Kevin looking frightened. He hears the baby cry-ing—

(I thought he was dead?)

—and suddenly he is standing over the crib again, only now he's taller and Jimmy is still alive and crying. He looks down at the wailing infant. As always, Jimmy's crying makes him wince. He reaches for Jimmy but picks up a large, egg-shaped mirror instead. The reflected face in it is his father's, and his eyes are full of terror. The mirror dissolves and a doorknob appears, painted and dripping with blood that falls in stringy drips onto his mother's black marble baker's rolling pin.

He looks up and is suddenly walking downstairs. At

the bottom he catches a glimpse of himself in another mirror; he's wearing the Spider-Man mask.

(You're The Monster!)

But this doesn't feel like the other times he was inside The Monster.

(You're right. This *is* different.)

The last image fades to gray, but his vision pulses with the pain in his head, and he has trouble focusing.

(Where are we?)

The last thing he remembers is being in his parents' bedroom, looking for The Monster—

(You mean Dad?)

—and seeing his father in the mirror, his face bruised and cut from his fall through the ceiling.

(Why did you turn around? You should have ducked!)

But he didn't, and The Monster punched him in the face.

(That's why your head hurts so much.)

But Billy remembers coming to shortly after . . .

(That's right!)

. . . as The Monster was dragging him downstairs by the hair . . .

(That's why your side hurts when you breathe.)

. . . but the moment was brief. He passed out again, and his mind was overwhelmed with images that flooded his senses. He experienced emotion, thought, sensation, and memory within those images as if they were his own experiences.

They aren't.

(Whose are they?)

He's not sure, but he thinks he knows.

(Who?)

The last of the blurring gray lifts from his vision—

(Speak of the devil.)

—and a face appears over him.

(*Dad!*)

* * *

The pain and fear John sees in his son's eyes nearly sends him over the edge.

How did I ever get to this point?

He sees the look in the child's eyes change. Is that sympathy he sees there? Understanding?

"You know, don't you?" John Teags whispers to his son, pleadingly. There's a flicker of uncertainty in the boy's eyes, then he nods slowly.

"You've known all along, haven't you, about . . . *him*."

The boy looks uncertain and frightened again.

"No. Shhh. Shhh. It's all right. Don't be afraid, Billy. Everything will be all right if you're not afraid. We can keep *him* away if we're not afraid, okay?"

Another uncertain nod. "You mean . . . The Monster?" his son asks, his voice nasal from his broken nose clogged with blood.

"Yeah, yeah . . . *The Monster*. That's right. That's what you call *him*, isn't it? That's a good name for *him* . . . *Monster*. That's what he is."

A look of hope appears on his son's face. "Then . . . The Monster . . . is real?" the boy whispers.

"Oh yes, son. He's real. He's *very* real."

"You're not The Monster? Oh Dad!" he sobs. "I been so scared! I thought *you* were The Monster."

His son tries to sit up and hug him, but his wrists and legs are bound with gray duct tape. The boy looks at him, confused.

"Aren't you going to free me, Dad? Aren't you here to rescue me?"

John Teags wants to break down and cry at the fear he hears in the request, and the hopeless hope he sees in his son's eyes. He'd like nothing more than to grant it, but . . .

"I can't, Billy. If I do, your monster will come back."

The boy lifts his head as much as he can and looks around warily. "Where is it?"

"Hiding," he answers.

The boy looks puzzled. "Where?"

"In here," John says and taps the side of his head with his index finger.

The boy is crestfallen at the news.

"No! No, don't be sad," John says quickly. "*He* won't hurt you anymore if you help me."

The boy looks more puzzled than before, but he nods and tries to smile even as he looks as though he might burst into tears at any moment.

"Just tell me where Jimmy is."

The boy looks wary.

(He's not buying it, Johnny-boy!)

"Billy," he whispers saying the boy's name like an apology. He says it again wistfully, "Billy, you don't understand. If you don't tell me, The Monster will kill you, but first he'll *hurt* you."

"I can't, Dad," the boy whispers and sobs.

(I'm confused!)

So is Billy.

(Don't trust him! Do you feel that? There's something wrong here.)

Billy can; the air is charged with a feeling like live electricity, reminding him of the time his mom took him to the Museum of Science in Hartford, and there was a room with a machine that created lightning. In that room he had felt the current in the air like a living thing. It made his skin buzz, and his hair stand on end and wave in the air. There was so much electricity in the air he could smell it.

If his nose wasn't broken, Billy is certain he'd be able to smell whatever is in the air now, it is so strong. It flows between him and his father, crackling with energy.

It floods Billy's mind with a feeling of anticipation and sets the hairs all over his body on end and every nerve to tingling. But even as Billy succumbs to the sensation, he notices his father appears to be unaffected. Billy searches his face for any sign that he senses what Billy feels, but sees none.

(Dad's too wrapped up in being crazy right now.)

His father leans closer, and the thing between them grows stronger. . . .

(Holy crap! What the hell is happening?)

He doesn't know. It's exhilarating and terrifying all at the same moment. It intensifies the pain in his face—

(Does your face hurt? It's killing me! l-o-l!)

—and all the other injured and bruised parts of his body. He takes short, gasping breaths, unable to breathe deeply without feeling like his left side is being blasted by a blowtorch and stabbed at the same time.

(The Monster did drag you down two flights of stairs to the cellar by your hair. That's got to be hard on the ribs.)

He remembers and flinches, causing more knives of pain to shoot fiercely through his throbbing head and side. The center of his face feels balloonish. He tastes blood. He can't breathe through his nose, and his vision is narrowed due to the swelling around his eyes.

(You're in deep doo-doo!)

His lips are swollen and blubbery, and his two top front teeth are loose.

(You're in worse than deep doo-doo. You're in deep *shit*!)

Billy knows that, and the knowledge terrifies him as much as the energy coursing between him and his father.

(Speaking of which: *Is* he The Monster or not?)

"I don't understand, Dad. If *you're* not The Monster,

then where does it come from?" he asks softly, lowering his voice to a whisper at the name of the thing he fears most. "How did it get *inside* you?" he asks, remembering the dream of The Monster absorbing his father.

His father grimaces at the questions. He starts to turn away, and his hand brushes against Billy's bare arm. To his father, it is casual contact, but Billy is nearly convulsed by it, as if jolted by a powerful electrical current. Alien images and memories again flood his young mind:

(Make the darkness your friend.)

He heard the voice and nearly screamed with fear. He was alone in the cellar. Anyway, he was supposed to be alone in the cellar. He'd always been alone in the cellar before.

Alone and terrified.

(You don't have to be afraid anymore.)

This time he did cry out faintly, but immediately clamped his hand over his mouth. No matter how frightened he was, no matter how scared, he couldn't make noise. Sir wouldn't like it. It was bad enough being locked in the cellar, made to lie motionless for hours in The Brig, the cramped, narrow shelf under Sir's workbench, but he didn't want Sir to come down and put him on the bench for a tune-up. Or worse: to balance his books.

"Do you need a tune-up, puke? Do you want me to balance your books?"

He shuddered at the thought.

(Why don't *we* give *him* a tune-up? Balance *his* books?)

"Who are you?" *he whispered to the darkness.*

The darkness giggled back.

(You know who I am.)

He didn't and didn't want to. It could only bring trouble. Sir wouldn't like it; him talking to someone right there in The Brig, in Sir's house, in Sir's cellar. He had learned long ago not to piss Sir off deliberately—of course he didn't need to do that. He could piss Sir off just by looking at him.

He scrambled out from under the workbench, even though to get caught doing so would mean both a tune-up and a full accounting of his books—what Sir called "Taking Inventory"—but he was terrified by the voice.

(Don't go!)

He fled. Quickly, but quietly, he went to the workshop doorway and looked longingly up the stairs to the light at the top seeping through around the edges of the door. Gingerly, he felt the side of his face and sucked in his breath, wincing at the pain even the lightest touch brought. It wasn't too bad though. He had got off easy tonight and he knew it. He just hoped Sir didn't realize it, too, and decide to "Take Inventory."

"The accountant's here, Johnny-boy! Time to examine your books! You got dividends comin' to you, puke."

Sir loved taking inventory and paying dividends, any excuse, any time.

"Gonna balance your books, Johnny-boy."

The last time Sir "balanced his books" he got a new tattoo— Sir's initials burned into the bottom of his right foot with a lit cigarette.

"Brand you like an animal, so's you won't forget who owns you."

(Welcome to Marlboro country! Makes you want to light up, don't it?)

"Go away! Leave me alone!"

Oh no! Too late! He forgot himself and shouted. Loudly.

"What the fuck is your problem, puke?"

He was frozen with fear. The words from above were muffled at first but grew louder as Sir got closer to the cellar door at the top of the stairs. The door banged open and light flooded down and over him where he sat huddled on the bottom step clinging to the rail post. The sight of him, as it often did, sent Sir into a rage.

"Goddamn it, you little son of a bitch! What the fuck are you doing out of The Brig?" *Sir roared in a guttural, animal growl, sounding as if some great beast were speaking.*

He trembled and felt his bowels loosen, their contents turning liquid, the muscles growing weak. He knew he couldn't mess himself, not again. Sir wouldn't stand for it. The last time Sir made him clean his soiled underwear with his . . . tongue.

"I told you, you had to do time in The Brig, didn't I, puke, and I meant stay in the fuckin' Brig!"

He scurried backward into the workshop and squeezed into the spidery darkness of the shelf beneath it. He huddled there trying not to mind the cobwebs that made him feel like bugs were crawling all over him in the dark. He didn't mind as long as Sir stayed upstairs and didn't come down.

Too late.

"You know, Johnny-boy," *Sir said as he started down the stairs. The tone of his voice had changed from bellowing rage to cool, quiet seriousness, which was much more frightening for what it forebode,* "you are about as dumb as a dog with a lobotomy."

Sir entered the workshop, taking off his belt. He whimpered. Sir was wrapping the leather end around his hand. He was going to use the buckle; he was going to get serious. Sir was going to do some accounting.

He flinched with dread anticipation.

Sir dragged him from beneath the workbench and dumped him on the cold, concrete floor at his feet. Sir's arm came up, the brass of the belt buckle caught the light streaming through the cellar windows, and he tried not to scream, tried not to cry. If he screamed it would only be worse, and if he cried . . . it would be horrible! *Screaming would piss Sir off but crying would make him crazy, and the beating would be worse than if he could just keep quiet and take it like a man.*

The belt fell. The buckle dug into the back of his shoulders, tearing and bruising the skin. He shuddered under the blow, letting out only the tiniest of whimpers.

"Shut up, Johnny-boy! Take it like a man, boy."

* * *

Still unaware of the effect his touch is having on the boy, John turns away. The boy takes a deep, painful breath, and his body relaxes.

"Take it like a man, boy," John says softly, the words slurring from his lips. He looks around quickly, furtively, as if expecting someone to be lurking in the shadows listening, or perhaps waiting to pounce. When he speaks again his voice is low, concentrated, urgent. "I never wanted any of this to happen, Billy. You've got to believe me. I never meant to hurt . . . anyone." He has to stop as the tears escape again. "I'm not *him*, Billy. I'm not the monster. You've got to understand." He looks at his son, but the boy's eyes are distant, glazed.

Like a smothering victim given a reprieve, Billy sucks air and coughs.

(What *is* that? Why does that keep happening?)

Billy can't think straight.

(That was *scary*!)

Billy's mind is awhirl with leftover images, impressions, memories, and thoughts: the hulking, frightening form of SIR; the touch of spiderwebs on his skin; the smell of his father's fear, and worse . . . the *feel* of his fear at being in The Brig.

(Maybe that's why The Monster puts all its victims in cellars! But what the heck's a *brig*?)

Billy shudders at the memory; it feels like his own, even though he knows it isn't.

(You always knew you had a special link with The Monster!)

But Dad?

(*Before*, you didn't *know* The Monster was inside Dad!)

That's it, Billy realizes; that's why he's connecting

with his father now—The Monster didn't *devour* and *absorb* Dad like he saw in his dream; The Monster got *inside* him, like the monster in *Alien*.

(Like that little girl in the movie, *The Exorcist*, that you watched with Dad and Kevin. She had the devil inside her!)

Dad's possessed.

(Maybe The Monster is really the Devil!)

His father's hand comes close to his arm. Invisible psychic sparks crackle between the hairs on their skin. Billy shivers at the sensation and tries to slide away without drawing attention. It doesn't matter; his father turns away.

"Dad . . ." Billy starts to say and flinches when his father's attention snaps back to him.

(Don't make him mad!)

"Sorry, Billy," his father says gently. "What did you ask me? You want to know how did *he* get inside me? The Monster? How did all this start?" He pauses and shakes his head. "He wasn't always a monster, you know. He was just . . . me. Just another part of me. I knew that . . . I knew that for a long time, but then . . . things changed." He hangs his head as tears of self-pity fall to the floor at his feet.

(They're crocodile tears—just like Mrs. Petrie always says! They're fake!)

Dad wipes at his eyes with the backs of his hands and sniffs back snot once, twice, and swallows it. He clears his throat, turns, and expectorates on the floor behind him. "I never told you guys much about my family, Billy, but I was an only child, and I had me an only parent, too, back when single parenthood wasn't fashionable." He laughs softly, wearily, and goes on. "I never knew my mother, not really. I have vague memories of her, but nothing I can grab hold of, you know? Sir always said, 'Your mother was a no-good worthless bitch sent from

Hell to torment me.' Sir told me that she had taken off after I was born because she couldn't stand the sound of my crying. I believed that for a long time . . . I thought it was my fault." He stops for a moment. His breathing is the only sound for several seconds before he goes on. "Years later, after I got sent to the hospital, I found out that she didn't run away; she didn't abandon me. Sir killed her. The police found her body buried in the backyard.

"I think I always knew, deep down, that Sir had killed her, 'cause before I ever found out she was actually dead, I used to make believe she was an angel. I used to imagine her in Heaven, waiting in line to get her wings—you know, like Clarence in *It's A Wonderful Life*, and as soon as she got them she would swoop down and carry me off with her." He blinks tears away. "There must have been a shortage of wings in Heaven back then. Sometimes I'd think she didn't come for me because of what Sir had said, about my crying. That made me feel bad . . . you know . . . responsible? I felt that for a long time, until I had you guys."

He looks at Billy and shakes his head.

"I could never understand what there was about a baby's crying that my mother couldn't stand until I had you and your brothers. Kevin's crying was bad, and your crying was worse, but you two were *nothing* compared to Jimmy. He's got that shrill cry that's like," he hesitates, groping for words. "You know what I mean? It's a sound that goes right through you. It sets you on edge. . . .It's like scraping your nails on a chalkboard, only worse . . . it's like scraping your *teeth* on a chalkboard!" he blurts out.

(That's exactly what it's like!)

His father's words speed up, and he starts to ramble. Billy's not sure he is even aware of him anymore.

"Like last Tuesday night. That was bad. Molly managed to get Jimmy to bed early, around seven o'clock, because he hadn't taken a nap that afternoon. We were able to steal a little bit of quality time then." He sighs. "A little bit of heaven after all the kids were in bed. We had a glass of wine, listened to some old Beatles tunes— Molly loves The Beatles. But, of course, we played it softly so as not to wake Jimmy. We were snuggling on the couch, just enjoying the wonderful quiet for a change.

"I took Molly in my arms." He smiles wistfully. "It was the way it was before she got pregnant with Jimmy. We sat on the couch, and I leaned over to kiss her, but that was as far as I got. Jimmy started crying. He was upstairs, in the nursery, as far from me as he could possibly get in this house, and the sound still went right through me as though it had been blasted directly in my ears. It was even worse than when he first came home from the hospital.

"Even though it was killing me, I forced myself to go up with Molly to check on Jimmy. Any hope that it was a minor interruption, though, didn't last. Jimmy started vomiting as soon as she picked him up."

Billy remembers that night. He woke to hear his mother's frightened voice: "He's got a fever, John! He's burning up!"

"Then Kevin, too, woke with a fever and started puking, too," his father went on. "I could deal with taking care of Kevin, even though he cried like a baby after he threw up all over his bedroom floor before he could make it to the bathroom, but his crying could never compare to Jimmy's, which went right through the base of my skull and up into my brain like a drill.

"Little Jimmy's crying went on relentlessly for hours that night. I honestly don't know how such a little body can cry for so long and so hard without ever getting tired. Molly, an angel as always, cleaned his vomit and rocked him, cooing to him in her arms—but it was no use. Jimmy just kept throwing up and crying—and crying and crying and crying!"

"But Dad, you can't blame Jimmy," Billy says softly, "He was sick. He's just a baby."

"Just a *baby*? *Just a baby!*" his father shouts and lets out a frightening monsterlike laugh—and just like that The Monster is there, glaring baleful hatred at Billy.

"*He's just a baby! You can't blame Jimmy!* Hah! You want to know who I can blame? You want to know who's *really* to blame for me, Billy-boy?" The Monster leers, sticking its face so close to Billy's he can smell sweat and bad breath. His skin vibrates at The Monster's nearness.

"You, Billy!" The Monster sneers. "*You* made me what I am, today! Your crying made me the monster that I am, puke, and Jimmy's crying just made me strong. It was like pouring gasoline on an already blazing fire!"

Billy shrinks from The Monster's accusation, but he can't escape what it brings to mind: the most frequent dream in the recurring series of dreams that he's had on or around his birthday. At least, he had *thought* they were dreams. Now, seen in the light of The Monster's words, he realizes they were memories, or at least inspired by a memory. A very old memory; an infant memory that was more than just a jumble of sensory detail. A memory of a baby crying shrilly. Voices yelling; adults arguing. Familiar, yet somehow incomprehensible sounds. He remembers not being able to understand what the voices he heard were saying. It was as if they were speaking a foreign language. He could feel his body, warmly bundled in fragrant softness. And just behind the pleasant smell were the odors of sour milk and the yellow pungent stink of dried urine. Over, under, and through it all he could hear the sound of music, of chiming little bells; a music box playing, "It's a Small World."

When he opened his eyes, Mickey Mouse and Donald Duck floated over him. Lazily they spiraled in the air above him. Goofy and Pluto were there, too, floating and bobbing along with Daisy Duck and Minnie Mouse, drifting round and round to the chiming Disney song.

But nothing was as loud as his thoughts—his needful, wanting thoughts; his hungry, crying thoughts; his cold, fearful, lonely thoughts. Thoughts like impulses, like reflexes—the involuntary muscle flexing of his mind—shot through with his jumbled consciousness in no apparent pattern and with no understandable insight. They were thoughts that could not be ignored, anticipated, or controlled.

His remembers his skin feeling dry in places, cold and sticky in others. He couldn't feel his arms and legs in a normal way but could sense them, moving, jerking about independently and spasmodically as if they were disconnected from him and had a life of their own.

Much like his thoughts.

(Like when you're in The Monster, too!)

The sensory details shifted, overlapped, and became mixed together. The scene changed, yet remained the same. It clarified and suddenly he remembers looking at the darkening blue of an early evening sky. Perfectly formed five-point stars shining with bright yellow rays glowing from their symmetrical arms.

No. Not the sky. A ceiling. A ceiling painted to look like a star-filled night sky. The stars look like they were plucked from an American flag they're so perfect and exactly alike. Meeting the sky ceiling at a right angle was a pale blue wall adorned with stenciled yellow bike-riding circus bears holding three red balloons each.

(The nursery! You're in the nursery!)

The wall stretched so far above it frightened him; it seemed to him that such a tall wall might be too heavy and collapse upon him. He remembers hearing the sound of the baby crying, and how he wanted it to stop, but the wailing only got louder. A small hand, fingers chubby and stubby, knuckles dimpled, waved in front of his eyes spastically before plunging into his mouth, fat knuckles first. The irritating crying ceased and was replaced by a half-strangled gurgling.

(It's you!)

He was the baby crying.

That's when the memory got scary; that was when he felt the bad thing, all locked up, stuffed into a box and forgotten. But the box opened and inside was an egg—

(The black Easter egg of your Disney dream!)

—and inside the egg was the bad thing, growing worse every time the baby cried.

(Every time *you* cried.)

The egg started to crack.

He remembers the voices, loud and arguing. They mingled with the sound of his own crying until he couldn't tell them apart—it was just a wall of noise. And the louder it got the worse the bad thing became. The cracks in the egg widened and ran down the sides.

His head throbbed with all the noise inside it and out. His privates were on fire, stinging and burning terribly.

The stench of urine and more was a pungent part of the memory.

His crying brought a light on—too bright after the dimness his eyes had become accustomed to, and his crying went up a notch. The egg cracked open to reveal glimpses of the bloody, black evil thing inside. A voice spoke; he remembers it as his mother but, strangely, he couldn't understand her words. He could sense her tone, though—tired, frustrated, on the edge of anger, but not with him. Never with her baby boy. She was speaking too loudly, too angrily to be speaking to him. Whenever she spoke to him—even when he'd been fussy and crying—

it was always gently and with love. Dad appeared in the doorway behind her, looking anxious and upset.

(Why couldn't you see The Monster inside him then?)

His crying went up a notch. The egg crumbled, revealing the horror inside it. And that's when the most important part of the memory occurred, and he knew— long before he learned to talk and understand language—he knew, from that point on, that the egg's hatchling was a child-hating monster that wanted to kill him every time he cried.

He quickly learned not to.

It's all my fault.

(No it isn't!)

It is! He knows it's true . . .

(Says who?)

. . . known it, deep down, ever since The Monster started killing mothers and their babies, and he discovered a link with its mind. He knew even before that, but he hadn't wanted to see.

All those people dead because of me.

(What? No way!)

All those poor innocent babies, like Jimmy.

(*You* didn't kill them!)

He didn't have to: *I created The Monster that did.*

(So? Doctor Frankenstein created a monster that killed, but *he* didn't get blamed for it.)

Like you said before: That isn't real; but this is.

There is a sound from the other side of the cellar, outside the house. John goes to the workshop doorway and looks across to the opposite windows. There is movement outside the right rear corner one. He leaves the boy and crosses the disaster area of junk between the workshop and the far window. It is open a crack. John peers through the dirty glass. Faint music reaches him— The Carpenter's, "Close to You." The music is leaking from the earphones the next-door neighbor—a bleached-blond, chubby, middle-age woman—is wearing along with too much makeup and too little clothing—

(Those pink hot pants and halter top are about a size too small.)

—for a woman her age and weight. She's doing stretching exercises in her driveway.

He is about to turn away when she stops and hurries toward him. He ducks back, but she hasn't seen him. She's picking something up. It looks like a folded paper airplane. She unfolds it. He wants to look closer—the paper looks familiar but is hard to see through the filthy glass and the weeds encroaching outside the window. The woman stares at the back of the unfolded airplane; the front looks to him like a photograph. Suddenly, she looks up at his house and shakes her head. Clutching the paper airplane, she turns around, crosses her driveway, and goes into her house.

John turns from the window at the sound of the boy moving on the workbench. Struggling. "I don't blame you, Billy. You had good reason to cry, I guess," John says loudly as he returns to the workshop. "You were sick. You got better, though. It was weird, but it seemed like you got better real fast after *he* became The Monster. It was as if you *knew* even then what your crying had given birth to. But that didn't happen with Jimmy. I don't feel any connection with him, not like I did with you. He just cries and cries and cries. Nothing satisfies him. Nothing seems to make him feel better for very long. That's when I knew what my mother must have felt. That's when I understood."

He frowns and looks down at his feet as if he's lost something. "Sir was different, though," he says to the floor and adds another furtive look behind him. "It took me a lot longer to understand him. He was such an enigma—a brutal man who was an expert auto mechanic, a successful CPA, and he liked to collect butterflies. Go figure, huh? He had framed displays all over the house filled with butterflies pinned to corkboard. He cared more about his damned butterflies than he did me." He looks at his son and caresses the side of his face with the back of his hand. "You have no idea what it was like. . . ."

(Wrong!)

Billy knows *exactly* what it was like as soon as his father touches him.

Huddled in the darkness of The Brig in the workshop at the bottom of the cellar stairs, crying. But Sir wouldn't stand for crying. Sir's ears are like radar when it comes to crying. The cellar door at the top of the stairs opened. He tried to retreat further under the bench, cringing under the growing shadow of Sir descending the stairs and coming into the workshop.

"Stop that sniveling! Stop it now!"

He tried to stop crying, but he couldn't. The pain was too much . . . the burning where his father had branded him— SIR—*in the heel of his left foot.*

"I can't stand that whining shit, puke. Cease and desist *now* or face the consequences."

He gulped back his sobs with a herculean effort and stopped his tears.

"That's better, Johnny-boy. Now get your ass upstairs. I need help with the collection."

He scrambled past, wincing at the prospect of a slap for no good reason as he did, and hurried up to the kitchen. The stereo was on in another room, but turned up loud so that Sir can hear Jimmy Buffett singing, "Margaritaville," while he works on his favorite pastime—next to hurting him that is—bug collecting.

A stack of corkboard, cut into eight-by-eleven-inch pieces, sat at the left edge of the kitchen table. A desk blotter was arranged in the middle of the table, right in front of the sole chair. To the right of the blotter a short stack of eight by eleven panes of glass sat, and just above the glass were several black, plastic picture frames, also eight by eleven. At the top edge of the blotter, five one-pint Ball jars were lined up like soldiers. Each was a-buzz with a live, trapped, flying insect. On the blotter, just below the jars, was a pincushion, loaded with shiny pins, and a pair of long-handled, narrow-tipped tweezers. On the table, against the right edge of the blotter, was a large magnifying glass.

"Take your post, puke."

He did, dutifully standing at attention to the right of Sir's chair despite the burning pain in his foot. He picked up the heavy magnifying glass and held it at the ready like a soldier at arms with his rifle.

The ritual began.

"Okay, what's first?" *Sir picked up one of the Ball jars. He held it close to his Coke-bottle-lens glasses.* "Magnification!" *Sir shouted.*

He put the magnifying glass between Sir's eyes and the jar. Sir grabbed his wrist and moved the glass back and forth, focusing.

"My eyes are the only thing about me that's weak," *Sir said softly and looked sideways at him.* "And don't you ever forget it, puke." *Sir chuckled and started humming along with Jimmy Buffett, who was looking for his lost shaker of salt. Sir sized up the prey in the jar. His reflection, distorted both in the surface of the jar, and in the magnifying glass, was grotesque, even monstrous.*

With a wave of his hand, Sir dismissed the magnifying glass. He put the jar down on the blotter in front of him and picked up one of the corkboards. Five narrow labels were af-

*fixed to its surface in a pentagonal pattern with ample space
between them.*

"Leucorrhinia proxima," *Sir said, reading the first label
in the bottom left corner of the corkboard.* "Otherwise known
as the red-winged dragonfly." *Carefully, he placed the cork
on the felt blotter in front of him and pulled the jar containing*
leucorrhinia proxima *over against its top edge. He un-
screwed the lid of the Ball jar and kept his left hand on it while
he picked up the long tweezers with his right. He opened the lid
just enough to allow the tweezers in with room to move.*

The concentration on Sir's face was intense. "Magnification!" *he called again.* "Come on, you little rat-bastard!"

*He was unsure if Sir was speaking to him or the bug, but
that was the least of his worries—his nose tickled. He could feel
a sneeze building. Fear coursed through him, making his nose
tickle more. To sneeze now would mean certain pain—serious
pain. He scrunched his upper lip into his nose and the feeling,
thankfully, passed.*

"Gotcha!" *Carefully, Sir removed the dragonfly from the
jar, its tail clamped between the pincers of the tweezers. The insect vibrated its iridescent quadruple wings in a futile effort to
fly away.* "A beauty," *Sir exclaimed. With deep concentration,
the tip of his tongue showing at the right corner of his lips, Sir
bent over the board and carefully placed the dragonfly in the
spot above its label. He held it to the cork with the tweezers in
his left hand while he pulled a pin from the cushion with his
right. Breathing heavily, his eyes gleaming with excitement, he
pushed the pin through the dragonfly, until the head of the pin
was flush with the still buzzing insect's body, and fastened it to
the board. The bug beat its wings faster than could be seen, but
it was in vain.*

*He felt bad for the dragonfly. He knew how it felt; trapped,
completely in Sir's control. Just like him.*

*Sir repeated the process with the tweezers and the next Ball
jar, removing a large dusty-colored moth.* "Calephelis bore-

alis," *he said as he snagged it with the pincers and withdrew it from the jar.*

His arm was getting tired; the magnifying glass was heavy, but he didn't dare put it down, or even let it droop a fraction of an inch. The last time he did, Sir had used the magnifying glass to burn him with focused, concentrated laser beams of sunlight. It was an experience he did not care to have again.

By the time Sir was done with the next two insects—a large, furry, black and yellow striped bumblebee stuck under the label Bombus ruderatus; *and a common yellow jacket pinned beneath the identification* Vespula vulgaris—*the muscles in his arms screamed for relief. Just when he thought he couldn't hold the glass up any longer, and was ready to let it drop no matter what Sir did to him, his father gave him a reprieve and waved the glass away.*

There was one jar, one insect, left.

"The pièce de résistance!" Sir breathed as he withdrew the final specimen from its jar. He held in to the place of honor, smack-dab in the middle of the corkboard, right above the label Danaus plexippus. *"This beauty is all yours, puke. Don't fuck it up, or I'll be pinning you to a fucking corkboard."*

Sir held out a pin for him. He took it, his hand trembling. He tried to keep it steady, but he couldn't. Sir knew he couldn't, and he knew Sir knew he couldn't; Sir was just doing it to have an excuse to dole out more punishment. Not that he ever needed an excuse.

"A beating a day keeps the whining away!" Sir often said.

He started to cry. The tears snuck up on him and caught him unawares. One moment he was concentrating with every fiber of his being on holding the pin steady, but the next his vision blurred as his eyes filled with water, and large, hot tears rolled down both cheeks. Once the tears started, he couldn't stop them. All he could do was keep silent and hope Sir didn't notice.

"Hold the pin steady and put it right through the center of the thorax," *Sir shouted at him, not taking his eyes from the bug.* "Come on! You've seen me do it hundreds of times."

Of course, that only makes his hand tremble more. Sir looked at him; saw the tears.

"What the hell are you crying about now? Stick the damn pin in and be quick about it."

"I-I don't w-want to kill the pretty b-b-butterfly!" *he sobbed, losing any pretense of self-control. He dropped the pin and covered his mouth with both hands, trying to squelch the rising torrent, but it was too late.*

Sir rubbed his temple with his free hand, as if he had a sudden headache. "What did I tell you about crying, puke? Huh? You want something to cry about? I'll fucking flay you alive! I'll give you something to cry about; I'll beat you to within an inch of your life!" *Sir shouted and then made good on his word, giving him plenty to shed tears for.*

When it was done, Sir stood over him, breathing heavily, the cut lamp cord dangling from his fist, and said, "Crying is what drove your mother out, puke. Not that I minded getting rid of the bitch. But she just didn't know how to handle little animals like you."

Then Sir showed his adeptness at handling animals like him: the way he handled him every day—roughly and violently—as he dragged him down to the workshop at the bottom of the cellar stairs, stuffed him into the shelf underneath the workbench, and left him there to wait for the next time . . . and the next . . . and the next. . . .

John removes his hand from his son's face and rubs it briskly over his own. Flakes of blood fall from his skin to the sound of his fingers scratching roughly over his beard stubble.

"It wasn't until recently, really, that I think I finally

got it—got Sir. I think he must have had a *voice*, too. . . ."
He drifts off and becomes lost in the corridors of the
past again. He jerks out of it suddenly like a soldier
snapping to attention, rigid and upright.

"Sir was an ex-Marine. My earliest memory of him is
him telling me to call him *Sir*." His voice becomes deep
and gruff, with just the hint of a Southern accent to it.
" 'None of this *Daddy* bullshit!' he said to me. He said,
'No *Dad, Pop*, or *Fah-ther*.' " The last is said with a haughty
British accent and a delicate wave of his hand.

"He said, 'In my corps, Johnny-boy, you call me *Sir*,
first, last, and foremost. In fact, I want you to call me Sir
as if it is in all capital letters, like, *SIR*!' And to make
sure I got it right he gave me my first tattoo." He pulls
up his sweatshirt and holds up his left arm, revealing
the soft flesh of his underarm. He pulls back the tuft of
wiry black hair and there, just above the center of his
armpit, the word *SIR* is tattooed in small dark blue
crudely drawn capital letters a quarter of an inch high.

"It took him an hour to do it. He used the tip of his
hunting knife and blue ink from a broken ballpoint
pen. But he sterilized the knife with fire and wiped his
work with rubbing alcohol constantly." He winces at the
memory. "Everything was clean. No chance of an infec-
tion. No chance of me getting sick and having to see a
doctor. That wouldn't do. He was good that way, good
at making sure no one ever knew . . . no one ever saw—
he never let me out of the house, not even for school.
Sir taught me the three R's. Later, I was easily able to
keep the scars hidden from your mother, Sir did such a
good job of choosing his spots. I was two or three when
he did this one. The next one was on the heel of my left
foot. Those were just two of many. He said it was so I'd
never forget what to call him, 'first, last, and foremost!' "
John laughs, but there is no joy in it. It is an empty, des-
perate sound, as dry as sand against wood.

"I give him credit, though. He stopped my crying. One way or another, he stopped it all right. He cured me of that endless, annoying bawling and sniveling. I never could have done the things to Jimmy to stop his crying that Sir did to me; for one thing your mother wouldn't have let me. But his tactics worked. I'll give him that. They worked pretty damned good."

John smiles grimly and walks to the rectangular cellar window set just below the ceiling at the end of the workbench. "You know, he could have just given me up. Put me in an orphanage or something. He could have dumped me on relatives. He could have killed me like . . ." He looks at the floor and doesn't finish the sentence. He glances up at the window. The sun peeps through for a moment then the clouds return. A shadow moves over everything like a dark blue bruise.

"But he didn't give up on me. He didn't give me up. I don't know why he didn't. Maybe because we were connected, too, you know? Like you and me." He looks at the boy, excitement burning in his eyes. "Do you remember that night? Huh?" Seeing no response he leans closer, looking his son in the eyes. "You have to remember! It was the night I realized that we're *connected*." He taps his head. "Up here. The night you looked like you sensed"—he pauses, checks behind him—"that *he*—*The Monster*—was with us. *Invisible*. Yeah. You knew, remember?" He smiles, mistaking his son's confused expression for a knowing look.

"It was wintertime. We were in the parlor watching TV. I think it was *American Idol*. You were lying on the floor in front of the television, and I was in my easy chair behind you. Your mother was on the couch reading a magazine. I think it was *Discover*. You know how she enjoys that science-y stuff like *National Geographic*. Anyway, you and me were watching the show, and she was reading and watching at the same time, which used to drive me crazy." He stops and smiles at the boy, showing a rare moment of happiness.

"She'd always end up missing something. Then she'd have to ask me what happened, and then I'd miss something while I explained what she had missed." He laughs, but the happiness no longer shows in his face nor sings in his laughter. The haunted, hunted look returns to his eyes, and the laughter becomes a sob. He remains quiet for several moments before straightening and staring at the wall like it is something new that he has never seen before. He continues; his voice soft.

"That night, though, she wasn't that interested in the show. It wasn't one of her favorite TV programs anyway. Not like you and me. Remember?" His speech quickens. "And Kevin, Kevin, Kevin was over at his friend Donny's house, yeah. And little Jimmy was still just a *quiet* lump in your mother's belly." He chuckles.

"It was such a . . . a . . . *profound* moment that I, I can see every detail. . . . There was a commercial for Twix candy bars on TV that your mother hated because it didn't advocate sharing. She thought it taught kids bad manners. The radiators were hissing with heat because it was below freezing outside. And you, you were wearing your Spider-Man pajamas. Remember those?" He has to stop for a breath; his words coming too quickly for his lungs to keep up. His face is flushed and his eyes are dancing with excitement.

He starts to speak, but stutters uncontrollably for several seconds and breaks into a high-pitched laughter that cuts off abruptly. "Okay. The commercial was on and your mother, sitting there with her legs curled up under her and wearing her blue terry cloth bathrobe over her red Dr. Denton's, said, 'Listen to this, hon.' I didn't though, not right away. She was always reading stuff to me from out of her magazines. Stuff that she thought I would find interesting but rarely did—not while I was watching *Idol* anyway." He rubs his chin furiously. His day-old beard sounds like sandpaper.

"But you perked right up and looked at her. You were always listening to things you shouldn't. Adult things. She told me about some study at the University of Oslo that found what they called a sort of *psychic* link between male children and their fathers, from right after birth all the way up to age seven. She thought that was so damned interesting." He laughs and shakes his head slowly. "But like I said, I was barely even listening, until you sat up on the floor and looked at me." John stops and looks at the boy with eyes full of wonder.

"It was the weirdest thing! I just looked at you, and I knew. I *knew*! It was almost like I could hear your voice in my head right there with, you know, *him*—The Monster. And I suddenly remembered that I could tell what Sir was thinking sometimes when I was little, when I was your age. If I hadn't been able to, I would have suffered a lot more than I did. I might not have even survived if I hadn't been able to tell what was going on in his head, if I hadn't been able to know when something was making Sir crazy.

"You know what I mean, don't you?" He asks the question and leans close to the boy. "It wasn't like I could actually read his mind. It was . . . more of a feeling. Like when you know you got to go to the bathroom, you get that tightness in your balls, or that tugging feeling. That's what it was like. And it didn't happen all the time, just when Sir was really mad about something or his voice was . . . well, you know. And when I wasn't able to sense what was on his mind, *he*— my other voice—still could a lot and used to warn me when Sir was about to go on a rampage. It's like that other me never lost the link to my father's mind.

"And you inherited it from me. Only you've got it worse. Stronger." He pauses, thinking. "That was the beginning of the end, you know. It's funny how things happened. . . ." John's voice trails off. He looks with concern at his son. "Even though you turned him into The Monster, Billy, he didn't get really bad until your mother brought little Jimmy home from the hospital . . . that's what caused all this, not you. After a while you stopped crying so much, and The Monster went to sleep. It was Jimmy that woke him up again" New tears shine in his eyes, and his voice grows husky.

"Jimmy just wouldn't stop crying, you know? It was worse than your crying ever was, and I thought your crying was pretty bad at the time you were born. Funny . . . Kevin almost never cried compared to you and Jimmy." He pauses. "But Jimmy's crying drove The Monster over the edge." He looks around and leans close to the bound boy on the workbench. "Jimmy's crying made The Monster do terrible things. . . . Jimmy's crying is like pins and needles in my brain. It's like a metal rake being dragged across a plate of glass. It makes my bones ache.

"*Can't* have crying," he exclaims, suddenly. "No! Can't have it! No *SIR*!" He looks at the boy, and tears run down his face. His voice is small and childlike. "I always *wanted* to stop crying, I really did. But I was so scared, and then there was the *pain*. . . . I knew my crying made Sir crazy angry. I knew it made him want to kill me, but I couldn't help it, especially when I was really little. It was so *dark* down there. . . ." He grabs at his underarm where the word *SIR* is scarred in the flesh. "It hurt so bad."

With a deep breath that brings a pained expression to his face, the boy asks a question in a voice so pathetic and sad it rends John's heart and weakens his knees.

"Dad . . . what happened to Mom and Kevin and Baby Jimmy?"

John passes a hand over his eyes, digging his index finger and thumb into the corners on either side of the bridge of his nose and rubbing hard and deep. He grunts, and his voice is harsh and raspy when he answers.

"I . . . I don't know, for sure, what happened, Billy. I came home from my trip early, and your mom had to go out and get medicine for the baby." He laughs sadly. "Big mistake. Jimmy started crying, and he wouldn't stop. One moment I was upstairs trying to get him to be quiet, and the next I was standing in the living room and . . . Molly . . . your mother . . . and Kevin and Jimmy . . . were all *dead*." He sobs and passes a hand over his eyes. "All I can tell you, Billy, is that The Monster got her. It wasn't my fault. If I could have done anything. . . . I loved her, Billy, so much." He smiles sadly.

"Did I ever tell you how we met? No, no of course I didn't. It's funny really. I met your mother at the state hospital the day I was released—the day I turned twenty-one—but she thought I worked there. It was a Saturday afternoon. Molly—your mom—was there visiting her cousin who had suffered a nervous breakdown. I had all my worldly belongings, meaning my clothes—two pairs of jeans, a few shirts and sweaters, socks and under-wear—stuffed in a backpack. Doctor Rathbone and the nurses and other patients on my ward had just thrown a 'Getting Out' party for me. After fourteen years in that place I was finally free and headed for a halfway house to stay in until I got a job and found a place of my own.

"I was kind of scared leaving the asylum. It had been my home since Sir died. I really didn't think I was going to make it on the outside, but then I saw your mother. She was standing in the garden outside the front en-trance of the hospital, hugging her cousin and saying good-bye. As I stepped outside, sunlight caught her hair and enveloped her head like a halo. It was like a vision of an angel or a saint—it was amazing. Her red hair *glowed* in the light, and it captivated me. It hypnotized me. That was enough—I was smitten—but then she looked at me, and I was done for. I was a goner for sure. There was no going back then."

He pauses and looks sadly around the workshop. "No going back. I can't *ever* go back." He sighs, but then brightens. "Your mother was so beautiful, she literally took my breath away. I couldn't take my eyes off her. I tripped over the low hedges lining the walk and fell over, right on my face. She burst out laughing and came running over to help. It was pretty funny. She was really concerned if I was okay or not, but she couldn't stop laughing.

"Needless to say I felt damned stupid. I was embarrassed and ashamed, but when she told me not to be—after she'd stopped laughing of course—I wasn't! Just like that"—he snaps his fingers—"she made everything all right. It was amazing. No one had ever affected me that way before, but she could do that. . . ." He looks down at his feet and adds softly, "most of the time, anyway." He takes a deep breath and continues in the same soft tone. "We had coffee at a Starbucks near the hospital. At first she wanted to go to the hospital coffee shop, but I said no. I was afraid someone might recognize me and talk to me and reveal that I had been a patient there.

"I don't think your mom ever found out that I had been a patient. She didn't know I had been committed. I let her go on that way. I never told her what happened. I gave her a phony name, then changed it legally soon after I got out so she'd never know. I didn't really have to do that because I had been in there so long no one on the outside remembered what I had done, but I wanted to start *over*. That was the magic of your mother! She made me feel like I *could* start over. She made me feel like I was okay, normal. She got me a job with her dad's insurance agency, and I moved into her apartment less than a month after I got out of the asylum. We were married a year later.

"You know, it's funny. I didn't know it when I was little, but going to the state hospital was the best thing for me. I was able to get help then. *He* didn't have any plan for us after Sir was . . . gone. Because I was just a kid, I was remanded to what we, the patients, called 'the asylum'—the state psychiatric hospital's special criminal pediatric ward. In fact, *he* got real quiet after what happened to Sir. . . . *He* didn't talk to me as much as he used to. *He* stopped telling me what to do. Then, over the course of the fourteen years that I was at the state hospital, *he* stopped talking altogether. I thought *he* was gone until . . . there was a rebirth, and *he* came back . . . *different*." He looks at Billy. "You . . . and then Jimmy. . . . But right after Sir died, I never could have gotten on in the world by myself. Not then. I had no idea what to do. No idea of what was normal—I was too messed up. I had never been out of the house alone. I had never been to regular school with other kids. I never had a friend other than *him*. I could barely read or write—Sir was a better disciplinarian than a teacher. I had never had contact with another human being other than Sir and people I saw on the television, and I didn't think *they* were real. I was only seven years old when . . . Sir . . . died.

"I went to school at the state hospital and learned everything Sir should have taught me—everything I would have learned in public school. I even got my GED in the hospital. I stayed until I was twenty-one. That's when they said I was ready to go out in the real world and be normal. I didn't believe Doctor Rathbone, didn't believe I could do it, but then, at just the right time, as I was walking out of the asylum—within *minutes* of my release—I met your mom. That was the luckiest thing—the only lucky thing—that has ever happened to me. I finally had a chance at a normal life . . . a normal life."

He suddenly barks out a hard despairing laugh and

shakes his head ruefully. He expels air forcefully through his nose. "I really thought that was all it would take to complete my cure—a name change and your mother's love." He grins sadly. "Stupid, huh? I should have known that it wasn't going to be that easy, *couldn't* be that easy. But then, I always believed Doctor Rathbone, my shrink in the asylum, when he said, 'Every problem has a solution, if only the right one can be found.' It took me a long time—too long—to realize that's not true. Some problems don't have solutions. They *can't* be solved, not by medicine or love.

"I'm a perfect example."

He attempts a laugh at his last comment. It is a strained sound.

Suddenly he scrambles to his feet and begins pounding his right fist on the top of the workbench next to his bound son.

(He's losing it! Do something! Distract him! Get him to keep talking about Mom!)

"Dad?" Billy asks meekly, but his father doesn't hear him. "Dad!" Billy says more forcefully, and pays for it with an increase in the intensity of the throbbing pain in his face and in his side. But he succeeds in getting his father's attention. He stops pounding on the workbench and looks at Billy as though dazed and confused about where he is and what he's doing there. "Dad?" Billy says again, softly. His father blinks and focuses on him. He smiles as if he's just noticed Billy's presence and is pleased by it.

"Yes? What is it, Bill?"

(Wow! He's nuttier than I thought.)

"Dad, when I . . . when I was in the attic, I found some old pictures of you and Mom from your honeymoon, I think."

"Really?" His father sounds amused. "We went to the Virgin Islands." He laughs. "Your mom said she wanted to get recycled." He laughs some more.

(I don't get it. What's so funny?)

Billy forces a laugh, too, though he's not sure what his father meant either.

(Something crazy probably. Just keep him talking and try to think of some way to escape.)

"There were some other pictures, too," Billy went on, "of you guys sitting around a table with some people I don't know. There were a lot of wine and beer bottles on the table."

"Yeah? That must have been from our first apartment. Those were your mom's friends from college, I'll bet. She was still in school when we met. She was studying to be an elementary schoolteacher, but she quit soon after we got married. She got her dad, your grampa, to make me a partner in his insurance agency so I'd make enough money that we could start a family. She always said the only thing she really wanted to do was stay home and have kids." He sighs. "She used to say the only reason she wanted to be a teacher was 'cause she loved kids so much and couldn't wait to have a bunch of her own. She wanted to have *six* kids. Six! Jesus, Mary, and Joseph on a fucking palomino! Can you believe that? Could you see *me* with *six* kids? I was ready to quit after you."

He looks at Billy. "But your mom wanted a girl so badly. She begged and begged me. It was inevitable, I guess, especially since I could never deny her anything."

(Except her life!)

Billy winces at that.

Tears fill his father's eyes and spill down his face again. "I wish I had. If we hadn't had Jimmy none of . . . this would have happened. I think *he*—your monster—

would have stayed asleep or hidden, if Jimmy hadn't come along."

Abruptly he stops and wipes the tears away vigorously with both hands, but it is no use; they pour faster from his eyes, and he finally succumbs to them and sobs woefully.

(Quick! Change the subject!)

"Dad? What happened to Sir? Your father?"

(What? Why'd you ask that?)

It was the only question he could think of.

His father strikes his thighs with his fists and shouts, "There wasn't any other solution!" His face is bright red and wet with flowing tears. "Something *had* to be done. Sir was getting worse." He staggers back and leans against the wall. A tear drips from his chin. "He was a bad man, Billy. He was bad. Bad to the bone. Just . . . *bad*. But . . . he was my father, and I didn't *know* he was bad. I thought *I* was bad. It took me a long time to figure that out. A lot of years of therapy. . . ."

(Which obviously didn't work.)

His father clears his throat and goes on. "He was drinking too much, and when he drank he *really* hated me. He was leaving me in The Brig for days at a time. He wasn't feeding me. I took to eating the moldy cheese I found in mousetraps under the cellar stairs.

An image—residue of the images that had flooded his mind at his father's touch—flashes before Billy's eyes for a moment: a small boy, maybe four or five, dressed in long underwear so filthy it appears charcoal colored. He is barefoot, and his dirty feet blend in seamlessly with the dirty leggings. He is in the bulkhead cavity of a cellar, on hands and knees under the wooden stairs, carefully disarming a mousetrap and wolfing down its greenish-yellow bait.

(I'm gonna puke!)

180   *R. Patrick Gates*

Oblivious, his father goes on. "I guess that's what brought *him* out. I would have died if he hadn't rescued me." He pauses, thinking and remembering. He wipes a stray tear from his eye before going on. "Like I said before, *he or him*—that's what I called the voice in my head—wasn't bad then, it was just a voice, my friend. He helped me. And he hated Sir. The more Sir hurt me the stronger he got, and the more his hatred grew.

"It's funny—not funny *ha-ha* but funny *weird*—that even though I'm pretty sure now that Sir must have had a similar voice in his head, he never knew about *him* until it was too late. Right up until just a few seconds before his death, he had no clue. But he learned real quick. And just before he died, I think Sir must have realized . . . that I wasn't *me!*"

(I think I hear the *cuckoo* clock striking twelve!)

He shakes his head and leans against the table. He looks down at Billy. "It's so hard to explain. Please tell me you know what I mean."

(Sure, sure. Tell him anything he wants to hear.)

Billy gives him a quick, though restrained, nod. "Did you . . . kill him, Dad?"

His father shakes his head and his expression hardens.

(Oh-Oh! Wrong question.)

"I thought you understood!" he shouts. "*I* didn't kill him. I've never killed anyone. It was *him! Him!*"

The doorbell rings.

John stops shouting, but remains unmoving, hands gripping the edge of the workbench, eyes on his son.

The doorbell rings again. He pales visibly and slowly removes his hands from the bench. He looks at the ceiling, then at the boy and puts a silencing finger over his own lips. "Shhh! They'll go away." He starts to repeat the phrase like a magic incantation, mumbling to himself, "They'll go away. They'll go away. They'll go away." Soon the litany changes to "*please* go away!" over and over.

(That ain't going to do it, Johnny-boy.)

Whoever is at the door is unaffected by his mumbled pleas. The bell rings again. John begins to tremble, and his voice takes on a screeching, whining tone. "Why-y don't they go away-ay?" he asks, sounding like an unhappy spoiled child. He waits, holding his breath for a few moments. The bell rings once more.

(You'd better do something about this, or I will!)

He swears softly and turns to his son. "Sorry, Bill, but this is for your own good." He gags his son with duct tape, winding it round the boy's head and over his mouth, not noticing how the boy assists him by lifting his head to avoid being touched by him. He goes upstairs and sidles over to the door. Being careful not to be seen, he leans forward and peeks around the edge of the curtain. It's the next-door neighbor.

(She of the too-tight hot pants.)

She rings the bell again and tries to peer through the glass and curtains on the door window. John ducks back. She looks at her watch; he glances at the clock: 9:30. She glances again at the door, but he can tell she's not trying to look inside now; she's caught her reflection. She smiles at herself and fixes her dyed blond hair with her right hand. She's got something in her other hand. She frowns and appears to be getting annoyed.

Good, he thinks, hoping she'll go away, but he has the sense that it is a futile hope.

(She's the nosy type, and a flirt to boot.)

On more than one occasion in the past she's flirted with him any time she saw him in his yard or on the street. She rings the bell again, stabbing at the button with her thumb, over and over, making it sound like bells in a bag being tossed about.

He covers his ears and starts to turn away when he sees what's in her other hand. He looks at it and understands why it looked so familiar when he saw it through the cellar window. It's a photograph of his family, taken last year at Sears.

(This can't be a good thing.)

The woman is startled when he opens the door abruptly, but she quickly composes herself and smiles seductively, flirtingly. She coquettishly bats her eyes at him.

"Can I help you?" John says, stiffly. She looks at him with her pale, ice-blue eyes, and he can see her taking in how haggard he looks with plaster dust in his hair and dried blood on his sweatshirt and a good-size lump and bruise on his forehead from when he fell through the ceiling and struck his head on the dresser in his and Molly's bedroom. He hopes she'll not notice, or think the blood is paint. He's seen her wearing glasses before, but she always took them off whenever she saw him. He imagines she believes the old Dorothy Parker adage that, "men don't make passes at girls who wear glasses."

Her smile widens, and she sticks out her ample bosom so that he can appreciate the cleavage revealed by her low-cut shirt. "I'm Barbra Luts," she says, her voice rich and husky. "Remember me? I live next door?" she asks to remind him when he doesn't respond. She holds up the folded photograph. "I found this in my driveway just now," she explains. "As jokes go, I don't think it's very funny."

He takes the photograph from her and reads the note scrawled in black crayon she points out on the back of it:

Help! I'm trapped in the house with a monster.
It killed my family. Everyone's dead
Call the police
Sincerely,
Billy Teags

John feels his face getting hot, knows that his color is rising. Mrs. Luts isn't smiling anymore. She looks suspicious.

(She *knows*, Johnny-boy! She knows!)

"Oh that kid!" John says quickly and laughs. To his ears, his words sound stilted and phony, and there is no way he thinks she will buy it. *He* is on the verge of pouncing, but John adds a winning smile and a wink and suddenly Mrs. Luts, the flirt, is all smiles again, a coquettish look in her eyes.

"I'm really sorry, Mrs. Luts. I've been away on business—I just got home. My son has an overactive imagination. I know Billy had a friend over yesterday—last evening—and they were playing up in his room when I called from the convention I was attending. They must have thrown this out his bedroom window. My oldest boy and the baby are sick . . . the flu or something. My wife and Billy probably have it, too, by now, I don't know. You didn't happen to see them all go out, did you? Like I said I just got home, and there doesn't seem to be anyone here."

(That's good.)

The woman gives him a confused expression and shakes her head, no.

(Real good.)

"Well, maybe my wife took them all to the doctor. I'm sure they'll show up. I'll be sure to speak to Billy about this as soon as I see him. I apologize if it upset you."

"No, no, no. No problem. And call me Barbra, please.

Believe me, I know how boys can be. I have four of them."

She stops and looks uncomfortable, as though she's afraid he'll lose his interest if he knows how many kids she has or, God forbid, how *old* she is. He takes advantage of her sudden uncertainty. "Well, thanks for being so nice. I'll make sure it doesn't happen again. And thanks for coming over and not, you know, calling the cops or anything." He laughs, and this time he thinks he sounds believable. "That would have been kind of funny."

She laughs with him and adds, "I tried to call you, and I kept getting a busy signal, but it was a weird, fast busy, you know? That means there's something wrong. But don't worry. I called the phone company for you. They checked the line and said you must have a receiver off the hook, and that I should tell you. So, actually, it's a good thing your son played this little joke, or I never would have called in the first place, and you wouldn't have known about your phone. The operator told me to call them back if you still have trouble after hanging up your phone, and they'll send someone out."

He looks at her and the old saying *if looks could kill . . .* crosses his mind.

(She's screwing everything up, Johnny-boy. She's making me mad. Why does she have to interfere?)

John swallows hard, trying to keep his composure. "Well, thanks," he says as evenly as possible and closes the door, but remains watching at the curtain.

She stares at the closed door, a baffled look on her face. Closing the door so abruptly seems to have caught her off guard.

Why doesn't she leave? John wonders.

(There's something not right with this bitch!)

"No," he whispers frantically, "she'll leave." He silently thanks God when she finally turns and bustles off the porch and back to her house.

At last, she's gone!

(Just what we need, a nosy neighbor.)

But he thinks he handled it well, considering.

(You did okay, Johnny-boy.)

He starts down the cellar stairs but stops midway.

"What am I going to do?"

(You know what to do. Everything will be all right if you can convince Billy. You were doing fine until we got interrupted. I'll stay out of the way while you convince the kid, then it'll be okay.)

John sits suddenly on the stairs. "What are you saying? Nothing will ever be okay again!"

(Yes, it will. Trust me.)

"I can't trust you. You got me into this. You're out of control."

(Listen, dumb-fuck, I've only done what had to be done. And I could have come out just now and ripped that old slut's throat out, but I didn't. Her coming over can help. She'll back up our story if you can get the kid to go along. She'll tell the cops we just got home.)

"No," John says. "We're forgetting something."

(No, we're not. We're playing it cool. I could have beaten the kid to find out where he put the baby, but I didn't. That doesn't matter now. What matters is there's still a way out of this if we just play it cool. That's what you got to do now with the kid. Play it cool. *Convince* him, or you won't like the alternative.)

John puts his head in his hands and feels physically ill. "If only I hadn't come home early from my trip, everything would be fine now." He can't even remember now why he left the insurance agents' convention in Boston and took the train home early, except that he'd

had one of his headaches, the kind that blur his vision
and pound in his ears like a beefy blacksmith hammering on an anvil.

"I can't do it," he whispers.

(You've *got* to do it, or else Billy—)

The sound of a car door slamming outside interrupts.
John gets up, ascends the stairs back to the kitchen. He
looks out the kitchen door, but sees no one. Walking on
tiptoes, he creeps through the house into the front hall
to the edge of the living room door. He peers around
the corner of the door frame. On the opposite wall is a
window facing Barbara Luts's home. Through it he can
see the flirtatious blonde looking at his house.

(The second floor!)

He rushes to the top of the stairs and lets out a groan.
The window shade and curtain on the window of his and
Molly's bedroom facing the Luts place are gone. They
lie in a mangled mess amid all the other debris that is a
result of his earlier rampaging search for the baby and
fall through the ceiling.

(The nosy bitch can see right inside! She'll see the
collapsed ceiling and wonder what's going on. Maybe
she'll call the cops!)

He steps gingerly, but quickly, over and through the
destroyed bedroom until he has a better view of Mrs. Luts
standing in her driveway, staring up at the window. He
keeps to the side, out of sight, and watches. She shakes
her head and takes out her cell phone.

(She's calling the cops! We got to stop her!)

He doesn't move; he notices something.

(She pressed more than three numbers on her
phone!)

She can't be dialing 911. She's also looking through
his downstairs window again, to and fro.

(She's calling *us* and looking to see if we answer.
When it doesn't work, she'll call the cops, or the phone

company, or *someone,* 'cause this nosy bitch just won't *leave it alone!*)

"Wait! Now she's going back into her house. We're okay."

But he quickly realizes he's wrong; Barbra Luts comes right back out again, carrying a blender pitcher full of a red liquid, and a large, clear plastic Tupperware canister filled with a dark brown liquid. She quickly crosses her driveway, heading for the back of his house.

John leaps over the ruins of his bedroom and sprints down the hallway to Kevin and Billy's room. He climbs over the piles of clothes and boxes from the closet and goes to the window overlooking the backyard and the garage. Barbra Luts goes to the garage and looks in the window.

"Why is she doing that?" he wonders aloud.

(Why do you think, idiot? Molly's car is still in there, right?)

She leaves the garage and goes around the side of the house.

"She's coming back," John says, fear in his voice.

(Good.)

While his father is occupied upstairs, Billy struggles against his bindings and tries to make sense out of what the hell is going on.

(Oh . . . the usual, trapped in the cellar with a monster who takes you on a trip to Loony Land every time he touches you.)

Should he believe his father is innocent like he claims to be? Should he believe that The Monster is really separate from Dad, able to act on its own without his knowledge?

(Sure! Why not? And while you're at it, why don't you write a letter to Santa Claus and the Easter Bunny?

Dad's loony tunes! Face it! He's gonzo! Off the deep end. He's lost his marbles. Got bats in his belfry. One pound shy of a full load. He's gone . . . *MAD!* Why would you believe *anything* he says?)

He doesn't see any other choice.

(Why?)

He has to believe that The Monster and his father *can* operate independently of each other because . . .

(Can they? The Monster is strong. . . .)

. . . it's his only hope.

(If only Dad could kill The Monster!)

He doubts that will happen. His father isn't strong enough to kill The Monster. The important thing is if *Dad* is completely *separate* from The Monster at times and doesn't know what it is doing and thinking during those times, then maybe the *vice versa* will apply.

(Like if there are times when Dad doesn't know what The Monster is doing, *vice versa,* there are times when The Monster doesn't know what Dad's doing?)

Exactly. And maybe, with Billy's help, together he and his dad can keep The Monster out long enough for . . .

(What? You think he'll let us just leave? Better yet, call the police?)

No, not the police . . . but maybe Dad could just let him go. . . .

(Yeah, and maybe kangaroos will hop out of your butt! Think of something else.)

There is nothing else. Billy considers that if he can convince Dad to help him escape during one of those times when The Monster doesn't know what he's doing, he might just have enough time to get out of there. The more he thinks about it the more the idea grows; the more convinced he becomes that it *will* work.

(Are you serious?)

No matter how crazy Dad is, he thinks, when he's

Dad, he doesn't want to hurt anyone. He didn't want to hurt Mom or Kevin or Jimmy; The Monster did it. Like Dad said, he didn't even know what was happening; if he had, he would have tried to stop it.

(Are you sure about that? Do you really believe him? Think about it; he's got a *monster* inside him.)

It's my only chance.

He *has* to get through to his dad and get him to help him escape. He knows, deep down, that his father loves him enough to do it. What he doesn't know is if it will work.

(What if Dad's lying, or you're wrong? What if The Monster is *always* watching? What're you going to do then?)

Billy doesn't know.

(I think you're going to be dead, that's what.)

That's why it had better work!

A shadow falls over Billy. He shuts his eyes, afraid it is The Monster returning, sneaking up on him silently as he lies bound on the workbench. He opens one eye a slit and looks around, but he's alone in the workshop.

(The Monster is still upstairs!)

The shadow is coming from the cellar window above him. Someone is outside, looking in.

He opens both eyes and recognizes Mrs. Luts, the drunk lady who lives next door. He heard his father call her a "lush" once and when Billy asked what that meant, he was told "a drunk."

Billy tries to cry out to her for help, but the duct tape wound round his head and over his mouth makes any attempt at speech futile. He hopes she will at least see him bound and gagged in the cellar and realize something is terribly wrong.

But she stares blankly at the glass, turning her head left then right as though she is having trouble seeing through the window. She straightens, and Billy notices she has a big round plastic container in one arm and a pitcher of some kind of red drink in the other.

(She's coming to visit!)

It certainly appears that way as she moves away from the window and heads in the direction of the kitchen porch.

Billy moans and struggles furiously against the tape.

In the upstairs hallway, on the very top stair, John stands, listening to the doorbell ringing.

(That fat bitch is screwing up our plans, Johnny-boy! We're running out of options!)

The bell rings again.

(You know what we have to do, don't you?)

John goes downstairs, stopping quickly in the living room to pick up Molly's bloody rolling pin sitting on the coffee table next to the couch, and goes into the kitchen. He places the black marble rolling pin on the counter and crosses to the door. He unlocks and opens it.

"Hello again!" Mrs. Luts says a little self-consciously. She holds up the pitcher. "I thought you looked like you could use a drink, so I made Bloody Marys. Guaranteed to cure what ails you. I know it's early but, to be honest, Mr. Teags, if anyone ever looked in need of a pick-me-up, it's you. I also brought some of my home-made chicken soup if you're hungry."

John stares at her blankly. Her flirtatious pose falters. She suddenly looks uncertain of what she is doing. She clears her throat and goes on nervously. "I also wanted to let you know that your phone is still out. I just tried calling on my cell and couldn't get through. I called the repair service again," she says, speaking rapidly and looking uncomfortable under his stare. "I told them it was an emergency so they'd send someone out quickly. I know how annoying it is not to have phone service. They said they'd send someone right away."

She pauses and looks as though she's struggling with some inner decision for a moment before she gives him a piercing look, takes a deep breath, and says, "Mr. Teags, I hope you won't think I'm being nosy." She leans toward him. "But I'd have to be an idiot not to sense that there's something very wrong. You see, I *know* you didn't come home today. I saw you running up the street yesterday in the rain, carrying your overnight bag and briefcase."

(She saw us!)

John realizes that's what he had forgotten—yesterday, as he'd hurried along in the rain past Mrs. Luts's house, he thought he had seen one of her window shades moving. And if she saw him, who knows who else did, too.

That seems like years ago, instead of just yesterday, before anything bad happened.

"And just now," Mrs. Luts goes on, "while I was in my driveway, I couldn't help notice that it looks like you've had some damage in your bedroom. Did something happen? Please forgive me, but . . . are you and your wife having . . . problems? I noticed her car still in the garage, too, though you said she was out. Would you like to talk about it?"

She squints at him and smiles nervously, obviously wondering if she's gone too far.

"It's that obvious, huh? You're a very observant woman, Mrs. Luts," *he* says with just the right touch of pathetic humility and sincerity.

"Please, call me Barbra," she says coquettishly.

"Okay . . . Barbra," *he* says and sighs. "You know, maybe

it *would* be a good thing for me to talk to someone about this. Why don't you come inside, and we'll have one of those delicious-looking drinks you've got there."

Mrs. Luts happily accepts and steps inside. She places the bag with the soup in it, and the blender pitcher of Bloody Marys, on the counter next to the marble baker's pin. Without her glasses she doesn't appear to notice the blood and tissue stuck to it. She turns to John and gasps in shock.

"Oh my God! Mr. Teags, don't cry!" she says, stepping closer to him. "I can't stand to see tears from anyone, but from a grown, *strong* man like you, it just about breaks my heart. Please, please don't cry, Mr. Teags. Talk to me," she implores, moving closer still.

He turns away, his hand over his face, and takes a few steps past her. *He* leans against the counter, head down, and continues to sob.

"Come on, now, John—if I may call you John—it'll be okay." She tentatively touches his shoulder. *He* sobs again. She rubs the top of *his* arm letting *him* know she is there for *him*. She moves to *his* side and slides her hand down *his* back, rubbing between *his* shoulder blades.

"Come on, it's always best to talk about these things. Is your wife cheating on you? Is that it? Did she leave and take the kids?"

The sobs quiet; *his* head comes up.

He looks at her. *His* hands shoot out—one clamping over her mouth, the other reaching around her and pulling her crushingly close until her face is an inch from *his*. This close, she can finally see *him* clearly, can see that *his* eyes are dry.

"You know, you fat bitch," *he* whispers in her ear, "you really should learn to mind your own business."

She bites *him*, opening her closed mouth under *his*

smothering hand and digging her left incisors into the soft flesh between *his* thumb and forefinger. *He* yelps and curses and pulls *his* hand away. She manages to twist from *his* grasp and swipe at *him* with her right hand. She gets in a good shot to the left side of *his* face with her nails. It catches *him* by surprise. *He* roars in pain as she drags her half-inch nails down through the flesh of *his* left cheek. With the clawing blow, Mrs. Luts manages to pull away, but only for a second. A single note of a scream escapes from her lips before *he* punches her in the mouth, cutting it off. Her head snaps back, blood spurts from her mouth, and she staggers under the blow.

He smiles smugly at her, confident that she is going down. But the woman surprises him. Despite looking weak in the knees, she suddenly lunges, nails brandished, scratching at *his* eyes. *He* is caught off guard and driven back against the counter. Lashing out, *he* grabs both her wrists, pulls her arms apart. Before she can react, *he* head butts her square in the mouth. There is the muffled crack of her teeth dislodging and the crunch of her jaw breaking. Her body goes limp. She falls to the floor at *his* feet.

"Didn't you ever hear about what happened to the curious cat?" *he* asks her as *he* reaches down, grabs a handful of her dark-rooted blond hair, and starts dragging her across the kitchen floor. A painful groan slips from her mangled mouth. *He* is startled again by her tenacity and strength in spite of her injuries when she reaches up and digs her nails into the back of *his* hand entwined in her hair.

He lets go, growling with pain and anger. Her head flops to the floor, banging hard, causing her eyes to flutter up into her head again.

"I'm through fucking around with you, bitch!" *he* says, going back to the counter and picking up the gore-smeared marble rolling pin. *He* bends over her and swings it, connecting with her face and head: once, twice . . . three times.

Billy shudders at the sounds from above.

(Someone's getting their butt kicked, and I bet it ain't The Monster!)

He struggles against the bindings, but it is no use. He cries, but his whimpers are muted by the tape over his mouth.

(Stop crying! Be glad it isn't you getting wupped.)

That thought doesn't help.

(You're right—soon enough you'll be on the receiving end.)

There is a cry of pain from above—

(The Monster!)

—accompanied by several loud, thick, wet and crunching, *smacking* sounds, followed by a noise he is familiar with . . .

(The Monster is dragging another body down here!)

Tears stream down John's face as he drags the blonde by the hair down the cellar stairs to the workshop. He deposits her incredibly heavy body on the floor by the wide wooden steps that lead up to the closed bulkhead door and drops the bloody rolling pin on top of her. The nosy neighbor's face is masked in blood that drips to the floor and quickly forms a pool. He throws an old paint-cleaning rag reeking of turpentine over the puddle and one over her face. As he does, he hears her breath still wheezing faintly in and out of her broken nose and smashed mouth and jaw.

(She's like the fucking Ever-Ready Bunny!)

"Why couldn't you just mind your own business?"

John asks the unmoving woman. His voice is half whisper, half sob. Exhausted, he sits heavily on her prone body—she moans—and wipes sweat from his brow.

(Christ! What a cow! We just did the neighborhood a favor, Johnny-boy!)

After a few minutes rest, he gets up and stands over the body. Her breathing has grown fainter, but it is still there.

(It doesn't matter. We've got more important things to take care of.)

"But it's over now. If she saw us come home yesterday, then other people did, too."

(Shut up, puke! It ain't over till it's over! It ain't over till the fat lady stops breathing.)

He hears laughter in his head. Or is it coming from his mouth? He's unsure, bewildered, scared . . . .

(Don't give up so easily, Johnny-boy. We can still make this work if *you* can convince the kid it's in his best interest to play along with a slight new twist to the story to accommodate our nosy neighbor's presence and anyone else seeing us yesterday.)

"Why don't we just get out of here, and leave him behind?"

(So's he can call the police? No. One way or another, Billy-boy's going to be very useful to us.)

Billy listens to his father whispering to himself by the bulkhead stairs.

(Not a good sign. Especially when he laughs.)

Something is wrong.

(The Monster killed someone again.)

In spite of that, Billy's heart soars at his father's last question, "Why don't we just get out of here and leave him behind?"

(But who's he talking to, The Monster? And is he — are they—talking about you?)

His father steps over to the workbench, leans over, and smiles at him. Billy looks into his father's eyes and sees sorrow there, sorrow and remorse and something else . . . *despair.*

But he sees no sign of The Monster and hopes that maybe Dad was just talking to himself, which means The Monster might be sleeping, or whatever it does when it's unaware of what Dad is doing.

(Be careful. I bet it's just hiding, watching, and waiting.)

His dad's eyes are red from crying. His face, clothes, and hands are stained with flecks of blood, and his left cheek is furrowed with deep, bloody scratches. Looking at him, Billy immediately knows Mrs. Luts fought back. He also knows she paid dearly for doing so.

"Let me take this off you," his father says, his voice hoarse as he grabs a pair of small, blunt-end scissors from the back of the workbench and cuts the duct tape wound around Billy's head and over his mouth. Carefully he pulls the tape back and unwinds it, gently lifting Billy's head to remove the tape from the back of his son's head. The tape tugs uncomfortably at Billy's lips and the flesh of his face and pulls painfully free of the back of his head, taking hair with it.

Billy cries out softly, both from the pain of the tape ripping free and from the sudden startling image of a bloody hand, stripped of all its skin, reaching for him, which accompanies his father's touch. As the image breaks apart, Billy quickly looks at his father's eyes, checking to see if his whimpering is bringing The Monster out.

Dad smiles back at him.

(That's a good sign.)

"We've got to talk, Billy," he says after the last strip of tape is removed. "I've got a big problem."

Billy shakes his head slowly. "I can't tell you where Jimmy is," he says tearfully and cowers.

"No, no. That's okay. That's not what I want to talk to you about. Right now I'm in trouble, Bill. Big trouble. You know that, right?"

Billy nods, but cautiously.

"You know I would never do anything to hurt your mother and Kevin or the baby, don't you? You know it wasn't my fault, right? I didn't know. *He* did it—The Monster."

(Here we go again.)

Billy nods slowly.

"Billy, I could go to jail for a long, long time—the rest of my life, all for something I didn't do. You see that, right? And if I have to go to jail for life, then you are going to end up living with one of your cousins—none of whom, I know, you really like—or they're going to put you in a foster home."

Billy hasn't considered that until now. He sees the truth of what his dad is saying.

(*If* you live!)

He is going to be all alone in the world.

(You'll always have me!)

"But it doesn't have to be that way, Billy. If you help me, I'll be able to stay with you. We could still be a family."

"What about the . . . you-know-who?" Billy asks, timidly.

"*Him?*" He looks around and leans a little closer and whispers, "The Monster? He . . . he'll go back to sleep and, and I can get some help and keep him asleep. Everything could be okay again."

(Except for the fact that he *killed* everyone!)

Billy ignores that and concentrates on his father. *Right now* might be one of those moments he's been hoping for, a moment when The Monster isn't around or aware of what Dad is doing.

His father looks at him and smiles sadly once more. There is no trace of The Monster, not the slightest hint.

"I've worked out a story we can tell the police. You want to hear it?"

(He'll kill you if you say no!)

Billy nods.

"Good! I'll call the cops and tell them that when I came home yesterday I found everyone dead, except for you. And the Baby Killer was still in the house. We'll say the killer stabbed you and thought he killed you, but you faked it. I found you hiding in the attic when I got home, but The Baby Killer was hiding up there, too, and attacked me. I managed to hurt him before he knocked me through the ceiling. We gotta make the cops think . . .

(Did he say, *stabbed you?*)

. . . that the Baby Killer tied me up and stayed in the house till today 'cause he was hurt and 'cause *you* wouldn't tell him where Baby Jimmy was until today!" He looks immensely proud of his fabrication.

(What was that about stabbing you?)

Before Billy can respond his father goes on. "If we both stick to the story, they'll never know. I mean, *what* would we tell them anyway? A *monster* killed everyone? They'd think we're crazy."

(Well, they'd be half right.)

His father pauses abruptly and scowls. Billy watches emotions struggle on his father's face and is certain The Monster's return is imminent, but his father stays and goes on as before, reinforcing Billy's belief that The Monster is temporarily out of the picture.

(*Temporarily* is the key word here. How long?)

"What do you say, Bill?" his father asks, smiling but not looking directly at Billy. His eyes are set on something beyond the workbench—the body over by the bulkhead stairs. "Oh. One other thing," he adds and looks at Billy again. "You have to say that Mrs. Luts from next door got killed by the Baby Killer, too." He bites his lip, shakes his head, then brightens. "Ooh! I know! You can say she came over with some soup 'cause she knew Mom was home alone taking care of the sick baby and Kevin. She brought some drinks, too, for her and Mom to share, but the Baby Killer was still here. And he killed her, too, just before he took off. Pretty good, huh?" His dad nods hopefully.

(Lie! Go along with it!)

"It won't work, Dad."

(What are you doing? He'll kill you!)

Billy disagrees. Now *is* one of those times when he can get through to his father without The Monster knowing; he's sure of it. He watches his father's face, waiting for a response.

"It will if we want it to, if *you* want it to, Bill," his father says softly, but there is a hardening tone to his voice.

"The police will find out, Dad. The detectives like on *CSI* will come, and they'll figure it all out." He pauses, looks deep, but still sees no sign of The Monster in his father's eyes. Encouraged, Billy goes on, "Dad, if you just let me go, I'll tell them—I'll tell the cops that you're sick. I'll *make* them understand that you have a monster in you, and *they'll* get you help."

"No they won't, Bill. They'll kill me or lock me away forever."

"No!" Billy says, but falters. He almost missed something. His father's voice changed a half second ago. There's been a subtle shift in his eyes.

Now The Monster stands over him, its mouth curled into a sneer.

"You think you're a smart-ass don't you? Hide the baby, now this? Big genius of the family. Older than your years! Hah!" The Monster laughs and growls as it exhales. "You should've been smart enough to go along 'cause now I got to balance your books. And you're going to pay dividends by telling where the baby is."

The Monster puts its thumb to his broken nose. "Tell me."

Billy closes his eyes and remains silent.

"Little puke," The monster says and presses its thumb into his nose. The explosion of pain knocks Billy unconscious before he can cry out.

You didn't have to do that!
(Shut up, Johnny-boy!)
He strides up the cellar stairs, two at a time.
Where are we going?
(The kid has a point. And without him, this has gone too far to make a story plausible enough for us to get away with it. If we stick around, the cops are going to catch us and know what we did.)
No! What you did!
(Yeah. Right. Whatever. It was stupid to think we can trust the kid. Now we have to take care of business.)

At the top of the stairs *he* stops and takes from the wall a long, pointed metal skewer that goes to the rotisserie barbecue grill.

No! You can't do that!
(Sorry Johnny-boy, but it's my signature—my trademark.)
You don't have the baby!
(Don't worry. Billy-boy will tell me where the brat is when I shove this—)

A loud groan comes from the workshop below.

(That *wasn't* the kid.)
Mrs. Luts!
(Doesn't that old cow know when to die?)

Carrying the rotisserie skewer like a sword, *he* returns to the workshop.

*   *   *

The pain that so quickly sent Billy reeling into black-ness also brings him back to consciousness. The hurt throbs through his skull and keeps his mind from fully disengaging, from completely escaping. Instead, it pulls him back to reality like a slumping marionette jerked to life with a tug on its strings.

Billy opens his eyes and quickly closes them again. He can't see anything with the world spinning like a top, not to mention the fact that the dizzying motion makes him want to throw up. The pain throbs in his head and pounds in his face. He can hear the squishing rush of blood through his heart with every beat and every beat brings new pain to his mangled nose.

He tries opening his eyes again. This time the spin-ning illusion isn't as bad. It stops after a moment, leav-ing everything around him lurching unsteadily and blurry until he rapidly blinks several times—with a good deal of effort and pain—and his vision returns to normal. Next to his head, so close to his eyes as to still be blurry but not unidentifiable, a small pool of congealed blood. Billy is pretty sure it is his. Nose blood.

(*Snot blood!*)

He smiles and winces with pain; just blinking his eyes is painful. He rests until the throbbing pain that accompanies every beat of his heart diminishes. Slowly, carefully, he turns his head to look around. The pain immediately shoots up to full volume again. He loses vision for a moment. When it returns, he is look-ing at the edge of the cellar window where the wooden frame meets the stone wall. He becomes aware of a sound that is keeping time with the beating of his heart. It is a blunt, wet, *thudding* sound—a *whacking* sound.

It stops, and he hears a soft, tuneless humming, punctuated with a sighing little grunt of satisfaction.

(The sound of someone happy in a job well done.)

Billy doesn't have to see to know who it is; the memory of what The Monster just did to him . . .

(That was just the start of the torture!)

. . . is as fresh as the pain in his face.

(You should have listened to me and gone along with him. Now you'll have to tell him where Jimmy is, or he's going to *hurt* you *real* bad.)

It doesn't matter, Billy thinks. What just happened . . .

(I hate to say I told you so, but . . .)

. . . seems to prove that his theory about Dad and the Monster being separate is wrong . . .

(The Monster was listening, kind of like it was looking over Dad's shoulder all the time, just like I said.)

. . . *or does it?*

(Huh?)

Just because it didn't work this time, he reasons, doesn't mean it won't work at all. He just has to find the right time to get through to his father. He just knows there have to be times when his father and The Monster are separate.

(Like when?)

He's not sure. He'll have to play it by ear.

(Okay, so what are you going to do?)

When the time is right, he has to try again to reach his father and, this time, *convince* him to make an effort to keep The Monster out.

(And what if he can't? You're not going along with that plan, are you?)

The Monster will keep on killing no matter whether he goes along with the plan or not.

(Let's say *not*—part of the plan is *stabbing* you!)

He hears The Monster speak over by the bulkhead stairs, but it isn't talking to him.

*   *   *

"Ah . . . you're still with the living? Now let's just see if we can do something about that, huh?" *he* says to the bloody, bruised body on the floor. Her face is barely recognizable; her hair, more red than blond.

(Doesn't matter—she bleaches it anyway.)

There is surprisingly little blood on her clothing, though. Her ample breasts are nearly coming out of her low-cut blouse. They remind John of an incident last summer when he was in the backyard trimming the low hedges that separate his yard from Mrs. Luts's. Within five minutes of his arrival in the backyard, Barbra Luts came out dressed in bright pink hot pants and a sheer white blouse that left nothing to the imagination and was cut so low he could see the very edges of her nipples, when she was standing, and her entire breasts— nipples and all—when she bent over, which she did as much as possible in his direction.

"I guess great minds think alike," she said, coquettishly, as she crossed to the hedges where John was working. "I was just coming out to trim *my* bush as well."

(Dressed like that? More likely she was looking to trim your you-know-what!)

For the next twenty minutes she made a point of keeping pace with him, trimming the side of the hedges that faced her property. She did so bent over, or kneeling, the entire time, giving him a continuous clear view of her bosom. John had to admit for a woman her age she appeared to still have full, firm breasts . . .

(She must be Middle Eastern, 'cause she's got a nice *Iraq*!)

. . . but underneath her breasts, he could see the wrinkled cellulite paunch of her belly.

(Whoa! That was a turn-off.)

Several times she winced in obvious back pain, but she stayed with it as long as John did, showing off her assets, making small talk that was full of innuendo. Uncomfortable with her blatant come-ons, John finished the hedges as quickly as possible and retreated to the garage to clean and oil the hedge trimmer. His next-door neighbor on Ledgemore Street, Byron Verdon, came over.

"I couldn't help but notice you were getting quite a show just now," he said with a lecherous grin. Byron was completely bald, intensely freckled, and obscenely obese—so fat he waddled instead of walked. Though only thirty-five, he had a raspy, worn-out, old voice. Molly once commented that if squirrels could articulate words, they'd sound like Byron.

"You ain't the first one, you know," Byron went on, chuckling. "I know of at least three guys in this neighborhood—all married—who have bonked Barbra Luts, or as *I* call her, Barbra *Sluts*." His grin widened. "In fact, you're looking at one of them," he stated proudly.

Incredulity must have been obvious on John's face, for Byron immediately became defensive.

"You don't believe me?" he asked.

John looked at his neighbor's ponderous bulk and a song that Sir used to sing, set to the tune of "Auld Lang Syne," came to mind.

(*For all we know it may be so, but it sounds so goddamned queer!*

We hate to doubt your honesty, but your bullshit don't go here!)

"It's true! Every word!" Byron rasped. "I'm dyin' if I'm lyin'. I was behind my shed—you know how it's right at the corner where my yard, your yard, and her yard meet—taking a leak when she came out of her house and came over to me, bold as brass. I think she was spying on me, just waiting for an opportunity. I didn't see her at first, but when I looked up there she was, practically drooling over my dick. 'Here, let me help you with that,' she says. Can you believe that?"

(Quite frankly . . . no!)

"Then—I swear to God—she dropped right to her knees and started sucking on my johnson like it was a freakin' Popsicle. I swear to God!"

John wasn't sure who made him more uncomfortable that day, Barbra Luts and her not-so-subtle-seduction, or Byron Verdon and his outrageously ridiculous story.

(If we're through strolling down *Mammary* Lane, Johnny-boy, we've got work to do.)

Though Billy can't see The Monster, its voice stabs deeply into him, reaching so far inside it turns his bowels liquid with fear, and he nearly messes himself. He doesn't want to do that; he doesn't want The Monster to know he's *that* scared. Billy defiantly wants to deny it the satisfaction of knowing it has scared him so badly he might easily crap his pants at any moment.

(You'll crap them for sure when he makes you tell where you hid the baby.)

No, he'll never tell. He shakes his head . . .

(Ouch!)

. . . and pays for it. The pain is centered in the middle of his face. His nose hurts the worst—he can't breathe through it at all—and the pain radiates out from there into both cheeks. Aching fault lines extend throughout the rest of his face and head, from his jaw to the top of his skull and down to the base of his neck. His lips feel huge, as if someone mistook them for water balloons and tried to fill them to the point of bursting. A term he's heard his mother use for big lips—"That guy's got Mick Jagger lips"—comes to mind. He used to laugh when she said that; now he feels like crying.

(That would hurt too much.)

Everything hurts; the simple act of *breathing* hurts. Do it too deeply, and he is tortured with agonizing pain in his left side. He fights back tears, refusing to cry. The Monster would like that too much, and Billy isn't about to give it any more pleasure than it's already taken in the pain and killing it's caused—*is* causing, he guesses by the noises it's making, grunting in exertion with every *whack*.

(So, what are we going to do?)

Cautiously, he probes the front of his mouth with his tongue.

(I wouldn't do that.)

His front teeth wobble—"Nothing to worry about. They're just your baby teeth," he can almost hear his mother say—and he tastes blood, sour and bitter. He probes a little too hard as . . .

(I said, "Don't do that!")

. . . a new knife of pain shoots up through his nose, making his eyes close tightly enough to squeeze out tears. He sucks air sharply and searing needles stab through his left side. They spread to every muscle and bone in his body, making him ache from head to toe.

(Told you!)

He tries to stay very still. The terrible weight of so much agony threatens to push him back into unconsciousness, and he can't let that happen.

(No, no, no! That happens and you're *dead*!)

He needs to stay awake. He has to try and reach his father again and get him to block out The Monster.

(You're as crazy as he is! Think of something else or say good night!)

It's his only chance; he doesn't know what else to do.

(You could try and get out of here!)

Bound and helpless as he is, he doesn't see how he can do that. He has to try to get through to his father again.

(You *are* nuts!)

He takes a slow, deep breath through his mouth, wincing at the piercing torture it brings, and tries to speak, but the pain reaches a new level of intensity. He faints for a moment but struggles back. He tries to ignore the pain as best he can and takes another shallow breath. He manages to speak, but his words sound more like painful sobs.

"Da-ad? Da-ad, are you there?"

His father's face comes into view. Billy feels faint looking at Dad's features splattered with so much blood it drips from his hair, his chin, and coagulates in blobs on his cheeks. It dries in thick rivulets on his neck. He looks as though he's been sprayed by blood; Billy can't help but guess it must be Mrs. Luts's.

(Don't think about that! He's going to *kill* you!)

"Dad?" Billy says, trying not to cry. "Please . . . please help me!"

His father looks at him. His white eyes showing through all that blood reminds Billy of how the giant ape's eyes looked in the old black-and-white movie, *King Kong*, only his eyes aren't scary like Kong's, they're full of sadness and horror at what he's done and terror at what he might still do.

(To you!)

"Billy," his father says haltingly, "I . . ."

He is interrupted by the sound of the doorbell ringing again.

"Oh for Christ's sake!"

The Monster is back, shouting and turning toward the sound. "That fat bitch really fucked things up." The Monster spins round to Billy. "I'll bet it's the telephone repair guy. Can you believe it?" he asks. "If I *really* needed them to fix the phone it would take fucking *days* for them to get out here!" The Monster fumes. The Monster swears loudly, "Fuck it!" and leaves the workshop. A moment later Billy hears it going up the cellar stairs.

(Looks like there's no way you're going to get through to Dad, so now what?)

He has no other plan. To keep panic and fear from pushing him into hysteria and terror, Billy tests his bonds—gray duct tape wrapped around his wrists and ankles. His hands are bound in front of him.

(You've got to get free! That's something you can do! Concentrate on that!)

Steeling himself against the pain in his side, he sits up on the bench top and puts his wrists to his mouth. Panting in short, tortured breaths, he finds the edge of the tape with his side teeth and starts to work it loose. After several attempts and several pauses, during which his consciousness grays under the intense pain his efforts cause, he manages to catch the edge of the tape between his right eyeteeth. Quickly, steadily, he pulls, unwinding the tape from his wrists while trying to slow his breathing.

(You're going to pass out if you don't!)

Twice the tape slips from between his teeth; they scrape against each other, and he comes away with strands of adhesive clinging to them and a hammering of pain so loud in his head it brings tears to his eyes. But he spits the sticky strings out and tries again. At last he unwinds enough of the tape that one last good pull will free his hands. He knows the pain will be excruciating, but he has to do it.

(Yeah, if you want to get out of here!)

Battling the pounding in his skull, Billy lies back and rests a moment. He gets up again and brings his head forward to meet his wrists. Holding them up in front of his face, he takes a short, painful breath through his mouth and chews a good portion of tape between his teeth. He clamps down on it as hard as he can with his right-side teeth, from his canine to his still buried molar. The action completely dislodges one of his bottom side teeth. It spills from the corner of his mouth and slides down his chin. He steels himself for one hard pull on the tape.

(Better get it right the first time—it's going to hurt like hell!)

Suddenly he jerks his head and body back while pushing his bound wrists away. The tape makes a ripping sound as it splits between his wrists. It is accompanied by a keening, painful exhalation from Billy as he lets go of the tape with his teeth, and his wrists come free. He gasps and falls back onto the workbench, unconscious.

John stands in the shadows of the kitchen near the door. Through the gauzy curtains he watches the man on the porch. By his uniform and the Verizon truck parked at the corner of Ledgemore Street next to the telephone pole, he can see he was right—it is the telephone repairman. John bows his head and concentrates all his willpower on making the man go away. When the guy rings the bell for the fifth time, he doesn't think the man is going to give up, isn't going to leave.

John looks down at himself.

(We can't answer the door and send the repairman away looking like this.)

He is robed in blood. He must clean up before he can deal with the man at the door. Another thought keeps John from moving. The repairman is going to want to come into the house and check the phones.

(Can't have that.)

Movement by the repairman distracts him, and he moves closer for a better look. The guy is hanging a piece of paper on the doorknob. Now the man is leaving.

He lets out a sigh of relief. There is no cause for alarm. Everything is going to be fine.

(For now.)

* * *

Billy regains consciousness like a diver frantic for air, swimming up from the murky depths. Only Billy rises, not into fresh air, but into *pain*. His face throbs, and he has the worst headache he's ever experienced. His left side feels as though it has a long, sharp, spike stuck in it. The sound of bells fills his head, and the taste of plastic and glue fill his mouth.

(Those aren't *bells,* dummy. It's the doorbell, and that's *tape* you're tasting.)

He opens his eyes, stares uncomprehendingly at the wooden beams of the ceiling in the corner, and realizes what he is looking at.

(That's right, it's the cellar ceiling. You're in The Monster's torture chamber, and if you don't get moving FAST he's going to t-o-r-t-u-r-e you!)

It all comes back to him. He picks the tape from his mouth with his right hand. It's free!

(You did it!)

Placing his hands on either side of his body, he pushes himself slowly up into a sitting position on the workbench. Despite the pain—everywhere, but especially in his left side—that the movement causes, he bows his knees outward, slides his ankles up until he can reach the tape wound around them, and picks at it. He can't quite get the edge, however, which is under his legs. The exertion makes him faint with pain again. He lies back to rest a moment.

(Don't stop now!)

The doorbell rings a fourth time.

Billy turns his head upward toward the shelves and sees the scissors his father used to cut the tape from his mouth. Sitting up again and fighting the wave of hurt the motion causes, Billy grabs them and goes to work on the tape holding his ankles. The scissors are sharp.

As the doorbell rings again, he cuts quickly through the tape, freeing his legs.

(All right!)

He slides his legs over the edge of the workbench and stops. He hears something and looks up. Whoever was at the door is leaving; he can hear the porch's rusted screen door squeaking as it opens, then slams closed with a bang like it always does.

(The Monster said there's a telephone repairman at the door.)

Billy pulls his legs up, and scrambles onto his knees. Standing on the workbench he reaches up and tries to open the rectangular window, but it won't budge. He tries again just as the legs of the telephone guy appear.

(If you yell, The Monster will hear!)

He hesitates . . .

(But this might be your last chance!)

. . . and bangs on the glass, shouting: "Hey! Help! Help me! Please help me!"

Billy hammers on the window as hard as he can without breaking it. Despite the pain in his head and broken nose, and especially the pain in his side when he takes a breath and shouts, he yells as loudly and clearly as possible through his mangled teeth and swollen lips. The effort is excruciating.

(The hurt The Monster is going to put on you will be worse!)

He knows that. He *has* to get the repairman's attention and get him to call the police. Then he has to hide again before The Monster comes back.

(If you don't . . . you're *dead*!)

John stiffens at the sound of the boy's voice calling for help and banging on the cellar workshop window.

(That little puke! You shoulda really let me balance his books, Johnny-boy!)

John unlocks and unbolts the porch door and opens it, knocking to the floor the repairman's preprinted note, stating the time he had been there. He steps out and over to the side screen window. Panic surges through him when he sees the repairman get down on one knee to peer through the dirty window and into the cellar. The guy leans closer, visoring his hand over his eyes to block his reflection

John hears his son cry, "Get help! Call the police before The Monster comes back!" but his speech is as mangled as his nose and lips. His plea sounds like: "Ged hep! Call da bolice afore da mawster gums bag!" It is obvious by the puzzled look on his face that the repairman can't figure out what the boy is saying.

(But he will! We've got to do something about this, Johnny-boy!)

"What's wrong?" the repairman yells. "What happened to you? Where's your mom?"

"Sheesh dead!" the boy shouts back. "Call da bolice! Pleesh!"

(That's it! Get out of the way, Johnny-boy!)

The telephone repairman leans closer to the window, trying to get a better look inside.

He looks down and spies a pile of rusty iron horseshoes stored in the corner of the porch over the winter. Next to them, even better, are the foot and a half long metal stakes for the game. *He* lifts one and hefts it in his hand, slapping it against his open palm. From outside he hears the repairman say, "What the fuck?"

With deadly swiftness, *he* opens the screen door and glances about—no one in sight. *He* leaps down the steps to the walk and charges around the side of the house. The telephone repairman catches his approach out of the corner of his eye, but it is too late—the horseshoe stake is falling, and crushing, and the blood is flying.

The boy's face—a picture of horrified disgust—is framed in the cellar window. *He* grins at the boy and delivers more skull-splintering blows.

Billy screams and draws back from the cellar window. The telephone repairman's head hits the house once, driven against it by The Monster's blow. The house shudders from the impact of the guy's head. The man falls facedown in the flower bed, the top of his bloody head resting against the glass of the cellar window. The man never cries out. The only sound is that of metal striking bone as The Monster finishes him off with two more whacks.

A fine sifting of dust floats from the cellar ceiling rafters.

Moving quickly, Billy slides off the workbench, loses his balance, and tumbles to the floor. Pain envelops him like a fog. His vision clears slowly, but the pain remains. He blinks and something just inches from his eyes comes into focus. With a start he realizes what he's looking at.

(A bloody rag!)

He reaches out and pulls the rag away . . .

(And beneath it . . .)

. . . the bloody face of Mrs. Luts, the lush.

Billy scrambles painfully to his feet and backs away until his foot strikes something behind him. A cloud of flies rises around him. He turns slowly. His mother and Kevin lie dead on the workshop floor, against the back wall, waiting for The Monster to bring Jimmy down and pin him to Mom like a human corsage. He reacts to the sight of their bloodied corpses as if struck by a blow. He flinches, steps back blindly. As the flies resettle, Billy can't take his eyes off their landing spot: his mother's misshapen head, dented and cracked with blood and bits of white bone showing through. He's glad he can't see her face; she's lying on her side and her long red hair, matted with blood and flesh, hides her features.

Kevin, however, lies on his back, with insects buzzing around his face. Dried blood cakes on his brother's chin and neck and stains the front of his Red Sox pajamas from collar to cuff. It looks like an upside-down palm tree on the front of his top and like weird footprints down the legs of the bottoms. He even has blood on his feet and between his toes.

But his face is the worst.

(Why do you do this to yourself? Don't look at him.)

That is impossible. Once Billy looks, he is frozen by the gory sight, unable to look away, like what his dad once told him about how deer will freeze in the road when caught in the headlights of a car.

(And you know what happens to those deer? *Splat!*)

Kevin has one eye open—a tiny black fly crawls over it—peeking out from behind a swollen mass of pulpy goo that might have been his nose. His other eye is buried beneath bloody, bruised, split, and inflated flesh. The middle of Kevin's face, from his eyebrows to his mouth, is caved in. The wound is deep, caked with blood, and lousy with bugs. Below it, Kevin's lips are split and swollen purple; his mouth is open. An ant crawls out of it, walking along his protruding tongue, which sticks out as if he had been in the act of speaking when his face had been crushed and sudden death froze his mouth that way.

(He was probably crying for help.)

Or begging for mercy.

(Fat chance!)

Not from The Monster, Billy knows, but he can't believe it of his father.

(You're a sap.)

A sound from upstairs breaks the mesmerizing hold Kevin's corpse has on him. Billy turns away and a hand grabs at his right leg. Fingers close around his ankle.

(It's Kevin come back to life as a brain-eating zombie!)

Wildly, Billy looks down. The hand clutching his ankle is not Kevin's; it's the next door neighbor's, Mrs. Luts.

(She's still alive? You've got to be kidding! Look at her!)

Mrs. Luts looks up at him through her one undamaged eye—the other is gone in a bruised mass of raw flesh. Though her lips are swollen and bloodied, they move. He hears a blubbering, sobbing, gurgling sound.

(She's trying to talk!)

Billy gets down on all fours next to her to hear. He exhales loudly, trying not to cry or be sick; he can see the bloody pulp of her face up close. She speaks again, but he can't understand her. It sounds like she's gargling.

(Blood, probably!)

He looks away, but she grabs at his wrist and won't let go. Her other hand is struggling to rise from the floor. She's clutching an object in it.

(Is that what I think it is?)

Billy reaches for her hand. As soon as his fingers touch her fingers, her fist relaxes and opens, revealing . . .

(Rescue!)

. . . a cell phone!

Mrs. Luts looks at Billy with her one good eye and her lips widen in what he guesses to be a smile of encouragement. A few more gurgling, mumbled sounds come from her mouth before her entire body suddenly arches with rigidity, then collapses, looking crumpled and deflated.

(I think she said call nine-one-one!)

Billy grabs the phone before it falls from the neighbor lady's suddenly lax grasp.

(Do it! Call the cops! Dial nine-one-one!)

Upstairs The Monster is swearing and grunting and banging against the kitchen door like it's moving something heavy into the house. Billy looks at the window over the workbench. The body of the repairman is gone.

(The Monster's busy! Make the call, then it's time to play hide-and-seek again.)

Billy agrees.

With one last titanic effort, John pulls the body of the repairman into the kitchen and slams the door. He drops the man's arms, and the guy's bloody head thuds on the linoleum. He sinks back against the counter and slides down until he is sitting on the floor. The bloody horseshoe stake falls to the floor beside him and rolls under the stove. John looks at the repairman and starts to cry.

"Everything's going wrong," he sobs. "You weren't supposed to show up. . . . Aw fuck!" He kicks the repairman and gets no response. He leans over and looks at the man. He turns the head and sees that the entire back of the repairman's skull is caved in. The back of his khaki repairman's shirt is soaked with blood. The man's face is chalk white. Blue circles are forming under his eyes. His lips, too, are turning blue.

"He's dead," John whispers and sinks back against the counter again. He wipes the tears from his eyes and looks at the front of the repairman's shirt. Stitched in yellow on the pocket is the man's name: DAVE.

"You're dead, Dave," he informs the corpse. "Sorry. You just picked the wrong fucking day to do your job adequately." John laughs out loud; it is a bitter sound. He gets up and goes to the door.

(Nobody saw!)

"You're wrong," John says as movement outside catches his eye. Across the street and down one house. Behind the hedges.

A head.

A boy's head pops up behind the bushes—looks this way.

John gasps. He recognizes the face. It's Donny Desmond, Kevin's best friend from just down the street.

(The little shit saw everything!)

"No!" John whispers fervently, almost pleadingly.

(Yes! Look at his face!)

He is right. The look of shock and fear on the child's face is unmistakably clear. He saw the attack on the telephone repairman.

"If he saw, then the other neighbors probably did, too! They'll call the police! He'll run home and tell his mother," John keens softly. "We should just leave everything and get out of here!"

(No! Look! Here he comes!)

Kevin's friend leaps over the low bushes and ducks behind a maple tree, then sprints to the corner of the house directly across the street.

John parts the curtains just enough to see more clearly. The kid disappears around the back of the opposite house and appears on the other side a few moments later. Running low and fast—looking as though he's playing a game—he sprints across the street and into the yard.

(He's playing spy and wants to look in the cellar!)

"He'll go away!"

(Yeah, when monkeys fly out of my ass.)

Wearily, John pushes the body of the dead telephone repairman aside and starts down the cellar stairs.

He can't get a signal.

(*Can you hear me now?*)

Billy's pretty sure he did everything just as his mother showed him last year when she got her new cell phone. "Just open the cover—it's just like *Star Trek*, huh?"

And it was. Billy and Kevin and Dad loved to watch old *Star Trek* reruns on the Sci Fi Channel.

"It will turn on automatically. Then you dial nine-one-one for *any* emergency—the police, fire department, or ambulance. After you dial nine-one-one, press the button that has the little green phone symbol on it."

He did that with Mrs. Luts's cell, but got nothing.

"If that doesn't work," his mother told him, "look at the little bars on the screen. Move around until you see at least three bars, then you'll have a signal."

Keeping his eyes on the cell phone in his hands, watching the bars on the LED instead of looking at the bodies on the floor, Billy carefully steps over the still breathing—

(And bleeding!)

—Mrs. Luts and creeps out of his father's workshop. He turns left, then right, seeking those elusive bars. He gets one that fades as fast as it appears. There is no sound now from the kitchen. He turns right, gets a bar.

(Keep going.)

Despite being numb with pain and shock, Billy staggers on. At the moment, he wants nothing more than to be able to just lie down and sleep—sleep, sleep, sleep, and forget *everything*.

(Why don't you just put a bullet in your head? That would be quicker and less painful than what The Monster's going to do when it catches you again.)

As he approaches the nearest wooden support post, a second bar appears. From upstairs he can hear hysterical laughter.

(It sounds like The Monster is having a good old time at least.)

Billy steps around the post, avoids tripping over a rolled-up inflatable pool toy, and gets a third bar.

(That's it! Call!)

His fingers are trembling so much he dials 9-9-1-1-1.

(No! Get it right! Stop shaking! Remember what Mom said: If you can't get through at first, keep trying. Press the button with the red phone on it and start over.)

He presses the red button and takes a deep breath. He tries to control the tremors that originate deep in the very marrow of his bones, and tries again. He can only manage 991 this time.

(Use your thumb!)

He does and it's much steadier. He gets the emergency number dialed.

"Nine-one-one: Blackstone Emergency. Your call is being recorded. Please state your name, address, and the nature of your emergency."

"Billy Teags. Sixty-two Warren Street. You got to help me!" Billy whispers as loudly as he can and still be whispering. "I'm trapped in my cellar. My dad's gone crazy."

"I recognize you! You made a prank call before—"

The cellar stairs creak.

(Hide that! If The Monster sees it you're *dead!*)

Billy jabs the red button, cutting the operator off, and snaps the lid closed. He stuffs the cell into his hip pocket.

* * *

Two steps down the stairs John hears his son whispering his name and their address furtively. He crouches and peers under the railing into the cellar just as the boy blurts out a plea for help and exclaims, "*My dad's gone crazy!*"

(The little puke got free, and he's got a cell phone!)

"Don't hurt him anymore," John whimpers, silently.

(You always hurt the ones you love, Johnny-boy!)

Billy looks back at the stairs and is startled by his father's bloody, sad face staring back at him. But only for a moment. The Monster's leering visage seeps quickly through. Suddenly, a sound behind Billy draws The Monster's attention. It looks over his head. Billy turns, too, toward the sound—one of the cellar windows facing the other side of the house is being pushed open. There is someone there, in the filthy window in the corner, on hands and knees, peering in. The face is freckled and narrow, the eyes wide, the nose short and pug, the hair long and dirty reddish brown.

(Kevin's friend!)

Donny Desmond.

(Yell! Warn him!)

But he can't. The Monster is down the stairs in a flash and sneaking around the left side of the cellar, approaching the window from an angle where Donny Desmond can't see it. The Monster puts a finger over its lips and winks at Billy.

Kevin's friend struggles with the window and finally manages to push it all the way open. He peers in and spies Billy. His eyes go wide at the sight of him.

"What happened to you?" Donny asks in a loud whisper.

It is the last thing he will ever say.

Before Billy can answer, or do anything but stare in horror, The Monster leaps forward, grabs Donny by the hair, and pulls him roughly through the window. Billy doesn't want to watch but can't pull his eyes away. He wants to help, but doesn't dare. He is too afraid to do anything but witness.

(You should *run!*)

Donny screams when The Monster grabs his hair, but it is quickly cut short by a sharp punch to his throat. Donny chokes loudly, coughs and gags; his breath wheezes horribly through his bruised windpipe.

The Monster pulls him into the cellar head first by his hair. Donny comes through the window to his waist, scraping the skin from his arms and tearing his T-shirt nearly off him, shearing patches of skin off his chest and back. With the second tug the rest of Donny's body comes through, pulling down his pants and shorts and scraping flesh from his buttocks and the front and back of his thighs as he tumbles headlong to the cellar floor and lies unmoving and half naked at The Monster's feet.

With a smiling glance toward Billy, The Monster nudges Donny over onto his back and steps on the boy's throat.

(Don't look!)

He can't help it. He watches in growing panic as The Monster slowly chokes Donny Desmond with its foot. A high-pitched, but stifled, scream keens at the back of Billy's throat as Donny's legs jerk spasmodically, his arms flail uselessly at the foot killing him, and blood gushes from his nose. Frantically, Billy tries to think of some way to stop The Monster.

(Find a weapon, *anything!*)

But he can't; all he can do is close his eyes, fall to his

knees, and put his hands over his ears to block out the sound of Donny choking to death. Oddly, it is that sound that brings to mind the last time Billy saw Donny Desmond. It was a week ago—exactly a week. Donny and Kevin were shooting hoops in Donny's driveway, and Billy was watching. Mom had told Kevin to keep an eye on him while she went shopping with the baby. Dad was working

Donny and Kevin were playing H-O-R-S-E. Donny, who was an inch taller than Kevin and better at sports, was winning. He had only an H, while Kevin had H-O-R. Donny made nearly every shot he threw up—hook shots, three-point shots, underhanded, free throws, and leaning-back-over-the-head-upside-down ones. Every time Kevin tried to shoot, Donny made choking noises. More than once it was obvious that Kevin missed because of Donny's goading.

Billy thought it hilarious and laughed gleefully every time Donny put his hand to his throat and hacked. His laughter increased to uproarious whenever Kevin missed a shot, which was a lot. Frustrated and angry, Kevin—

(Who never did like to lose!)

—took it out on Billy.

"Shut up, Baby Einstein," he yelled and grabbed Billy's arm. Forming a fist of his right hand, with the middle knuckle protruding sharply, he punched Billy in the upper arm and ground his knuckle deep, seeking the bone amidst the muscle, delivering what he called, "The Japanese Bone Bruise." It was one of the most painful—

(Of many!)

—torments that Kevin had in his sadistic bag of tortures.

"Hey! Leave him alone!" Donny cried.

"Shut up and mind your own business!" Kevin shot

back. But unlike other kids, Donny was not cowed by Kevin. He came over and pushed Kevin away.

"Leave him alone. Why are you such a jerk to him? You should be glad you got a brother. I wish I had a brother. You don't know how lucky you are."

Kevin did a rare thing then, he actually backed off and left Billy alone, for a little while anyway, but not before he got in a parting shot on Billy with another quick punch to the shoulder, and to Donny with, "You want a brother so bad I'll sell you mine. Better yet you can marry him since you like him so much."

"I'm not a fag like you!" Donny retorted and the game of H-O-R-S-E resumed.

Billy brimmed with gratitude for what Donny had done.

(And it wasn't the first time either. Remember Christmas?)

Last year, Christmas Day, Donny had again come to Billy's aid against Kevin. He'd come over to play with Kevin on the new PlayStation 3. The video game system was supposed to be for both Kevin and Billy, but Kevin had immediately staked a claim of sole ownership to it. In an aside to Billy when their parents were in the kitchen, he said, "I don't care what Mom and Dad said, Baby Einstein, the PlayStation is *mine*. And if you tell them I said that, you'll wish you had never been born. You can use it *only* when I'm not around, and then you better not mess with any of *my* games."

Billy was outraged but helpless. In the fall months leading up to Christmas, Kevin had employed Billy's help in getting their folks to buy the video game system for them.

"We'll have a blast playing together with it!" Kevin told him repeatedly as he egged him on to ask their parents for the gift right up until Christmas Eve; his rea-

soning being that since Billy was the baby of the family
he had a better chance of getting what he asked for.

(Kevin was always figuring every angle.)

And Billy had faithfully, earnestly, and with great enthusiasm, done what Kevin asked.

(And then he screwed you.)

But Kevin hadn't counted on Donny.

Christmas afternoon, after the family had gorged
themselves on turkey with all the fixings and holiday veg-
etables, not to mention a good array of pies topped with
whipped cream, or ice cream, or both, Donny came over
to play.

Having been set straight by Kevin, Billy moped in the
background playing with the new Transformer action
figures he'd got that morning, but really watching the
progress of the video game, the latest version of *Mortal
Combat*. After an hour of nonstop game play, Donny
wanted to take a break.

"No," Kevin said. "Finish the game first."

Donny had noticed Billy watching avidly and offered
him the controller.

"Why don't you take over for me, Billy," he said, "and
see if you can kick your brother's butt."

Billy leaped at the offer, but Kevin would have none
of it. "No!" he said adamantly to Donny. "I'll put it on
pause, you wuss!"

"Let the kid take my place," Donny demanded. "I *want*
him to take my place!" he insisted, shoving the controller into Billy's hands and pulling him over in front
of the TV. "Or are you afraid your *little* brother will beat
you?"

"Fat chance!" Kevin shouted, but ripped the controller
from Billy's hands. Billy burst into tears and Mom came
running.

"What's wrong?" she asked, looking from Billy to Kevin.

"Mom, Billy's being a pest!" Kevin accused before Billy could stop sobbing long enough to say anything. "He won't leave us alone!"

Donny Desmond shook his head at Kevin, as if to say, "You liar!" but he remained silent.

"Kevin won't let me play, but Donny said I could!" Billy bawled in protest.

"It's okay," his mother soothed, picking him up and carrying him into the kitchen. "You can play later," she said. "Let Kevin and his friend play now. Come and help me wrap presents for your cousins. Remember, we're going to Grampy's tonight." As she carried him out of the room, Donny looked at him and shrugged. He gave Billy a wink and a smile that did more to make him feel better than even his mother's doting.

Billy had always wanted to thank Donny for being so nice to him, but had never had the chance since Kevin was always around, and he didn't want his brother to label him a fag. Now, as Donny's choking dies away, Billy wishes he had.

"Hey," The Monster says. "Look at me, kid."

Billy does. It no longer has its foot on Donny's neck. It stands over the unmoving boy who makes no sound.

"It had to be done, kiddo. It's just the way it is." The Monster bends over and grabs Donny's right arm. It lifts him and drapes him over its hunched shoulders in the fireman's carry. Walking stooped under the low ceiling and stepping over and kicking through the junk strewn about the cellar, The Monster carries the bloody body around the furnace and hot water tank to the workshop. There, it unceremoniously dumps him on the floor next to the unmoving Mrs. Luts, who lets out a soft groan as Donny Desmond's falling body nudges her.

A car door slams outside, followed by the muffled crackle of an unintelligible radio transmission.

(That didn't take long!)

The Monster looks shocked.

(And scared!)

Billy knows it knows what that sound is as well as he does. Billy heard it for the first time, not that long ago, outside school during a fire drill when a police car and the fire trucks were parked out front, their radios squawking loudly.

The Monster glares at Billy. It steps over Donny Desmond and holds out its hand. "Give me the phone, puke."

(Better do it.)

Timidly, Billy takes the cell phone out of his pocket and holds it out to The Monster. It takes it and growls, "This does not bode well. I think you need your books balanced." The Monster lashes out, and Billy goes down, the right side of his already bruised face bleeding fresh from The Monster's blow. He blacks out for a second, comes to, and blacks out again. He opens his eyes and, through excruciatingly painful triple, then double, vision, watches as The Monster steps over him, as if he is no longer there, and charges up the cellar stairs.

(Get up!)

Billy struggles to his knees and nearly passes out.

(Breathe deep!)

He gulps air through his gaping mouth like a fish out of water, gasping at the riot of pain in his head and knifing through his side. He breathes as deeply as he can, and his head clears a little with the intake of oxygen. Painfully, he crawls to the bottom of the stairs. He looks up through the small window there just in time to see a pair of legs in dark blue trousers with a light blue stripe down the side, go up the porch steps. He hears the screen door open.

(You're saved!)

He hopes so, but he doesn't like how the knot of dread that he's been carrying around since coming home from school yesterday has suddenly swelled so that he's finding it hard to breathe.

(Take it easy! That's just from getting hit, and seeing Mom and Kevin, and what The Monster did to Donny! Everything's going to be okay now! The cops are here!)

Saturday afternoon

Just as the clock in the front hallway chimes out the noon hour, John reaches the top of the cellar stairs and ducks into the kitchen, keeping low so as to stay under the window in the door. The porch screen door slams and the doorbell rings

"Hello?" a voice calls from the porch. "Mister Teags?"

(Don't make a sound!)

The bell rings again, backed up by a knock on the glass.

"Mister Teags? This is the police. Hello? Anybody home?" The cop takes off his hat and puts his face to the window with his hands cupped over his eyes.

(Stay down! Don't move!)

The cop steps back, then reaches for the door. The doorknob rattles.

John suddenly remembers he forgot to relock the door after dragging the repairman inside.

(Big mistake, Johnny-boy!)

The doorknob turns.

John stares at it, panic momentarily immobilizing him.

(Move, you stupid puke!)

The latch slips open.

A gleaming ray of sun appears from behind a cloud and pours through the small rectangular window over the sink. It sparkles on the chrome handle of Molly's largest butcher knife, plunged into its wooden block holder, on the counter next to the stovetop, within easy reach, awaiting the call to butchery.

(Like a vision from fucking God!)

The door starts to open but sticks for a moment, as it always does when it's rained for a while and the bottom swells and rubs against the equally swollen floor jamb. With one fluid motion—a synchronous, balletlike movement of arm and body—*he* reaches out and grabs the knife off the counter. *He* takes two steps forward, grabs the doorknob with his left hand, and yanks it open hard. Grasping the outside doorknob too tightly, the cop is pulled off balance.

"Hello? It's the po—!"

There is a flash of dark blue. *He* thrusts the knife straight, hard, and deep into the policeman's throat, well above the bulky bulletproof vest obvious under the officer's dark blue shirt.

The cop finishes his sentence in a faint whisper directed awkwardly down at the knife sticking out of his neck, which he is regarding with some amazement as he finishes his sentence: "—leeeeeeece." The sound escapes him like air from a punctured tire. He falls to his knees just inside the door and grabs the edge of it with his right hand. His head hangs back and blood gushes from around the blade. It runs down the front of his shirt. His mouth opens and closes slowly. The cop looks up at *him* and tries to speak, but no words come. He can only lick feebly at his lips. His breathing slows. It rattles in his chest as he exhales. He tries to take another, but can't. Like a freshly cut tree he sways, totters, and falls to the kitchen floor. The impact pushes the handle and blade of the butcher knife further into his throat, nearly to the shaft, so that a good two inches of the bloody blade pokes through the back of his neck.

Stillness and silence reign for several minutes.

"You killed a cop," John says, finally, to the air. He looks down at the dead policeman at his feet and shakes his head.

"How could you be so stupid? You know what they do to cop killers?"

(So the other cops won't like it . . . tough shit!)

A car goes by outside. He tries to close the door, but the cop's body is in the way. He bends over and grabs the corpse under the arms and pulls it into the kitchen, rolling it onto its left side against the base of the counter. He tries to slam the door again, but the body's feet are still in the way. He kicks them aside, but one swings back, and the toe of the cop's shoe catches him squarely on the anklebone.

"Shit!" John swears loudly and hops on one foot, rubbing the hurt with his left hand while he steadies himself against the cellar door to his right. Angrily, he again kicks the cop's feet out of the way and slams the door.

Billy hears the calling voice suddenly cut off then a loud *thump* of something hitting the kitchen floor above.

(My guess is a body!)

There is dead silence.

(The Monster killed the cop who came to rescue you!)

Billy doesn't want to believe it.

(You knew it was going to happen!)

Billy sobs, crying as much for the cop as from the pain wracking his face, head, and body.

Another death.

"Another person is dead because of me," he whispers. "Mrs. Luts. Donny. The telephone guy. . . ."

(There you go again. Look, instead of blaming yourself, you should be looking for a hiding place and a weapon.)

Billy shakes his throbbing head slowly, blinking tears from his eyes.

(You don't have a choice!)

He sighs and shrugs and battles back his tears as he halfheartedly looks around.

(You know where to look!)

He knows. His father's workshop. But with the bodies of Mom, Kevin and Mrs. Luts, and now Donny in there, too, it's the last place he wants to go.

(If you don't want to end up like them, you'd better go back in there.)

Grimacing, Billy struggles to his feet and shuffles to the doorway where he scans the workbench, its shelves, and rack of tools while doing his best not to look at the mutilated bodies on the floor at the edges of his vision. The workbench is a treasure trove of possible weapons— screwdrivers, hammers, wrenches, the scissors he used to free himself. Any of them would be great if he was a lot bigger. But the best he can do with any of them is to inflict minor wounds on The Monster.

(You need something to at least put it out of commission . . . if not *kill* it!)

He ignores the latter; he doesn't want to even think about the possibility that the only way he might survive is by killing The Monster inside his father . . .

(Either that or die!)

. . . and probably kill his father, too, in the process.

(Ya gotta do what ya gotta do!)

He reels at the thought. "No," he gasps. "I can't!

(Yes, you can.)

"I can't . . . I don't know how . . ."

Just then his eyes happen upon the answer—

(Yes!)

—in the corner, hanging on a hook on the rear wall, right next to the workbench—

(Right over Mom and Kevin—don't look!)

—his father's electric nail gun. Giving the bodies of Mrs. Luts and Donny as wide a berth as possible—

(Keep your eyes on the prize!)

—Billy goes to the workbench and, without looking at them, leans over the bodies on the floor to take the nail gun from its hook. The tool is heavy, but he can handle it with two hands. He's seen his father use it several times and was always scared by it, yet, at the same time, enthralled by its loudness and power. His father explained to him once that the nail gun works on the same principle as a regular gun, but with specially made bullets that fire nails. Looking at it now, he remembers how his father used it.

(You can do this! All you have to do is plug it in, turn it on, point it, pull the trigger, and . . .)

He sees an immediate problem: the cord on the nail gun is only about three feet long, and the nearest outlet is out of Billy's reach high on the back of the work-bench. He'll have to climb onto the bench top again to plug it in and stay there while he fires it.

(You can surprise The Monster when it comes back.)

The sound of the cellar door opening upstairs makes him keenly aware that he's out of time.

(The Monster's coming down the stairs!)

Billy puts the nail gun on the workbench and tries to scramble up after it, but he's too exhausted and in too much pain to climb fast enough. He barely reaches the top as The Monster's shadow fills the doorway behind him.

He twists around and looks at it. The Monster is looking at the nail gun on the bench next to him. It grins.

"What have you got there?" The Monster asks, as if speaking to a very young child.

(Oh . . . nothing . . .)

"Let me see," The Monster says and crosses to the bench where it picks up the nail gun. "You see, Billy-boy, you've got to have cartridges in here before it will work," it tells him, opening the breech of the gun. It reaches up to the top shelf of the workbench and pulls down a box from which it takes a plastic ammo belt holding cartridges with nails sticking out of them. He loads the belt into the breach and snaps it closed.

"Then you have to have power, Billy-boy. Instead of a hammer to spark and fire the gun powder in the cartridges, which propels the nails, this uses an electrical charge, so you got to plug it in." The Monster takes an orange extension cord from a hook on the side of the shelves, plugs it into the gun's cord, and then into the workbench outlet.

"See? And last, but not least," The Monster says with a flourish, holding up the nail gun as though it were a product in a commercial, "ya gots ta turn it o-on." It finishes in an exaggerated voice, adding, "Du-uh!" for added insult. The Monster flicks the switch on the handle. The tool hums to life.

(Uh-oh.)

The Monster points the nail gun directly at Billy's forehead. "So . . . before we were so rudely interrupted, I noticed that you managed to escape, *and* you called the police with this." The Monster holds up Mrs. Luts's cell phone. "And all you managed to do by that is get someone else killed," it says solemnly, as it sights along the top of the nail gun. "Ah! Ah!" it says quickly, reacting to the look of fear on Billy's face. "It's okay. I mean it, kid. I know I was mad at first—

(Mad? You got that right. You're *insane*!)

—but you've impressed me. Believe me, *I* know how hard it is to escape from duct tape. It practically takes your skin right off, doesn't it? And don't feel too bad about the cop . . . I don't!" The Monster laughs.

Crazily, Billy finds himself nodding in agreement . . .

(As if this isn't an insane conversation!)

. . . but he never takes his eyes off the hole where the nail will come out.

"Escaping, though, that's something," The Monster

says with what seems like genuine admiration for Billy.
"Many a time was I bound in the cellar with duct tape
and tried to escape, just like you, though I never did. It
hurt too much, and if Sir had caught me . . ." The Monster pauses, grins, and moves closer to Billy. "But Sir got
what was coming to him."

It is all Billy can do not to cry out at The Monster's
nearness, fearing its touch.

"You and I are a lot alike, kiddo. Sometimes I think
I've got more in common with you than I do with that
retard you call, 'Dad.'" The Monster laughs abruptly at
that, and then turns serious just as quickly. "So," it muses,
wiping a tear of laughter from its eye, "I bet you're
wondering what happens now, right, kiddo?" The Monster cocks its head at an angle and looks askance at Billy.
"We can still get out of this, can still get away, but we've
got to get moving. And you've got to start cooperating,
Billy-boy." The Monster looks up at the ceiling and speaks
softly to itself. "There'll be more cops coming soon. You
can bet on it."

A surge of hope courses through Billy.

(That's right! *More* cops will come!)

The Monster looks at its bloody hands and chuckles.
"I'm starting to feel like Lady Macbeth."

Billy has no idea who that is . . .

(Probably someone else he killed.)

With the nail gun in hand, The Monster goes over to
Mrs. Luts's body lying on the stone floor. Billy is shocked
and surprised to see her bloody, mutilated head moving. Her one good eye opens, and she looks up at The
Monster. A garbled, faint scream comes from deep in
her throat, unable to make it all the way out.

(I thought she was toast!)

"What have we here?" The Monster grabs the skewer
off her body and grimaces at the blood and gore on it.
He holds it up for Billy to see then tosses it aside. "My,

my, my! She's a spunky old cow, isn't she?" The Monster clucks its tongue reproachfully. It raises the nail gun and points it at Mrs. Luts's one good eye. "You know," The Monster says, "seeing your determination, lady, really gets me," The Monster touches the middle of its chest with its free hand, "right here." The Monster looks at Billy. "What do you say, Billy-boy? Are you going to help me out, or do I put a nail in the feisty fat broad's eye?"

"Dad, please, don't."

The Monster shakes its head and looks sadly at Mrs. Luts. "I wish I didn't have to do this . . . but . . . I guess the 'eyes' have it."

Billy screams and looks away at the *thump!* of the nail gun firing. It's followed by another *thump* as the neighbor lady's head bounces off the floor once when the nail penetrates her skull via her left eye socket. She lets out a gargling groan that dies away slowly.

"Nailed her," The Monster deadpans, but it can't keep a straight face for long. A smirk starts and grows into bust-out laughter. "I kill myself sometimes!" The Monster wisecracks.

(If only!)

"What the hell is wrong with *you*?" The Monster says, the mirth gone from its voice, replaced with irritation. "These are the *jokes*, kid, why aren't you laughing? That was funny!" The Monster places the nail gun on the floor and grabs Donny Desmond's limp body, propping him up against Mrs. Luts's corpse.

"Now what's it going to be, Billy?" The Monster says. "Donny here is still alive. I can hear him breathing. He's got a pulse." The Monster picks up the nail gun and kneels next to Donny. The Monster nudges Donny's face with the tip of the nail gun, eliciting a faint, hoarse croak from the boy. The Monster looks at Billy and nods. "See? He's still alive. Now you tell me where Jimmy is.

I'm not fucking around, puke! You want *another* person to die because of you?"

(Liar!)

"Dad, don't let him do it, please." Pleading is all Billy can do, with tears streaming down his face, and his words broken with sobs.

"Come on, Billy-boy," The Monster urges, enthusiasm in its voice. But that enthusiasm is quelled by the doorbell ringing again.

"What the fuck? Is this Grand-fucking-Central or what?" The Monster exclaims. It stands and, in the same motion casually—even *carelessly*—fires a three-inch nail into Donny Desmond's forehead.

Billy reels at the shot and turns away again, gasping, sick, and faint as The Monster lays down the nail gun and goes upstairs.

John steps quietly, cautiously, from the cellar door to the edge of the kitchen door. At first glance he is relieved to see it is a woman and not another cop, but then he really looks at her: five-foot-five; a pretty, freckled face; short, curly black hair; big chest and big hips. She's been over the house dozens of times—Donny Desmond's mother, Ellen.

Looking at her, John is reminded of last New Year's Eve. He and Molly had shipped Kevin and Billy over to Molly's sister's for the night and were hosting a party. Molly had become friends with Ellen Desmond soon after she and John had moved to Blackstone from Poughkeepsie, where Molly had been going to school. Kevin was four at the time, the same age as her son, Donny. The two women became friends after meeting at the local Hannaford's Supermarket and discovered they lived within a few houses of each other.

About twenty people had attended and the house was full. John cued up the stereo with seven CDs—The Beatles' White Album; Crosby, Stills, and Nash's first album; Neil Young with Crazy Horse; Jefferson Airplane's "Volunteer"; The Beatles's "Let It Be" and "Abbey Road"; and, to cap it off, Jefferson Starships's "Blows against the Empire." Next to the stereo he had piled all the CDs—other hippie-era bands that he and Molly shared an affinity for—that he wanted to play for the night.

The party was going well; people were even dancing in the living room. Just before midnight John went upstairs to use the bathroom since the downstairs one had a line of three women waiting to use it. After zipping up and washing his hands, he stepped out of the bathroom and right into a very drunk Ellen Desmond. Downstairs, a chorus of loud voices was counting down the last five seconds of the New Year. Immediately following *one*, shouts of "Happy New Year" filled the house.

Ellen Desmond, whose husband, John had learned through Molly and her friendship with Ellen, had recently left her for another woman, threw herself into his arms and kissed him passionately, her mouth open and tongue hungrily seeking out his. Clumsy from drink, she fumbled with his right hand and awkwardly placed it on her left breast. That was when Molly called from downstairs, looking for John to share a New Year's kiss with. He left Ellen Desmond standing in the upstairs hallway, breathing hard and crying silently. Since then he's avoided her as much as possible.

(We can't avoid her now, Johnny-boy.)

She casts a worried look over her shoulder at the empty police car parked out front.

"She's looking for Donny. He must have told her he was coming over here to see Kevin. Then she saw the police car," he whispers silently.

(Open the door, Johnny-boy.)

On his knees John pushes the dead policeman over next to the repairman in front of the refrigerator. He crawls back to the door, and is about to regain his feet and open the door, but stops. He holds up his hands, brown with dried blood, and turns over to look up at his reflection in the toaster on the counter. He winces at the sight of his gory visage.

Ellen Desmond jabs the doorbell again. John slides to the side of the door and stands to peek past the edge of the curtain again. Ellen Desmond casts another glance back at the cruiser. She moves toward the glass and John leans away. The fuzzy shadow of her head stains the kitchen linoleum then disappears.

He leans back to the window. She's reaching in her pocket . . .

(Open the door, Johnny!)

. . . pulling out a small, black plastic object . . .

(Open the fucking door, puke!)

. . . a cell phone. She flips it open and thumbs the key pad three times.

(She's calling 911!)

Before she can put the phone to her ear, *he* pulls the door open and lunges. A shriek escapes her lips at the sight of his bloody visage. The phone falls to the porch floor. She backpedals, her hand grasping wildly for the screen door handle behind her.

He nearly grabs her, but the door hits the dead policeman again and rebounds, striking his shoulder hard enough to knock him aside just as his fingertips brush down Ellen Desmond's left arm.

She finds the handle as *he* bounces off the side of the door frame and stumbles onto the porch, stepping on and crushing her cell phone. She pulls the screen door open and flees, tripping down the stairs in her panic and falling to one knee at the bottom. She quickly regains her feet and runs down the walk as fast as possible. Her high-pitched shrieking is punctuated with garbled cries for help—" 'Ell me! 'Leez! " 'Elp!"—as she bolts down the front walk and stairs to the sidewalk. She doesn't stop there and keeps screaming as she runs past the parked police car and into the street. She keeps screaming right up to the moment she is struck by a speeding yellow 1968 Road Runner in cherry condition.

Like an acrobatic clown, she flies in the air and does a rag-dollish cartwheel over the hood and into the windshield, which shatters. She flips up and over the rest of the car racing by beneath her. She performs a graceful, elongated somersault high in the air that ends when she hits the road, and the somersault becomes a wild tumble of limbs, clothing, and blood.

The Road Runner veers off the road and plows into a maple tree ten yards farther down on the opposite side of the street. The crash is brief but explosive; a second filled with the sound of crushing metal, broken glass, and one short, half-second blast from the horn.

John ducks back inside and closes the door but remains at the window. He recognizes the car. It belongs to seventeen-year-old Pete Simpson, who lives around the corner on Ledgemore Street in the biggest, most ostentatious house on the block. Both he and his father—who drives a Jaguar—have a habit of *racing* through the neighborhood as if it were their own private little NASCAR speedway.

Across the street, Mrs. Canard, the neighborhood gossip, comes out her front door. She is short and round, dressed in a too-tight white sweatsuit that accentuates the rolls of cellulite around her stomach and hips, making her look like a female version of the Michelin Man, made of rubber tires. Her hair, normally a brilliant orange and bushing around her head, is subdued by curlers.

From the corner of her mouth hangs her perpetual cigarette. John remembers Molly telling him that she smokes
unfiltered Camels.

"Her fingers and teeth are brown from nicotine,"
Molly said.

Mrs. Canard, being closer to Ellen Desmond, goes
toward her. She takes a few steps, bending sideways awkwardly, trying to see her neighbor's face.

From the house next to Mrs. Canard's, Joe Velardo,
another neighbor, ventures forth dressed in a quilted
gray housecoat, Red Sox cap, unlaced construction boots,
and working his heavily bearded jaw furiously as he
chomps on a burnt-out cigar. He looks from the smashed,
smoking wreck to Mrs. Canard, to the torn and crumpled body of Ellen Desmond in the street, and back again.
The attraction, and closer proximity of the car, which
crashed into the maple tree at the edge of his front
lawn, proves stronger and he moves toward it, but slowly,
as if unconsciously trying to fight off its draw.

Mrs. Canard reaches Ellen Desmond's body and suddenly cries out, "Oh my God!" She turns away, looking
as though she is going to be sick. Instead she takes out a
cell phone. Seconds later she is screaming into it, re-
porting the accident.

(He killed Donny! Again!)

Losing the meager contents of his nearly empty
stomach—mostly water and yellow bile—does not make
Billy feel any better.

(He was almost dead anyway. Mrs. Luts, too.)

Billy shakes his head and sobs. Everywhere he looks
there is blood and death—Donny and Mrs. Luts, Mom
and Kevin. He closes his eyes and climbs down from the
workbench. Opening his lids just a slit to see directly in

front of him until he's out of the workshop, Billy leaves and goes to the bottom of the steps. He stands there watching and listening.

He hears The Monster growling and swearing as it opens the kitchen door. Through the window at the bottom of the stairs, he sees the legs of a woman stumbling down the porch steps and falling to a knee on the walk.

(It's Donny's mom!)

Billy starts crying again for a split second when he sees her frightened face and hears her prolonged screams—until they're cut off by a terrible *thunk!* The sound of glass and metal smashing is brief but terrible. All is quiet for a short spell, but the quiet is broken by the sound of The Monster slamming the door. It passes by the open cellar door, then back again a few moments later carrying a gun.

(Where'd it get a gun?)

Billy figures it must belong to the policeman that The Monster killed.

The Monster stops in the doorway and looks down at Billy. "You want to live, right Billy-boy?"

Billy nods nervously.

"Then get up here!"

Defiantly, Billy shakes his head. The Monster starts down the stairs toward him.

"Dad?" Billy says softly, imploringly. "I need you, Dad."

The Monster grunts with disgust and shakes its head.

"I call the shots, Billy-boy, not him. Thanks to you, kiddo—thanks to you *and* Jimmy—I'm strong. Which is why you have to tell me where he is!"

"Dad! Please, *please* come out and help me!" Billy pleads.

(This is crazy!)

The Monster laughs.

(But then . . . *he is insane!*)

The Monster's laughter cuts off abruptly. A few steps from the bottom it stops, looks confused.

(Can it be?)

With a swelling of hope, Billy senses his father's return.

"Dad?"

His father smiles at him, but the smile falters at the sound of far sirens coming closer.

"Dad, listen to me, please," Billy implores.

(It's no use!)

The sirens grow louder until they are blaring right outside. Rubber tires shriek to a halt and the sirens die. Billy can see blue and red lights flashing on the kitchen walls behind his father. He turns and sees them, too.

(And he don't look happy!)

His face fraught with anxiety, Dad retreats back upstairs to the kitchen.

"Shit!" John swears, looking out through the back door window. There is another cop car out front and two cops getting out of it. As he watches, another cruiser and an ambulance arrive from the other direction and pull to a halt, blocking the street.

(Don't worry about that. We can still get out.)

The house is on the corner of Warren and Ledgemore with the garage and driveway accessed by the side street, Ledgemore; the cops are on Warren. From the ambulance two EMTs emerge and split up—one going to Ellen Desmond and the other to the driver of the wreck. Another two cops get out of the recent cruiser and the four policemen meet briefly in the road and split up as well: one each going with the EMTs and the other two separating to interview Joe Velardo and Mrs. Canard.

John leaves the window and hurries through the kitchen and the hallway to the front door. The lock and

handle are stiff from disuse, and he is sure it will let out
a rusty screech that will give him away, but it doesn't.
The swollen edge of the door lets out only a soft moan
as it brushes against the jamb. He opens it just enough
to slip through, pulling it lightly closed behind him. He
crouches and crosses to the tall screen windows and listens. Amidst the crackle of random transmissions on the
police radios, he can hear Mrs. Canard's gravelly voice,
loud, clear, and tearful. "I called you, Officer. I saw the
whole thing!"

John rises enough to peer over the sill. He quickly
spies Mrs. Canard—she's not hard to spot. She's standing on her front lawn, a few yards from the wreck, with
a police officer. Her eyes are puffy and smeared with
mascara. Her nose is red and running. Her bulbous lips
tremble with the onset of fresh tears as she blubbers:

"I saw the whole thing. I saw him run her down like
she wasn't even there!"

The cop, a young guy with a face so smooth it looks
as though it's never been touched by a razor, appears
taken aback by the deep, rasping masculine voice coming from the woman.

"Um . . . ah . . . Sarge?" he calls to the cop checking
out the crashed Road Runner with the EMT. The other
cop is older and regards the younger officer with a scowl.
"Uh, this woman says she saw the accident," the young
cop stammers.

The older cop nods patronizingly at Mrs. Canard,
then glares at young cop. "So, you're supposed to be
taking her statement! *Jezus*, Rook, you know how to do
that, don't you? Or didn't they teach you *anything* at the
academy?" he says with so much disdain the young cop
blushes.

John feels sorry for the kid.

(That guy's a prick. I like him.)

The rookie cop smiles halfheartedly at John's neighbor and takes out a flip-top spiral notebook and ballpoint pen. "Can I have your name please, ma'am?"

"Mary. Mary Canard. I live right here." The woman points to her house, the large white ranch behind her.

"Okay. And do you know the victim? Can you tell me her name?"

"It's Ellen, Ellen Desmond. Ellen Desmond," Mrs. Canard repeats and wipes her eyes, smearing the mascara even more across the bridge of her nose.

(She looks like a fat, orange-haired raccoon!)

"And do you know where Mrs. Desmond lives?" the cop asks.

"Yes, oh yes. Right over there." She points to a white house a few down on the left side of Warren Street, past Ledgemore. "She lives there with her son, Donny. He's ten or eleven. Her husband left her." Mrs. Canard's voice takes on a gossipy tone that is, surprisingly, even deeper than her normal voice. "He ran off with a younger woman. His secretary, I heard." She rolls her eyes. "It's *always* the secretary."

The cop looks impatient, then distracted as the EMT pulls his head out of the driver's window of the Road Runner and says to the older cop, "He's dead, but we're going to need the Jaws of Life to get his body out of there. I'll call it in."

"Okay, ma'am," the young cop says, wearily, turning his attention back to Mrs. Canard. "You should just tell me what you saw."

Mrs. Canard wriggles her body up as straight as her rotund form will allow. Her face is flushed, and even from across the street John can see that her eyes are gleaming with more than tears—*excitement.* John guesses her husband doesn't listen to her much.

(Probably too busy screwing his young secretary.)

"I just got back from the health club where I work out every Saturday from ten to twelve while my girls take ballet and gymnastics classes till one. My husband is working. I was going to mix up some tuna fish for lunch for me and the girls when they get home. They're twins, you know—"

"What time was this?" the cop interrupts.

Mrs. Canard looks at him as if he just said something offensive. "I just told you, lunchtime. Aren't you listening? What are you writing?" she asks loudly, leaning forward to look at the cop's notebook, but he holds it away.

"I'm sorry, ma'am," the rookie stammers and glances sidelong to see if the older cop is watching. He isn't. He's got his head in the window of the wreck, frisking the dead driver for identification. "I'm kind of new at this," the young cop says to Mrs. Canard. "I've only been on the force for about a week."

Mrs. Canard smiles and winks at him. "Oh! Don't worry! And don't mind me! It's easy *not* to listen to me. My husband *never* hears a thing I say. I have to write him notes and stick them where he'll find them. I should buy stock in Post-it pads I use so many."

The young cop relaxes and smiles.

"Anyway," Mrs. Canard says waving her hand as if to dismiss her rambling, "I do know the exact time 'cause I looked at the clock just before I heard the god-awful noise of that car racing down the street because there's a clock on the counter where I was making the sandwiches. It was 12:30 and I was thinking I had just enough time to finish making the sandwiches and change before I have to go pick up the twins at dance school. I was looking at the clock when I heard the car. Did I just say that? Of course I did. Where was I? I had noticed the police car over there when I got home, so when I heard the car racing down the street I ran to the door to see if the cop was going to nab the kid. Oh, I've yelled at that kid many a time. I knew it was that yellow hot rod when I heard it. I've called the police before to complain about it. Actually I kind of wondered if that's why the cop car was here. I thought maybe you had a speed trap set up, but I guess not. The cop who belongs to that car was nowhere to be seen when that kid ran her down. Actually I'm not surprised the boy hit Ellen—he drives just like his father. Like father like son, you know? We've got small children in this neighborhood. We can't have people driving like that. Anyway, so I looked out and was surprised to see Ellen run into the street. A second later, the car hit her. It was awful. It was the most awful thing I've ever seen." Mrs. Canard chokes up and can't go on. New tears blubber to the surface, and she wipes her runny nose on the back of her hand.

The young cop looks uncomfortable. "She ran *into* the street?" he asks.

Mrs. Canard nods, sniffling.

"You mean she was running *up* the street from her house?" the rookie cop asks, looking down to the Desmond place that Mrs. Canard had pointed out to him.

"No, she was coming from the Teags's house. Over there."

John ducks as Mrs. Canard points toward the house. He stays down and catches the voice of Joe Velardo giving his statement: "I don't know what the hell happened. Me and Margaret were sitting there watching the noon news, waitin' for the Red Sox to come on at one, when *bang!* then, *crash!* We got up to look and seen this. Other than that, I don't know what's going on."

"Sarge?" The voice of the young cop again.

"Yeah, what-a-ya got, Sherlock?" The older cop.

"The lady told me the victim came running out of the house across the street, number sixty-two. The Teags family lives there."

"Yeah. That's Barry Lumpski's unit parked out front. He took the first call here to check out a prank call from some kid. Dispatch has had bogus calls from this address before. Why don't you go help load the bodies while I go check it out?"

John chances another peek. The older cop crosses the street to the first cruiser to have arrived on the scene, and looks inside. The young cop goes over and holds the doors of the ambulance open while the EMTs load Ellen Desmond, encased in a black plastic body bag. John takes advantage of the moment and scrambles back inside. He gently closes the door and hurries through the house to the open cellar door.

Billy's dad appears in the doorway again at the top of the stairs. The pistol is still in his hand, hanging by his side.

"I need you, Billy," his father says, nearly sobbing the words.

Billy takes one step up the stairs.

(No! It's another trick!)

"I need you up here, son. You're our ticket out of here now, Billy. We can get away and nobody else has to get hurt. I promise. Are you with me?" His words are charged with emotion and the threat of tears.

(When he says *our* and *we*, does he mean *us* and him, or him and The Monster? Don't trust him!)

He has no choice. He *has* to believe his father.

A sound from outside and motion in the window near the stairs catch Billy's ear and eye. He looks just in time to see another pair of uniformed legs go up the porch steps. The screen door opens, and they step inside.

(The cops are here to save us! Again!)

Billy looks back at his father with hope, but The Monster suddenly snaps back into his face.

"Forgot to lock the fucking door again, puke!" it growls.

At first, Billy thinks it is talking to him, but then realizes it isn't. It holds the policeman's pistol up and looks toward the kitchen door. For a split second Billy thinks of screaming a warning to the cop, but The Monster looks at him as if it reads his mind.

"Be good now," it whispers, "And nobody else has to get hurt."

Billy shivers at how *nice* it can speak and be about to *kill* someone. He squats at the bottom of the stairs and hugs his knees to his chest, hoping he's wrong, hoping The Monster means what it said.

(Like Kevin would say: "Fat chance!")

Billy scrunches his eyes closed as tightly as possible, but can still hear The Monster breathing and grunting and softly mumbling up in the kitchen. The next sound is the doorbell, then the doorknob turning slowly. He hears the door open quickly.

"Oh shit—" a strange voice exclaims. It is cut off by shots—one, two, a pause, then a third.

Billy whimpers and covers his ears, but he is too late to keep out the sound of a body hitting the floor and The Monster's gleeful laughter.

The cops outside react with confusion at the sound of the shots coming from the back porch. Even though the rookie cop knew his older partner was coming to knock on the Teags's door, he still looks around as if thinking the noise came from somewhere else.

(The gun!)

He steps onto the porch and retrieves the newest dead cop's pistol.

(Another Glock—forty caliber with a fifteen-round clip!)

Straightening, a gun in each hand, he looks out at the street just as the rookie cop pops up. Their eyes lock. *He* raises both pistols . . .

"Take cover!" one of the other cops shouts and tackles the rookie, forcing him down behind the first patrol car parked in front of the house just as *he* squeezes off a shot from each pistol. The first shot goes wild and plows unnoticed into the edge of Joe Velardo's lawn; the second grazes the windshield of the cop car hard enough to star the glass.

There is pandemonium in the street. The two EMTs, having just hurriedly finished loading Ellen Desmond's body into the back of the ambulance, duck behind their vehicle. The cop who was measuring the skid marks in the street ducks around the front of the ambulance. Across the street, Mrs. Canard stands on her front walk, hands to her face, frozen in an expression of shock, shrieking at the top of her lungs.

"Get back in your house!" the cop who saved the rookie yells, waving his hand at Mrs. Canard as if it could push her back into her home. It takes the hysterical woman a minute to follow his command, during which time *he* draws a bead on her. Just as he is about to blow her away, she turns and hightails it back inside. Next door to her, Joe Velardo needs no such instruction from the police. As soon as he hears the shots and sees the cops diving for cover, he disappears inside his house, slamming his door and loudly locking it behind him. Other neighbors, whose curiosity drew them from their houses along the street, wisely copy Joe Velardo.

John steps back into the kitchen and starts to close the door. Before it shuts he hears, "I'm calling for backup. Get your twelve-gauge!"

John hurries through the house to the front door. He opens it a crack and peers out. He can see the very tops of the heads of the two cops behind the patrol car closest to the house. While the older cop, who has a bushy black mustache, talks frantically into his radio— "We have an officer down! I repeat! Officer down!"—

the young cop duck walks backward until he can open the cruiser's door. He slides onto the front seat on his stomach, reaches for something under the dash, and slides back out again, closing the door. In his hands he holds a shotgun.

The older cop puts his radio away, looks at the shotgun and the rookie, and nods. Nervously, he peeks at the back porch over the hood of the car. "Cover me," he tells the rookie.

"What are you going to do?" the rookie asks. His voice is high pitched, on the edge of hysteria.

"I'm going to get Bud. I can't leave him on that porch. He might still be alive," the mustached cop says, ducking down again. Before the rookie can protest or make any reply at all, the older cop ducks around the front end of the cruiser and sprints, staying bent over, across the sidewalk and up the three steps to the flag-stone walk that will take him to the back porch.

The front door swings open slowly, and *he* steps through, both pistols up, firing through the large screened windows to the left. The cop dashing along the walk doesn't have a chance. Bullets tear into the side of his neck, his left arm just above the elbow, and the base of his spine, while the rest zing off the stone walk or plow into the soft green grass bordering it. One wild shot ricochets off the trunk of the thick oak tree next to the walk and plunges into the side of the Verizon truck at the corner of Warren and Ledgemore, a good fifteen yards away.

The rookie cop training the shotgun on the back porch is caught completely off guard by the attack from the front. He jerks back in shock and loses his balance. As he falls on his ass, he accidentally pulls the trigger and the shotgun blows a hole in the squad car's front fender and tire. A rush of air escapes the latter like a gust of wind.

Before *he* can bring the pistols around to catch the exposed rookie, slugs tear through the front window screens, and gouge the shingles less than three feet behind his head. The cop who initially ducked around the ambulance is shooting at him. *He* fires, ducks, and lunges back through the open door into the front hallway. He kicks the front door closed behind him just as a shot rips into the wood with a *crack* and another shatters the oval, smoked-glass window in it. Pieces shower him.

From outside a scream of pain mingles with a plea for help.

For a moment Billy thinks—

(Hopeless!)

—his father will come back and will finally listen to him long enough to be able to overcome The Monster.

I came so close just now!

(Doubt it!)

"Oh man! That was a fucking rush!" The Monster cries in the house above, weakening Billy's hope. It sounds jubilant.

(See what I mean? Sounds like he's having too much fun killing cops. It sounds like he's having a blast!)

At the bottom of the cellar stairs, Billy remains huddled in the fetal position, his eyes closed, but he can hear the cellar door squeak on its hinges when The Monster pushes it open and calls down to him. "I'm not fooling around anymore, Billy-boy. Get the fuck up here."

(Don't piss him off!)

Billy looks up into The Monster's eyes. "You lied to me! You said no one else would get hurt."

(Oh-oh, you're dead now.)

The Monster sings, *"You made me do it; it didn't wanna do it, I didn't wanna do it!"*

"Dad!" Billy cries. "You can fight it, Dad. You got to try."

(Oh yeah that'll work—*not*! You should run and *hide* before it does to you what it did to Donny and Mrs. Luts!)

"Okay, enough fun and games. I'm getting tired of this bullshit, puke. Let's move it!" Irritation is beginning to show in The Monster's voice.

Billy still doesn't move. "I want my daddy. Please come out, Dad. Please try, Dad! Please!"

The Monster's irritation quickly turns to anger. "Shut up! If you think I'm leaving you behind or letting you go, you're crazier than your father! Like I said, Billy-boy, you're my ticket past those cops out there. *Now get up here or else!*" The Monster growls the last words, sending a chill through Billy.

The Monster takes two steps down the stairs. The wood beneath it creaks loudly.

From outside, comes another scream of agony followed by a plea, "Help me God! Please, somebody help me!" Billy whimpers in his throat at the sound, but The Monster suddenly stops and stares out the window. It clucks its tongue like an old lady.

"Someone really should help that poor man and put him out of his misery," it exclaims, grinning maliciously.

"Dad! No!" Billy cries to no avail. The Monster turns around and goes back up to the kitchen.

(You better do something—*hide* while you can! It's better than nothing. Better than dying.)

Billy shakes his head. He's tired—too tired to hide. He doesn't want to think anymore, doesn't want to be afraid anymore, doesn't want to feel *anything* anymore.

(You'll feel plenty if you give up.)

He can't help wondering, what's the use?

More shots sound from upstairs. Billy cringes and

whimpers. He backs away from the stairs, receding into the cellar until he bumps into an overturned folding card table.

"I have to do something to stop The Monster or else it will just keep killing," he says softly. With every killing The Monster seems to be getting crazier and hungrier for more murder.

(You're right about that! The Monster's having a jolly old time spreading death and destruction, all right.)

I came so close to reaching Dad.

(And yet . . . so far.)

I have to stop The Monster, Billy thinks again. *I'm responsible.*

(How many times do I have to tell you? You were a *baby*! It's not your fault!)

Billy knows that, but it doesn't change anything.

(What about Jimmy? He's the one that made The Monster really evil. Your dad said so himself. If it's anyone's fault, it's his!)

It doesn't matter.

"It's my fault," he mumbles, tears filling his eyes. "*My* crying made the thing inside Dad turn into The Monster and made it start killing."

(Baloney! He's *crazy*! Don't you get it? Besides it's like a *vice versa*! *Any* baby's crying would have done that! Look what Jimmy's crying made it do!)

"It's not Jimmy's fault," Billy whispers to himself, "and it's not Dad's fault either, really." Tears large and slow run down both cheeks.

(It sure as hell ain't *your* fault either. If it's anyone's fault it's *Sir's* and there's nothing you can do about that now!)

Still . . .

(*Nothing!* So quit feeling sorry and quit blaming yourself! Concentrate on staying alive!)

. . . he can't help but feel guilty . . .

(Oh, for crying out loud!)

The thought *The Monster is my responsibility* won't go away.

(No! Your only responsibility is staying alive!)

He can argue with himself forever, but deep down Billy knows what he knows, and nothing his alter ego can say will ever change that. He has to do what he has to do. If he can't reason with his father to make The Monster stop killing, or trick it so that he can escape, then Billy knows he is going to have to find some way to stop it *physically*, even if it means hurting, or even *killing* his father.

(Now you're talking.)

"Oh God! Please help me!"

The wounded cop's cries are getting hoarse and weak. John slides over to the kitchen door and looks out. He can just see the downed policeman's ankles and shoes moving sluggishly on the flagstone. Beyond him, on the other side of the cruiser, the rookie cop bobs up to cast a worried glance at his injured partner, then ducks down again, like a spooked rabbit in a hole.

"Oh no. Look what you've done," John whispers.

(It was bound to happen sooner or later, Johnny-boy. You watch all the cop shows on the boob tube. You know they had to be figuring things out.)

John supposes it's true—it was just a matter of time.

(Sure . . . considering the nature of our . . . work . . . it's not much of a stretch to guess they probably started checking couples who have had babies within a month or two of any of the women and babies we killed.)

"*You* killed!"

(Whatever. You know, Johnny, *denial* ain't just a river in Egypt.)

"I wish they had caught you sooner."

(Yeah, well, that and a nickel will get you squat, Johnny-boy. I'm sure they tried real hard—dragnets, FBI profilers, but you know, maybe I'm just too good to get caught. Ever think of that?)

"If that were true, we wouldn't be in the situation we're in now," John argues as he goes to the front door. Glass crunches beneath his feet as he sidles up to the curtain blowing in the breeze pouring through the shattered door window. He quickly scans the street but can't see the other cop who shot at him from behind the ambulance. A moment more, however, and he hears him; his voice comes from behind the ambulance.

"Terry! Terry!" he calls. The rookie cop behind the cruiser responds with a loud affirmation that is a cross between a grunt and a sob.

"Terry," the cop behind the ambulance says, "can you get to Officer Farr? We've got to get him out of there! I'll cover you!"

The rookie shakes his head vehemently and stays put. The whine of multiple sirens grows louder and closer, mingling with the intermittent squawking of the police radios.

Ducking away from the door, John runs up to the second-floor window at the top of the stairs. It overlooks the left front half of the house before its view of Warren Street is blocked by the front porch roof. From here, John can see the dying cop on the walk below, barely moving or making any more sounds, lying in a pool of slowly spreading blood.

"Listen," the cop behind the ambulance shouts. "I'll get him, but you've got to cover me!"

The rookie cop nods rapidly and pulls the shotgun close. The other cop suddenly sprints from behind the ambulance, over to where the rookie crouches.

John puts the pistols down on the sill and slowly draws

the blind up. None of the cops seem to notice. He struggles with the window. With a hard yank, he pulls it open. Cool air flows in. There is no screen or storm window—it's the one upstairs window that has neither, and thus, is rarely opened, even in the summer for fear of mosquitoes getting in. The sound opening the window makes seems to him to be as loud as an explosion, but the cops do not notice in their panic. He figures the approaching sirens must have covered the noise.

John strains to hear and tries to read the cop's lips. "Okay, try not to shoot me," he thinks the older one says to the rookie, looking as though he is only half-joking. The rookie nods some more. His hands are bloodless white gripping the shotgun. The other cop looks back at the ambulance and waves. Now John can see one of the EMTs peeking around the back end of the vehicle.

"Get ready!" the cop shouts. "As soon as I carry him over to you, get him in and get out of here pronto!"

The EMT's head nods slightly and disappears.

Fascinated, John watches the ambulance cop creep to the front of the cruiser and dart forward, across the sidewalk and up the stairs with one hand on the wrought-iron railing, pulling him along. A short sprint and he's to his fallen comrade, lying on the flagstone directly under John's window. The cop moves around to squat over the injured policeman's head and put his hands under his shoulders so that he can roll him over.

"Easy now, Ron. This is going to hurt, but I've got to move you," John can hear the cop below him say as he turns the hurt man over.

John flinches as the wounded officer screams in pain at the movement.

"Take it easy," the cop gasps, cringing at the volume of the hurt man's cry. He leans over him again and looks into the face contorted with pain. "I got to get you out of here, Ron," he says anxiously. He looks fearfully at the front porch, then over his shoulder at the back. "I'm sorry, but I've got no choice; I've got to get you to the ambulance, or you're going to bleed to death. I'll try not to hurt you, but you've got to stop screaming."

The cop glances over at the cruiser where the rookie, shotgun in hand, is propped on the hood, pointing the weapon at the house. "Here we go," the cop says. He puts his hands firmly under the wounded man's arms and lifts him. The bleeding policeman grits his teeth but cannot keep from emitting a guttural cry of pain.

He picks the weapons up but uses only the left one. From the right side of the window frame, he squeezes off three shots that form a triangle around the two cops on the walk below. The rescuing cop immediately dives to the right of the walk and scrambles around the back of the oak tree.

What are you doing?

(Keeping 'em put, Johnny-boy. As long as they got wounded exposed and in danger like that, we got leverage. That and Billy-boy may be enough to get us some demands granted so we can get the hell out of here with a chance of getting away. We might come out of this smelling like roses yet!)

In the cellar, Billy whimpers at the sound of each new scream. With reluctance he goes back to the stairs. Voices and the sound of The Monster running up to the second floor spur him on. With a great deal of effort and pain, Billy climbs the cellar stairs.

(What are you doing?)

At the top he steps into the kitchen and winces at the sight of the bodies—a dead policeman and the telephone repairman, lying on the floor in front of the refrigerator.

More people dead because of me.

(There you go again! Forget that and try the door.)

The sound of footsteps coming down the stairs overrides his guilt and prevents movement. A moment later The Monster appears in the doorway between the kitchen and the front hall. It looks surprised to see him.

"Well, well, well," it says approvingly. "Glad to see you're finally living up to your genius reputation, Billy-boy. I was just coming to get you."

"Dad?" Billy says, quickly. "Please listen to me. I know none of this is your fault. I know what Sir did to you, but—"

"You know *nothing* about Sir!" The Monster barks harshly. It laughs. "But he got what was coming to him all right."

Before Billy can plead any further, The Monster grabs his arm and drags him upstairs. The effect of The Monster's touch is immediate, terrifying, and overwhelming. Billy's body stiffens, his eyes dim, and his pupils focus somewhere on a far place in a far time.

"What are you going to do?"

(What do you think I'm going to do? I'm doing what you never could! If I don't, we'll die down here.)

Billy watched from a place deep inside his head-that-was-not-his-head as his body-that-was-not-his-body performed without him. He saw hands take some fishing line from Sir's tackle box in his workshop and string it across the top of the stairs, at ankle level. He retreated to the doorway of Sir's workshop, at the bottom of the stairs. He listened as his voice—but not his voice—started hollering, sounding strange, like that kid, Stewey on that cartoon, Family Guy, *long before that show was ever on.*

"Oh Fah-ther, you old fuck-face! Come down here so I can kick your ass!"

There was a loud bang from upstairs that sounded like a chair being toppled. Heavy footsteps made the basement ceiling shudder and creak. The door at the top of the narrow stairs opened, bathing him in light.

"What did you say, puke?" *Sir growled, drunkenly standing in the open doorway.*

Again his voice came as if from someone else: "You heard me, you old fuck!"

"So you finally decided to grow a set, huh?" *Sir asked in a quiet, scary voice.* "But now you got to be a man and pay for your balls." *He took a step forward.* "I'm gonna balance your books, big-time, puke. Time for a tune-up. Time to take fucking *inventory!*"

As though seeing it all in stop-action animation through a kid's 3-D viewfinder, Billy saw Sir come charging through the door at the top of the cellar stairs. His leg hit the fishing line, and he went over like a lemming off a cliff. He pitched forward, hands out, and hit the middle steps with his chin. There was a loud crack. Sir bounced twice—Billy counted them— and his bones crunched and snapped. There was more snapping and cracking as Sir's body somersaulted down the stairs, and his back hit the bottom few steps with his left arm twisted around and trapped beneath. He slammed headfirst into the stone floor at the bottom of the stairs. There was a sickening crunch! Sir's body jerked once, and he slumped onto his side, legs twisted on the stairs behind him, face pressed into the dirty floor. Both his arms and most of his ribs appeared broken. He could see bloody bones sticking out the elbow of his right arm and poking through his T-shirt on his left side. His head was twisted at an unnatural angle.

The spell is broken as soon as The Monster pushes him into the corner of the hallway on the second floor by the window and lets go of him. Billy's rigid body relaxes. The images fade more slowly this time.

"Dad was right. *You* . . . killed Sir," Billy whispers.

The Monster regards him curiously. "Duh! Like that was any big secret."

(I don't think The Monster knows you were just in its head!)

Outside, the pinned cops haven't moved. The rookie hasn't shown his face behind the cruiser out front. The wounded one on the walk is still moving, though barely and still pleading, though faintly. His would-be rescuer remains behind the oak tree, but he has unwittingly left the bottom half of his right leg exposed.

(Target practice!)

Before *he* can take aim, the distraction of more sirens wailing to a deafening end outside as another police car and ambulance arrive, stop him. They come up Warren Street and pull onto Ledgemore Street.

(No! Are they blocking the driveway?)

Roughly grabbing the boy's arm, *he* drags him down the hallway to the nursery where the windows overlook the garage and driveway and out over the kitchen roof at Ledgemore Street.

(Oh fuck!)

Because of the telephone repair truck parked at the corner by the telephone pole, the newly arrived cruiser and ambulance have to park farther along the street. The cruiser is parked on the sidewalk behind the telephone truck and the ambulance is right in front of the driveway.

(This may be a fight to the death, Johnny-boy.)

In The Monster's grip again, Billy experiences another onslaught of thoughts, feelings, images, and desires that coalesce into vivid memory.

Laughter. Shrieking, braying laughter. Laughter that became sobbing. Hysterical.

Before Billy's eyes, but at the same time seen as if from a panoramic viewpoint, lay the broken and bleeding body of Sir at the bottom of the cellar stairs right outside the workshop doorway.

"He's still alive," *he heard a voice, not unlike his own, say, and winced at the inner voice that answered:*

(Not for long!)

As though watching an incredible virtual reality movie, he moved toward the body.

(Don't trust him!)

With his foot, he poked Sir's leg lightly. There was no response. He reached out with his foot again and poked his broken arm. There was a response, like an eruption—a scream of pain and a bellow of anger.

He jumped back, but Sir didn't reach for him, didn't climb to his feet and take off his belt, didn't threaten to "balance his books."

(He can't move! He's paralyzed!)

Sir's body was heavy, but he moved it, pulling on his pants legs until he could grab both his ankles and drag him from the bottom of the stairs into the workshop. Sir screamed and fainted, then woke, screamed, and fainted again as he dragged him the few feet to the workbench. He left him on the floor in front of the bench, paralyzed, back and neck apparently broken.

With an air of calm determination, he climbed on a stool and grabbed a razor knife off the top of the workbench. Sensing what was coming, Billy wanted to close his eyes against the scene, but it was impossible. He was forced to watch the hands use the razor on Sir's exposed flesh, cutting away a strip from his neck and shoving it into Sir's screaming mouth.

(Serves him right.)

Methodically, slowly, he skinned Sir alive. One strip at a time.

Curses, threats, and finally pleas came from Sir. Inside, Billy felt and shared in all the pent-up anger and pain being released; the vengeful desire to make Sir pay for all the times he showered abuse and humiliation upon him. All the times he treated him like an animal.

By the time he was done flaying him, Sir was barely coherent, but that didn't end it. He got a rusty pan of water from the sink in the workshop and poured it over Sir, reviving him for more torture. Sir pleaded for mercy, and he felt a surge of hatred remembering all the times he had begged his father for mercy and had got his "books balanced."

"No," he said. "I'm going to balance your books for a change. Once and for all."

Through his excruciating pain, Sir looked at him oddly, as though he sensed the presence of more than his son.

"Look, it's your 'lost shaker of salt,' " *he said to Sir, quoting Sir's favorite recording artist, Jimmy Buffett. He held the salt shaker out over Sir's skinless body and sprinkled. The salt took a moment to have an effect, but when it did, it was immense. Sir had looked close to death, but the salt in his wounds revived him—screaming—even better than the water, while, strangely, at the same time, weakening him more.*

Sir begged to be left alone. "Please, Johnny, stop. . . ."

More salt on his raw, bloody flesh was his answer.

"You don't know who you're talking to, do you?" *he asked Sir.*

That odd look of confusion again on Sir's face.

"I'm not your little puke, Johnny-boy," *he said and shook a little more salt over Sir's hamburger legs.*

"I'll do anything you want. I'll give you anything, just please, stop," *Sir pleaded.*

"Will you let me go outside, Daddy?" *he asked in a childish voice.* "Can I have friends? Can I go to school with other kids?"

"Yes," *Sir groans.* "Anything."

"Hah! Idiot! I'm an animal, remember? That's what you always call me—a little animal. And animals can't go to school! Animals don't have friends!"

*He looked around. Strips of Sir's hide hung everywhere,
drying in the cool air of the cellar. Billy felt a jumble of things,
revulsion at the sight of the skin mixed with angry joy at having payback on Sir.*

*"If you won't stop, then kill me, Johnny, please," Sir begged,
softly, calmly.*

*Billy saw the rest then; saw how Sir would die, slowly, so
slowly, and just before the end, the recognition in Sir's eyes as
he saw what was inside his son.*

The Monster unceremoniously dumps Billy on the
floor against the overturned bureau. For a moment
Billy thinks he hears a cry from within the piece of furniture, but realizes he's hearing the echoes of Sir's pathetic cries in his head.

(So that's what "to flay someone alive" means! It's
enough to gag a maggot!)

Even though The Monster takes its hand away, the
residue of its mind—the shock of Sir's torture and murder—leaves Billy muddle-headed and disoriented. He
lies limp and dazed against Baby Jimmy's hiding place.

The Monster opens the window overlooking the
kitchen roof and takes aim.

(The baby-faced blond EMT who just got out of the
ambulance.)

He fires. He is aiming for the ground—a warning
shot—in front of the EMT, but the bullet strikes the
side of the ambulance less than a foot behind the medical technician's posterior. The man—

He's just a kid!

—dives to the ground on the lawn, unsure of where
the bullet came from. The two cops who just got out of
the cruiser behind the Verizon truck rush to the ranch

fence at the edge of the yard, take up positions, and open fire.

Bullets *thunk* into the side of the house. The top glass of the window shatters, sending shards everywhere. *He* cries out and ducks as glass tears fine gashes in his arms and face. A bullet strikes the Mickey Mouse clock on the opposite wall, above the closet. It falls, hits the overturned crib mattress, bounces off, and shatters at the edge of the dried puddle of blood on the floor partially covered by the mattress. Its two C-batteries pop free and roll until they hit the edge of the overturned bureau.

(They're shooting at us, Johnny-boy!)

He is gleeful as if the bullets are long-awaited presents. *He* pops up into the window and fires back. By sheer luck his first shot finds a policeman. The one on the right is thrown backward by the force of the bullet. A spray of blood hangs in the air for a moment. The other cop screams his partner's name—"Ja-a-a-a-ack!"—and returns fire again.

He laughs at the breeze produced by the bullet passing within a quarter inch of his ear. In the corner of his vision there is movement. *He* turns and fires before looking. The EMT, who had been trying to get away from the shooting, goes down with a bloody hole in his side. He cries like a child, screaming and wailing for his mother.

Bullets rip into the wall opposite the window again, and into the ceiling above his head, showering plaster onto him and the boy lying in a heap behind him, apparently senseless.

(Come on, Johnny! Time to check the front!)

I don't want to do this anymore!

He steps over the boy and sprints down the hallway to the front window.

(Damn it!)

The cop's body is gone, as is the ambulance.

(They took him while we were busy in the back!)

He searches the street out front.

(Where's the cop who was hiding behind the tree? Where's the rookie?)

A sound from below. . . .

(They're in the house!)

The kitchen!

He moves to the other end of the landing where two feet of the shattered railing is still attached to the wall. From there, by leaning forward a little, he can look straight down on the stairs and see anyone coming up.

A floorboard creaks below.

(It's a cop!)

He holds his breath. Another creak. He can hear breathing in the hallway downstairs. *He* leans forward and peers over the only part of the railing still standing. A head appears below him. It looks up just as he squeezes the trigger and sends a bullet straight down through the upturned face.

A black hole, the size of a dime, appears in the cop's left cheek, nestled right up against his nose like a monster blackhead. At the same time, a spray of blood, bone, and flesh bursts from the back of his head. The *bang* of the gun is followed by a *thunk* as the bullet passes through the cop's face out the back of his head, and into the wooden stair below him. A wet gushing sound, as the contents of his head escape through the hole in the back of his skull, follows close behind. The dead policeman collapses on the stairs like a dropped sack of laundry. There is a frightened cry from the hallway below and the sound of someone—

(My guess is the rookie—)

—beating a hasty retreat through the kitchen and out the back door.

He runs to the window just in time to see the rookie hightailing it down the walk to the cruiser parked out front. The cop is an easy target—

No!

(We'll let him go. He reminds me of you, Johnny-boy.)

—but not for long. From behind the wrecked Road Runner, another cop fires on the house. *He* ducks back and grins.

In the distance, the renewal of more approaching sirens. Lots of them.

(More cops—more fun! Don't worry, Johnny-boy, now it gets interesting.)

Are you nuts? After killing cops we'll never get out of here alive.

(Sure we will. We got Billy-boy—our ace in the hole. The cops won't be too quick to shoot at us when they see we got him.)

I won't let you hurt him.

He laughs and sidles up to the window.

(Relax. He won't get hurt. The cops won't hurt him, and we have no need to hurt him now. He's our ticket out of here. Still . . . I would like to know where the baby is . . . you know how I hate to leave things unfinished, Johnny.)

You're crazy. You don't want to get out of here. You just want to keep on killing, 'cause you like it. I won't let you use Billy as a hostage and put him in danger.

(And what's wrong with killing? Don't be such a hypocrite—you like it as much as I do.)

Billy crawls to the doorway of the nursery and leans against the right side of the door frame. He struggles to his feet and nearly passes out with the effort. He hangs on to the doorjamb and gently leans his bruised and bleeding head against the cool wood. Slowly, painfully, he takes a step into the hallway.

(What are you doing? You should be hiding?)

"Nowhere to hide. Not anymore," Billy mumbles.

*   *   *

John hugs the wall and breathes rapidly, feeling faint.
(Tell them we have a hostage, Johnny-boy!)

John leans forward and a bullet grazes the very tip of
his nose. It burns the tender flesh there as though it
had been touched with the tip of a hot iron.

John ducks, but *he* jumps right up again and thrusts
both pistols forward, firing rapidly in the direction of
the wrecked Road Runner.

As soon as *he* shoots, the rookie jumps up from behind the cruiser with the shotgun pointed at the second-
floor window. The young cop fires, but the shot is wild
and rips up the siding to the left of the window at the
corner of the house.

He fires back, just as wildly, as he quickly steps into the
window, then back. Bullets *ping* and ricochet off the roof
of the cruiser and the blacktop of the street. There is a
clattering sound—like something dropped in haste. *He*
ventures a peek at the edge of the window. The rookie,
his shotgun by his side, is lying in the road, arms splayed,
one eye gone, replaced by blood pooling in the cavity
where it had been.

The cop behind the Road Runner fires and keeps on
firing as he rushes into the street to the rookie cop's
side. One look at the rookie and he lets out a cry of anguish and rage. He fires at the house and keeps firing
until his weapon is empty. The sound of his shots is
overwhelmed by the blaring siren of another police
cruiser, lights flashing, pulling up in the middle of Warren Street a few feet away. Two more uniformed police
officers get out. The driver immediately lends a hand
with the rookie. The other takes up position behind his
cruiser, aiming his pistol over the roof at the house.

He takes a shot at him and misses, but it has the de-
sired effect. The new cop, a heavyset, jowly man with a

decent beer gut, and the other cop quickly grab the
rookie and drag him behind the nearest cruiser. His
partner—an equally beer-bellied veteran with a face that
is all nose—ducks down behind his squad car in the
street. *He* turns and runs down the hallway, past Billy
clinging to the wall opposite the bathroom like a drunk
barely able to stand, and back to the nursery. Stepping
over pieces of the broken crib and the fallen bureau
lying facedown on the floor, he goes to the rear window
and looks at the garage and the driveway that leads to
Ledgemore Street. Two Blackstone police cruisers and
three Connecticut State Police cars are now there behind the ambulance, blocking the street and the end of
the driveway even more.

"Shit!"

(It's that little puke's fault! We could have been out
of here by now!)

As The Monster runs past him in the hallway, its hand
brushes across Billy's chest. Even through his clothes he
feels the energy piercing him. Like the Monster rushing past him, the images and memories it imparts to
him do the same.

The headline of a newspaper from seven years ago:

First Murder in Blackstone
since 1830!

*He saw the date—just a few days after the day he was born.
There was a picture with a caption identifying one Antonio
Baldacci, the husband of the victim, accused of murder. The
scene slid away, replaced by another. He was sitting in a dark
car on a dark street. A man—the man in the newspaper photo—
came walking down the middle of the street. His hands and
clothes were covered with blood, and he appeared to be in shock.*

A police car pulled up; its spotlight blinded him as two officers knocked him to his knees and handcuffed him.

This scene, too, slipped away, replaced by a dimly lit one where a woman was spread-eagle on a table saw in the cellar of a house. Her skull was crushed, and the saw was embedded in her womb as though it had stuck there as it had been cutting her in half.

The scene went dark, as if he had closed his eyes very slowly, and then brightened again to reveal he was standing in front of a television set.

"The trial of Antonio Baldacci came to a sensational close today," *a TV reporter in front of the Blackstone Court House said.* "TV crews from as far away as Boston, New York City, and Philadelphia were on hand expecting to report a guilty verdict due to the overwhelming evidence against Mr. Baldacci, but the case was thrown out by Judge Thomas O'Neal, when it was learned that another young woman has been found murdered in the cellar of her own home, in the same manner as Mrs. Baldacci, less than five miles from where the Baldaccis lived."

A shift of imagery and he was treated to a quick glimpse of a bespectacled, mousy woman, lying on a concrete cellar floor, her skull crushed with a large adjustable wrench still wedged in her skull, and her womb mutilated in a similar way to Mrs. Baldacci's with a pair of gardening shears, also still stuck in her.

A third glimpse of murder slipped by as the scene bled into a roadside—a transient woman hitchhiking. He pulled over. She got in, and a moment later he was standing in a hole in an abandoned burned-out shack along Interstate 95, looking down at her naked, mutilated body. It was too dark to see everything that had been done to her, all of her wounds, but he knew they were there—the sharpened branch thrust through her repeatedly was still in her like a macabre road sign.

The scene changed again . . .

*A young woman, her belly swollen with pregnancy, in the
lowest level of a parking garage on the outskirts of Blackstone.
Her head was crushed with a tire iron which had then been
used to stab her repeatedly in an apparent attempt to cut out
her unborn baby. The tire iron had been left behind, sticking
out of her like a post . . . or a pin.*

The scenes fly by so fast they blur and become a gray
haze, and then they are gone. Billy is left breathless and
weak.

(Those were the women he killed before he started
murdering babies, too!)

"Right after I was born," Billy mutters sadly. More
proof that he is to blame for The Monster.

(No—there's something else, something you're overlooking—when he was killing Sir. Couldn't you feel it?)

It doesn't matter.

(Yes, it does!)

No.

The Monster is shooting out the nursery window and
more people are going to die unless he does something.
Right now.

(I got an idea, Johnny-boy, that ought to keep you
happy, for a while anyway. We're going to use the fat
broad and Kevin's friend as hostages to buy some time
while you find out where the baby is.)

He leans into the window frame and fires with no specific aim at the police cars blocking the driveway. Stepping back he shouts, "Coppers!" over his shoulder.

(Don't I sound like Jimmy Cagney?)

"I got hostages! Anyone tries to get inside again, and
I start killing them!"

He risks a look. The cops look confused, even doubtful.

(Where's that little puke? Show them!)

He runs to the doorway just as the boy steps into the room. He grabs his arm and pushes him to the window. *He* crouches behind the boy.

"The kid gets it first if anyone tries to get inside!" he yells.

For a fleeting moment Billy catches a glimpse of police cars and ambulances and policemen moving about, looking at him with shocked faces, before his mind succumbs to The Monster's touch and is invaded once more. Another memory strikes like a bolt of lightning splintering a tall tree.

In the dark of the cellar, in the deep dark loneliness of The Brig, he lay curled up on the shelf under Sir's workbench, his four-year-old fists doubled up and pressed into his groin, his teeth clenched, trying through sheer force of will to keep the inevitable from happening.

But he couldn't.

He'd been in the cellar too long.

Far too long.

He inhaled a speck of dust into his nose and it tickled. He reached to clench the nostrils closed, but he wasn't quick enough. The sneeze burst forth, and he stained the seat of his underwear. At the same moment a spurt of urine escaped.

The door at the top of the stairs opened. Sir heard, and when he was in The Brig, noise of ANY kind was prohibited. Fluorescent light from upstairs penetrated the workshop, reaching him in The Brig, revealing what he'd done. There was no hope of covering his shame now; no hope of hiding it. He could smell himself, and he stunk. If Sir couldn't smell him at the top of the stairs, by the time he reached the workshop he would.

But Sir's olfactory sense was predatory.

"You filthy little animal!" *Sir bellowed as he started down the stairs.*

Terror dissolved whatever control he retained, and he added to the mess in his pants, completely relieving both bowel and bladder before Sir reached him. The stench was awful.

"You filthy fucking animal! You puke!"

But he wouldn't be smelling it for long.

Before he could say a word—not that any apology or pleading would make a difference—Sir reached in, grabbed him by the scruff of the neck, and pulled him from The Brig. Sir switched his grasp to his throat, choking him senseless, before knocking him down with a backhand blow. Blood spurted from his nose, and his face grew cold and numb as Sir spun away into a gray, swirling mist.

When he came to, he was lying in the tub, half-immersed in scalding water, and Sir was scrubbing his backside and privates with a Brillo pad. The water was bright red with blood. His face felt as though there was a huge bone sticking out of it where his nose should have been. He gingerly touched it and pain exploded in his head, knocking him out again and bringing a fresh torrent of blood gushing over his mouth and chin to color the water an even deeper crimson around him.

Billy slumps against the windowsill, staring blankly as two cops run over to the EMT lying on the grass near the end of the driveway. They pick the man up and start to carry him off. He is suddenly aware of The Monster standing behind and over him, aiming at the men and shooting at them.

He crows triumphantly seeing the cops drop the wounded medical technician in order to take cover. *He* looks at the gun and smiles.

(I'm pretty good with this.)

Bet you can't shoot yourself in the head!

He laughs.

(Good one, Johnny-boy, but not too fucking bright. Remember, if I go, you come with me. Besides, we're not dead yet—you see their faces when I held up the kid? Believe me, we'll get what we want.)

I don't want anything. I just want this to end.

(In for a penny, in for a pound, Johnny-boy. You've killed too many people.)

No! I didn't kill anyone! You did!

The Monster laughs again.

(What? Are you starting to believe the bullshit you've been feeding the kid? Look in the mirror, fuck-face, and tell me who *I* am?)

As Billy continues to watch, unable to move, another cop car pulls up. The siren dies, but the lights remain flashing. A man in a suit gets out. He surveys the situation and immediately springs into action. He pulls out a gun and dashes to cover behind the Verizon truck. Running fast and low, he vaults the wooden ranch fence that partially encloses the yard and sprints across the lawn to the downed EMT.

"That guy's got balls," The Monster says behind Billy. Another ambulance appears on Ledgemore Street, backing up toward the cop and the EMT. It stops short of the driveway, and the driver gets out.

"Another guy with balls," The Monster says.

The suited cop and the ambulance driver lift the wounded man, who starts screaming in pain. Together they carry the man to the ambulance and get him inside.

"Captain Burke!" one of the uniformed officers yells to the guy in the suit. "We got wounded out front, too! I don't know if there's more than one shooter in there, but he's got hostages."

"The front of the house!" The Monster cries suddenly and runs from the room. Billy lets go of the windowsill and slowly slides to the floor.

He ducks to the right as he reaches the front window. The cops there are quickly helping EMTs load the rookie into an ambulance. A policeman providing cover from behind the cruiser parked in the middle of Warren Street spies him in the window and sends a bullet smashing into the window frame less than a foot from his head.

He retaliates—firing, ducking back, firing again. *His* second salvo catches the cop in the forehead just as he rises above the edge of the car roof for another shot. As if by magic, a hole appears just below his hairline. His hat flies off, accompanied by a spray of flesh and blood, and he falls to the asphalt.

Across the street, Mrs. Canard screams so loudly it makes him jump. "Oh my God!" she cries, as the cop goes down. "The back of his head exploded!"

He peers across the street and sees the fat woman on her porch, framed in the screen door, a bag of microwave popcorn in her hands.

(She's watching this like it's a fucking movie!)

Mrs. Canard suddenly turns and spews popcorn all over her porch floor. The sound of it dredges up a memory that overwhelms and stupefies *Him* for a moment:

Hungry.
Thirsty.
In the dark a long time. How long exactly, he didn't know.

But it was certainly long enough that he felt weak from lack of food and water.

Necessity made him move from The Brig under the workbench. The ancient instinctual drive to survive made him brave enough to crawl out of the dark, cobwebby space and go lick drops of water from the faucet in the sink by the door. He didn't dare turn the water on—Sir would hear and wouldn't like it. Thankfully, the faucet leaked and he could quietly lick water from it if he was patient.

Those meager drips, however, barely quenched his thirst. He was about to risk turning on the water for a quick drink when he noticed something in the large trash barrel in the corner—a small bag of salted cashews, half full. Unable to believe his good fortune, he grabbed the bag and devoured the nuts.

The initial pleasure of the food gave way to increased thirst as the salt on the nuts worked on him. Unable to stand it anymore, he took the ultimate risk: turning on the faucet and drinking from the tap.

The consequences were immediate.

"Don't tell me you're getting a drink!" *Sir yelled from the kitchen above. The cellar door opened.*

"You are not where you are supposed to be, puke. Who gave you permission to get out of The Brig?"

He was frozen with fright. A cold sweat broke from every pore on his body. Even Sir's heavy footsteps descending the stairs couldn't get him moving. He awaited his fate in dreadful silence.

Sir stopped in the doorway of the workshop, his hands up above his head, on either side of the frame. The light from the workshop's two windows reflected off the lenses of his square, black plastic-frame glasses, turning them silvery white and blind. Sir's crew cut seemed to bristle as he looked down at the empty cashew wrapper on the floor, and then the water dripping rapidly from the faucet he hadn't closed tightly enough.

"You've been breaking regulations again, puke. Now . . . you're going to *do* what you *are—puke*!"

Sir grabbed him by the back of the head, roughly entwining his fingertips in the dirty, knotted hair, and dragged him to the sink. He thrust his head into the basin.

"Open your mouth!"

He did as he was told. Sir immediately jammed a finger down his throat until he retched. Sir kept his finger there until he vomited.

(I can't stand that sound!)

He draws a bead on the shadowy form of Mrs. Canard framed in the doorway, bent over as she continues to throw up. *He* squeezes off a shot. In mid-retch Mrs. Canard lets out a deep groan and flops to her porch floor.

(Bingo! We just did the neighborhood a favor, Johnny-boy! Give that man a see-gar!)

The cops out front return fire again, but he ducks to the side. Just as he's about to retaliate, the air is filled with a loud, amplified metallic voice: "Cease Fire!" it orders and the police obey. Then it speaks to him.

"John Teags? This is Captain Tim Burke of the Connecticut State Police! I'd like to talk to you."

Billy is startled by the bullhorn. He pulls himself up to the windowsill just enough to look over the edge. The police are all hiding, except for the man with the bullhorn; the policeman in the business suit who saved the EMT.

(The one The Monster said had balls!)

The approach of The Monster from behind makes him cower, but he is surprised when he hears his father answer the policeman.

"What do you want?" he shouts.

A burst of scratchy, electrical crackling gives way to a metallic voice. "We want a cease-fire, John. We want to know what's wrong. We want to help you. But first, you've got to let us get help to our wounded. In good faith, John, let us get them to the ambulances, then we can talk."

His father looks at him. Billy nods. His father nods back.

"Okay!" he shouts from the left side of the window.

"Thank you, John," comes the static-filled reply.

There is the sound of movement outside—feet running, sprinkled with commands to bring up stretchers and get EMTs, mingled with the cries and screams of the wounded as they are moved. Billy lifts his head above the sill again and watches as cops, both local and state, plus several EMTs, scurry about trying to get all the people killed or hurt by The Monster out of harm's way as soon as possible. His father watches, too, then slides down the wall until he's sitting on the floor on the left side of the window. Billy sits back on the right side and looks at his father, his face still streaked with blood . . .

(Other peoples' blood!)

. . . his hair tangled and matted with blood, his clothes stained with blood.

(Ditto!)

Billy smiles sadly. Dad taught him the meaning and use of "ditto" back in a happier time.

(Before The Monster.)

Now his father looks so sad Billy is tempted to crawl into his arms and hug him.

(I wouldn't do that—he could turn back into The Monster at any moment!)

"I'm so sorry, Billy," his dad says. "I'm so sorry for everything that's happened." Tears run down his face, the drops turning red as they gather blood from his skin.

Billy can't help himself; he cries, too.

(You are such a *baby*!)

"I'm sorry, too, Dad," Billy says.

(What've you got to be sorry for?)

His father shakes his head. "No, Billy. You've got nothing to be sorry about."

(See? Told you.)

Billy shakes his head in disagreement. "I created The Monster. *My* crying did it."

His father sighs deeply and slowly. "But you couldn't help that, Billy, you were just a baby." He stares at the floor; his eyes far away. "Why did he do it?" he asks softly, vaguely.

Billy, confused, looks around. "Who, Dad?" he ventures.

His father looks at him. "Sir. Why did he do the things he did to me? Why did he hurt me so bad?"

(We could ask the same thing of you!)

"Why did he hate me so much? Was it just the crying? I don't hate Jimmy, and I never hated you, Bill."

Billy doesn't know what to say.

"I never wanted to hurt Sir, but in the end I didn't have a choice." His father looks at him and cocks his head to the right. A faraway remembering look comes over him. Emotions flit over his face. "You ever feel like you're in a movie, or on TV? Like everything that's happening *looks* real, but it's all just special effects? That's how it was the day Sir died. I listened to *him* yelling and swearing and hurling insults up at Sir in the kitchen, then Sir bellowing back, all in a rage. I wanted to stop *him* from yelling, but I was too weak."

A look of panic suddenly crosses his face, and he struggles to breathe. "It struck me as funny," he gasps. "I couldn't stop laughing . . . . I didn't want to hurt Sir, I swear—much less kill him! But *he* said we were going to *die* if we didn't do something.

"You know, I never told anyone about *him* before.

Not the police when they took me away as a child, not the social workers, not my friends at the asylum, not even Doctor Rathbone, my psychiatrist. I told *you*. Only you. You know why? 'Cause I know you've got the same *voice* in your head."

(Me?)

"You hear it, too, don't you, Bill?" He looks at Billy intently. "You hear it, don't you?"

(Is he talking about me?)

Billy nods.

"I knew it! I knew you had a voice, too." He looks around secretively and whispers, "You hear the voice of the . . . *other* . . . *you*! You hear the voice of *him*!"

(Hey! I'm not *him*! I'm no monster!)

Billy nods again.

(What? Don't just sit there, bobbing your head up and down like an idiot. Tell him!)

"I knew it! I knew it! We're so much alike!" He grins proudly.

(Tell him I'm not The Monster!)

"When did *you* start hearing it?" Dad asks, looking at him intensely

"I don't know," Billy answers truthfully. "I guess it's always been there."

(I am not an *it*!)

"Dad," Billy goes on, ignoring his alter ego, and changing the subject, "You've got to help me. And I can help you, too, Dad. Together we can stop The Monster. We can't let it kill anyone else."

Before his father can answer, the conversation is abruptly interrupted by the bullhorn: "John! John Teags. Are you there, John? Can you hear me?"

* * *

John groans and looks at the boy. "What do you want?" he shouts, raising his eyes to the window.

"I tried calling your telephone, John, but it's out of order!"

(No shit!)

"Do you have a cell phone that I can call you on so we can work this out with nobody else getting hurt?"

John looks doubtful for a moment until he sees his son looking eagerly at him, and he remembers Mrs. Luts's cell phone in his pocket. He places one of the pistols on the floor and rolls onto his side to dig the phone out of his pants pocket.

"Yeah!" he yells up toward the window, "I got a cell!" He pulls it out.

"Good!" the bullhorn voice answers. "Call nine-one-one and tell the operator who you are so you can be patched through to my cell. Then we can talk privately and work things out, okay?"

John shouts the policeman's last word back at him and looks at the boy. "I think everything is going to be all right now," he says. He holds up the cell phone. "We've got a new plan."

He gets off the floor, picks up the pistol, and stuffs it into his waistband. He winks at the boy and goes into the hallway.

(He's lying.)

Billy remains on the floor by the window.

(He said: "We got a new plan!" If he and The Monster are separate, how come he's always saying *we*?)

Billy isn't sure what to think anymore. His father's use of *we* and talking to himself in the voice of The Monster certainly seem to indicate they are inseparable.

(And if he lied about that, your little plan goes out the window.)

"It doesn't matter," Billy mumbles, almost too exhausted to speak. "The cops are here, and he's going to talk to them. They'll get him to give up."

(You think so? I think he likes killing too much to just give up. Anyway, you know what's going to happen if he *doesn't* give up, don't you?)

Billy knows, and he doesn't want to think about it.

John goes down the hallway to his and Molly's bedroom and dials 911 on the cell phone. Before the emergency operator can say more than a word, *he* interrupts, "This is John Teags!"

"Hold on one moment, please, while I transfer you." She sounds nervous.

"Mister Teags?" A male voice comes on the line. "John? Can I call you John?"

"Sure," *he* answers. "You can call me anything you want as long as you don't call me late for dinner."

There is silence on the line.

"That's a joke, son," *he* says, impersonating Foghorn Leghorn's Southern drawl.

"Um, yeah," the cop sounds nonplussed. "John? My name is Tim, Tim Burke, and I want to help you."

"Then listen, Timmy-boy, and listen good," *he* growls into the cell phone. "I've got hostages, so you're going to give me what I want then back off and let me go, or I start throwing dead bodies out the window. *Capisce?*"

"I'm sure we can work this out," the cop replies calmly.

"Good. I want a vehicle—something big like an SUV—and I want the roads cleared to Blackstone Airport, where you're going to have a commercial airliner fueled and waiting for me and my hostages to get on board." *He* pauses and looks at John's watch. "And if that's not happening within fifteen minutes, someone in here is going to die, and it won't be me."

"Okay. Take it easy, John. You don't want to hurt anyone in there—isn't your son in there with you, John? You don't want to hurt him."

"I don't give a shit about him! Besides, I've got other hostages—the next-door neighbor, Luts, and the telephone repairman, Dave something, and Donny Desmond, the son of the woman who got hit by the car out front. Not to mention I think a couple of the cops in here might still be alive, so don't fuck with me!"

"Okay! Okay, John," Burke replies hastily, nervously.

He smiles, sensing victory.

"I'll see what I can do, John, but it's going to take longer than fifteen minutes. I'm going to need an hour, maybe an hour and a half, to make all the arrangements you want."

"Bullshit! I'll give you half an hour." *He* hangs up.

(What'd I tell you, Johnny-boy? Like taking candy from a dead baby.)

But where are we going to go?

(Mexico. South America. Colombia. How about Afghanistan? We'll say we're Muslims.)

You're crazy. This is crazy. They're never going to meet your demands.

(I think you're wrong there, Johnny-boy. You'd be surprised what they'll do to save the lives of the innocent.)

But Misses Luts and Donny and the phone guy are all dead. You said they were hostages.

(They don't know that! Smarten up, puke! Besides, the kid's our ace-in-the-hole.)

You can't hurt Billy.

(I won't . . . have to if he tells us where the baby is. We're not going anywhere until I finish business. You got to get it out of him, Johnny-boy . . . or *I* will.)

* * *

"Billy, we need to talk."

(Careful!)

His father stands in the nursery doorway. He leans forward enough to look out the side window and drops to a crouch. He duckwalks over and between the ruins of the crib and by the toppled bureau, to where Billy still sits by the window.

"Billy?" he whispers and looks over his shoulder. "I've got an idea."

(Watch it! Don't trust him.)

Billy looks hopeful. "Yeah?"

His father looks around again before going on. "I think I've figured out a way for you to escape."

Billy's hopefulness turns wary. "But, Dad . . . the police. . . . Didn't you just talk to them?"

"Yeah, yeah, sure," his father says quickly. "But still, I'd rather get you out of harm's way before . . ." He hesitates and looks toward the window. "I just want you to be safe," he finishes, smiling sadly at Billy.

(If the plan involves *stabbing* you, forget it!)

"What are you going to do?" Billy asks, watching his father's face closely.

"*He*—The Monster—wants Jimmy, Billy. *He* wants Jimmy real bad."

Billy refuses with an adamant shake of his head.

"No, no, no. It's okay. I know how you feel, Bill. It's just that . . ." His father pauses and lowers his head and his voice. "It's just that if you tell him where Jimmy is, then I can help you escape while *He*'s distracted with the baby."

(Hell–o! We have just gone way beyond *The Twilight Zone.*)

"No," Billy says with a note of resignation.

His father winces at the denial. Billy waits for The Monster, but it doesn't come.

"Billy . . . you don't understand," his father says, exasperated. "*He* will hurt you . . . and worse." He thinks for a moment and adds, "Besides, once you're out of the house the police will be able to come in and arrest *him*."

(This is nuts—by him he means . . . him, right?)

"Dad, I don't want anyone else to get killed," Billy says, feeling the tears build again.

"Neither do I, Billy, neither do I," his father replies quickly and anxiously. "And nobody has to. I promise this will work."

(Play along! Maybe he's just nuts enough to be able to do it.)

The phone in John's shirt pocket bursts into song, "Close to You," by The Carpenters. John pulls Mrs. Luts's cell from his pocket and opens it.

"Hello?"

"John? It's Tim Burke again, John. How are you doing?"

John shakes his head, bemused at the policeman's attempt to turn their communication into a casual conversation.

(As if we're old-fucking-buddies!)

His son looks at him with such despair he can't bear it. He gets up and goes into the hallway, then the bathroom, and closes the broken door as best he can.

"I'm . . . I'm fine," he says awkwardly. "Who's this again?"

"It's Tim Burke. Is that you, John? John Teags?"

"Yeah," John replies weakly.

"You sound different, John. Are you all right?"

"Yeah."

"Okay . . . um, John, we almost have everything ready for you, but we need more time to get a plane into the airport. I don't know if you're familiar with Blackstone Airport, but it caters to small craft. No commercial airlines run out of there. We've got to find one willing to land here and take you out." When there is no reply after several seconds, the policeman says, "We're going to need more time, John."

(Okay. That'll give us time to finish business.)

John looks at his watch. "How much more time?"

"Another thirty to forty-five minutes, that's all. We've got a plane on the way from Logan Airport in Boston."

(See? I told you they'd do what we want.)

"Okay," John agrees.

"John . . ." The detective pauses as if unsure of how to proceed. "John, it would be an act of goodwill on your part if you let us get my wounded officers out of there."

He answers, "Sorry, Timmy-boy, but I lied. They ain't wounded. They're all dead."

What'd you say that for? Now they're really going to get us.

There is an extended silence on the line. *He* thinks the cop hung up, but Tim Burke speaks again, his voice strained.

"What about the hostages, then, John? How about you let the hostages go and take me, or one of my men, as your hostage instead. I'll be a lot more use to you as a hostage than any civilian, especially when you get to the airport, or when you want to land somewhere. Why don't you let them go and be safe . . . especially your son. Think about him, John. How about it? We trade—me for them."

(Time for stall tactics.)

"I'll think about it." *He* hangs up.

(You better get the kid to tell you where the baby is, Johnny-boy. Make like the nice daddy or I'll make like the *bad* daddy.)

Don't do this. Please don't do this.

(Chill. Once I take care of business, we can get away and spend lots of quality time with the kid. It'll be on the run, of course, but what the hell? We can't have everything.)

But the cops want to trade. They won't let us leave with Billy. Why'd you tell him his men are dead?

(Fuck the cops. They'll let us go if the boy is our shield, and they think the rest of the hostages are alive and tied up in the cellar. Now go back and find out where the baby is.)

(He's coming back!)

Billy painfully rises to his knees as his father returns to the nursery. Dad looks out the window, then at Billy, and crouches in front of his son. He smiles.

"The police want us to let you go. This is great, Billy. I think if you tell *him* where Jimmy is, in exchange, he'll let you go. Then all this can end."

(Whatever you do, don't try to talk to him anymore! He's crazy! Just play along. You can't talk to crazy people.)

Billy doesn't say anything. The sense of dread and despair that has been his constant companion since yesterday afternoon—

(Seems like a thousand years ago!)

—thickens.

"What do you say, Bill?" his father asks, his voice urgent and nervous.

A shout from outside catches his father's attention, and he rises on his haunches to look out the window. Billy shivers as The Monster's voice comes out of his father's mouth again. "Those double-crossing bastards!"

On Warren Street, just past Ledgemore, two large black delivery-type vans are parked in the street. From the back and side doors of both vehicles, men in paramilitary gear, complete with helmets, gas masks, and automatic rifles, are exiting.

(There's a SWAT team out there!)

With a cry of, "Fuck you!" *he* jumps up to a standing position and opens fire with both pistols. The SWAT team cops are too far away, so *he* aims closer to home and wings his first target—a policeman standing at the back of the Verizon truck. Only a portion of his back is visible, but the shot tears into the middle of the visible area. He clutches at the spot and falls to the street, but is quickly dragged back under cover by Burke, the cop in the suit.

At the first shot, the police scatter.

His second shot shatters the side window of one of the cruisers parked on Ledgemore Street. Several cops in the road had ducked behind the squad car, but when the window blows out they run pell-mell for better coverage. *He* gets one of them on the fly. He isn't sure where the man is hit, but in mid-run he suddenly does an arm-flailing pirouette and spins to a heap in the middle of the road.

At the third shot—within the space of two seconds—the police return fire. The SWAT team divides into two lines that come charging up Warren to the corner of Ledgemore where they spread out. *He* ducks to the left and shoots around the window frame at them, but the gun clicks emptily. He tosses it aside and tries the other. It, too, is empty. He stuffs it into the waistband of his pants

"Don't go anywhere, Billy-boy!" *he* says to the boy and scrabbles on his hands and knees into the hallway, crawling to the stairs and down.

As the police return fire, Billy screams and curls into a ball on the floor, hugging his knees to his chest. The room is alive with bullets slamming into the walls and ceiling, knocking out chunks of plaster that shower down upon him. The air in the room is full of *zinging, whizzing* sounds. Outside he can hear odd popping noises that he realizes must be gunshots, even though they sound like cap guns.

As soon as The Monster goes downstairs and stops shooting, the police stop, too. After a few moments of quiet, broken only by the squawking of numerous police radios, Billy gets off the floor and ventures a peek out the window. He is surprised to see a group of what look like army guys taking up positions along Ledgemore Street and training their rifles on the house. Another group of army guys are weaving up Warren Street, running from car to car, tree to tree, telephone pole to car wreck, and so on, taking up similar positions as they make their way to the front of the house.

(They must be the SWAT team The Monster was just talking about.)

As Billy watches, the EMTs and other local police run to the wounded and hurry them to safety. Billy realizes the SWAT team cops are providing cover so that the wounded can be rescued. As soon as that's done . . .

(Uh-oh!)

. . . he's pretty sure the cops will storm the house . . .

(Especially since Dad keeps killing them!)

. . . and more of them will die. His father, too.

(Nothing you can do. You should just hide until it's all over.)

Billy can't do that.

(Don't give me that, "It's my fault," crap again.)

But it is.

Somehow he has to find a way to stop The Monster from killing anyone else.

At the bottom of the stairs John comes upon the cop he killed. The man's face is hidden in blood. The last four steps are slick with his brains and the red stuff. Weeping silently, battling back nausea, John pries the cop's gun from his hand with a good deal of effort. He then checks the cop's belt and finds two extra ammo clips. He puts them in his pocket.

(Good work, Johnny-boy. I think we're going to need lots of ammo before this day is done.)

John steps over the dead cop, being careful not to expose himself in the smashed window of the front door. He can hear activity out in the street. The tread of many boots. Metal clicking and clacking as guns are checked, cocked, and aimed.

(The SWAT team's getting ready to make a move.)

"Why did you have to shoot at them again? They were negotiating!"

(Don't be such a dumb ass, Johnny-boy. It's over. They never had any intention of negotiating. They've been fucking with us, stalling for time until the SWAT team was ready to take us out.)

John steps into the kitchen, staying low, and awkwardly crosses to the dead cop lying on the floor next to the telephone repairman in front of the refrigerator. He takes the two spare gun cartridges off the policeman's belt and pockets them as well. On elbows and knees—gun in his right hand—he crawls to the breakfast nook windows. He lifts his head just enough to see out at the backyard and the driveway. Just as he notices a SWAT commando at the far rear corner of the garage taking a bead on him with his high-powered rifle, the man fires at him.

John dives to the floor as the bullet smashes through the screen and window and creates a crater in the wall behind him. A framed, colored ink drawing of radishes falls off the wall and shatters on the floor, adding its glass to the shards from the window.

(Whew! That was fucking close!)

With one of the breakfast nook windows shot out, it's easy for *him* to pop up and fire two shots and duck again. This immediately draws heavy fire again from all sides of the house. The air is thick with the sound of bullets flying and smashing into walls, furniture, lights, and ceilings in every room. The noise is incredibly loud and abrasive; it hurts the ears. The house shudders under the onslaught.

(Enough fucking around, Johnny-boy! We need to show them we mean business.)

He shoves the pistol in his pants, next to the empty one, and crawls on his stomach to the cellar door, pulls it open, and scrambles through and down.

Billy is on his feet, at the nursery door, about to go down and make one last plea with his father to give up, even though he fears—

(Dad's crazy as a bedbug.)

—it's useless. But one step into the hallway and the world explodes. Just in time he throws himself to the carpeted hallway floor as a bullet rips into the wall where his head had just been.

(You should get under cover!)

Billy lies on the floor, hands over his ears. He doesn't dare move. The assault of gunfire on the house grows worse. He can feel the house shaking with the impact of all the bullets striking it. The noise is so loud and awful he screams in a futile attempt to drown it out.

Abruptly, the hail of bullets is interrupted by a repeated command from the bullhorn: "Cease fire! Cease fire!" Silence descends.

Billy tries to raise his head, but he is too dazed and dizzy to succeed for several moments. His shell-shocked ears are ringing.

(But I can still hear The Monster coming!)

Billy looks up as The Monster reaches the top of the stairs.

(He's got Donny!)

In its arms The Monster does indeed carry the limp, lifeless body of Donny Desmond, still sporting the nail protruding from his forehead. The Monster stops at the top of the stairs next to the shot-out window and shouts, "Hey coppers! I got a present for you. Nice work! There's more where this came from. Just keep it up!"

Grunting with exertion, The Monster swings Donny Desmond's body back and forth a couple of times and tosses him out the open window. The sound of his body hitting the ground is accompanied by cries of shock and disbelief from outside. The Monster peers around the edge of the window frame and chuckles gleefully.

"Here they come!" The Monster says softly. "That's it. Pick the kid up. Yeah, that's it. See what we did to him? Nailed him good, didn't we? Now you'll fucking listen, won't you? Now you know we're not fucking kidding around here. Go, go on. Carry the kid off. I ain't gonna shoot you." The Monster chuckles again. "Not yet anyway." It cups one hand around its mouth for amplification and shouts, "Back off, or I will kill another hostage!"

The Monster looks over its shoulder at Billy and suddenly runs toward him, hunched over, face wearing a fierce and cruel grin under the dried blood. Billy shudders once again at how different The Monster can make his father's face look.

(I'll never get used to how he can look like a whole new person. Um, monster.)

Billy struggles up to a sitting position, his back against the nursery door frame. The Monster crouches in front of him. It sniffs. Billy watches a drop of bloody sweat at the end of The Monster's nose go up its nostril.

The Monster sneezes.

"God bless you," Billy says automatically.

The Monster looks at him strangely, then sadly, and Billy sees his father shine through.

"Dad?" he calls immediately, pleadingly. "I know you're in there, Dad. I know you are!" he blurts out. "You got to be stronger than The Monster, Dad. You can do it. I know you can!" His voice, distorted by dried blood caked in his broken nose, still sounds as though he has a bad cold. The effort of speaking hurts. His vision wavers and grays. For a few moments he can hear nothing but the pounding of his heartbeat. Slowly his vision returns only to reveal The Monster just inches from his face, laughing at him.

"I doh you're in dare, Da-ad! I doh you are!" The Monster mimics him. It leans back on its haunches. Its smile disappears. "I'm tired of this game, kid. It's over. I guess I don't have time to give a shit about the baby anymore. Things have gone way beyond that. Right now, you're my coat of invincibility, my suit of armor, and my ticket out of this. So forget about your father coming out and helping you. You can't call your father out to rescue you like in one of those stupid movies he used to watch with you because he *never left*! Get it? *He never left*!"

(Tell me something I don't know.)

But Billy shakes his head in vehement denial. "No," he croaks, but it comes out as "Doh!"

(You sound like Homer Simpson!)

"Yes, Homer," The Monster quips, too, and giggles. "I'm sorry to say that what we have here are not two personalities. I'm not Sybil. This isn't *The Three Faces of John*."

Billy has no knowledge of the references The Monster is making, but he understands its meaning too perfectly.

The Monster laughs. "Or you can think of it as a *vice versa*—I'm the real John Teags, and your dad is the monster. It doesn't really matter." The Monster laughs again, but stops abruptly and looks at Billy with confusion, as if it suddenly lost its train of thought.

"You're a liar!" Billy sobs, his side burning with pain. "You're not my father! My father is good and nice. He would never do anything to hurt anyone. You're not my father." The last word comes out as *fahder.* "You're not," he finishes softly. Tears flow from his eyes, and he can't keep his facial muscles from creasing as he cries. The movement brings pain, causing more tears, which, in turn, increases the hurt.

The Monster throws its hands up in the air, looks at the ceiling, and shakes its head. "I only wish that were true, my boy. I only wish that were true!" *it* cries with exaggeration and looks at him. "There's no denying it: You are the fruit of *my* loins. Whether you like it or not, this is kinda like *Star Wars.* You know the part when Darth Vader says, 'Luke, I am your father!' Only now it's 'Billyboy! I am your father!' " The Monster stands. "Sorry, kid. There's only one way out now." It looks around. "Bestlaid plans of mice and monsters," *it* says and chuckles.

Billy can hear his father in the laugh. The Monster grabs his arm and lifts him off his feet. As it drags him downstairs, Billy faints from the pain and succumbs to the overpowering connection between their two minds as he is plummeted senses-first into hell.

The air was thick with flies; the stench terrible. Twice in the past two days Sir messed himself—the first time while being skinned; the second time when bleach was added to the salt on his raw flesh. Sir hadn't moved since then, despite being prodded with his foot, poked with a screwdriver, stabbed with the same screwdriver, and finally burned with wooden matches from a box Sir kept on the workbench.

Sir was still breathing, though; his chest moved up and down, barely perceptible to the eye. He can hear the air whistling in and out of Sir's open mouth. A pulse could be seen in the exposed veins in his arms and neck.

He looked around for something suitable to put a fitting end to Sir's life. He knew what he wanted and found it in one of Sir's ski poles stored in the cellar. He broke off the round, plastic bottom piece, so that it resembled a giant pin.

"Now you can be just like one of your damned insects," he said as he plunged the pole into Sir's chest, pulled it out, and thrust it in again and again until his arms felt like lead, and he could no longer lift the ski pole.

Walking like *The Hunchback of Notre Dame*—another horror-night movie Billy watched with his father—The Monster drags Billy into the kitchen and shoves him into the corner nearest the door to the front hallway before it cautiously ducks through the breakfast nook to the windows.

Billy's vision clears and the memory fades, but something remains . . .

(I knew it!)

. . . something that has been nagging at the edges of his mind but now becomes clear—while he was witnessing Sir's torture and death, he was inside the mind of *The Monster*, not his father, and not some alter ego of his father's, but the real, live, full-blown—

(Evil, baby-killing—)

—terrifying *Monster*.

(And if The Monster was alive back then, it means *you* didn't create it.)

The Monster had been there, inside his father, right from the start.

(It was always there!)

The Monster has always been inside Dad!

(And vice versa!)

Dad lied.

(If he's lying about this, then he's lying about everything.)

The realization hurts and . . .

(I hate to say I told you so but . . .)

. . . the implications are too shocking for Billy to
think about right now.

(Then there's only one thing left to do!)

Reluctantly, Billy agrees. He's avoided thinking about
it, but now . . .

(You have no choice.)

. . . he knows he has to stop The Monster somehow,
someway . . . but how?

(Isn't it obvious? The Monster showed you!)

The cell phone in John's shirt pocket erupts into
"Close to You." *He* answers it.

"It's your dime, go ahead."

There is hesitation on the line, then, "John? Is this
John Teags?"

"The one and only."

"John, what's going on? Why did you kill the boy,
John?" The cop, Burke, sounds sad, weary.

(Yeah, like he gave a rat's ass about the kid!)

"I thought we had an understanding, John."

"Fuck your understanding," *he* replies. "You've got a
SWAT team in position to take me out. But if they don't
back off, another hostage will die!"

"Listen John—"

"No! You listen, puke! If I want any shit from you I'll
whistle, and you can come sliding in! If I don't get what
I want and soon, more hostages are going to die, and
their blood will be on your head! I want a car with a full
tank of gas, and I want it now. I want every cop in the

neighborhood gone. You've got fifteen minutes." *He* snaps the cell phone shut.

"Get over here, Billy-boy."

"Dad," the boy whimpers, "please just give up. Dad, can you hear me?"

"You know, for someone who's supposed to be so smart, you're a bit thick," *he* says with a sigh.

"You're not my father!" the boy blurts out. "Dad said you were separate."

"Really? Let me see . . ." *He* says with exaggerated thoughtfulness, hand on chin. "Gee—do you think he might have . . . *lied?*" A sound outside draws his attention. *He* looks to the window. "They're not going for it. They're moving in for the kill, the fuckers. This is it. Get over here, Billy-boy."

The boy defiantly shakes his head.

"Wrong answer, puke."

(Move! Run! Get down to the cellar before he grabs you again!)

Before Billy can do anything, there is a crash and a round canister smashes through the remaining unbroken glass in the far left breakfast nook window. It clatters to the floor and emits a thick, billowing cloud of acrid green smoke. Gunfire from outside renews as The Monster picks up the canister—howling in pain as it does—and throws it back through the window and outside as two more smoking cylinders come smashing through the window over the sink and the broken window on the front door in the hallway. The house fills with smoke.

(Now! Go!)

Behind the choking green cloud, Billy runs to the cellar door as fast as his injured body can manage.

Somewhere in the fog, The Monster roars with rage and what sounds like pain as bullets whiz through the kitchen, attacking the walls again.

(Maybe he got shot!)

Billy finds the doorknob of the cellar door amid the foul smoke and flings it open. He plunges down the stairs, nearly falling in his panic to get out of the line of fire.

(Go! Go! Go!)

At the bottom he pauses and whispers aloud, "There's no fishing line down here."

(Something in the workshop, then.)

Upstairs the sound of The Monster's return fire is loud and strung together by its equally loud curses.

Billy goes to the workshop door and looks around, doing his best again not to look at Mrs. Luts, his mom, and Kevin. On the floor of the workshop by the bulkhead stairs next to where the Monster originally dumped Mrs. Luts's body, he spies what he needs.

(That'll work!)

But the thing is slick with blood . . .

(Don't think about that.)

. . . and there are clumps of bleached blond hair, like Mrs. Luts's stuck to it and more—*red* hair the same color as . . .

(I said don't think about that!)

. . . his mother's.

(Way to go! You *never* listen to me!)

Despite an urge to look at his mother's body and confirm that it is her hair—and probably her blood—on the marble rolling pin, he keeps his eyes averted and picks up the pin by its relatively clean end—the end The Monster must have held it by when it was killing Mrs. Luts and his . . .

(Don't do this again!)

He doesn't. He shakes most of the hair and bloody

clumps off and carries the rolling pin like a thing diseased to the stairs. As quietly as possible he climbs the steps, holding the thing away from him, afraid to let it touch more than his hand and even more afraid of dropping it lest The Monster should hear.

Thin tendrils of putrid smoke seep under the door at the top of the stairs. On the other side of it—so close, so loud—The Monster is screaming with pain and anger and cursing at the same time until it is all just a jumble of incoherent noise. It never stops firing its weapon as it jabbers.

(Better work fast!)

Carefully, using both hands even though it means he has to touch the blood and gore on the rolling pin, he lays it on the very top step of the cellar stairs. It rolls a few inches, making him panic and fear that the step isn't level enough to hold the round pin without it rolling off, but then it stops and remains still. As quietly as he climbed, Billy descends to the bottom of the stairs and runs to the workshop, where he grabs the nail gun. Playing the extension cord out as he carries the gun, he takes it as far as he can—just reaching the bottom of the stairs. He raises it and sights along the top the way The Monster did when he aimed it at him before.

(Can you really shoot that thing?)

Billy isn't sure, but he thinks he can. He saw how The Monster did it.

(No, I mean can *you* really shoot *that* Thing? The Monster . . . who also happens to be Dad! If the fall doesn't stop him . . . can you?)

Billy has to admit he doesn't know.

He looks to the door at the top of the stairs and wonders how to get The Monster to come down after him, especially when the cops outside are shooting at it and keeping it occupied.

(You make it come down, just like The Monster did to Sir.)

"I don't think I can do that," Billy whispers.

(Don't worry. Let me handle it. *I* know *exactly* what to say.)

The first canister of tear gas is so hot it sears *his* palm as he throws it out the window. The pain is enraging. Oblivious to the bullets flying, he lets loose with a scream of babbled curses, screams, and grunts and shoots back. Brandishing one of the police pistols in his good left hand he fires so fast the gun jams. *He* tosses it aside and pulls the other from his waistband. Fumbling it with his injured hand, *he* manages to discharge the empty clip and pull a fresh one from his pocket. *He* rams it home into the handle of the pistol.

He ducks against the kitchen door as the room fills with tear gas. *He* stands and smashes out the window in the door with the butt of the gun in an attempt to get some air. A slug rips into *his* right bicep. It spins him around, and he falls to the floor with a cry of pain, dropping the gun. Grabbing at his arm, groaning, *he* pushes himself up to a sitting position against the space of wall between the porch door and the cellar door. Coughing and choking, *he* leans over and retrieves the gun before it disappears from view in the encroaching noxious green fog.

(This is it, Johnny-boy. Do-or-die time. Just remember it ain't over till it's over.)

He looks around, his eyes burning and tearing. Gas surrounds him, making him blind as well.

(Where's the kid?)

"Time to haul ass, Billy-boy!" *he* shouts, laughing and coughing at the same time. "We got to make like a banana and split!"

From far away, nearly drowned out by the gunfire, he thinks he hears a baby crying.

(Jimmy?)

It sounds like it's coming from upstairs, from the nursery.

"Hey! You old fuck-face! Why don't you come down here and get me so I can kick your ass?"

The voice from the cellar distracts him from the faint crying.

(That doesn't sound like Billy-boy!)

"What did you say?" *He* coughs and asks, hesitantly, as he reaches for the cellar door.

(That sounded like—)

"You heard me, *puke*! Clean the shit out of your ears!"

(—*me*! That sounds like *me*! That little bastard! He's got to pay now, Johnny-boy. Now he's got to *really* pay.)

Billy listens to the voice coming out of his mouth and is fascinated and *terrified* by it at the same time. He's lived a long time with the voice in his head—since he was born and became aware of The Monster, he realizes—but he's never heard the voice *speak* outside his head. He has *never* let it out, never vocalized it. Though it has always felt like him, and he's always accepted it as the wisecracking side of him that is too afraid to speak out and really say what he is thinking, he is surprised at how *different* it sounds outside his head. He is frightened by how *alien* it feels. Suddenly it's as though there is a whole other *person* inside him—the voice of his alter ego is the voice of a completely *new* person even as he knows it is still just him, still in *his* head.

Billy flinches as the cellar door is whipped open. Coughing from the green tear gas swirling around it, The Monster shoots at him. Bullets slam into the wooden railing about halfway down, sending splinters flying in every direction. Just as Billy ducks and tumbles to the side,

The Monster starts down the stairs and steps on the rolling pin.

The entire fall happens loudly and violently in the space of a few seconds, but feels much longer to Billy. The Monster's left foot rolls on the pin and slides off the step. The rolling pin flies off the side of the stairs and disappears into the cellar's mess. The Monster crashes into the left wall, knocking down the rest of the barbecuing implements hanging there, and careens forward, holding the gun up as if afraid the pistol might break in the fall.

The gun doesn't, but The Monster does, even though it never utters a sound as it tumbles down the stairs.

Its left foot gets caught for a moment between the second and third stair from the top and the anklebone snaps before the foot twists free. Still The Monster doesn't cry out. It hits the stairs on its left side—a snapping of ribs—and somersaults the rest of the way until, with a loud *crack*, its head strikes the stone wall opposite the bottom of the stairs. The gun flies from its hand and clatters away behind the nearest pile of overturned newspapers. The Monster lies on its left side, blood seeping out from under its bent head, its legs twisted on the three bottom steps above it, a jagged bone jutting out of its left ankle through its bloody sock. It doesn't move.

(He's still breathing.)

Billy can see its chest rising and falling. Moving slowly, never taking his eyes off The Monster, Billy bends down and picks up the nail gun. He raises the electric tool and points it with shaking hands.

(Get closer! You might miss from here!)

Billy obeys the voice now as though it belongs to someone older, someone wiser who knows what to do and to whom he should listen.

He takes a step closer. The trembling of his hands increases, and the nail gun rattles.

(Closer! Shoot it right in the forehead just like it did to Donny.)

Billy takes another step. He's a foot away.

(Now! Do it now! Nail the bastard!)

Billy tries to pull the trigger, but he can't do it. No matter how much he wills his finger to move and squeeze the trigger, he can't do it . . .

(Don't trust it—)

. . . he has no choice.

(—just shoot it!)

He can't *see* The Monster anymore.

(No! It's a trick!)

There is only his father, unconscious; no sign of The Monster in his face. Billy just *can't* shoot him.

(This is a mistake!)

The eyes open and his father looks at him . . .

(He's still The Monster—)

. . . and smiles weakly.

(—even if he looks and acts like Dad, haven't you learned anything?)

Billy sees no sign whatsoever of The Monster in his father's eyes.

(He's still there! I'm warning you!)

He sees only his father looking sadder, despite the smile, than Billy has ever seen him . . .

(Don't—)

. . . looking as lost and frightened as a little child about to start bawling.

(—trust—)

"Billy," his father whispers. A look of pain crosses his face.

(—him!)

Billy lets go of the nail gun. It clatters to the cellar floor. He goes to his father and drops to his knees at the bottom of the stairs next to him.

"I'm sorry, Dad," Billy sobs, tears running freely

down his cheeks. "I had to do it. I had to stop The Monster."

"I know, Bill," his father replies, his face and voice strained and full of pain. "It's okay. It's okay. I'm sorry, too. You know I'd never hurt you or your mom, or Kevin or Jimmy . . . I just . . . couldn't . . ." His voice trails off. He closes his eyes for a moment.

"Billy," his father gasps, and opens his eyes again, trying to focus. "That voice—the one you just used to lure The Monster—that's the voice you hear in your head, isn't it?"

Billy nods and blubbers tears.

"That's Sir's voice, Billy. I know that voice seems like a part of you, like a close friend, but . . . be careful of it." Pain fills his face and his words end in a moan.

Billy reaches for him—

(Watch it!)

—without thinking. He takes his father's hand and his father's memory takes him. Billy stiffens. His breath catches in his throat. He is immersed in his father's mind more completely than at any previous time—so completely he is almost submerged. He almost drowns. This time he not only sees a memory through his father's eyes, he understands *everything* else in his father's mind as well, every detail, every moment, every memory of his life . . . and The Monster's as well. It dissolves into Billy's mind like a cube of sugar dropped in a glass of lemonade, and he sees . . .

Molly in the kitchen when he walked through the back door early Friday afternoon. Both Kevin and the baby were still sick. Both of them had come down with the flu Tuesday night and had been miserable since. Molly was just about to give Jimmy, who was thankfully quiet though he didn't look well, a bottle of Pedialyte to keep him hydrated; he'd suffered from vomiting and diarrhea for two days. The baby was in his highchair in the breakfast nook, against the left wall, near the table.

Molly was pleasantly surprised to see her husband home early from his trip and asked him to watch Jimmy while she went to CVS to get more children's Tylenol and Pedialyte that the doctor had recommended.

He should have said no. He knew as soon as she asked that he should say no. The thought of spending time alone with little Jimmy made him cringe inwardly. He had purposefully avoided situations like this since the baby came home from the hospital a little over four weeks ago.

Before he could panic, Molly gave Jimmy his bottle, picked up her bag, and kissed his cheek, promising to be right back. Before he could protest, she told him Kevin was sleeping up in his bedroom, and then she was out the door. He stood in the kitchen, arms hanging at his side, staring after her. The house was still. Jimmy quietly sucked on his bottle. He was thankful for that. The tightness in his gut loosened a little. As long as Jimmy remained quiet, or even better, went to sleep, everything would be fine. As long as Jimmy didn't start bawling. . . .

He was okay for the first twenty minutes or so after Molly left. While Jimmy was still greedily, and quietly, sucking on his bottle of Pedialyte, getting hydrated. He picked up his youngest son and carefully carried him up to the nursery where he laid Jimmy in his crib. The infant was close to finishing the bottle and drowsy. As he watched, Jimmy fell asleep, the bottle slipping onto the crib mattress by his side. He closed the door and checked on Kevin in the next room. He, too, was asleep, propped up on pillows on the bottom bunk bed with several comic books strewn about him.

Moving like a burglar, he crept back down the hallway, walking on eggshells, aware that anything—a loose floorboard creaking, a cough, a sneeze, a disturbance in the air—might wake Jimmy. He wasn't going to risk it. Holding his breath, he went down the stairs as slowly and quietly as possible. Not until he was back in the kitchen did he relax.

He sat at the kitchen table for the next ten minutes, eating a bowl of double Dutch chocolate ice cream and staring at the clock, willing Molly to return on time for a change. He knew from experience that when she said she'd be right back it could be anything from a few minutes to a few hours. Usually that was no problem; usually she took Jimmy with her. He likened it to when he'd say there were ten minutes left in a basketball game and still be saying it half an hour later. But this was different; this was the first time since Jimmy was born that he was alone with the baby. He knew he'd been lucky to avoid it for that long. It was inevitable . . . just as he knew it was inevitable that as soon as he was left alone with the baby, Jimmy would cry.

And Jimmy did.

He was sliding the last spoonful of ice cream into his mouth when he heard movement from Kevin's room upstairs. He thought nothing of it at first; as long as it wasn't the baby, everything was hunky-dory. Even when he heard the door to Kevin's and Billy's bedroom, next to the nursery, open, he didn't think there was anything wrong, nothing to worry about. Kevin was just getting up to go to the bathroom; the poor kid was sick with the flu. He had it coming out of both ends and going to the bathroom was a frequent and necessary action.

But the more he thought about it—the more he heard the hallway floorboards creaking and the bathroom door squeaking—the more he got worried that the baby would hear and wake up. He quickly got up and started for the hallway to hurry upstairs and tell Kevin to be extra quiet, when the unthinkable happened.

"Mom?" *Kevin shouted from the bathroom.* "Mom? We're all out of toilet paper!"

He cringed and winced at the sound of Kevin shouting. He wanted to scream, "Shut up, you little idiot! You'll wake the baby!" *But that would have been just as bad. Moving as quickly and as quietly as he could, he ran upstairs.*

"Mo-om? Are you there?" *Kevin shouted again just as*

he reached the hallway. Incredibly, there was still no sound from the baby.

"Shhh! Shhh!" he hissed at his oldest son as he dashed to the bathroom. "Kevin, be quiet!" he whispered as loudly as he dared through the partially closed door.

"Dad? Is that you?" Kevin said loudly.

"Shhh!" he hissed again, but it was too late. The next moment the air was split with the baby's scream.

"No!" he cried in anguish. He put his hands over his ears, but it was futile. "Goddamned fucking son of a bitch!" he bellowed.

The toilet flushed and Kevin opened the bathroom door, his face pale from more than just the flu, his eyes full of fear. Staring at his father, Kevin dashed across the hall to his bedroom and closed the door

He flew downstairs to the kitchen. He had to get another bottle for the baby. It was the only thing he could think of: shove another bottle in Jimmy's mouth, and maybe everything would be okay, maybe he'd shut up. Because if the baby didn't take the bottle, he knew he was in trouble—knew it from the moment the baby had emitted the first high-pitched needling cry.

He couldn't think clearly. Had Jimmy just finished a bottle of Pedialyte? He tried to give him formula anyway, but Jimmy just kept crying. The poor kid just didn't feel well, that's why he was crying; he had a right to cry . . . but did it have to be so . . . excruciating, so abrasive that it left him dazed and unsure if in getting the bottle ready he had bothered to check the temperature of the milk or squeeze the inner bag to be sure only milk came through the nipple and not air. For all he knew he could have given Jimmy steaming hot formula or freezing cold. He couldn't be sure. In the pain brought on by Jimmy's crying, he couldn't even remember what temperature setting and heating time he punched into the microwave oven. Everything that happened after the baby started crying was fuzzy.

His confusion, pain, and irritation did not help to quiet Jimmy. He knew children can sense their parents' feelings and thoughts. He always felt the same way around babies that he felt around cats—afraid. Cats always seemed to sense his fear and knew that they had the upper hand with him and wouldn't leave him alone. It never failed. Put him in a room with a lot of people and a cat and the cat would end up rubbing against him and trying to sit in his lap.

It was the opposite with infants. They sensed his fear of them and that, in turn, made them afraid. Infants don't like fear, especially in adults. They like security, and he could never provide that. If he could just pick little Jimmy up and hold him securely and burp him or cradle him, change him if need be— but he couldn't do that when he was alone. When Molly was around, yes—she made him feel secure; if anything went wrong he knew she could handle it—but not when he was alone.

After Jimmy refused to take the bottle, John pleaded with him to be quiet. When that didn't work he picked the baby up and jiggled him as he nervously shifted from foot to foot and scanned the crib for the baby's pacifier—what Molly called a "tuttoo." Jimmy wouldn't take that either when he laid him down or tried to cram it into his son's mouth. He felt Jimmy's diaper, but it was dry.

"Goddamned kid just likes to fucking cry!" *he fumed in a low voice. The pitch of Jimmy's crying went up a notch as if in answer.*

That was when He *came out. . . .*

It was like a very bright and painful flashbulb went off just behind his eyes. Billy had the sensation of stepping back, but not disconnecting. He was aware of everything, felt everything, and experienced everything with all of his senses. He watched his father's arms and hands reach into the crib for Jimmy. Detached, but not powerless, he continued to watch as his hands slid under the baby's armpits and his arms bent, lifting the child out of the crib. The baby was still crying. It stabbed into his brain.

He heard a voice, yelling and shouting. At first he was too shocked at who the voice sounded like—

(Sir!)

—to understand that the voice was shouting, "Shut up! Shut up, you little puke! Shut the fuck up!"

He watched as his father's arms and hands punctuated each word with a quick jolting shake of the baby, making the infant's little arms and legs flail around and his neck-less head flop back and forth. Miraculously, the baby quieted, but instead of making him feel better, he felt worse for a few moments, nauseous and faint. Slowly the feeling passed. He thanked God that the baby had stopped crying and laid his youngest son back in the crib. He let out a sigh of relief.

As he left the nursery, he looked in on Kevin. He was lying on his bed, a look of fear on his pale face. It was obvious he had heard him *swearing at the baby in the nursery next door.*

"Everything's okay now, Kevin. Sorry I yelled," *he said to the boy.*

The baby not crying was proof that all was okay.

"But if you get up, be quiet!" *he told his oldest son.*

He left and went back to his room at the end of the hall, across from the top of the stairs. Lying on his bed, he heard Kevin get up again. He tensed, but there was no more sound. Whatever Kevin was doing he was being quiet about it.

He relaxed and stared at the ceiling, not thinking of anything in particular, just enjoying the quiet and hoping it would last until Molly came home, when he heard Kevin's footsteps thumping down the hallway. He immediately sat up and swung his legs and feet off the bed, ready to tell Kevin as loudly and quietly as he could to be quiet or else he'd wake the baby again. He never got the chance to say it.

"Dad! I think there's something wrong with Jimmy! He's not moving or breathing or nothing!"

A chill went through him even as he opened his mouth and said, matter-of-factly, "He's okay. He's just sleeping."

Kevin shook his head and looked back down the hall. "I don't think so, Dad. He's not breathing. I went in and checked him. Honest."

The chill took root deep in his spine. He tried to reiterate that Jimmy was only asleep, but the image of him shaking Jimmy belied that. For a long moment he hoped, maybe even believed—actually believed—that just by saying that the baby was fine, time would be reversed and his actions taken back, and there would be little Jimmy lying in his crib . . . crying!

He got off the bed and followed Kevin down the hall to the nursery. Kevin went to the side of the crib and looked down at his baby brother. "See Dad? There's something wrong with him." *Tears filled his eyes and words sobbed from his mouth:* "I think he's . . . d-dead, Dad."

He looked at the baby but said nothing, made no move.

"Dad! Dad! What's wrong with Jimmy?" *Kevin shouted at him; standing by his side, his voice fearful and on the edge of hysteria. He wanted to answer his son, but he wasn't able to focus or concentrate. All he could think about was how peaceful it was when the baby wasn't crying!*

But Kevin disturbed that peace. His voice became shrill as his tears flowed stronger. He began to panic and shouted at his father to do something.

"Dad! The baby isn't breathing! We got to call Mom . . . or . . . or . . . a . . . a ambulance! Where's Mom? Dad! Answer me!" *Over and over, yelling until he had a headache, and couldn't take it any more. Then he came to the rescue again.*

"Shut the fuck up!"

Billy watched his father's arm come up, his right hand shoot out, and his knuckles connect with the side of Kevin's face. The boy spun around, flew off his feet, and hit the doorknob on the nursery's closet door facefirst with a squishy, crunching, splat! He grabbed the hair on the back of Kevin's head before the boy could fall and slammed his face repeatedly into the doorknob.

The sound of Kevin's face against the metal handle was nauseating. The sound was so loud that he automatically looked over his shoulder at the baby, afraid that the noise would wake him, and he would start crying any second.

Baby Jimmy lay in the crib, quiet and unmoving.

He looked down at Kevin lying at the foot of the closet door, facedown on the circus-tent-patterned carpet that covered the nursery floor. His right arm was twisted under him at an odd angle. Beneath his crushed face, the circus print carpet grew dark with blood. He knelt by Kevin and looked at the closet doorknob. It dripped blood and gobs of sopping red flesh. He reached down and carefully rolled his son over and gasped.

He picked Kevin up—the boy's blood rained upon the carpet softly—and carried him into the hallway. He carried Kevin downstairs. Blood ran from Kevin's wounds and left a trail. As he reached the bottom of the stairs, Molly came in the kitchen door. His panic reached a new level. Quickly, he carried Kevin through the living room to the dining room and quietly rolled his body under the edge of the table.

Hearing him in the other room she called softly, "Honey, I'm back. Sorry I took so long. I decided to go to the grocery store and pick up a few things." *She went out again.*

He quickly ran into the kitchen and glanced out the window. Molly was going back to the garage for more shopping bags. He looked desperately for a weapon and found it in Molly's black marble rolling pin, in its white granite holding stand on the counter next to the stove. He stood just inside the door, then thought better of it; someone passing on the street might see. Before Molly returned he went back to the living room and waited.

Molly came in and placed shopping bags on the counter.

"John?" *she called, not too loudly.* "Did you hear me?"

The clink of her keys hitting the kitchen table, as she tossed them there the way she always did, came next.

"I'm in the living room with the baby," *he called.* "Could you give me a hand?"

Billy wanted to warn his mother; wanted to tell her to run but, trapped within The Monster, was unable to do anything except watch, and realize that while he, himself, couldn't do anything—

(This already happened yesterday, after all!)

—his father could have done something. Just as Billy shared his father's memory and felt, smelled, saw, tasted, and heard as his father did, he knew his father was capable of stopping The Monster . . . knew that his father could easily have stopped it . . . but he chose to do nothing!

As he beat his wife to death with her own rolling pin, his father cried, "No! No! No!" over and over, his voice keeping time with the blows, but that was all he did. Billy kept hoping, even though he knew the truth, that Dad would do something, but he didn't. He never made a move to stop his hand from driving the heavy marble roller into Billy's mother's head until the top of her skull turned to mush.

And at the last, when Molly fell to the floor, blood pouring from her broken head like water from a broken pipe, he looked into her dead eyes, saw the silent question, "Why?" frozen there . . . and was unable to do anything but listen to The Monster—his father—laugh, like the madman that he is, in her dying face.

(The rotten bastard!)

Once and for all, finally, Billy understands a simple truth that he can no longer run from . . .

(Dad killed Mom!)

His father tries to shift his body toward Billy and cries out in agony. Billy pulls his hand away and the images disappear, but the knowledge remains.

"You lied to me," Billy sobs. "You *knew.* You saw . . . *everything* The Monster did to Mom, to everyone, but you didn't do anything to stop it and *you could have*! You could have! But you didn't do *anything*!" Tears stream down Billy's face. "*You* killed Mom. You were there, and you didn't even *try* to stop it, Dad. The Monster is right—you are him and vice versa." The last word drags out into a long, winding whine.

His father closes his eyes again and takes a shuddering breath.

Hands over his face, Billy bawls into them and doesn't see the left hand slowly reaching for him.

"Boo-fucking-hoo!" his father grunts as he grabs Billy by the throat, only now his father's voice is indistinguishable from The Monster's. "I told you before, Billy," he says as he squeezes, cutting off Billy's air, "that your dad is a liar, didn't I?"

Billy is paralyzed in the stranglehold, unable to breathe or talk . . .

But amidst the pain, fear, and despair that fill him, a sudden epiphany. Everything he's seen and felt through his father and The Monster—from killing Sir to setting a fellow patient on fire in the hospital, to the series of rapes that graduated into the murders of women and eventually mothers and babies—comes together in one devastating realization: his father has been planning to murder everyone in the family for some time.

And that truth, that realization, is the final straw added to the weight of the knowledge that everyone he loves is gone. Everyone he loves is dead.

(Or crazy.)

Nothing will ever be the same again.

(Does it matter? In case you hadn't noticed, you're *dying* here.)

He does notice something else. In the cellar window—combat boot-clad feet charging up the porch stairs and into the house. Far, far away, as Billy grows weaker and his mind recedes from the images of his father's memory, he hears the kitchen door bang open, then one of the SWAT team is coming down the cellar stairs amidst the green fog which has been rolling down from the kitchen and spilling over the side of the stairs into the cellar. The cop wears a gas mask and is unbothered by the smoke. He has a rifle in his arms, pointed straight at Billy's father.

(Shoot him! He's choking here!)

"Let the boy go now!" the policeman shouts, his voice muffled by the gas mask.

Billy's father ignores him.

"Let him go now or I *will* shoot!" the cop bellows.

Billy's vision is getting dark around the edges, as though nightfall were approaching but only inside his head. He can feel his legs and body jerking spasmodically, but it is as if they are stretched out way below him and by the time the spasms reach him they are little more than tremors. There is a distant pop, and a reddish, black smoking hole erupts just above his father's right eyebrow. His head and body jerk once, simultaneously, and he slowly turns his face away from Billy.

Far away, the connection with Billy's mind fades.

But his father doesn't let go.

(You're a goner.)

As if viewing some interesting goings-on from the top of a distant mountain, Billy watches the SWAT team cop charge down the stairs, grab his father's arm, and try to pry each finger from his neck.

The circle of Billy's vision grows ever smaller.

The cop pries the index finger loose.

Billy can hear ocean waves crashing against the shore.

The cop pries the ring finger loose and grabs the thumb.

Billy's vision circle is no bigger than a baseball, and the sound of the ocean gives way to music played at superfast speed, rushing through his head like a jet.

(See you later alligator . . .)

The SWAT cop loosens Billy's father's thumb, the rest of his fingers finally let go.

(In a while crocodile. . . .)

As the circle shrinks to darkness, Billy falls to the floor.

After the fact

He walks into the kitchen and sees the newspaper on the table. No one is around. He goes over and looks at it. It is one of the New York City tabloids with the blaring headline:

Father Knows Death!

He reads the first paragraph of the article.

BLACKSTONE, CT—Local and state police are being called on the carpet for their bungling of a confrontation with a Blackstone, Connecticut, insurance agent believed to be the notorious Baby Killer. In a wild shoot-out with the alleged serial killer, several police officers and civilians were killed and wounded.

"This was the most inept handling of a hostage situation that I have ever seen," said Blackstone District Attorney, L. Theodore Wysk. (For more on the DA's comments and the investigation into police actions, turn to D5.)

Killed in the fray were Patrolmen Barry Lumpski, Boniface "Bud" D'Amato, Bob Panapoulis, Sgt. Ron Farr, Patrolmen Jerry Robb, Steve Kahn, Joshua Stork, and Terry Galloway, a rookie on only his third day with the force, along with an EMT, Bruce "Bib" Baker. Police later discovered that alleged Baby Killer John Teags had also murdered his next-door neighbor, Mrs. Barbra Luts, a telephone repairman, Dave LaPierre, his eldest son's best friend, Donald Desmond, and his own wife and child, Molly and Kevin Teags. The latter two bodies and Mrs. Luts were discovered in the cellar of the Teags's house. During the shootout, Teags tossed Donald Desmond's body from a second-floor window after killing the child with a nail gun. Mr. LaPierre's and Officer Lumpski's bodies were found in the kitchen.

The police responded to a prank call from the Teags house that turned out to be the real thing. Shortly after that call, another concerning a motor vehicle/pedestrian accident brought more officers to the scene to find Mrs. Ellen Desmond, mother of the above hostage victim murdered by John Teags, had been struck and killed by an automobile, apparently while fleeing from the Teags home.

Tears come. He scans down.

The body of Mrs. Thelma Canard—an innocent bystander—who lived across the street from the Teags and called in the accident, was found on her front porch by her daughters nearly an hour after the shoot-out. According to the Blackstone County Coroner Mrs. Canard was apparently a victim of a stray bullet.

He goes to the bottom of the page and reads more. He wipes away the tears and smiles.

> Surviving the murderous rampage were William Teags, the seven-year-old son of Baby Killer suspect John Teags, and his baby brother, one-month-old James Teags. According to doctors who examined the children, both had been victims of brutal abuse at the hands of their father. Seven-year-old William was treated for a broken nose, bruised larynx, fractured cheekbone and ribs, and various cuts and bruises to his body. The baby, James Teags, was reportedly found exhibiting injuries consistent with "shaken-infant syndrome." Both children, however, are expected to recover.

He looks up from the paper and sees his reflection in the kitchen window. His neck is still bruised purple, turning yellow at the edges, but it has stopped hurting and the swelling has gone down. He can still hear and feel a *click* in his throat whenever he swallows, and his voice is still hoarse and raspy, but the doctor says that will all go away with time.

(It could have been worse, right?)

From the upstairs of his Aunt Phyllis and Uncle Jim's house comes the sudden piercing cry of his baby brother, Jimmy. Despite the way it jars his nerves and hurts his ears, he smiles again.

"Maybe we'll be all right after all," he whispers.

(And maybe we *won't*! How can you stand it? I swear that kid's crying is going to drive me *crazy*!)

GREAT BOOKS,
GREAT SAVINGS!

When You Visit Our Website:
www.kensingtonbooks.com

You Can Save Money Off The Retail Price
Of Any Book You Purchase!

- **All Your Favorite Kensington Authors**
- **New Releases & Timeless Classics**
- **Overnight Shipping Available**
- **eBooks Available For Many Titles**
- **All Major Credit Cards Accepted**

Visit Us Today To Start Saving!
www.kensingtonbooks.com

When Darkness Falls
Grab One of These
Pinnacle Horrors

More Nail-Biting Suspense From Your Favorite Thriller Authors